Isles of the Blind

Robert Rosenberg

Fomite
Burlington, VT

Copyright 2015 © by Robert Rosenberg
Cover design: Gina Rossi, ginarossidesign.com
Cover photograph: Merve Ates
Author photo: Bill Cardoni

All rights reserved. No part of this book may be reproduced in any form or by any means without the prior written consent of the publisher, except in the case of brief quotations used in reviews and certain other noncommercial uses permitted by copyright law.

This is a work of fiction. Any resemblance between the characters of this novel and real people, living or dead, is merely coincidental.

ISBN-13: 978-1-942515-18-0
Library of Congress Control Number: 2015952153

Fomite
58 Peru Street
Burlington, VT 05401
www.fomitepress.com

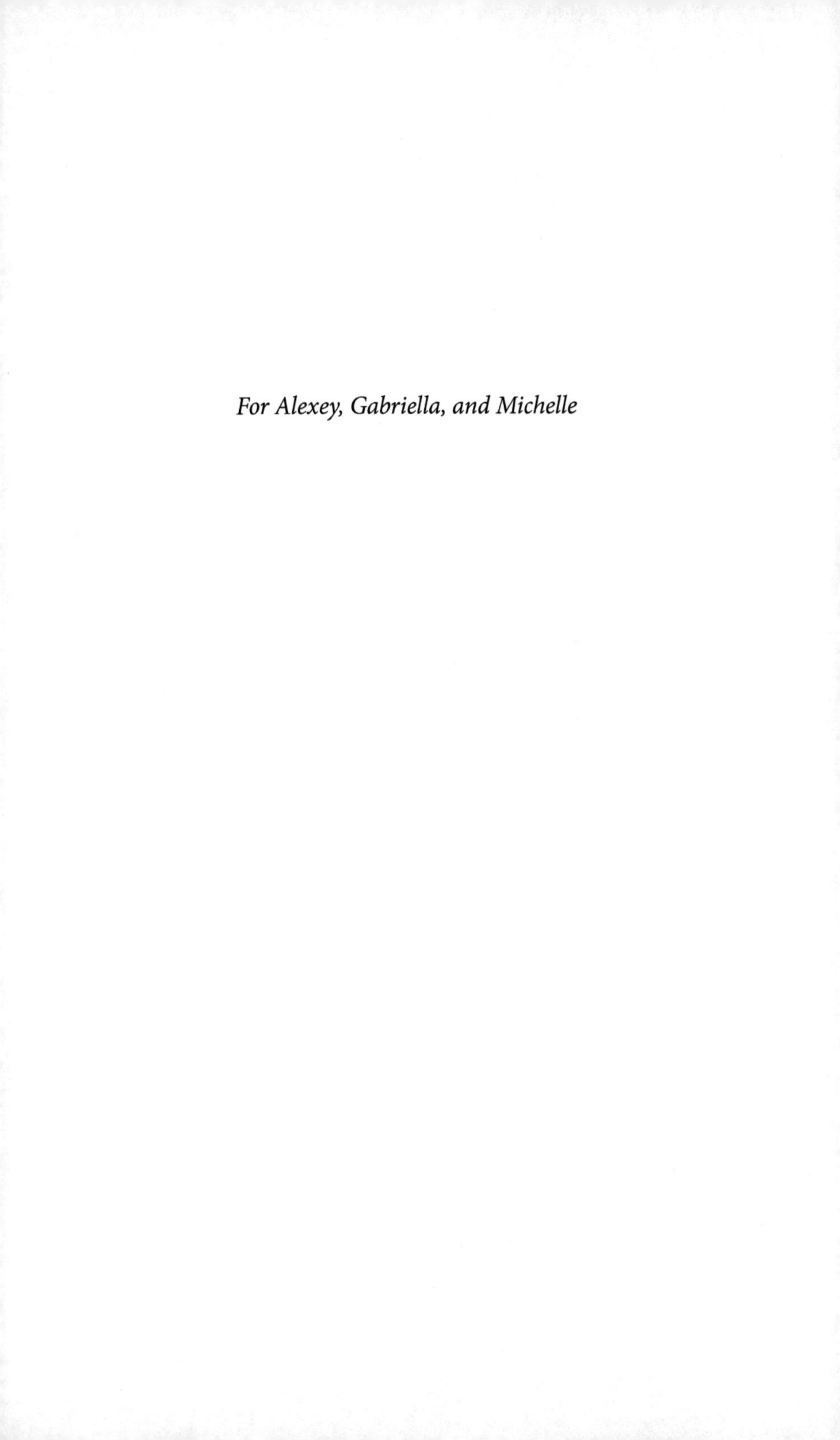

For Alexey, Gabriella, and Michelle

"He says that the only way we can survive is really by us shouting all the time, so that we don't fall asleep, because if we fall asleep we will not, we will never wake up any longer. So we were sitting back to back on this bench and yelling all night. And as the, the night came...as the day came along, we were already exhausted of yelling. And then we stopped, and then I felt that he is not any longer on my back. I turned around and he, he fell from the bench on to the deck and his head was in the water, like...on his belly. In other words, he could not possibly breathe any longer. He was dead. And...but he was very close to me, but just a corpse..."

> — David Stoliar, sole survivor of the 1942
> sinking of the Struma,
> interviewed by the U.S. Holocaust
> Memorial Museum

The scribe, after taking down these dangerous words for the thousandth time, would patiently write the explications concerning why
the Prince's royal brothers had gone mad, why
they were obliged to go mad, and why Ottoman
princes were incapable of doing anything else
besides going mad.

– Orhan Pamuk, The Black Book

Spring 2005

The night before he was lost at sea, my brother called at 3 AM.

For five years I would replay the moment, trying to beat back the guilt. Had I not seen this telephone call coming? Had I not rehearsed it in my mind so many times that my response was necessary and inevitable, given our troubled history? What could I have said that might have saved him?

In our apartment in the capital I'd been dead asleep. Naomi, naked beside me, was hogging the cotton sheets. Our daughters were curled up in the next room over, one thin wall away, their lips moving in their dreams. The cordless phone had rung out twice, shaking the night. I'd slapped my palm along the bedstand until it hit the receiver. "*Alo?*" I called, pressing the phone to my ear. "*Efendim?*"

"Who is it?" Naomi murmured into her pillow.

Half awake, I'd called out again, "*Alo? Alo?*" In the dark I realized I was holding the receiver upside down. I straightened it, and I heard my name. Fourteen years since we had spoken, but I knew Yusuf's thorny voice immediately. My legs stiffened, I jolted up, and though I was certain, asked who was calling.

"Come on Avram, it's me. Listen, quickly."

"What do they want?" Naomi, still groggy, was mumbling. She rolled over, her bare shoulder grazing my side, and from the other side of sleep said, "Tell them it's too late."

"Avram?" he was saying. "Are you there? A word. Just a word."

Off balance, I held the phone to my chest and whispered, in wonder, "It's my brother."

"Your brother?" Naomi's voice registered its first alarm.

"Yes. It's Yusuf."

She lifted her head and glanced at the clock. "Tell him he's waking the twins. Please Avram, hang up. By the power of God, hang up."

"Yusuf," I muttered into the phone, "do you even know the time?"

"What's time between brothers?"

"Avram, please. For the girls." Naomi placed her hand on my knee. She had every right to fear such a call. Yusuf had no business attaching us to the trouble he was stirring.

I patted her elbow and said into the phone, "Can you call back in the morning? You've woken us…"

"Just a moment. Listen. Just one word." The rising authority in my brother's voice brought everything rushing back. He had always demanded more than I could offer. I was always at a loss to keep up with him. Yusuf might have achieved greatness; but at what cost to our family? Even one word at this late hour was too much to give him. Maybe it was simply the bad connection (and five years on I was still unsure), but I thought I'd heard a woman's high-pitched laughter in the background. The usual confusion of sex, power, and jealousy when it came to my brother.

Then nothing: my thumb had found the off button. I held it for a second, its resonant tone sang into my ear. A chill settled over me, and I rattled the phone into its cradle.

"No end to his selfishness," Naomi was whispering. "I'm sorry Avram. I don't care what he's suffering. He brought this on himself."

"You're right."

"Three o'clock in the morning!"

"You're right. You've always been right about him."

After this I couldn't sleep. Naomi slept only fitfully, wrapping the sheets taut around her body as if bandaging a wound. The call had jarred us, and I had forgotten, until the soft light of dawn broke through the shades and I left the comfort of bed for the toilet, that it was April 23rd: my birthday. In the frigid bathroom, urinating the scattered spray of a forty-year-old man, I wondered if Yusuf could have remembered.

I left the bathroom, and from down the hall I swore I heard a familiar hacking cough. At the twins' room I pushed the door quietly open. The coughing had stopped, the air was heavy with sleep, but I felt a lingering presence. I fixed the covers over my five-year-old girls, and for a moment it seemed to me Estella, lips half-parted, wasn't breathing. I watched for the rise of her chest beneath the sheets, then hunched down by the bed and moved my face closer to hers, listening for it. She coughed out once, startling me. I stood and stepped back. In the shadows of the curtains past her bed something stirred, a presence in the darkness. I waited, watching the curtains. Then stillness. I could hear Estella's breaths come normally again.

✳✳✳

FOR FOURTEEN YEARS I had tried to forget him. I'd see his world-beater smile gracing the Life section in the Sunday papers and beaming out at us from celebrity gossip TV programs. I'd catch him interviewed Friday afternoons on CNNTurk's BusinessWeek, spot him guest-starring on 20 Billion Lira Pyramid. The financial pages estimated his net worth. Tossing aside those pages for the Style section, I'd stumble across his name:

Ottoman Disco Bling!

For one hot summer night only, the Queen City was transformed into Saturday Night Fever with the launch of the New Yorker Disco Party co-sponsored by Jack Daniels and Teletürk.

Held earlier this month on the 47th floor of the Teletürk Tower, with a panoramic view of the ancient mosques below and the glittering skyscrapers of Levent behind, the New York 70's DISCO — THEMED event came complete with thumping beats, explosive hip-hop dancers, a star-studded guest list and more than 500 throbbing partiers blinged out in sequined Disco style.

Miami's South Beach deejays Jake Blundercross and Forest Y kept the partiers hopping with funky house beats and disco classics. Hip hop emcee MasktIntruder collected objects offered up by the pulsing crowd — a 50 lira note, a lipstick container, a Beckham Football Jersey — and churned these into an off-the-cuff rap that had the audience chanting for more.

To rev up the New York City atmosphere, graffiti

Despite myself I'd kept track of these banquets and charity
balls. I'd noted the foolhardy Teletürk publicity stunts: the failed
expedition to climb Mt. Everest, the sand-boarding video filmed
in Namibia, his heli-diving trip to the Great Barrier Reef. So he
was familiar to me, even at that distance. I'd seen him aging, but
still fit, clearly testing the limits of his disease.

In these ways and others I'd measured his storied public life
against my private contentment. Only on my return to Istanbul
five years after his death — my marriage failing, my career in
shards — would I see what Yusuf had truly left behind. I had
known him across two decades through the prism of the media.
The tabloid facts could never fully illuminate a life so extraor-
dinary, or justify a death so strange. I'd been measuring myself
against a public invention.

***

IN AS MANY ways as Yusuf's life had been remarkable, my own

had lacked distinction. I was an architect, charged with supervising my Ankara firm's government contracts for the construction of prisons. No architect goes into the field hoping to spend his best years drafting latrines and cells. But I had found with jails, like with all things, the more attention I gave them, the more their nuances grew on me. I'd tell myself that I was performing a service for our nation's fraught international image. Jails primarily need to be secure, but they also support life, and it may well be an unlucky journalist, activist, or university professor who winds up locked in the cell my teams designed. The few square meters of wall around him might be home for many, many years. So every consideration becomes important: how large a space for a bed, the opacity of the windows, the pacing length of the floor, the kind of bolted-down furniture (not too comfortable, but comfortable enough), all of these concerns limited by what public money a municipality budgets. And they never budget enough. Security does not come cheaply; neither do modern amenities. For murderers an architect might be less inclined to care. Perhaps it was my sympathetic upbringing, but in nearly two decades with the firm I'd done everything in my power to ensure each space met a minimum standard of human compassion. I could never sign the blue-prints without picturing myself in the cell.

When word had first reached me that my brother was no longer merely well-off, but had been ranked by *Servet* magazine as the seventh richest man in the nation, I was stunned, intrigued, amazed. With the arrival of the pocket telephone in our country Teletürk Holdings had come across its second boom, larger than the first. Yusuf had continued to place large bets on nascent industries. His cellular company had diversified into the burgeoning empire that would come to include discount airlines, textiles, Internet banks, and designer condoms. Teletürk had completed its border-to-border fiber backbone network, with plans to offer broadband services to far flung villages in Anatolia. Shepherds crouched on dusty hilltops, amid their flocks, typing on laptops.

The more famous Yusuf grew, the more I saw his face staring out at me from the papers and billboards, taunting me with the determined visage of his greatness. He was everywhere; I couldn't shake him. Yusuf was saying: Look at you! The loving father, the harried husband, the loyal employee, designing your jails by hand. Is this what you have to show for our parents' sacrifices?

By the time I'd heard that my brother was in serious political trouble, on trial for crimes against the nation, what had once been the background noise of my adulthood had become the thunder of the world calling out to me, in tabloids and cable news specials: Witness what happened to the brother you once hoped to erase. See how his life grew so large, while yours only shrank. Behold how your diseased little brother was redefining telecommunications and challenging the historical record of a nation, while you were cutting your little girls' toenails, and zippering pajamas, and singing "Ali Baba Has a Big Farm."

***

THE SCATTERED SPRAY of a forty-year old man. Barefoot on the cold tile of the bathroom. Life reduced to a vision of myself through my famous brother's eyes. I spent that Saturday morning in Ankara celebrating my birthday with my two daughters and Naomi. The question of the previous night's phone call hung in the air, weighing on my mind like a word I couldn't summon. Naomi had gotten me fresh packages of underwear and business socks, which she knew I always needed, and which she knew I'd never buy. With outstretched hands the twins presented me gifts wrapped in identical green tissue paper, tied with identical blue bows. Sara's was a plastic comb; Estela's a wooden hairbrush inscribed "TK" — initials that were not mine. They had saved for and had chosen and had overwrapped the presents themselves, in layer after layer of tape. Opening these gifts, feigning delight, I was ignorant of the drama unfolding four hours west, back on the island of my youth. I found out only that afternoon, on TGRT Breaking News, that Teletürk CEO Yusuf Elmas had suffered a high-speed boating accident.

I stood numb before the television, watching coverage of Coast Guard rescue ships circling the Sea of Marmara. They were colorful toy boats, festive almost, and below them, as if swimming underwater, Yusuf's name scrolled across the bottom of the screen in a recursive loop. Every time it disappeared to the left, reappeared to the right, something plummeted inside me. *A word. Just a word.* I'd denied him even that, the smallest of atonements.

In the days to come we were force-fed the official story by the national media. He was gone, the Jewish Billionaire — drowned in the Marmara — taking with him some young whore of his, one of his playthings, a 19 year-old by the name of Yasemin Demopoulous. She was half his age, the daughter of a foreign Coca Cola executive — and Greek, of all things! Scandal! A public denigration of our Republic! An insult to the national identity!

I did not believe the official story then, and I still did not believe it five years later, when I set out to search for the truth myself. We were a nation living in fear and distrust, knowing we were being lied to. We could afford no faith in anyone, not the police, not the military, least of all the rich and powerful who claimed to have the people's interests at heart. Something rotten was happening up in those rarefied political heights, of which the average citizen had no understanding. How could I accept my brother's made-for-TV death as just an accident? Not an accident with such providential timing for the State. Nobody could buy an explanation so simple.

Genocide. Genocide. Genocide. Yusuf had spoken the word freely, one too many times.

Book I

1

A Return to the Islands

At the port in Kadıköy on that overcast Saturday the ferry engine hummed, vibrating the padded wooden bench beneath me, and I set off for the islands as I had with Yusuf and my parents so many times, so many years ago. The early afternoon loomed cold and gray with relentless drizzles. I slid closer to the radiator and zippered my jacket. A few scattered passengers were reading newspapers, hunching over their crosswords and word-searches. The front page article of a man on the bench across from me described a new breast implant technology designed in America, and the accompanying illustrations distracted me momentarily from my mission. I turned to the ferry window. Outside the scratched glass the gulls swam in the wind, circled in a wet glide, dove; and in a rush of air were jolted upwards.

"*Chai? Tost? Kahve?*" called the steward, pouring steaming cups, then passing again.

We sailed by the deserted beaches of Kınalıada and the

saddle-bag hills of Heybeliada. In forty-five minutes the boat sidled up to the largest island, growled, and then exhaled a final great sigh. The ferry terminal, I saw, had been newly restored, with Iznik tiles of interconnected vines gloriously strangling the edifice. It was four in the afternoon by my gold watch. Here the rain had stopped. One of the largest buildings on the waterfront, a beaux arts hotel I remembered from my childhood, had suffered a fire, and new construction had begun. I'd have to look up which architects had won the contract. Outside I walked along, the salt mist heavy in the air. To my left the water smacked the pier, slapping waves up onto the concrete. Gulls wheeled overhead in the wake of the departing ferry. It moaned away from the dock and hurried back towards the city, wasting no time to flee the winter desolation of these islands. Plunging into the foam the squeaking birds followed the boat, and with them took the last signs of life.

I was alone, the city sixteen kilometers across the sea to my right, invisible now in the mist of a leaden sky. Down the street I asked directions to the new police station from the only person I could find: a crazy-eyed man who, wearing mittens without fingers, was roasting *köfte* over a charcoal grill. He pointed through the smoke up a hill, in the direction of the clock tower, which showed the wrong time: 7:50.

Adalar İlçe Emniyet Müdürlüğü — Polis announced the painted sign at the station. A worn flag, red with the crescent moon and star, wagged on its pole. At a marble basin a kneeling officer was unraveling a knotted garden hose from its spigot. He wore a pistol in his holster and handcuffs tucked into a leather pocket hanging off his belt. He saw me, waved, flung the hose into the weeds, and came to meet me at the steps. In the center of the lawn a single palm tree had been planted — a tree not from this climate. For all its summer beauty, for all the resonance of my childhood memories, the island now seemed artificial, a place where pretty things were brought from great distances and planted for show. An artificial beauty but — I managed to calm myself, inhaling the resinous pine air — pleasant still.

"Too long, too long," Officer Ceber said, grabbing my shoulder with a forceful squeeze.

"Too long," I replied.

We'd known each other from a distance during my army days. He was the most enthusiastic hazer of new recruits, delighting in "corrective training" rituals that involved chili pepper and sand paper. I remembered him as the worst kind of bully — a bully with an outsized smile. In pickup football matches he'd use his arms to trap the ball against his chest, then throw a fit if we called him on it. He'd cheated at cards, but was the first to accuse others. Now he protected the law on these islands.

Officer Ceber been expecting me, and I showed him the list of names Yusuf's lawyer suggested I track down, should I be looking for help.

"Nılay Gören. Mustafa Faik," he read aloud. "What do you want with this one — Flora Demirkan?"

"I was told one of them might show me around the house."

"Yusuf's house? It's not much anymore. I can take you there myself, Avram, if you'd like. This one. Flora Demirkan — " he tapped the paper with a dirty nail — "won't talk to anyone about the house."

"I was told these people might be interested in some off-season work."

"You were misinformed."

I held my palm out for the list of names. He frowned and glanced again at it. "What kind of work, do you say?"

"Cleaning. Caretaking."

Ceber broke into a full-throated laugh, and when I asked what was so funny said, "You have more than cleaning on your hands. Follow me then. You can always try."

He led me into a winding back alley of the seaside village, behind the street of a few waiting phaetons, onto Cınar Sokak. On the walk Ceber chatted, rambling on about a report he had read just this morning that claimed the hairy men in our country went balder, faster, than any other men, in any other nation. Did I know why this was? "Testosterone!" The officer removed his *POLIS* cap, and I saw that he had combed over a few long tendrils of greasy hair in an attempt to cover the balding summit of his head. "World record levels of testosterone! Eh? Eh? When did yours start going?"

"Mine? It hasn't yet."

"In denial, eh? You wait. Nothing to be ashamed of." He lifted his police cap, scratching at his smooth head as he walked me three blocks further, then stopped. With both hands he grasped the ramshackle gate of a two-story cement hovel. Black leggings and wet ladies undergarments flopped from a line off the balcony. An ancient exercise bike crouched rusting in a corner. The house, surrounded by melancholy plants potted in rusted olive oil tins, had not been painted in years. Between each plant lazed a cat — at least twenty of them — poised like sentinels charged with guarding the ferns. Amid the filth floated the smell onions and garlic, and some kind of pastry.

"The caretaker?" I asked.

Officer Ceber chuckled to humor me, then raised one bushy eyebrow. He called out "Flora" in a voice now filled with caution. A middle-aged woman dressed in cleaning clothes, her hair pulled back behind a scarf, threw open the front door, peered out at us, and disappeared back inside. She reemerged a moment later bearing a tray of butter cookies. Her hair was now loose, tumbling in a brown sheen to her shoulders. The door she passed through, barely attached by its hinges, fell at a slant, banged against the wall, and lay off-balance as she descended the steps. Behind her, three tangle-haired boys sprinted around the house and halted at the corner, watching their mother approach us.

"*Hoş geldiniz,*" she called. "Officer Ceber, try these, will you?"

She swung the tray of cookies at the policeman's head. He took one, looked at her for permission, and snatched a second one.

"A new recipe," she said. "Tell me what you think. Still warm."

The policeman popped an entire cookie into his mouth, and was nodding.

"Good?" she asked. "Good? That's right. Of course they're good. *Afiyet olsun.*" She thrust the tray in my direction. "*Buyurun!*" I held my hand to my heart. I never cared much for desserts. "What," she said, "You don't trust me? I'm offering you poison? Take!"

So I took, and in the cold of the late afternoon I ate the sweet warm dough. Officer Ceber was scratching crumbs off his lips and explaining who I was. Assuming an official tone, he asked the woman if she would be so kind as to accompany me to the villa of her former employer. At this request her expression hardened, the hospitality eclipsed. "Yusuf's brother?"

"Yes."

"And what, you're here to see the house too?"

"Yes."

She grew quiet, eyeing me, then the policeman, with a hostile look I would, over the following months, come to expect and then dread. She lowered the tray of cookies and called inside, "Feride!" A younger woman appeared in the doorway, wiping her hands on a cloth. The daughter was pretty; her own features echoing the fading light of her mother's face. Her black T-shirt read in English, in yellow letters, *Good Girls are Bad Girls who haven't been Caught.*

"Finish dinner," Flora ordered. "I have to show this gentleman to the Halim Pasha House." She looked back, scanning me from shoes to collar. "Like a woman who has nothing better in this world to do with her time."

Officer Ceber removed his cap, bowed his bare head, took a third cookie, and took his leave. Flora Demirkan hurried back into her hovel, and returned, smock removed, in worn sandals and tight Mavi jeans, which her ample hips and thighs now filled to nearly bursting. She did not speak, but as she led me off that misbegotten street she kept glancing at me with dark Asiatic eyes, the black pupils shrouding a connection between us I did not yet grasp. She walked in surprisingly light, long steps, at the same pace uphill or down, and behind her back her thick glossy hair swung from shoulder to shoulder. Only as she beckoned me to follow more quickly uphill did I realize, despite the poverty, despite the makeup, how striking she once might have been. For a few minutes I huffed to keep up; and trying to slow her I called out, "What'd you used to do for my brother?"

"Mostly I cooked for him."

"For how long?"

The question rankled her. "Ages," she said, "More years than I admit to people like you." She hurried forward now, faster, mumbling about these endless inquisitions.

Finally we came to it: the wooden gingerbread mansion, built at the turn of the previous century by an Ottoman merchant, occupying a sloping plot of coastline ten minutes' walk from the pier. Through the black wrought-iron fence the three-story house possessed the quality of tragedy. Salt air had peeled thick white paint off the façade in chunks. Strips of blanched, graying wood were visible. Bougainvillea vines had overtaken the southeastern corner, and wet browning palms filled the grounds running up to the porch. In the statue garden a wild rose-bed retained only the hint of green; beyond it a marble white fountain marked the center of a wide patio before the colonnaded portico. A busted-in security panel hung off the front gate — which wailed when Flora swung it forward, and whined in response when I eased it back behind me. We followed flagstones obscured by thrusts of weeds, beyond a tangled herb garden thick with the scent of wild sage, up to the marble steps. Filigreed windows of red and green glass outlined the front door. Two of these panes were cracked. Spray painted black on the floor of the front porch were the words: *Jewish Trash. You will PAY the bill.*

So there it was — my welcome, my first hint of what was to come. I had not yet caught my breath. I wondered, pausing on the steps, straddling those spray-painted letters, how many times life presented a man with such an opportunity. Not the fantasy world of movies or the fading glories of our football teams, but life, actual life, lived on a grand scale — love, death, money, dreams, lust — all there to be explored, if I was up to the task.

That was how I felt approaching my dead brother's villa five years after his death, strangely alive again in that long grey winter, on the verge of something large and brave, though I could hardly have said what it was. We had only just discovered that he had left Father this home. Let it rot, Naomi had insisted. And now it was clear, without even knowing, we had done just that.

2

The Drowned Girl

THE MOLDY TILED porch encircled the house, overlooking the cracking cement of a helipad on the western lawn. Flora Demirkan directed me to the front door, showed me how and on which locks to use the keys. The door stuck hard. I resorted to a shove of the shoulder. Inside an enormous foyer opened to more marble stairs. The lights did not work: I'd have to order the electricity switched on. Above us two pigeons were perched in two high windows, facing inside, their heads tucked coyly into their bodies. At intervals they cooed lazy warnings to each other. Flora and I pulled off our shoes and slipped our feet into mismatched pairs of ancient guest-slippers. Down the echoing hallway a collection of early photographs of the city and engravings of maps in gilded frames had bubbled and drooped with the humidity. Small blue *nazar* trinkets hung over every door — protecting the ruined home from the evil eye. Along the walls of the foyer, and occupying every corner of the living room and even the dining room, sat enormous antique bird cages. Near the stairs one of them had fallen over onto the floor; its shredded newspaper lining spilling out. The stench as we passed was still foul.

"What happened to the birds?" I asked Flora, my finger under my nose. She stared at her feet and shrugged. She was resisting the urge to look around herself.

I made my slow way down the hall and through the first door to my right came upon the library. The books had been raided, and the half-empty shelves had the shattered look of a face missing teeth. I thumbed through a fading paperback of Nazim Hikmet's poetry. A high-school hardcover of *To Kill a Mockingbird* still contained a folded up draft of a three-page English essay — not in his handwriting. Perhaps he'd copied from it. I'd known him to do such things. I ran my hand across a few more stale titles: Mark Twain, Descartes, Stendhal, the philosopher Rumi, and came upon a leather-bound prayer book. I slid it off the shelf. It had not been opened in a long time, and after a moment it struck me that this was the *haftora* Yusuf had used, thirty-two years ago, to prepare for his Bar Mitzvah. He had kept this book in our room as a teenager, on the top of the bookshelf beside his swimming trophies. I turned it over in my hands, measuring the weight of it, and found myself smiling, stupidly, in wonder. I sat in the dust of a creaking wooden chair near the window and cracked the volume. Fumbling through the brittle pages I found what might have been a bookmark — a receipt for a meal at Günaydın Restaurant. I ran my fingers up and down the crinkled paper. The receipt's blue print was faded, but I could make out that the bill had been less than two lira, drinks included, and that Yusuf had ordered *ezogelin* soup. Only my brother would take a copy of his haftora to lunch at a *kebap* shop, and order lentil soup between his practiced prayers.

I placed the book on his desk beside a brushed nickel antique phone, like something I'd seen once in Dolmabahçe Palace, with a rotary dial and mechanical bell. I lifted the receiver — dead, of course — and followed the frayed cloth chord to where it had been yanked from the wall. Could he have called me from here, this very desk, on his final night? And what was the CEO of Teletürk, our nation's cutting-edge cellular company, even doing with a rotary telephone? He had always been exasperating. It occurred to me that if I could better understand the man who had sat in this chair, better understand who he had become over those missing years, and what he had died for, I might figure out how my own life had veered so wildly off course. I might finally resolve the puzzle that had been our relationship, and come to terms with my dead brother for good.

The woman, Flora, was watching me with her arms crossed, scraping one slipper back and forth on the hardwood floor. I stood, gathered myself, and brushed my grimy hands on my now grimy pants. "We'll need to clean," I said, scraping a line through the dust with my own slippered heel. "I'm hoping to get it into shape for my father to move in. He's retiring."

She was silent.

"Quite a project," I muttered. I noticed through the shadows the faded intricacies of arabesque scrolling over a chipped door-way, in dire need of repair. I couldn't contain a grin. "A hell of a project."

She raised her head as if to nod, but her chin hung in the air — a momentary gesture of defiance or curiosity, I couldn't be sure.

I swung both hands out, indicating the house. "Can you help me, Flora? Do you have the time for this?" I'd raised my voice as if I were talking to someone who didn't speak our language. My question echoed too loudly off the half-empty bookcases.

Through the dim light from the windows she stared at me with large and tender eyes, and quickly those eyes lost focus, darkened, and looked beyond me. She clicked her tongue. "*Beyefendim*, I'm afraid I can't." She was facing me, only a meter away, and I took in Flora Demirkan at this distance. She was a thick-limbed, buxom woman, with firm lips, a fierce and handsome face, the hint of a double chin, and a husky voice that in other circumstances, lowered like this, might have bordered on sultry.

"I'll pay you well," I said. "That daughter of yours can help. Your sons, too. Your husband, if he needs work?"

"There is no husband."

"I apologize."

"There's never been a husband."

"Look, I'm saying it makes no difference to me. Whatever you want. No? No time for this? I'll find someone else then." I took from my pocket the scribbled list of names of the former staff, and clumsily unfolded it. "Do you know who might be interested? Nılay Gören, maybe? Mustafa Faik, his old security guard? This one — the boat mechanic — Hakan Öztürk?"

I didn't realize then the pain I was causing her. Had I understood how deeply the grief went, that she had been more than my brother's cook, I would never have asked her to help. But Yusuf's lawyer had told me his former staff, still suffering, might be grateful for winter work. I was simply inquiring. My intentions with Flora Demirkan had begun as innocently as that.

She stared hard into the floor again, considering my offer. "It'd be an insult to Yasemin's memory. I don't think I could bear it."

"Yasemin's memory?"

"My daughter, Yasemin."

I was confused, trying to work out her reservations. "Yasemin?"

"Yasemin Demopoulous. Who do you think I'm talking about?"

My arm, holding the paper, fell to my side. "Your daughter?" I asked. "Forgive me Flora, I didn't make the connection."

"Don't take me for a fool."

"But I always understood…the young woman was foreign. Your last names…"

"The young woman was as foreign as you are." Flora glared at me. Clearly she thought I'd planned this; that Officer Ceber was in on it as well. It looked bad — even malicious. Vaguely I remembered reading the drowned girl had family on the island, but I hadn't heard her mother had been employed by Yusuf. Not here, in this very house. "I promise you," I repeated, "I didn't know. Flora, I hardly knew him."

"You shake down my door with the cops, hound me with questions, force me to come here with you, and this simple fact you don't know?"

"We didn't shake down your door. Nobody warned me. Give me a moment. Let me get this straight. Yasemin Demopoulous, the girl who went down with him…"

"Are you satisfied? You, your police friends, have had your fun, testing me."

"Nobody's testing you." I took a step back and raised my palms out. "Just one second…tell me then…if you don't mind my asking…"

"I mind your asking. I mind your *bringing* me here. It's shameful!"

"Flora," I said. "You're mistaken." But my confusion had emboldened her. She was already making her way through the dark hall of memories back to the front door.

3

Twin Laments

Yusuf was five when he was diagnosed with *kistik fibroz*. He had always coughed a lot in our room, and sometimes woke me with his wheezing. My brother was gassy, and I learned at an early age to avoid the toilet after he'd just gone. Doctors at Marmara University's Division of Pulmonology had utilized a sweat test for the diagnosis, and this was how our parents first presented the problem to me: your brother just sweats too much, inside and out, and fluid gets into his lungs. I was only seven at the time, and in those years it hardly seemed more serious than that. For Yusuf's was a strange death sentence. Our parents were told the disease took the lives of many children young — the majority never reached twenty. But they were also assured that Yusuf had a mild version of KF, and could just as well live twice that long. Doctors didn't yet know the cause, a flawed gene identified only a decade later, in 1989, one that had been passed down from each of our parents: a deadly inheritance. So when I first asked Mother why I, too, did not have *kistik fibroz*, she could tell me only to be grateful the Good Lord had spared me. I was the Lucky Son.

For a brother with a debilitating chronic disease, Yusuf seemed relatively asymptomatic: just a kid with a perpetual phlegmy cough. And what was the big deal? I coughed all winter as well — partly because our dry, dusty apartment was always overheated, and partly in response to my brother's constant hacking from the bed across the room. Like a ticking clock the rhythm of all-night throat-clearing gets inside your head. You come to expect it, you find you can't sleep without it, and the provocation builds until your own throat becomes scratchy and you feel the urge to clear it too. All-night coughing, hacking, throat-clearing, first my brother's, then my own: the call-and-response of our childhood.

Treatments for KF were rudimentary in our country then, there were none of the electric vests and antibiotic nebulizers a wealthy Yusuf would later have access to; so we had to focus on loosening his phlegm manually. It was an exhausting procedure. Mother taught me at a young age how to clap Yusuf's back with cupped palms. "Like this," she'd say, piling the pillows, rolling the blankets, arranging my brother in various yogic angles best suited for postural drainage — first on the bed, then across my lap. She showed me how to lean Yusuf forward into a seated bow, or how to pull him back so that his head lay lower than his torso. Yusuf was long and thin for his age, his spine slightly bowed, and I came to know, better than my own, the geometry of moles and birthmarks on his neck. Mother showed me how to flop him over the pillow, to the front, to the side, to the other side. She showed me how to tap the back of his shoulders, then the front of each shoulder, one side of his ribs, then the other, and finally the top of his chest: tapping out all six positions for five minutes each with a firm, steady five-beat count. Clap clap clap — clap

clap! "Make sure he has nothing in his mouth. Switch positions. Don't be gentle. Harder! *Haydi*, make him cough again. Yusuf, cough! Louder! That's it. Three big breaths. Blow out. That's it. *Aferin!*" This percussion, our special song: pummeling my brother to keep him alive.

Obsessively Mother worried over Yusuf. Obsessively she forced her worry upon us. Yet the Herculean effort required to structure her life around her son's mucus flow would become clear only after she was gone. For over a decade, every day, she woke Yusuf an hour early and ran him through his physiopulmonary therapy, then administered his antibiotics. Mother met him at school for lunch in the nurse's office, clapped his back for thirty minutes and administered his enzyme tablets. I relieved her when Yusuf did his homework after dinner, pounding his back under her weary supervision. She sat next to us, timing the positions, reading everything she could find on the disease. Exercise, she learned, would keep Yusuf's lungs strong; and she bribed him into joining the youth football leagues he had until then avoided. Religiously she attended every practice. Common colds or the flu could lead to life-threatening complications, and Mother became the family hypochondriac. She forced me to sleep on the living room couch if I exhibited the slightest runny nose. She stopped smoking in the apartment for the most part, and took her furtive cigarettes only on the balcony. When doctors suggested that it was important, whenever possible, for Yusuf to spend time out of the city's coal-polluted air, she entreated Father to stretch our meager finances toward that cause.

That same year we bought a vacation house on the largest of the Princes' Islands.

We already knew many families who owned island homes. The city's dwindling Jewish population, those of us who had resisted the gravitational pull of Israel, was an ever-tightening community. Five centuries after our common ancestors had fled the persecution of Queen Isabella's Inquisition, had wandered the Mediterranean and found safe haven under the Ottoman sultans, many in our households still spoke Judeo-Espanyol. At home as children Yusuf and I spoke the language with our parents, but in our private schools we didn't. We rooted for the national football teams. We listened to *arabesk* and *fasil*. We snuck helpings of grilled offal from Taksim vendors. Steadily, without a thought, we were tossing away five centuries of tradition.

Mother's twin laments: Yusuf's KF and the family's assimilation. Not only then did she view the island as a sanatorium for her sick son, but the waters around it would now demarcate new boundaries for our indiscriminate social lives. On the island we'd have primarily Jewish friends and one day, with the Lord's help, Jewish girlfriends.

The wooded isle, the largest of a small archipelago off the Asian coast, had become a vacation ghetto for the city's prosperous minorities. Its two steep mountains were separated by a wide valley, and at the peak of each mountain an ancient Greek monastery commanded magisterial views. In Byzantine times the archipelago drew its name, the Priests' Isles, from these monasteries. Later, new monarchs established the brutal practice of exiling their predecessors to the islands — where they were blinded, then manacled into the cells of the churches, never to rule again — and the archipelago became known as the Princes' Islands. Across the years the horrors dissipated. By the

19th century the merchants of our city were building spectacular wooden mansions high on its hills. Now the island's close winter community of simple Muslim villagers was overridden each summer by what was left of the city's Jews, Greeks, and Armenians. In the safety of neighbors and numbers, the island would go some way towards assuaging Mother's fears.

Through my earliest childhood memories, arriving from the tumult of the city, I'd always been struck by the clean air and slower pace. Mediterranean pine blanketed the rocky slopes. A single road twisted around the shore, through the valley and back to the main village — whose narrow side-streets were crammed with clapboard shacks of simple families who'd lived here for generations, and who owned its restaurants, markets, and hardware stores. But the town's wider avenues, extending in an axis out from the main square, were lined with ornate wooden palaces and scented gardens of magnolia, lilac, and honeysuckle. In the ruins of one such home Leon Trotsky wiled away his first years of exile in our country, fishing in caiques off the steep coastline. In another mansion Mustafa Atatürk established the Anadolu Club, an elite British-style gambling hotel. Despite the fading glamour, to this day the island is still known for its tranquility. Cars are banned, so one must walk, or bicycle, or take a horse-drawn carriage. It remains a place stuck in time.

Father purchased the vacation home from the oldest of his fourteen cousins, Semuel Naim, who had recently moved to Haifa. "My cousin was looking to unload," Father would always recall, remembering those optimistic days. "We couldn't afford it…but how could I not buy? It was exactly what we needed. We did it for your brother. When I say that I mean, we did *everything* for your brother."

Father was Semuel Naim's favorite relation, and he sold it to us for a loss. "Our summer villa," Father called it with a smile, rubbing his rough-shaven cheeks. It was more cottage than villa: there were only two bedrooms, a kitchen whose mildewed tile was long due for replacement, a back patio that faced inland to hills overgrown with umbrella pine rather than outward to the sea. Nonetheless, Father took possession of it that spring with all the triumph of a West Bank settler. Yusuf and I helped him bang home the nails on the front right doorframe for Mother's mezuzah. On the opposite side of the door, at Yusuf's urging, we also hung the Turkish *nazar*.

But twenty-one years later, on his triumphant return to the island, Yusuf would hang only the *nazar* on his mansion gates, next to the metal sign that said *Beware of Dog*. Our cousin Byanka reported this after his death. "He'd forgotten who he was by then, the rich jerk! *No con quien naces sino con quien paces*," she said. It's not among whom you were born, but among whom you live.

4

Home Improvements

EXERCISE AND FRESH air were critical for Yusuf's health, and as a result all summer Father engaged us in a series of home improvement projects. He made us measure the walkway of uneven flagstones. We dug those up, wheeled them away, and leveled the earth, then covered it with a fresh coat of concrete carted in by horse from the Marmara Havuz pool service. Our parents allowed Yusuf, after much begging, to despoil the new, perfectly even walkway by pressing his hands and writing his name into the cement. He convinced me to join him. For pens we ripped twigs off the linden tree that shaded the north side of the house. Beside my handprint I wrote only my first name in block letters. Below mine Yusuf attempted the script he had perfected in third grade, and carved both his first and last name with the flourish of a man who would go on to sign multi-billion lira payouts. On my return to the island three decades later I'd search out those signatures. The cottage was there, painted now an obnoxious shade of Ottoman Rose, and I knew the exact location we had used for the hand-prints: in the upper right corner of the furthest slab as it approached the rusted sidewalk. I looked and looked, questioning my recall, but the names and prints had long been cemented over.

The cottage had been Mother's idea, but we never knew Father happier than he was that summer setting up house. Within a month he'd built us a bunk bed out of yellow pine slats he'd hauled in from the Moon Club stable on the far side of the island. I let Yusuf claim the top bunk, both because he wanted it so badly, and because I was secretly afraid of rolling off in my sleep and breaking my neck.

My cousins Mert and Byanka often spent the night with us, and they once convinced me to play a joke on Yusuf. Late evening, when he was sleeping, we took the mattress from the lower bed, positioned it on the floor, climbed the edges of the bunk and levered the top platform, higher and higher, until Yusuf rolled over. Slowly he turned, then swiftly, with a disturbing twist, flopped two meters and landed with a violent crash on the mattress below. Silence. It was a rougher fall than I had imagined; he could easily have broken his back. I expected him to be furious, to wake startled and screaming, but in the dim light my little brother was blinking at each of my cousins. He curled up and fell into a jerking fit of coughing. I came over and patted his upper back. "*Tamam, tamam,*" I kept saying. "You're OK. You just fell. You coughed yourself out of bed, Yusuf." I straightened his mattress, then helped him climb the ladder onto his upper perch. My heart was racing.

Three times that first summer it rained. The roof leaked. Yet no earthly power would persuade Mother to let Yusuf climb the house and help Father with the repairs. "Let the boys have their summer," she'd argue. "It's their *holiday* Emil, not the Gulag." Yusuf, fascinated by the workings of the roof and our father's ability to fix anything, liked to watch from the ground and hold the ladder for Father when he descended. I had to pull my brother off to play. From a distance, riding our bicycles in loops around the hill, or pedaling to the top of the hill and gliding down with no hands past the house, we'd scream for our father's attention. We could see him up there, shirtless, soaked with perspiration, his maternal belly sagging, his long, flabby arms covered in dark hair, straining against the heavy bricks. These he would pry off and toss on the ground with a steady thud.

By late August the roof was fixed, and the next time it rained Father and Yusuf celebrated a dry kitchen floor. On its cool tiles our dad did his version of a Black Sea dance, crossing his arms, slapping his sides, squatting and spinning and kicking out his feet, while Yusuf clapped for him. Mother came in smiling, and suggested they stop the foolishness before they broke something. Father stood with a rare grin and ruffled Yusuf's hair. The two of them had fallen into contagious hysterics. Then Father, despite the warnings, was dancing again, and we were all clapping for him. It's the only time I can remember the four of us laughing together like that.

5

Leek Meatballs

BACK THEN THE Sea of Marmara was clean. It suffered none of the pollution from all these years of oil spills and industrial ship traffic. You could see dolphins in the waves, and though there were rumors of sharks, they were said to ply only the deeper waters, out past Heybeli Island, where the Greeks swam. Sharks, I'd thought from a young age, liked Greeks best. It was fun to toss steel *kuruş* coins into the shallows to retrieve, and as kids we used to skim the surface with enormous rubber face-masks no one in their right mind would wear today.

Prodded by Mother, our dad had taken it into his head that swimming was the best exercise to bolster his infirm son's lung capacity. He promised Yusuf if he swam every day he would live as long as anyone. Over the three weeks of July then, when he stayed with us full-time before returning to work in the city, Father doubled as our swim coach, teaching us with great seriousness the crawl, then the side and breast strokes. The weekend the roof was finished we celebrated with swimming lessons, followed by a picnic on Seferoğlu Beach with our maternal aunts and uncles.

The windy day made for a chaotic scene: blankets flopping, children running, mini-tornadoes kicking up from the sand. Uncle Abud, sprawled on his towel, his great hairy chest and weightlifter's arms a comic sight, kept popping Mother's leek meatballs into his mouth whenever she wasn't looking. Once, catching my stare, my uncle winked, raised a stubby finger to his lips, and pointed to my mother. She would have slapped her brother if she had seen him stealing the product of a full morning's labor. Secretly I admired his guiltless crime. A thief among us! A Leek Meatball Thief! That was my Uncle Abud, and in my mind that's what he'd always be.

Aunt Grazya had brought along two expansive cotton tablecloths for her brimming family, and had sent four of my cousins off to find rocks to place on the corners so the hot wind would not upset the picnic. Uncle Tobya looked uncomfortable on the beach; he kept standing up and rearranging himself, then sitting down, crossing his legs and uncrossing them. "My husband," Grazya announced, arranging the olives stuffed with peppers, "has never learned how to relax. Give him an account book to balance and he's the happiest man alive. Give him the sun, the sea, a delicious breeze, and you'd think he was being tortured."

"I'm relaxed," Tobya grumbled, pulling at his shirt collar. "I'm *relaxed!*"

Grazya sent him off to make sure the children weren't drowning themselves, and got busy organizing our mother's dishes. It was while Grazya's husband walked away, while Mother was spreading the plates on the second tablecloth and Father was tossing a shrieking Yusuf into the waves that I saw Uncle Abud again stretch his great arm in the direction of Mother's *mezes*. He lifted a *filika* between thumb and forefinger and shoved the cheese-filled pastry into his mouth. Then he glanced at me. I had caught him a second time. Abud stopped chewing, rolled the pastry in his cheeks, swallowed it in one enormous gulp, and with a great lion's roar charged out to the water and belly-flopped in. I said nothing about the small crime to my mother. I'd wonder later, if I had said something — if I had exposed Abud at that moment for the man he was — what I might have changed.

After lunch Father bragged that his sons had perfected their swimming strokes and were ready to race any challengers. He paced the rocky beach to a spot twenty meters away. Yusuf and I joined three other teeth-chattering cousins lined up side by side, chest-deep in the water. Uncle Tobya stood at the finish line, holding up his glinting watch, first to his eye, then to his ear. Father raised one arm, pointed a finger in the air, counted to three, and mimed the gunshot. We sucked huge breaths, and off we went, racing to Tobya in a desperate display of coughing and splashing and gagging. Yusuf, less coordinated, handicapped by lungs that were already scarring, would nevertheless grow to be the strongest swimmer among us, with thoughtful, efficient strokes. But I was older and had greater endurance; and in that first race, flapping wildly, I beat him.

"It's the last time you ever could have done that," my cousin Byanka, now a middle-aged mother of two, reminded me many years later, sitting on that same beach. And it was true: Yusuf went on to become a first-class swimmer, so strong that the initial reports of his drowning at sea at the age of thirty-eight would be met by friends and relations with stern incredulity. "I myself never believed it," Byanka always maintained. "He had to be dead by the time he hit the water. Or else he would've simply swum back to Kadıköy. That kid could out-swim a torpedo."

She remembered correctly. By the time he was seventeen Yusuf would be competing in four events in the city championships — the breast-stroke his strongest. His name and weekly swim-meet times appeared in the youth group newsletters, always beside the same black and white photo: chin forever tucked, arms forever reaching, body perpetually suspended in mid-air off a starting block. The caption: *Yusuf Benezra, despite his battles with cystic fibrosis, trains with the Adalar Spor Kulübü year round. He remains a serious prospect to make the national junior team.*

For my part I grew to hate swimming. All that first summer I had to swallow my fears of the sea, of the unseen creatures that prowled its depths, and each time I felt the slime of seaweed skim my ankle I was convinced a jellyfish had stung me.

We raced once more that day — the breast stroke. This time I made a point of letting Yusuf keep up with me. Still it was close. Father was an indecisive judge though, and spacey Uncle Tobya had gotten lost in some speed calculation. We called to Mother up on the beach, who signaled with her cigarette that Yusuf was the winner. From under her striped blue umbrella she tensed her neck and gazed at me with a look that meant: you're older, healthy, and you can accept defeat better at your age. The Lucky Son.

Father lined us up, and raised Yusuf's long bony arm.

6

No Room

AFTER THE SWIMMING, after a dessert of cold melon, after a beach tackle-football match, I spotted Father resting on the rocks, legs pulled up nearly to his chest. Yusuf had sprawled beside him on a towel. Together, enjoying the warmth of the late afternoon sun, inhaling the scent of the sea, they seemed lost in thought. I took a seat beside Yusuf. Father drew his arm around both of us, hugged us close, and let go again. For a few minutes I joined their reverie. Heat and sweat coated our sunburnt skin.

"Beautiful, isn't it?" Father asked, waving his arm out to the beads of light dappling the waters. We nodded.

"Listen." His tone grew somber.

I glanced up. Yusuf too was quiet, waiting.

Father scratched his eyebrow with his thumb. "What you have to go through is bad," he said, looking down at my brother. "It won't be easy. You didn't ask for any of this, I know. But remember those journeys. Remember what real suffering was. Ship after ship, fleeing

Europe. Packed ships. Cattle ships. Wooden boats hardly capable of floating down a river. Jews, our brothers. Packed like rice in grapeleaves. No room to turn, to walk. No room to lie down, to stand, to use the toilet. Trying to get from Hitler to Palestine."

"Palestine," Yusuf repeated with a nod.

"The British ran it back then, and they didn't want us there yet. They were afraid for their oil, they needed the Arabs. They had a war to win, you see. What was one ship of Jews worth, when the fate of the world was at stake? And our brothers, our uncles, our aunts, buying their way on. And here, in-between, this country of ours, this crippled little country trying to take care of its own mess, barely able to wipe its own behind, unable to take sides. Unwilling."

I could only half understand the veiled references to history. I doubted my brother understood any more than me.

Father paused, shaking his head. "Boat after boat, plying their way down the coast of the Black Sea, through the straits, right here into the Marmara. They would have passed this very island, you see. It wouldn't have meant anything to them. A summer retreat! What was a summer retreat to these people, crammed five to a berth? In a winter storm, one of these boats — a cattle ship, nothing more — one of these boat's engines fail. It gets towed out there, way out, to the city coast. Winds rocking it. Rain and sleet pelting it. People sick inside, the smell of vomit thick in the air. Coughing and hunger and misery. Adrift at sea in a boat with no engines. And it slams into rocks — right out there, along the coast."

Yusuf, coughing again, covered his eyes in the sun, trying to see where Father was pointing. Mechanically I patted my brother's back.

Father looked down at us. "*"Gudio ki no ayuda a otro non ay,"* the saying goes. There's not a Jew who does not help another. An alert sounds back in town; and your grandfather — your mom's dad — comes to help. One of many, a young man himself. Off the rocks near the beach he wades in with the rescue workers, pulling bodies in the snow and freezing rain. His coat is soaked, you see, weighing him down. The wind is churning up waves, you see. Waist deep, shoulder deep, he's stretching his arms and dragging bodies by their hair and belts and shredded clothes. Such suffering! Two children and three women he pulled ashore, he once told me. He didn't like to remember. You had to drag it out of him. And corpses, he said. Floating corpses. The ones who couldn't swim. Those he didn't count. The water was so cold it burnt. Some of the rescued died even later. He was sick for weeks."

Father looked down at each of us in turn. "Two hundred drowned that night fleeing the Nazis. And you remember what that boat's name was?"

We shook our heads.

"The *Salvador.* Don't forget. It was called the *Salvador.*"

We shifted on the rocks, failing to digest the magnitude of our father's words, too young to understand the ceaseless horrors of the past. Yusuf asked, "Some lived though, right?"

Father's voice thickened. "Of course, of course. Some always live, to tell the story. More than a hundred and thirty were rescued. They sent them on to Palestine. Then the British — well, they wanted to ship them off to an island in the Indian Ocean. But that's another story, for another time." Father whistled lightly. "What a disaster the world can be."

"And grandmother?" I asked. I'd heard some of this before, and was connecting the pieces.

"She stayed." Father smiled, just barely. "Married your grandfather, the man who had dragged her from the water. The man who had saved her from the *Salvador*."

"But her parents?"

Father looked out and motioned with a flat palm across the sea. "This, too, is our cemetery."

Yusuf and I sat straighter on the rocks, respectfully silent, looking out across the Marmara. Our legs we pulled up now to our chests, our hands we locked round our wrists. The sun slunk lower, its movement closer to the horizon almost visible. The metallic waters glistened, mocking us.

In the summers to come Father would repeat the story. He spoke of the sea in those haunted terms. All he wanted was for us to swim — swim well, swim every day, swim for our lives. We were now a family at leisure, satisfied with the ups and downs of our fate in this city we had made our home, this city which five hundred years before had taken in one side of our family and had continued, in recent memory, to offer salvation to the other side. We must never forget. Our great grandparents, trying to get to Israel, had perished off this coastline. Now we vacationed here, a few kilometers away, diving and splashing in the same temperamental waves.

For three summers, despite Yusuf's severe diagnosis, this was the happy rhythm of our lives: the mornings working on the house, the afternoon picnics on the beach, the swimming races, the (admittedly terrifying) contests to see who could hold our breaths longest underwater, the football in the Golf Park, the twice-weekly movies at the open-air cinema, the melon ice-cream cones from Yunus's cart. In the evenings during Yusuf's therapy, out on the porch he and I would challenge my cousins to backgammon. We'd play as a team, with Yusuf rolling the dice, with me straddling him over the bench, clapping his back between turns. Clap clap clap — clap clap! My memory sometimes deceives me, but I don't believe it's romanticized how for three summers we'd lived this way, still a family, our health and finances stretched but intact; and I don't believe it's exaggerated how decisively everything changed once we lost the cottage.

"You all were ruined," my great-aunt Donna Linda recalled to me in the Dormitory for the Aging, where I used to visit her in my college years. She was delirious with age by then, and to my mind raving mad, and her remembering this with so much clarity made it seem like the only truth that ever mattered. "Ruined," she said, "because of your thieving dad."

7

Who Are You Going to Believe?

WHEN RELATIVES PLACED the blame on Father for the great rifts that divided the family I'd find myself defending him — first against my own doubts, and late at night, from across the bedroom, against Yusuf's. We were too young to grasp what would take me half a lifetime to work out, but we argued about it anyway, as brothers do.

I was only thirteen, Yusuf eleven, so how could we understand the stakes here, the patterns of history unspiraling? Five centuries ago our people, exiled, rootless, had sailed directly towards these trials. Since the year we had washed up on the shores of the Ottoman Empire we'd been guests in a Muslim land. The fault-lines had always existed. How could we understand that we had been living on borrowed time, and that this time, in my parents' generation, had simply run its course? Two World Wars. The Wealth Taxes. The anti-Minority Riots. Under all this pressure the slightest fissure — some misplaced blame, some slipping trust — could splinter and cleave the bedrock of religion and family and language on which our community had long stood. Yes, the ground was shifting again; we had to flexibly adapt to the strong motion of a new nation, or leave it behind for brighter shores.

Late at night Yusuf and I would hash it out. Our twin beds were lined up against the far wall of our city bedroom, the only wall in the room without a radiator or window. We slept head to head, separated by a ceiling-high sheet of plywood whose respective sides we used as bulletin boards for school calendars, Chiclet comics, and clipped headlines of our football teams' victories. Father had built the wall to afford us the illusion of privacy, but we could talk right through it.

"Avram, you think he has nothing to do with it! That only *our* father is innocent! Why more innocent than Uncle Tobya? Or Uncle Abud?"

"Because he's not a thief."

"I hope to God," my brother said, "he wouldn't do this for me."

"Listen to me Yusuf. He didn't *do* anything — not for you, not for me, not for anyone else."

"Israel," Yusuf would mutter. "Mother's threatening us with Israel again."

Friends were advising my parents to leave, as our paternal ancestors had once fled Spain, as our mother's grandparents had fled Romania, as so many among us were doing every year. Father believed flight was not the answer. He saw our family's challenges not as the cruel end of a long stay in a once hospitable land, but as the opportunity to make something still better of ourselves. Father stared into the cracking mirror of our national identity and never wavered.

"If he did it," I'd whisper, "he'd admit it to us."

"You're only taking his side because he's our dad," my brother would call out. "You want that to be true, Avram, even if it's not."

"If you can't believe your own father, who are you going to believe?"

Through the plywood came the sound of Yusuf's scratched breathing, and then a forced cough. I knew it wasn't a real one; I could always tell.

I'd learn the entire story only in the year after Mother's death. By then Yusuf had abandoned us, and straight through our lonely dinners Father, so distraught, so riddled by guilt, would talk at me, repeating the sordid details, dredging his memory for first causes.

This is where Father spotted that initial rupture: The year I was born my uncles had opened a jewelry shop in the southeast corner of the Old Bedestan, in the Covered Bazaar. They could barely keep it afloat. Mother had pressed Father to give up his study of architecture and help her brothers save the struggling business. He took on the challenge, dropped out of school, and managed the shop in equal parts with Abud and Tobya. With his help they made a success of it — a fact that would, through all of the finger-pointing that followed, be forgotten.

Tobya, Mother's older brother, was a frail man who wore a pair of thick reading glasses on a silver necklace that hung below his salt and pepper beard. The accountant of the group, Tobya kept the books and figures in a black leather ledger which was always shedding sheets of onionskin. This ledger seemed full of dark secrets. It sat on the desk behind the counter, next to the clacking metal register, and Yusuf and I took turns flipping through it, staring at Tobya's dense numeric scribbling, trying to decipher how much money our parents earned each week. Uncle Tobya, whose goal in school had been to study finance and work his way into one of the multinationals beginning to invest in our country, had instead, for lack of coursework, backed into an accounting degree. He was a man who'd never achieved the high standards he set for himself. He went about life convinced he was being undermined, but at the same time doing things which undermined his own natural talents: an early loveless marriage to Aunt Grazya (arranged by his parents), four children in five years (more than he was ready to support), then the purchase of a Chrysler he could not afford and, before he was ready, investment in a summer house on the island a block from our own. But the jewelry venture he had fallen into made it all work out in the end. Pressured by Abud, rescued by Father, Uncle Tobya stumbled into the lifestyle he later convinced himself he'd always imagined.

Tobya displayed self-confidence only when he was reciting numbers from his head. He was capable of great calculations, and whenever we came to the shop Yusuf would try to catch him off guard with a pre-arranged figure. "One hundred forty-five thousand nine hundred and ninety-nine…divided by fifty-four," Yusuf would shout. A moment would pass. Tobya would stand perfectly still, then with nervous hands pretend to clean the counter or rearrange the gems beneath the glass shelf. Before long he'd murmur, "Two thousand seven hundred and four… rounding up." We stared at him, wondering at his gift.

Sometimes in the shop Tobya, in return, used to challenge me and Yusuf to mathematical competitions of long division. "Fourteen twenty-five divided by sixteen?" he'd call out, glancing

up from behind his ledger, the slightest curl on his thin, brillian-
tined mustache. The race was on. I would press my fingers to
my temple. Sixteen into one-forty-two. Nine was too much. Try
eight. I was looking at my brother, and by then I could hear the
machine whirring in Yusuf's head, and I'd completely lost track
of the figures. Yusuf would announce the quotient before I was
even close.

"Bravo, son," Tobya whispered, and was back to his figures.

Tobya always had a stormy relationship with our mother,
who was in the middle of him and Abud, and who treated her
abstracted older brother in a maternal way he found insulting.
"Oh, when we were teenagers," Mother used to say, "we fought
epic battles. Tobya would gather me into a wrestling hold while I
pummeled his legs with my fists. What a wimp, to fight a girl like
that, and his sister yet!" Tobya stood only 1.7 meters — 1.8 on his
tiptoes. I remember him eternally hunched over the glass cases,
writing his accounts. He could hardly be bothered even with the
excitement of football. He always cheered "for a good game." A
good game! Yusuf and I laughed at that, and from an early age
we accepted that Tobya would never be invited over to watch a
match, the way Abud, a fellow Fenerbahçe fanatic, often was.

Abud, our bachelor uncle, was a tall stocky man with broad
hunters' shoulders and a thick gut. He suffered from chronic
back problems which he claimed were the result of weight-lift-
ing in the army, when he had once aspired to make the Olympic
team and become the nation's first gold medalist Jew. Abud was
the store's salesman. He was handsome, with fine rounded features — an eyeful for the female customers. With the baritone
voice of a disc jockey and the curly brown hair of Adonis, he

stationed himself at the entranceway, cat calling to women, teasing couples, giving paper flowers to babies, asking didn't that young man's girlfriend deserve a new necklace? He was the one who traveled to Antwerp twice a year with a group of salesmen from Jeweler's Row to purchase that season's stones: rubies and diamonds and sapphire, all the birthday pieces, jade for the earrings. Abud had an eye, and after three visits his connections in Brussels were established enough to eliminate the possibility of either Tobya or Father, both family men, from going.

Abud was close with Mother. His voice would grow high and sweet when they spoke, and he never turned down a request for anything she asked of him. Despite Abud's garrulousness he was forever single. So at Father's urging the splenetic Tobya and the distant Aunt Grazya were named our godparents. As a young boy I used to imagine with horror our fate should something happen to Mother and Father, and it was doubly horrifying to know that the accountant and his standoffish wife would be responsible for us when the impending ferry crashes and trolley accidents of my imagination took our parents to the grave.

Tobya overseeing the books. Abud the salesman. Father played the artisan: he took care of the sizing of rings, the correction of watchbands, the repairs of defective clasps. He enjoyed working at the back desk beneath a strong jeweler's light which, Yusuf and I marveled, was miraculously adjustable in all directions. Below that a line of miniature wrenches hung upside down from a metal wire — tools that had always looked to me like instruments of exquisite torture. Father possessed a wondrous facility for working with his hands, an endless capacity for repair. The shop got a yearly fresh coat of paint, and new wainscoting, and he loved fashioning and leveling the jewel cases. For him the continual reorganizing of the displays seemed less a business concern than a pet project.

In this way the three men shared the duties of a slowly growing business. "None of us imbeciles could have done it ourselves," Father would say. Between the families the rotation shifted, so that all three men had two days off. On weekends Mother helped behind the counter, and I have fond memories of afternoons spent in the store, Yusuf and I gazing up as a world of foreigners paraded in. The business with tourists was brisk, especially in the summertime when cruise ships docked at Kabataş, leaving only three hours for passengers to rush up the winding streets to the Grand Bazaar and search out the Treasures of the East. They tried on antique rings and bargained over harem mirrors. When Mother's quiet attitude or Father's pressed lips indicated they had gotten the better of some European snob, we too contained our smiles. Five centuries of rejection, we'd take our small revenge.

8

A Thief

Late on a Thursday evening in August — our family was
out of the city, summering on the island for the third straight
year — Father had returned to the store unannounced to check
on a re-sizing for a friend. The bazaar was set to close, and he
was expecting to find Tobya hunched over the counter. Then he
remembered that Tobya had duties as treasurer of the Cultural
Club, and Grazya was covering. Yet one hour before closing time
he found the corrugated steel gate already drawn.

Selfish Grazya. This was just like her, to try to get away with
closing up early when no one was watching. He viewed his sis-
ter-in-law with disdain. He could hardly hold a conversation
with her — but who could? She seemed aloof, always pulling at
the waves in her long curly hair, or touching her modest nose
to check it was still in its perfectly repaired place. Her eyebrows
were severely tweaked. You spoke to her, but you realized she
was only ever half-listening. "Perhaps it was the pressure of four
children?" Father would wonder years later, alone with me at
our dinner table. "And the lengths she would go to make herself

up — for whom? For Tobya! With his face pressed into his account ledgers, he never even noticed her. I couldn't understand that marriage, but I said nothing. Especially to your mother. You can't know the depths of other people's hearts."

Still, closing up shop an hour early? Father imagined Grazya off bargaining in the rug stores, or spending her husband's money on a new leather jacket, or sitting at the Havuzlu Café, one intensely moisturized hand propping up her chin, the other paging through *Mutfak* and her interior design magazines. He'd have to tell Tobya.

Father unlocked the store gate and drew it crashing up. He could see that a light in the back room had strangely been left on. This was unlike any of them — Tobya or his wife — who were careful about the electric bill. His next thought was: a thief.

The store was a small cluttered space, with two long glass cases containing mostly rings (platinum and white gold) and objects of art: menorahs, Koran stands, necklaces of the Star of David and the cross, *hanukiyas*, an antique red-glass *kidduş* set that was the centerpiece of the front window. Purple velvet curtains covering the dark walls gave the room less the atmosphere of a shop than of a medieval bordello.

If you pulled the curtain on the far wall, a short door led to the storage area, which was nearly as large as the front room itself. Father's plan had always been to finish this back room, knock down the right side of the wall, and double the size of the shop. This never happened; he never found time for it, and the back room became the place where the men would eat their lunches of salty black olives and grilled meatballs brought in from Sevim Lokantası. In the second year after Father joined them Uncle Abud installed a full-sized cot against the back wall, so that during slow times one of the men could take a nap. The former weightlifter claimed that a full day on his feet or even sitting on the tall wooden stool behind the counter took its toll on his back. He stiffened the mattress by laying two sheets of plywood between the pads and springs. Abud had the unique ability to sleep at will. Mid-afternoon, from the front of the shop we could hear his hippopotamus snores through the walls. He slept, the great beast, on his stomach in a fetal position, his bowling pin arms tucked under his face, a transistor radio tuned to jazz propped on the shelf behind him. On weekends Mother kicked him off the cot for the afternoon chest therapy she had me administer to Yusuf. I wiled away winter Saturdays, straddling my brother on that infamous cot, clapping his back with cupped hands, while out front our yawning uncles sold jewels to Scandinavians.

Now the light at the door frightened Father. Later he would acknowledge his first suspicion was foolish. The inner bazaar had been impenetrable since Ottoman times, when the entire Bedestan closed down nightly and was protected by the Sultan's private police force. Still, a thief was what Father suspected, and it was why he grasped the first weapon in sight: a long Shabat candle holder. Its cold silver lay heavy in his fist; its rounded grooves offered a solid grip, like the hilt of a sword.

Father turned the brass knob, pushing it down with his full weight until the door flew open and the stale black air of that room, sawdust and packing tape and epoxy, engulfed him. From his right came a high-pitched gasp.

His brother-in-law was hopping on one leg, trying to push his left foot through the twisted opening of his trousers. The harder he pushed the tighter the pants seemed to twist, until he stood still, his trousers down at his knees. His frightened gaze met Father's. Behind Abud, sprawled on the cot, a person Father had not recognized in her nakedness came into focus. Aunt Grazya was fumbling with a brassiere. She held Father's eyes for a long moment. From the rush of the opened door the bare bulb was still swinging. It illuminated Grazya's red and scornful face; the rest of her body lay deep in shadow. Jazz played tinnily from the transistor radio on the shelf. Grazya tugged the wool blanket up to her bare shoulders. Her hair was scattered loose in silky rivulets down her back. Abud had managed to pull up his pants and was trying to secure the zipper, but in his haste it had snagged. "Emil," he kept repeating, hobbling forward, one thick arm extended palm out, the other working the zipper. Father stepped back. "Emil. Emil." Abud's voice lowered from surprise to anger to a beseeching threat. "Listen. *Emil.*"

Father realized only then that the Shabat candle holder was still raised over his shoulder. "I think Grazya was shaking with the fear that I was going to beat her," he remembered. "Abud was stepping forward to disarm me. I had forgotten I was even holding the damn thing. I was thinking — of poor Tobya."

His arm fell to his side, his grip loosened on the silver candle holder. He looked away, then looked back to convince himself he was seeing what he was seeing. Abud reached for a shirt from a pile on the floor, but accidentally pulled up a blouse, and tossed it to Grazya with a grunt. She did not let go of the blanket clutched to her chest — by now she'd begun sobbing, her enormous mouth taking in long wild breaths. Father felt an anger and disgust swelling inside him. Abud stepped closer and placed a hand on his shoulder. "I had the strongest impulse to bite it," Father later admitted, "something I've never done to another human being."

He jerked away at Abud's touch. "I've seen nothing." He stared up at the swinging light bulb. "Forget I've been here."

"But brother," Abud pleaded, "wait!"

Father pivoted slowly on his heels, stepped out of the room, and pulled the door handle until the bolt's tongue clicked into place. Ridiculously, he drew the velvet curtain to cover the light under the back room door, replaced the Shabat candle holder, adjusted its angle, and rumbled the steel security gate closed. It fell against the tiled walkway of the Old Bedestan with a rousing crash.

On the walk back to the Eminönü ferry his fury rose. "It occurred to me in that moment that Grazya and Abud had not only risked their own happiness, but had staked the entire livelihood of the family. It was a disaster. I would have done anything not to have known." He sensed the end of the string of good years. His only hope was that Abud would be discreet. Father told himself that none of it had anything to do with him. He would keep his mouth utterly shut. *Hablad la verdad, perded la amistad.* Speak the truth and lose the friendship.

9

Cast Adrift

THE GUILT SWELLED though, especially on Thursdays and Saturdays, when Father shared the shop with Tobya, the cuckold in thick reading glasses pathetically scribbling the accounts. "I couldn't face your Aunt Grazya," Father recalled to me. "I could hardly look at your mother, knowing I'd have to unburden myself. I was miserable. The whole affair, you see, now I had some part in it. Abud suddenly generous. Offering to cover for me on Saturdays. Offering season football tickets. Rubbing my shoulder and laughing at tired jokes. His touch — I couldn't take it. I could hardly make it through a shift with him. I was quiet. Abud sensed it. He got suspicious, you see. He was certain I would say something to your mother, she would tell Tobya. I was at the edge of an abyss. Still, I held out. I never said a word. That was my one mistake."

By September the silent animosity could no longer be borne. Father had covered for his partners a full week while they vacationed on the island. He had worked those long days alone. He later claimed it had been a relief, that he realized only then what a liberation working alone would one day be. It had been a lucrative week. Business at the bazaar had steadily been improving, recovering in the years after the 1980 military coup, and buoyed by a surge in overseas advertising by the Board of Tourism. There had been a steady stream of customers: the Germans with their army rucksacks, the Italians with fine belts and slicked back hair, the English hunting the rug shops of Sultanahmet before a mass-migration south to the Irish Pubs of the Turquoise Coast. Father maintained he'd taken in more that week than the previous month. The money was locked in the safe in the rear of the store at the end of the night, then deposited in the Ak Bank branch along Nuruosmaniye Street on Friday afternoons, a task assigned to Tobya. And this was where, even for those of us wanting to believe him, Father's story grew murky. The money never made it in for deposit. That Friday morning the week's earnings were cleaned out of the safe.

"Of all the weeks when we might have been robbed — and we had never been robbed before — why under my watch?" Father demanded, immediately defensive whenever friends or family brought it up. He cast the accusing finger at Abud. "And why had they taken none of the jewelry? I was being set up. I've said that a thousand times."

Abud accused Father of taking the cash himself, of using the week alone to pull off the crime, of tossing the money he stole towards Yusuf's mounting medical bills, which by that summer had become a pressing issue. Tobya's ledgers and inventories showed over 400,000 lira worth of jewelry had been sold. Father was outnumbered, and it looked bad, even to us. Mother insisted she believed him; but she wore her addled grief openly. In those weeks I'd catch her alone on the balcony in the mornings, staring into the hazy sky, an unlit cigarette hanging from her mouth, her lips twitching. I'd quietly run Yusuf through his morning therapy myself. Whatever my doubts, I was willing to trust my father. What choice did I have? Yusuf was the one who could never move past his constant calculations.

"I hope to God," my brother would say, "he wouldn't do it for me."

The Bazaar police were called in. Dusting revealed all three men's prints on the counter locks and safe. Father was in a suspicious position, but untenable as well, for now if he were to accuse Abud or bring up Grazya's marital indiscretions it would seem he was throwing off the accusations. Despairing, he sought out Tobya at his home.

The apartment was a dimly lit three-bedroom affair four blocks from our own in Şişli, on whose shag orange carpet we had slept many weekends when our parents went out to weddings or to *meldados*. Father knocked. Tobya, answering, stood at the doorway blocking entrance with his arm.

"I'm your brother-in-law, Tobya. I just want to talk."

The diminutive man held his hand high on the door, gripping it with white fingers. Footsteps came from the kitchen, and Grazya appeared with a wet apron around her waist, a kerchief covering her pulled-back hair. Her face was tanned from her summer of island sun and she looked, even in her ragged house dress, perfectly made-up. Registering who it was her eyes revealed only the briefest glimmer of terror.

"Emil!" Her tone said it all: he had come, she believed, to tell Tobya what he knew. It was the end. To Grazya's credit she didn't hesitate. "Aren't you going to let your brother in?" she asked. She tugged Tobya aside, cast a prolonged glare at Father, and ushered him into the apartment.

"Tea? Biscuits?" she asked. "You'll stay for lunch, I hope."

"Nothing for me." He sat on the couch, leaned over his knees, scratched at his eyebrows. She brought him tea and sesame *biscochos* anyway. "Drink, brother."

The three sat in silence, sipping, nibbling. "God knows what each of us was thinking," Father remembered. "I wanted their forgiveness for a crime I hadn't committed. Tobya? Tobya might have believed I was there to confess. Grazya — she didn't know what to expect."

"It's been nine good years together," he began. "I didn't do it, Tobya. You have to believe me. When have I failed you before?"

"You've been acting so strangely. Where'd the jewelry go then? Are you saying you didn't make those sales?"

"I made the sales all right." Father shook his head. A sesame seed had lodged itself in his throat. He shifted in his seat and coughed into his fist. "I don't know. I don't know." He was approaching this the wrong way, he realized. "I'm family. We're brothers. Partners in this. You have to trust me. What idiot would do such a thing?"

Tobya stood, thrust one hand in his pocket and paced the room. "I've always trusted. I've never doubted." His voice wilted. "But Emil…nobody else had access."

"I know it looks bad. Think about it! I would have faked the robbery. Turned things over, covered my traces, something sharper than this. *Gudio bovo no hay.* There is no stupid Jew. You're not the only one with brains, Tobya."

Grazya, wide-eyed, implored her husband: "You should believe him already."

Tobya's voice hardened again. "Stay out of this."

"Don't speak to me like that. He's always speaking to me like that."

"This doesn't concern you."

"Why would Emil do such a thing? To hurt his own business?"

Tobya glared at his wife and snapped, "Why *anybody* does *anything* is a mystery to me."

Father looked at them both, and understood Tobya already sensed it. Deep down Tobya knew what his wife was doing, knew even whom she was doing it with, and in the morass of his weakness and through the blindness of his fears he could not confront her. It was simpler to believe in lies. The question was: did Tobya know *he* knew as well? Did he blame him for bearing witness to his shame?

"I felt the family crumbling then and there," Father claimed to me, remembering. "What would I tell my wife, bless her soul? How would you kids play with your cousins again? How could I stay in business with two men who despised me? And for nothing I had even done? My good name, you see. My marriage! Why would I have risked any of it? For a little money?"

Tobya had perched himself on the low radiator, his back to the curtained window. Over his shoulder a beam of afternoon light cut through the dusty air. "I can forgive you, Emil. That doesn't bring us out of this. 400,000 — it's quite a sum! If you needed a loan, for your son —"

"Brother, I don't need your forgiveness. I didn't take it."

"You can admit it. Pay us back. As long as it takes. We can move on."

"Admit it! It would be a lie."

"We could get by. We could work through this, if you admit it.

We could forget and look forward." He spiraled a finger towards the ceiling. "Only forward."

"I have my pride, Tobya. I'm a father, a husband, not a criminal." His eyes slid briefly towards Grazya.

"Nobody's calling you a criminal," Grazya murmured. "We understand what pressures you're under."

Father stood, crumbling his felt hat in his hand. "I'll leave."

"Go then."

"The shop…I'm leaving the shop. Give me my share of what it's worth. I'll never set foot in the godforsaken place again. It's yours."

"We owe you nothing, Emil. You're the one who owes *us*."

"You'll send me packing — your family, your own sister, a nephew who's suffering — with nothing?"

"You've taken your share!"

"Fools!" Father waved his crushed hat at them both. "Fools!" he cried.

He left the apartment in a rush, head spinning. That evening he returned to the shop. "I felt like a thief myself, stealing jewelry that already belonged to me. What was I supposed to do? I took only a third of it, enough for us to start fresh, to keep up with Yusuf's doctors' bills. I was the one who had been robbed, you see. My reputation! My livelihood! I'd been cheated, and you, both my children, were cheated too. We wouldn't stoop to their level. I wouldn't toss accusations at your aunt and uncles. If that was the kind of family I married into, it was family I no longer needed. When I explained it to your mother, I saw doubt even in her eyes. Even your mother! I realized then how alone we men are in this world."

Father recounted all this to me in the midst of my own grief, and at that time I didn't want to hear it. I wondered what the use of it was, this perpetual turning over of the past, this digging and digging in an attempt to figure out the precise moment one's life had gone wrong. Did it serve any purpose at all? It was so long ago, who even cared anymore? But across the years I'd listen with increasing compassion to him rooting through these memories. He couldn't move on. I still wondered — God forgive me! — if the man could have done it. Could he have stolen so much money and, pulled along by the current of his story, emptied out a third of the family jewelry store? Could he have lied to his own wife and sons? It seemed impossible. Not my good father. And yet, here was a man still prodding deeper and deeper through the layers of muck, searching for a truth that might exonerate him. It had stained his life. It was always with him.

For the rift was there, never to be bridged. We were cast adrift from Mother's family.

10

A Little Spoonful of a Little Urine

It was too late to complete his architectural studies (I'd make that up for him a decade later), but with the value of the jewels he had stolen from his own store, Father attempted one failed venture after another. Eventually he opened a mildly profitable school-supply shop, a ten-minute walk up the hill through the gypsy neighborhood from our apartment. August was our big season: the back-to-school month, when mothers dragged their children in to buy colored pencils and drawing pads, notebooks and compasses, pencil sharpeners and carbon paper, dossiers, erasers, glue, ink, labels, punches, staplers, string, and watercolors. Father took pride in knowing the neighborhood children, in keeping track of what grade they were in, of what teacher they would have, of who had passed their entrance exams to which private school. "It's the business," he would intone with forced optimism. "Never forget it! A vinegar seller with a smile earns more than a honey seller with a sour look." Yusuf and I understood that our father's use of business clichés would never compensate for his lack of business sense. The store advertised

Back-to-School Packs, which Father sold for a discount. You got your six pens, a ruler, compass, pencil bag, and spiral notebook for only seven lira. Yusuf warned him that it was too little profit. Father intoned, "Give the people what they need at a discount; guarantee the quality." Pencils that broke or pens that ran he was in a habit of replacing free of charge. "If I only sell a needle, I still check on its metal." He began to sell Korans and Koran holders for the children of the local madrassa, a practice that raised sharp eyebrows among friends at the synagogue. "*Vende pipinos, vende halvah, i no asperes a nedavah,*" he said. Sell cucumbers, sell halvah, but don't expect anything from charity.

His was the first stationery store in the neighborhood, and we got by on savings. That very year a slum was cleared in the far corner of the quarter, and the petrochemical tycoon Mustafa Toprak bought up the land to open a branch of his Islamic university. The new college would be the boon to business Father had long been hoping for: the traffic of a thousand students, all in need of school supplies! A lucky break. Father bragged about plans to expand the summer cottage on the island with a sunroom in back.

That winter Toprak University sprang open with its very own bookstore. They imported products from Germany and Japan. They stocked Iranian notebooks and colorful dictionaries from England and France, and sold everything for minimal profit. It was a bright, two-story bookstore; the front doors opened with a magical rush when you hopped onto the rubber entrance-pad. (Yusuf and I secretly took turns.) The new shop was easily ten times the size of our own, and lit by fluorescent lights, and open until nine every evening, and it had digital electronic cash registers perched on shining glass cases, and textured globes we could touch, and a toy department that sold electronic handheld sports games with beeping lights. On all three floors Egyptian pop-music was piped in. The store carried posters of Mecca and Damascus, printed football T-shirts emblazoned with the university's logo. A rack of magazines seemed a kilometer long — longer than you could find in the bookstores of Kadıköy.

Six months later we were helping our parents box up what was left unsold in the Going-Out-Of-Business Sale. Mother had been quiet all day, and we sensed the tension between them in the ferocity of that silence. At one point Father grew distracted taping a carton, and unaware that the dispenser had run out, he ran its blade over his finger — slicing his thumb to the bone. A barrage of curses followed, filling the empty shelves with fresh obscenities. Yusuf and I stopped. Mother rushed over, hushed him, and bandaged his thumb with her scarf. She urged one of us to run to the *eczane* for antiseptic. Yusuf, who knew the pharmacist well by this point, sprinted out. Helpless, I stood there. My father was pressing his finger, bobbing his head forward like a rabbi davening. Mother tightened the scarf and held it, her lips twitching, and then murmured something in my father's ear. Pretending to count rulers and tie them with rubber bands, I couldn't make out what she had whispered.

"Estela, not in front of the child."

"Semuel needs to know by the end of the week. Why won't you talk about it?"

"When the time's right."

She lowered her voice to a strained whisper. "You've said that three times."

I glanced up at them. Mother's eyes met my own. "Uncle Semuel knows an apartment in his building in Haifa."

"Estela."

"It's open. He's arranged it for us, if we'll move there."

"Estela!"

"This is a decision for the whole family. This concerns Avram too." She let go of my father's bloody finger and stepped over a box towards me. "What do you think Avram? Wouldn't you like to go to Israel? Wouldn't you like to make a move?" She had often mentioned a move to Israel. Her grandparents had lost their lives in the effort. It was a journey left incomplete in her mind.

I was only thirteen. I looked around at the failed shop, at the empty shelve, at the blinking lights and scratched tiled floor. I weighed all this against our seats at Fenerbahçe stadium, my friends at school, our summers on the island; and I lifted my chin and clicked my tongue no.

"Enough!" Father yelled. "They've grown up here. They speak the language better than their Muslim friends. This is the boys' country."

"You're afraid."

"My family's been here longer than half the people in this city. We've made good on it. It's our city. We've helped build it up. Our friends are here. Our life's here. Your own mother found safety on these shores."

"Her parents were trying to get her to Israel."

Father waved his bloody hand around the failed stationery shop. "It's a shame she didn't make it– is that what you're saying? All your problems would have been solved there. The Promised Land. None of this."

"That's not what I'm saying. It's just — we could use a fresh start, Emil. There are good doctors for Yusuf. It's going to get harder here for him. Semuel says in Israel — "

"Israel Israel Israel." Father pried open the bandage to check his finger, and wincing, lifted his head. "We hardly know anyone there. The boys will have no friends. And such violence!"

Father would never let us forget what our country, despite its faults, had offered us. As friends and relations emigrated one by one, he kept us staunchly rooted. Yes, the Jews finally had their own state, a spiritual homeland, but the diaspora must dig its heels into the sands of other nations as well. One of his favorite sayings was: "From inside of a watermelon, out came a Jew!" Starting life over in an unfamiliar land, perpetually at war with its neighbors, bereft of everything we knew, made no sense. It was Father's great fear, a fear three decades later, on the verge of a divorce, I would realize I'd inherited.

"There's violence everywhere, Emil," Mother was saying. "National Unification. Citizen, speak Turkish! That's always been the government's answer. You want to unify? Well, you'll see. The boys will forget who we are. It's all going before we can blink. We're losing ourselves."

With her clear moist eyes she was entreating him. She stepped back over to Father and clicking her tongue, unwound the kerchief again. It had soaked up ovals of dark blood, and the tip of his thumb was still wet with it. Father thrust it into his mouth.

"Here." She pulled it out again and wrapped it afresh. "*Una kutcharika de pisha dika.*" A little spoonful of a little urine: the remedy our grandmother used to prescribe, now no more than a running family joke. Mother recited the old prayer. "In the name of God, Abraham, Isaac, and Jacob, I remove from you, Emil Benezra, the evil eye, evil talk, all evil, all fright; let them go to the bottom of the sea."

Yusuf came running in with a clean bandage and antiseptic. Mother sprayed it on and Father, eyes watering, howled. In his pain he was so pathetic that soon they were laughing at each other, and we were staring at them, thoroughly confused.

Mother tsked and said, "Old man, I think we need to get this finger to a hospital." She pulled him up from his squat, and aimed him by the elbow around the empty counter towards the door. "Come. A little urine, a few stitches, all the same thing." They maneuvered together through the sad rows of half-filled boxes.

Under my supervision, we, their good sons, finished packing the rulers.

11

Off the Princes' Islands

Dᴜʀɪɴɢ ᴛʜᴇ ᴡᴇᴀʟᴛʜ taxes of 1942 my paternal grandfather had lost everything. When he couldn't pay the draconian taxes leveled on minorities, the family's textile factory was seized, and grandfather was sentenced to hard labor in Aşkale, breaking rocks with Armenians in the frigid mountains out east. Father, a young boy then, hadn't known if he would ever see his dad again. My grandmother had no word from her husband for over a year, and was convinced he had succumbed to a more subtle version of the ovens. But no ovens existed in our nation, thank the Lord, and my grandfather returned home after two years, a beaten man, a specter of his former self, but alive, gloriously alive. He was pardoned for defaulting on the discriminatory tax code, and spent the rest of his days quietly working as a tailor — mending the neighbors' pants, pressing the neighbors' slacks. The country forgave us once again our religion, granted us once again the lives we had peacefully led here on the edge of Europe for five centuries.

Now Father reminded us boys that we had survived that trial, and greater trials still. A failed stationery store was nothing! "My own dad dug in the mines in Aşkale, and my people built this city, and no one's going to drive us out of it. We're going to stay here and enjoy a part of it just like any of them. It's yours too. Understand? This country is yours too." He refused Semuel's offer to pursue the Haifa apartment. To keep our heads above water, he sold the only thing we owned of any value.

"*Prove de moneda no es prove, prove de* ideas *es prove,*" he said to us when the deal was complete. Poverty of money is not poor; poverty of *ideas* is poor.

I was glad not to be moving to Israel; but I had not imagined it would come to this. We'd owned the island house for three summers. Yusuf and I had refused to believe that Father, who loved his summer 'villa' more than any of us, would part with it. Before we knew it though we were helping empty the cottage. It took four consecutive weekend ferry trips to clear our summer belongings. Seeing our beach towels and goggles and inflatable rafts packed on the highest shelf in our cramped city bedroom, seeing our picnic table disassembled and propped against the bricks of the concrete balcony, seeing our *kebap* grill boxed and wrapped securely in packing tape (never, I felt, to be used again), seeing Mother offer the plastic patio chairs to our Muslim neighbors, seeing Yusuf angrily binding his French comic books in cellophane and piling them into a shoebox, seeing all of this, I sensed a blow we might not endure.

Off the Princes' Islands, on that last winter ferry ride Father tried to get Yusuf to come inside, to sit down on a bench, to huddle close and drink a hot *sahlep* with the rest of us. My brother refused to sit, and wandered in the direction of the toilet. After a few minutes I went looking for him. I found him outside at the rear of the ferry, exposed to the whipping cold and mist, leaning over the rail, coughing spasmodically into his elbow. He was watching the white-washed mansions of the islands recede. "Who needs it?" I said. "Not me," he answered, clearing his throat and spitting. I huddled beside him, leaned my own arms on the rail, my own mouth into the crook of my elbow, and together we watched the green hills of the Princes' Islands slip into the distance.

Two brothers, shoulder to shoulder on the rear of the ferry, the wet wool smell of Yusuf's jacket, the water churning white beneath us, the peaking waves dappled with rain. In losing the island house we were losing something important to who we were, but who could have predicted we'd spend the rest of our lives — first my brother, then me — trying to reclaim it?

12

Bedrock Architecture Consulting Ltd.

For my part the stirring had begun long before Yusuf's tragedy. Back in the early nineties our young republic was climbing out of its long and slothful isolation. The firm I worked for was expanding, and our two founding architects, happy to focus on business, shifted project management onto capable shoulders like mine. From assistant to lead drafter to drafting supervisor — my responsibilities had risen steadily, as had my hours and commitment to the job. Living now in the capital, four hours from home, I'd sunk myself into routine: my noble wife and stable job a refuge from a rocky past.

But following the 1999 Marmara earthquake the lira crashed again. Business slid, and our newest hires had to be laid off. The founding partners returned, demoralized, to supervising our understaffed drafting tables. Neither of my bosses had picked up a slide rule in a decade. The soft life, once tasted, had changed them. They no longer saw themselves as merely architects. Now they were artists, with vision — a precarious line to cross in our field, and the downfall of many solidly conceived projects. From me they insisted on beautiful prisons. They wanted our firm to leave a mark in the architectural history of the nation.

"Get out," said Omer, my best friend in the office, who had graduated in my class and had risen the ranks with me (he worked primarily on courthouses). "Get out while the getting's good. Style! It's all about style now. The walls will be falling in." In whispers and after-hour phone calls Omer tried to lure me with him back to the city of our youth. With the national tragedy, he smelled opportunity there: the potential for an upstart architectural consulting practice. The Marmara earthquake had sent our government pouring money into the field, as much as it took. Kids afraid to enter schools. Nurses afraid to enter hospitals. Everyone concerned another quake would send the ancient buildings and famous mosques toppling around them. What Omer smelled was a wealth of contracts for the inspection and structural consultations needed to certify buildings were "quake-proof." He pressed me for a starting cut of the investment: one year's salary. It sounded like a racket, mildly sleazy, and I hadn't forgotten my own father's business ventures. I didn't know if I could chance it.

A scheme to pack up and return to the city of my birth was not a risk I could force on Naomi or my girls. A return home seemed like a step backwards to a more unsettled time of my life. My wife's friends and relations lived in the capital. She was a talented watercolorist with a growing reputation here. We had built a comfortable life in which to raise our young daughters. The steady money I'd made in long hours planning jails had, after all these years, bought us this pleasant fifteenth-floor, three-bedroom apartment, in a micro-city with its own grocery, a private pool, and a state-of-the-art playground. Our complex even had its own meat restaurant, where on nights I picked them up from ballet class I treated the twins to *içli köfte*. (Sara ate only the outside pastry, which she loved, and Estela would polish off two of her own, plus her sister's leftover minced lamb filling.) Ballet lessons, *içli köfte*: we'd become a family of new traditions. I'd slowly done well. Nothing glamorous. But nothing glamorous was needed.

"Why relocate to an earthquake zone?" I said to Naomi at the dinner table on the night of Omer's offer. "Why should I risk all the years at the job, maybe one day partnership in the firm, on a gamble? We have everything we need right here." I gestured to our full spread: meat on the plates, salads in the bowls, wine in the glasses.

"Maybe you should think about it for a night or two," Naomi replied, cutting into her grape leaves. "Who knows? It could lead to something better for you."

I found her casual implication that there *was* something better, her willingness to toss aside the life I'd worked so patiently to build, worrisome. Indignation snuck up on me, a familiar feeling that had long lain dormant. Once I tasted it, once I felt it stirring like glass in my gut, I knew what I would tell Omer.

So off went my closest colleague with two associates from a rival firm to found over the next year what would prove a lucrative venture: BEDROCK ARCHITECTURE CONSULTING LTD. For my part I quickly got back to work, and refused to look back at a missed opportunity.

13

Blessed is He

THINGS BEGAN UNRAVELING more rapidly the year of my brother's accident. The burden of unanswered questions, the echoes of that final telephone call, the incessant reminder of who he was — in our gossip columns, on our television specials — kept me up at nights. I'd wake at three in the morning, my heart racing crazily, and go and check on the girls. I lived my life surrounded by a grayish haze, unable to move on. At the office, too, there were the constant signs of change bearing down on us. Distracted by my brother's drama, I was slow to acknowledge the firm's shrinking accounts, the mismanagement of contracts, the layoffs of mid-level employees, the loss of projects to younger firms making better use of software and the latest drafting technology, firms whose partners were not filching their time on considerations of "art" and "beauty." Only when the managing director assured me, "We value you immensely. Don't you worry, Avram. You, of all people, we need here with us." — only when I heard that did it finally hit me that I was working on a sinking ship. Still, day after day I averted my eyes from the bucking realities and focused on the portrait above the drafting table: the Father of the Republic, beaming down at me with his fierce and wolfish gaze. The gold-plated inscription: Blessed is he who can say I am a Turk.

Then things broke. One of our partners dissolved his share to move to Frankfurt, where it was rumored he had a second wife. He wanted to dive into the installation art scene, which he told me over a tearful goodbye lunch had always been his true calling ("Not the design of municipal property, Avram, but filling a room with sound and color. Sound and color!") The following review period no one on my team received the raises we'd been promised. Over a dark winter three clients sent lawyers to negotiate terms of backing out of contracts, including a prison in Kayseri whose working drawings I had sunk two lousy years of my life into, trying to meet some ethereal "vision." The boss offered me a salary cut and hinted he might have to let me go. If it came to that I had a year and a half of severance pay accumulated — but then what?

I hung on to the wreckage, clinging to my position while I looked for others. But the sad truth was, designing jails, I'd become too specialized; and I was having no luck landing inter-views. Naomi told me not to worry, she had complete confidence I'd fall on my feet — as if merely by pronouncing these words it would happen. I replayed how I should have left the company with Omer while the going was good. BEDROCK LTD. Omer was boldly making a killing now on post-earthquake structural inspections back home, a vital service in the most important city in the nation. And what was I left doing? Holding fast to a posi-tion I no longer wanted. I'd tell Naomi over dinner, after the girls had left the table, how trapped I felt. "I was too cautious. Yusuf would have taken the risk."

"We'll be fine Avram," she'd tell me, wagging her fork, sick of hearing it. "We'll be fine. Things aren't all bleak. I'm selling enough to cover until you find something. Take the severance. There's a world out there. Open your eyes, mister. You're not even considering your options."

I knew what she was implying. Two years ago her parents had emigrated to Tel Aviv, to an airy fifth-floor condominium seven blocks from the Mediterranean. Since then Naomi had dreamed of following them, of opening a gallery there, where the art scene was more vibrant than our own, and where she insisted good architects were always needed. "Of course they are," I'd tell her. "All those bombs."

"Think about it Avram. A new life."

"What new life? In the Promised Land? It's better there?"

I was still looking for work the next fall when Al Qaeda blasts tore through synagogues in Istanbul, killing three people and destroying the façade of Tiferet Israel. This was the temple Naomi had attended during university, in her years as an art student. She was visibly upset that entire week — unusual for a woman who normally took the world in stride. "Allah Allah!" she started saying, "If we're going to face synagogue bombs here, for God's sake, we may as well face them in Israel." A move. A change. The tide of the country was turning against us. An Islamic party was hijacking the nation. Was this really the place we wanted to raise our daughters anymore? "You're an architect, Avram," she reminded me. "You could be helping build your homeland."

"This is my homeland," I said. "This is where we were born."

"This will never be our home. Can't you see that now?"

14

The Wrecking Ball

LIKE EVERYONE I was shocked, outraged, and terribly saddened
for our community, but caught up in my own difficulties I failed
to summon the proper extremes of horror over the destruction
of a place half a country away, so distant from our lives. I had
long been conflicted in my commitment to the religion. When
I was a kid, on Friday nights Mother had lit the Shabat candles
and Yusuf and I had kissed our parents' hands and said the
kidduş. We celebrated *Pesa* and the High Holy days; we sent generous *Roşaşana* donation cards to the Dormitory for the Elderly.
For twenty years now since Mother's death I'd been steadily losing faith. I no longer kept even mildly kosher. I no longer went
to temple. And only at Naomi's insistence did I acknowledge
Shabat once or twice a month. For me the bombing of Tiferet
Israel was not the world-changing event it was for my wife; and
I could not pretend otherwise.

Naomi funneled her distress into long hours at the easel. I
stayed late at the office to comb online want-ads. Naomi would
be frustrated that I missed dinner with the girls. When I got

home I'd rush into the twins' room to lift the sheets to their shoulders and kiss them goodnight. Coming out to the kitchen, I'd find Naomi had put away the dishes and left nothing for me to eat. "There was plenty of warm food for you," she'd say, "two hours ago." I would noisily heat myself a can of Piyale tomato soup. Most nights Naomi holed herself up in the office, where she painted her furious landscapes late into the evening. I'd watch the television news — enlightening investigations on weighty subjects, like which football player on the National Team had the sexiest wife. Naomi would slip off to bed without a word. It took everything I had, fighting the thick glue of my grudges, to lift myself off the couch to join her. I stopped bothering. I'd fall asleep to the television. On any given night I could never put my finger on what, exactly, we were fighting about; but I understood we had stumbled into a darker, more dangerous region of our marriage.

Three weeks after the synagogue bombs, Naomi received a call from a gallery in Jerusalem interested in arranging a show of painters from our country — an expression of solidarity with our grief-stricken community. They wanted to exhibit her watercolors in what would be her first international showing. With the offer, her career threatened to break beyond her regional reputation among local collectors and interior designers. It was good news. I did my best to act pleased.

That night Naomi came and sat on the couch beside me. I shut off the television. She laid her head in my lap, as she used to in those days when our dreams had seemed mutually, securely, unattainable. "I'd like to go," she said. "I'd like to do this."

"Go then. It's a wonderful opportunity. It's an honor for you." Mechanically I stroked her hair. I had forgotten its softness. I had forgotten the roundness of her face, her dark eyebrows, the delicacy of her nose, the pleasures of her body. "It's an honor for us."

"I'd like to take the girls."

I stopped stroking her hair. She meant, I understood, something longer, and more permanent.

"No, Naomi. Absolutely not. My daughters don't leave this country. Go, do your show this winter. You're not taking them away."

She held me tightly around the waist and buried her face into my sweater. "Then come with us," she whispered into my stomach.

We had invested too much energy in anger, and had held out too long from apologizing, for either of us to retreat now. We couldn't admit fault for any of a hundred things we had said to one another, and even more that we had not. Neither of us could acquiesce to the other's fervent needs. This, I understood, was how a marriage crumbled. My inflexibility was like a slow-motion wrecking ball destroying us. I watched the walls slide in, and couldn't muster the compassion — a kiss on her brow, a tender grasp of her hand — that might shut the damn thing off.

"They're all I have." My entire body stiffened. I couldn't touch her hair anymore. I didn't, honestly, know where to place my hands. I stretched them up above my head, then crossed them over my chest. "I forbid it. Are you listening to me? I'm saying no."

15

These Black Months

WE'D ARGUED UNDER our breaths about that Jerusalem show for a week, and in the midst of these muted battles I received an urgent phone call from back home. It was my old downstairs neighbor, frightened, calling to report that my father had suffered an accident. The old man had been climbing the stairs to the apartment building. The lights on the timer had gone out. Fumbling for the switch, he had tripped down a half-flight of stairs, where the neighbor's son had found him, lying there, holding his thigh and groaning, "I'm dying. I'm dying." They had taken him to the emergency room at the German Hospital. Minor bruises, nothing broken. But a reminder still of another familial drama I'd long put off thinking about.

Ever since he'd lost my mother it had seemed to me that Father had been defeated in some large way. He'd returned as a jeweler to a shop in the Grand Bazaar — not as owner or manager, but as a simple artisan. He no longer had the motivation of pride. For over two decades now he'd sized and cut platinum rings in a store no bigger than a closet, just off the rug merchants' lane.

The dingy jeweler's floor was covered in a metallic dust, and its screaming machinery emitted wild ear-piercing shrieks. The noise was exacerbated by the pounding of metal from the nearby *han*, and the call to prayer that stormed beneath the stone archways. Father had lost much of his hearing, and his eyesight was going. Since Yusuf's accident Naomi and I had been trying to get him to retire and move to the capital to live with us. "Retirement is death," he'd say. "*Dingun lavoro no te dezenora, ma te proveca i te onora.*" No work dishonors you, but it raises you and honors you. Work, Father claimed, was the only thing keeping him alive. So we had let the idea go. Like him I had always placed stock in simple perseverance, in refusing to let go of what you held most familiar and true.

Father stuck a "Fenerbahçe Gold" bumper sticker I'd once given him on the window of the shop. He still enjoyed meeting the bridal couples who searched him out; he enjoyed the bargaining, offering a deal that undermined his benevolent Assyrian boss, an old friend from days long gone. "A matrimonial present," he would say with a wink to some young bride-to-be, having resized a wedding band for her at a miniscule profit. I encouraged our relations and friends to send Father their business, not so that he made more money — he didn't earn a cut — but so that hardly an hour might pass when he was alone in the shop. He spent, after all, his evenings by himself in our old Şişli apartment. The overly-furnished rooms seemed perpetually unkempt, though I paid, at Naomi's insistence, for a weekly cleaning woman. Cockroaches scuttled under the faded green living room couch. Father claimed he didn't notice them. He watched the football matches alone, a meter from the television set, and rarely made it past halftime before he fell asleep, his long thin mouth open, his gray head bobbing. For *Roşaşana* one year we subscribed him to Digitürk cable — 157 channels — and bought him a new, larger television to replace his small screen. When he could not negotiate the intricacies of the universal remote, we returned the whole damn thing. Naomi voiced concern that my father was increasingly frail. Yet he still managed temple on High Holy days. He still dressed for work in a worn herringbone jacket. He still had his nightly meal delivered up by Hasan's Lokanta. Two years ago he had called us with news: an impressive growth halfway down his spine. "Cancer," he boasted. There was hope, even a thrill, in the way he pronounced the word. A round of lab tests and biopsies proved the mass benign.

Now a fall: another in a long list of trials, in these black months of my life. I hung up the phone, and tapped open the office door with my elbow, like an intruder. Naomi murmured something, and I pushed it further open. She stood with her back to me before her easel, continuing to paint what looked like a squash or a gourd drenched in wet moonlight. But she was listening, and as I described Father's accident she lowered her paintbrush, bowed her head, and sighed.

"He can live with us." She turned, chin raised, and stared at some vague space over my shoulder. "He's always been welcome. Maybe this will finally scare him into it. The girls would enjoy having him here. I can take care of him."

"He has no friends here."

"He has friends in Tel Aviv. Uncles. His cousins in Haifa." Her bright eyes had come alive.

I wouldn't be baited. "He likes his independence. He likes

his job. You'd have to look after him full-time. How would you paint? It'd be too much."

"The girls are old enough to help. Look Avram, the man is half-deaf. How long can you expect your father to live alone, at this rate? Three flights he has to climb, every day, up and down. I worry for him."

"And I don't?"

She rinsed off her paintbrush, clacking it against the edges of a stained porcelain bowl.

"Maybe the Dormitory for the Aging?" I asked. I knew she'd never agree to such a thing. As a daughter-in-law it would shame her, and Naomi was not one to be shamed. "He's been in that apartment for forty years," I said, arguing with myself. "He's not going to agree to a move."

"Sometimes your time just runs out." Hesitating, she finally looked up into my face. "Why don't you take a trip to the city?" Her voice, calm now, was past exasperation. "Why don't you see what you can do for him? After a scare like this he needs his son." She thought for a moment, itching her high cheek with the back of her brush. "It'd be good for you too. To see him."

I understood. She meant my leaving would be good for *us*. A little distance, a little time. This was the closest to a civil conversation we'd had in weeks of silent feuding. She was watching me for an answer, her cheek freckled now with drops of white paint.

And so in this quiet way Naomi nudged me out the door. I took the severance: more than I expected, but more distressing still because it was clear the firm, after seventeen good years, would hardly miss me. The morning of my departure I kissed the twins goodbye on their warm foreheads. None of us at that moment had any idea how permanent that goodbye would be. Estela and Sara were only nine-years-old, but they sensed the gloom. It was a sullen moment. Each twin clung to one of my belt loops as I made my way to the door with my bags. When I promised I'd return soon my voice caught. "With new video games?" Estela asked. Yes, with new video games. "With chocolate-covered Turkish Delights," Sara reminded me. Yes, with chocolate-covered Turkish Delights. "No nuts," Estela demanded, with her mother's relentless hard-headedness. No nuts. Absolutely no nuts. Never any nuts. They hugged me; and for the sake of the girls Naomi and I exchanged a light kiss on each cheek as well: the kisses of strangers.

Staring out the half-tinted windows of a Varan bus, I arrived late that afternoon after an eight-hour ride. The city of my youth was unfathomably vast and bustling, a different place from the dull streets of weathered Ottoman architecture and endless rains that clouded my childhood memories. Skyscrapers stood at attention above the sunny northern hills; chain hotels hugged the cliffs above the gleaming straits. This place was now a modern European center for the arts, and film, and music; and looking out the windows I thought how, in the middle of this grinding storm of culture and industry, my brother had once lived with abandon, dancing disco on the 47th floor of that reflective glass monstrosity, the Teletürk Tower.

Forty-five years old. I took up house in our childhood apartment in Şişli. With only my father's company the apartment felt large, empty, mournful. The stairwell seemed precariously dark and steep. I'd never noticed this before. And Father, unharmed but predictably stubborn, refused to consider the Dormitory for the Aging, or entertain giving up work and moving to the capital. So we compromised, and with the help of a real estate agent I located a smaller two-bedroom basement apartment in Cihangir, near Firuzağa Mosque. It was a more practical and convenient space for an elderly man living alone on limited wages. Over two weeks we packed Father's yellowed books and musty woolen clothes and frayed sheets and threadbare towels, and moved it all by van in one fell swoop. Half the furniture was delivered, the older stuff we sold off to Gypsies, and we spent another week unpacking the new apartment.

Initially I had called Naomi each evening to report on this glacial progress; and to chat with the twins over speakerphone. Approaching December I was offering excuses for not coming home to see the girls.

"Baba sick of you yet?" Naomi would say. "How is my favorite father-in-law?"

"He's fine. He's fine. The girls?"

Our nightly telephone calls grew shorter. Naomi had stopped asking when I would return. I didn't tell her that I had gotten back in touch with Omer, to see if he could take me on as a consultant with BEDROCK Ltd.. If it panned out the job would require a permanent move back here to the city. It now seemed like my only good option. Neither Naomi nor I mentioned what lay foremost on our minds: divorce. Soon I was calling every other night. Before long I had missed a week.

In the new apartment building, a 1950's Bauhaus five-story with a fading stucco exterior, even the half-flight down to the basement proved a challenge for Father. The flat had been advertised as having a "winter garden," but this turned out to be a meter-wide gutter that flooded in the rains. The electricity went out once a day. Hot water arrived in blasts and cut off without reason. Bars lined the frosted window of the guest bedroom. Through the bars I could see the tires of cars and trucks, and the legs of people clopping amid puddles down the mud-slicked hill. Father was upset by the move, disoriented. He admonished me to keep the window closed or stray cats would crawl in and piss on our beds again. Each night that first week, to get some air, I climbed the six flights of stairs to the rain-soaked rooftop, where graduate students half my age in plastic chairs smoked endless joints, and from whose perch I could see the hotel high-rises in Taksim, and the traffic stalled along the Bosphorus Bridge, and on one clear evening, out over the edge of the Asian continent, across the sea, to the Princes' Islands.

16

The Halim Pasha House

I WAS SORTING THROUGH Father's recent correspondence, dumped during the move into a small shoebox, concerned that over the commotion of unpacking there might have been an outstanding bill we'd missed paying. What I found instead was an opened envelope from a law firm representing the Adalar Municipality. The letter inside asked Emil Benezra to get in touch immediately: a confidential matter concerning his deceased son, Yusuf.

"They've been after me since he died, Father told me that night in the bedroom. In the glare of the desk light he held the letter close to his glasses, shaking his head as he read it. "I never answer these people. Vultures!"

"It says important business. Confidential."

"A scam. No business is important when you reach my age. If it was important they'd tell you what it was. You answer it, Avram, if you'd still like to be involved." He handed back the letter, and began unbuttoning his dress shirt with uneasy fingers. "It's better when I don't think of him."

To set my mind at ease the next morning I called Gursel Uluca and Partners.

"An Avram Benezra?" the lawyer boomed over the phone.

"Yes."

"I'm speaking with an Avram Benezra, brother of Yusuf Elmas?"

I hesitated, and then said yes again.

"And you are calling on behalf of your father Emil?"

"That's correct."

"Mr. Benezra, I've been trying to reach out one last time to your father, to see if he's made a decision on the house."

"The house?"

"Sir. The police have been receiving complaints from the *Belediyesi*. Burglaries. Vandalism. On several occasions possible squatters. The Mayor has asked me, once again, through your brother's executor, to track down the owners. Should your father remain unable to see to the necessary maintenance of the historic property, the municipality is willing to take over administrative jurisdiction. The Touring and Automobile Society has expressed interest in developing the space as a cultural center. According to the mayor it's become an unsightly property. A mess, if you will. In imminent danger of arson and other abuse. The municipality is willing to fix it up."

"I don't understand how this involves my father."

"He is the owner of the Halim Pasha House, at number 25 Yilmaztürk Caddesi."

"I don't think he knows anything about this."

"Sir, that's impossible. We have copies of dated correspondence. Records of telephone calls. I see it has taken some time for your brother's lawyers to get back to us on this matter; but now they want a response immediately. They're trying to close the estate. Your father has never signed off on the deed. They're eager to put all this behind them once and for all."

"My brother died five years ago."

"I'm sorry for any delay you've experienced. These lawyers on your brother's side were not the original executors."

"I don't follow."

"They're not eager to wade into all this again. Nobody wants to touch it. Settlement had to be held up until all charges had been cleared. You understand, I'm sure."

"Yusuf wouldn't have left our father anything. They hadn't spoken in years."

"Mr. Benezra, your brother left your father, in his will, his island villa. We've written Emil a number of times on this. We've talked to him personally."

"He knows nothing about it. He doesn't hear very well anymore. He's never mentioned anything to me."

"I see there has been some kind of confusion." The lawyer fell silent. I heard him shuffling through papers. And then he asked again, as if rubbing it in, if he was indeed speaking to the brother of Yusuf Elmas, former CEO of Teletürk Holdings. *That* Yusuf Elmas, as if there could be any other.

"You say you've left phone messages?" I asked. "You say there's been correspondence?"

"Multiple inquiries, sir. Recent notices from your brother's lawyers as well. I was informed by my secretary that the last time we got him on the phone, Emil Benezra politely told us to go fuck ourselves. A man unafraid to speak his mind. What your father doesn't understand is that we're only trying to take this mess off his hands. We do have to clear up the inheritance and property transfer taxes for this to move forward."

"Taxes?"

"Emil's declaration on the land has yet to be made to the municipality. And of course, lapsed maintenance and security bills."

"We didn't know anything about this."

"As I said, should your father be unwilling or unable to assume responsibility, the Mayor assures me the municipality will gladly-"

"Yes, I know what you said. Give me a minute. Give me a minute please. You're telling me my father owns this house?"

"It's necessary, without delay, to have the deed signed, and sent to us by your father's lawyer. And then you can discuss declaration on the land, or what you'd like to do with it."

"My father doesn't have a lawyer."

"Please wait a second." I heard him shuffling more pages, then yelling to his secretary about an *arsa* tax form. I didn't know if I should believe any of this.

I called into the phone, "You're telling me that my brother left my father his island home. In his will. You have that in black and white. My brother's house."

"That's correct sir." He rifled through more papers on his end of the line, paused, and repeated, "Mr. Benezra, what would you like me to tell the *Belediyesi*? The Mayor's office is waiting. There's a limit to their patience."

My pulse was pounding. "Tell them I'll be out there tomorrow to sign whatever you need me to sign. Tell them not to touch anything. Give me your direct number. I'll get back to you."

When Father returned that night from the jewelry shop he admitted it: he'd not told me about the phone calls. Any inquiries by telephone that ever mentioned my brother he had, out of mournful habit, quickly dismissed. Any papers that had arrived with Yusuf's name on it he'd torn up. Father had shut himself off to the blizzard of phone calls and correspondence and knocks on the door that followed Yusuf's death. A bunker mentality. I understood the caution. Naomi and I had assumed it as well, determined to insulate the twins from the fallout. Naomi wouldn't let any of us comment to the press, or discuss Yusuf with the human rights organizations hounding us for inside information. She wouldn't let biographers speak to our family. I had accepted her caution as the safest route. Five years ago my brother was nobody we wanted clear ties to.

But now this was different. Here I was moving my hobbling father into a second-class basement apartment so that he might ride out his meager savings. I was approaching a winter of forced unemployment and thinning bank accounts. And all this time Father owned, without acknowledging it, a property of serious value on the Princes' Islands.

"Let it rot," Naomi said over the phone that night, when I filled her in on the situation. "Really, Avram, you should. Who needs it? Your father certainly doesn't. It's the last thing he needs."

"This is my brother's gift to him. It might help out."

"Your brother, a man who abused you in a hundred ways."

"We couldn't get along. A lot of brothers can't get along."

"For fourteen years you didn't talk to him. He leaves his own father living in a rat-hole, while he tosses money to the wind. And now that he's gone you'll swallow your pride, take his table scraps.

What would you tell your daughters? What kind of lesson is this?"

"This isn't about the twins. This is about my father. He's living in a basement apartment here, like a grave. Table scraps! You're telling me we should turn our backs on a gift this generous?"

"Please listen to yourself, Avram. The last thing we need is to attach ourselves to black money. Taxes. Insurance already. Legal fees. It'd be ridiculous."

"We could swing it for a few years. The girls could summer there, with their grandfather. It'd be an investment. I'll use my severance."

She was laughing at me now. "Don't you see? It's toxic. It was one of his maneuvers. I'd rather we were poor. I'd rather your father moved in with us than expose him to what your brother left behind."

"Let me check out the property. They're going to steal this from him. From us."

"From you." Her voice grew softer, pleading. "Avram, let them have it. Please. As my husband, listen to me. Let them donate the house to the Touring and Automobile Society. Let the Mayor take it off our hands. Let the island do something useful with it. A library. An orphanage. A concert space. A good cause. It's no business of ours. You become a whole different person when your brother's involved. You always have."

I recognized the tone of reason I'd found refuge in all these years. But the truth of it stung.

"Is this simply about the money?" she asked.

"He was my brother, for God's sake. It was kind of him. I thought you'd see this like I do. It might help the old man out. I thought you'd be excited. We could summer there ourselves, as a family."

"Kind of him? Avram, there was always a reason behind everything he did."

"We're finally getting a little bit back here. Here's proof. Even if you won't accept it, he remembered us. You didn't know him like I did, in his better days. You never saw us like that. With Yusuf, we all put in our time."

The memories, long dammed up, flooded through. I saw my little brother swimming out to sea, waving to our mother beyond the rocks of Seferoğlu Beach. Playing football together in the Golf Park, his standing in goal for our team. Tossing a comic book he'd finished across the room, onto my bed, to share with me. Standing shoulder to shoulder with me on the ferry, in the mist off the Princes' Islands.

Naomi, who could read my mind, seemed frightened. "Please don't take this on. I put in my time too, and I don't forget."

I was silent now, thinking.

"Are you listening to me Avram? It's a trap. Please listen to me."

"I'm listening," I said, fingering the envelope with Gursel Uluca and Partners' address on it.

Starting the next day I set to work straightening out the mess of the inheritance. In a single exhausting week I found Father a lawyer, tracked down the proper municipal signatures, agreed, in his name, to assume temporary costs for repairs until we could decide what to do with the place. I compiled a list of Yusuf's former caretakers who might be willing to take on work. I used half my severance to establish an escrow account for future taxes, and looked into terms of a loan for possible renovations, then settled on an insurance policy. On the last Saturday in November I received from the lawyer the keys to Yusuf's villa, and returned for the first time in three decades to the island. I was free now to go and assess the state of the property myself.

Yusuf's grand island home — the Halim Pasha House. This was not some cursed prison project I'd have to slave away at, cowing to my superiors, trying to please twenty separate parties at once, only to have the whole damn thing yanked out from under my feet without a moment's notice. This was a historic villa — in need, perhaps, of a little care. This was far better use of a man's talents.

Book II

1

Polite Opinions

Naomi, finalizing her watercolors for her Israeli show, knew nothing at the moment about what I was doing. She could not have minded having me gone. Omer was dangling the hope that late winter, if new contracts came in, he'd take me on as a consultant with BEDROCK Ltd. Until then I began visiting the island over three or four day blocks to see to the villa's restorations. I met and hired on Nılay Gören, my brother's diabetic live-in maid, and Mustafa Faik, his longest serving security guard — both of them desperate for off-season employment — to help clear debris and clean the mansion. I had yet to see my brother's cook again, though I kept an eye out for her, and as a shortcut to the ferry I made a point of passing down her misbegotten street, past her leaning hovel, half hoping that I'd run into her.

In those first weeks of December I stayed over at the damp Hotel Saydam Planet. In the evenings when the day's work was done I walked the village as my brother might have — long steps, hands behind my back — dropping into its stores and post office and cafés, talking to whoever I could about him.

"He stopped in each day on his way to the ferry," the grocer İlhan Saracoğlu boasted to me from behind a stack of blue plastic cartons filled with the day's first bread. "Each morning he asked for an orange juice. I gave him the best we had. He'd open the can and drink it right here by the register, shuffling through the newspapers. Your brother and me, we'd laugh together at the half-naked women on the front covers. He always preferred the one on the *Resim*. I preferred the *Çevap* myself." The grocer scratched his well-shaven chin with the back of his fingers, recalling these useless details as if any one of them might resolve the enigma of my brother's final morning. "He drank that damn orange juice every day, but he hated it, you know. Yusuf used to smack his lips: 'This orange juice is bitter! Terrible! Can't we Turks make some decent orange juice? What does it take? Just squeeze some damn oranges?' I think he liked to complain. 'In America,' he'd tell me. America America America. 'In America — Miami! — you've got the sweetest orange juice in the world.' 'Well, Yusuf, go live in Miami, if you like it so much.' But he said he'd miss me, how could he live in Miami? That was his way. He smiled. Such a smile! He made you feel, you know, warm, even though he was always complaining. It was a good-natured complaining. He had a gift for it. Some people complain. But Yusuf's complaining wasn't complaining. It was an art. A trick to make you like him. You knew he had more serious things on his mind. That orange juice. Naked newspaper women. *Beyefendim*, I used to forget he was so rich! I should have charged him double for his bread!"

The grocer, a wily, middle-aged man, had thick black brows and veins that pushed out from a muscular neck. At the time

Yusuf drowned, İlhan's two doe-eyed daughters were approaching the age when they should be married, and he admitted he often sent them to the cash register when Yusuf entered. Five years later the daughters, still single, were still working the cash register. They were shy however, and plump, and I knew my brother wouldn't have flirted under the watchful eyes of their father. That had never been his way.

The islanders treated me with a deference I'd rarely known. I had always understood Yusuf's reputation, but I only *felt* his authority, his success, when these people, on learning who I was, called me, too, *beyefendim*. It was as if they were speaking not to an unemployed architectural hack from the capital, but to a man of standing.

Everyone had their polite opinions. Every islander I met who had ever bumped shoulders with Yusuf claimed, five years on, to have known him intimately. Everyone understood the man my brother had become. Everyone was somehow complicit in or had some insight into or harbored some unique theory worked out in lucid detail concerning events that had precipitated the Jewish billionaire's untimely death. On the island I had stumbled upon an unholy mess of rumor and innuendo and trash. Eagerly I waded through it.

In the one-room post office on a dreary Monday I happened to mention I was restoring the Halim Pasha House, and the bearded post-master grew nervous. With his deformed left hand — one finger, one thumb — he removed from a high cabinet a cardboard box filled with yellowed stacks of envelopes. "Yusuf's brother? Of all things!" He offered me tea and, rattling the sugar cubes in his glass with his little silver spoon, vouched that when

Yusuf's personal mail used to pile up he would religiously send a boy to the Halim Pasha House with the whole box of it. "*Vallahi!* A special delivery, the only one on the island. But these envelopes," he said, drawing them one by one from the box, "kept trickling in after the…well, you see. Mostly foreign addresses. I'd forward them, but look, sometimes they'd return to me. I'd forward them again. And back they'd come. What could I do? *Beyefendim*, you're his brother; please, take them." He thrust one at me between his knobby fingers, a little too eager, it seemed, to unburden himself.

Back to the Saydam Planet I hustled, carrying with two hands that box of dead letters, my heart fluttering with the excitement of a reclamation. All that night in the hotel room I rummaged through the box. There were seventy-four letters. Some looked torn open and resealed. I found mostly junk mail, a few bills, and invitations to panels and conventions in Turkish, French, Russian, and Portuguese, mixed up with forms in other languages I could not at first recognize. One gold-bordered card officially congratulated Yusuf for his election to a second term as Trustee of the Friends of the Islands. In another letter I read how he had joined the island priests in their perpetual campaign to prevent the cobblestone trail up to St. George's Monastery (still used by pilgrims) from being paved. In a follow-up note an organization of conservationists had thanked Yusuf for stopping dead in its tracks a misguided proposal to introduce a motorized tram to the island. The gracious, if cloying, handwritten note praised Yusuf for his stubborn vision.

Personal mail. The trappings of a respected life on the island. I didn't know what I had expected to find, but nothing here hinted at murder, or vengeance, or any of a hundred reasons for his speedboat going down. There were no implied threats that I could discern.

The postmaster had organized that heap of old letters with rubber bands in the order they'd been returned. The next night I flipped through them yet again, and sorted them chronologically by the date they'd been written. In doing this I discovered one small thread that struck me as an odd coincidence. It seemed Yusuf had taken a serious interest in post-earthquake island reconstruction. A report his office had requested only two months before his accident, written in English, was titled: *Excessive Seismicity of the Marmara Region: One of the Most Seismically Active Zones of the World.* In its abstract it predicted: *Remaining fault strain to be released by some future seismic event....Grabens, fault offsets, and structural topomorphological features at the bottom of the Marmara confirm branch movement of the North Anatolian fault....* From the same address, a follow-up survey dated two weeks before his disappearance insisted: "*Urgent effective mitigation endeavors must be initiated with a goal of reinforcing the buildings on the Princes' Islands. Leaving vulnerable structures as they stand and blindly organizing for emergency response is **not** an option for the archipelago, just as it is no longer an option for the greater municipality.*"

Strange that I never heard about the Elmas Foundation's reconstruction efforts — which in my line of business I would have found interesting. Equally strange: I'd begun inspecting the mansion myself, and had found no signs of structural renovations — though clearly the property could benefit, like much of the aged building stock on the island, from modern reinforcement. Had he simply never gotten around to it, or had he run out of time?

2

Earthquake Science

Aﬁﬀﬃﬂ After the 1999 earthquake seismologists around the world had converged on our city in an attempt to predict where the next quake would hit. They agreed the fault line had not completely broken, and that within thirty years the Marmara region was in danger of a complete catastrophe. Most predictions still put the epicenter out at sea, directly beneath these Princes' Islands. As I understood it, if the entire fault line moved together the next quake would be more powerful than the one which had, in the last year of the millennium, taken twenty thousand lives. An earthquake of that size would sink the archipelago. We'd all been warned; we'd all chosen to forget.

"Your brother couldn't get it out of his mind," the Mayor of the Islands told me the following Saturday, in the Office of the District Governor. I had come to submit permits for renovations, but also asked to examine the property's records, to see if the mansion had ever been inspected for vulnerabilities. In the Zoning and City Planning Department's library the Mayor had entered, introduced himself, and ordered his staff to bring up two Nescafés.

He sat down uninvited opposite me at the long wooden table. "We'd begun discussing a plan for reinforcement of the oldest wooden mansions," the Mayor was saying. He was a lanky man with a runner's build and a well-honed air of self-importance. "Your brother wanted to strengthen the houses. As many as possible, as quickly as he could. He promised the cooperation of his steel-joist company, and was offering to subsidize the costs himself, fifty percent, through the Foundation." The Mayor sighed; his eyes saddened. "*Yuru be*! Yusuf had a penchant for tossing money at a problem. I was supposed to round up matching public funds for the project. To show municipal support of his efforts, see? As if it were that easy. He'd snap his fingers, and expect it to be done."

Our Nescafés had come, and without asking the Mayor prepared mine just as he prepared his own, with two sugars and cream. He stirred both glasses with his pen, and pushed one in my direction. I was explaining that I knew too well the delays involved in public financing. "But what was your objection?" I asked. "Half of these old homes are falling to pieces."

"True. But it was the attitude of invincibility that always disturbed me. That his money could take on an earthquake." The Mayor had a habit of biting his upper lip when he disagreed with something, as if the mere suggestion of disagreement pained him physically. I liked him for it. "Yusuf wanted to bring it all public, far too quickly, before I was ready or able to help. He commissioned dive after dive to assess risks in the Marmara, then asked me to get the results to the press. I wasn't comfortable with the speed he was moving. He had his nose in everything here. Second opinions, Avram. Third opinions. Topographic surveys of the sea floor. He'd go out on the research vessels with the scientists himself. Busy, busy, busy. It was unbelievable."

"It seems like a reasonable cause."

"Avram, we've only just met, but I know you'll understand. You and me — we have limits. There were never any limits for Yusuf. Once he hitched his mind to some big idea…well, it was then I worried most for him. We went at it once at a Friends board meeting. I told him we had to prioritize and think *practically.* Earthquake science is the worst science in the world. They don't get anything right. And it wasn't only the mansions. We had an old village here too. People who couldn't afford to be dislocated, who didn't want to be reminded daily their lives were in danger. Look, my work is always the law first, the law second, and then justice and equality. We couldn't just toss around public money at the speed he wanted. Based on what? Some vague geological threat? Our government doesn't work that way. How we'd go at it, him and me! "Yusuf Bey," I said, "you fool. What good would it do to reinforce every single building here, if our damn island sinks? *Kismet.* Some things you leave in the hands of God.""

According to the Mayor Yusuf had taken things into his own hands. He'd opened a subsidiary Elmas Foundation office on a back street of the village, advertising private assistance for anyone, of any income, who wished to earthquake-proof his home. The Mayor claimed that at the time of Yusuf's death twenty wooden mansions on the island and thirty properties on the neighboring smaller islands were slated to be structurally reinforced with steel beams and elastic features: the most modern methods. I recalled for the mayor one of the reports I'd found among the correspondence: the alarming study evaluating the seismic hazards of the region. I spoke passable English, but the study's technical French and German (with citations in Japanese) had been beyond me.

I asked the Mayor, "Do you know what a *narrow beam echo sounder system* specifically was used for?"

The Mayor's eyes drooped. "I have no idea."

"Could my brother really have understood references to *high resolution multi-beam swath bathymetry data*?" I'd looked that up myself.

The Mayor clicked his tongue sadly. "Yusuf was always in over his head. You remember, no?"

And I did, but as an architect I couldn't help take some pride in my brother's concern for the preservation of historic homes, and his dedication to the fate of these islands. Already I was feeling our missing years coming into better focus. My brother had lived here contentedly in his crumbling mansion, performing civic duties I'd heard little about, tossing money in every direction but his own, as immune to criticism from government bureaucrats, from doomsayers, from those who claimed to know better, as he had always been in more personal battles.

3

No Matter How Big You Get

Iɴ ᴛʜᴇ Gᴏᴠᴇʀɴᴏʀ's Mansion I thanked the Mayor for the Nescafe, said I knew how busy he must be, and stood to leave. To my surprise he accompanied me out of the library, down the two creaking flights of stairs, and along the shaded side streets all the way back to the Halim Pasha House, talking of Yusuf.

We were discussing my brother's return to the islands. I had not been at all surprised on learning through relatives, in the year after my wedding, that Yusuf had bought a home here. "He'd always loved the romance of this island," I told the Mayor. "As a kid he used to vow one day he would buy this famous *kiosk* or that historic villa and live in it year-round." I didn't say that my mother and I just laughed at Yusuf's nonsense. Nobody, we knew, except the poor villagers lived here on the island in the wintertime, when it was a cold wet miserable place, with eternal rains and unforgiving winds and irregular ferries to the mainland. Plus the historical houses cost a large fortune. "I'd listen to my brother spouting his garbage and think: Yusuf, you don't know what you're talking about."

"But he did it," the Mayor said. "He did exactly what he promised you."

According the Mayor, Cıhan İpekoğlu, the agent at İpekoğlu Emlakası, was the first to have spoken with the young entrepreneur in his smoke-filled real-estate office. "He asked Cıhan which houses were up for sale. The market in the nineties was not like it is today, after the earthquake, when everyone's trying to sell. Back then people were still holding onto property here: it was the smartest investment. Nobody trusted the national banks. Forget the stock market. You own a home, especially an antique home, the value is in your pocket, correct? Cıhan must have shown him five or six of the larger *yalıs*. But Yusuf wasn't satisfied. He said he would see to things himself, and left the realtor as quickly as he'd come."

For three weekends in a row he was spotted sauntering up and down the avenues, considering his options. Nothing on the market had suited my brother's ethereal vision. He'd appeared next at the Governor's Mansion. "He came in on a Monday in September," the Mayor recalled. "I didn't know who he thought he was, strolling in without an appointment like that, dressed like some dandified prince — the pinstripe suit, the white kerchief in the pocket, *hepsi*, the whole shebang. He requested from my office the names and owners of the ten oldest homes on the island. Yusuf knew exactly what he wanted. The problem was, what he wanted didn't exist here any longer."

Only my brother would have appreciated that two of those historic villas were the property of Vehbi Özakin, publisher of the *Resim* and the *Çevap*. Özakin was a prideful secularist who despised the slightest criticism of the state, and adjusted the news in his tabloid rags accordingly. The publisher had unreasonable hopes that his only son, Erdan, would one day take over management of his media empire. Yusuf had known Erdan Özakin as a twenty-three year radical near the end of their college days, when they had both attended the State Technical University and, as I recalled, had spent Sundays tutoring impoverished Kurds and drumming up ridiculous Leftist schemes. He'd once described the famous publisher's kid to me as "a hippy, a complete fuck-up, but fun enough."

Yusuf set his sights on Vehbi Özakin's smaller airy mansion, based on convenience of location: it lay on a street shaded by walnut trees only a kilometer west of the clock tower square, and it had its own floating dock, and it had room enough in the garden for a helicopter pad, and it had a timeless empire-baroque facade. Yusuf contacted the publisher through the son under the pretexts of business, and took both men to dinner at the Çırağan Palace. Bent over servings of lamb tenderloin they discussed a series of Teletürk advertisements to appear daily on the back pages of Özakin's *Sports* and *Life* sections.

Yusuf had charmed the men. The small deal was set. But more usefully, according to the Mayor, my brother had noted Vehbi's deferral to his son in matters of business. He'd noted the silent, hopeful glances passed across the table, how determined the aging publisher was for Erdan to take responsibility, any responsibility, for the newspaper business. Yusuf must have noted too the generational gap, how indifferent the son seemed to his father's attentions, how reluctant Erdan was to participate in even these minor business negotiations, how he paid more attention to his perfectly grilled lamb and pale-white asparagus and beaded glass of artisanal pilsner than to the potentially lucrative partnership being forged. Erdan Özakin, still clinging to his youthful vision of a Marxist state, had little interest in inheriting newspapers that were barely more than an arm of the National Security Council.

Erdan had always remembered that business dinner with bemusement. He and his father had expected high-stakes discussion of acquisitions or takeovers; but Yusuf had let them down with what seemed an inconsequential offer of a renewable contract for a year's worth of Teletürk ads. On the father's return from the bathroom Yusuf had suggested his team might run some designs by Erdan. The father looked at the son. The son shrugged and said he'd do it. Vehbi had until that moment considered the evening a waste of his time, but suddenly he was excited. "My father always got excited if I'd do something capitalistic," Erdan used to tell the Mayor.

Who can forget the now famous Teletürk ad campaign that sprang from that dinner? Each week a different celebrity or musician or politician or model, dialing a telephone, asking for their mother. The caption: **No Matter How Big You Get, She Still Needs To Hear From You.** The ads ran in this format for over three years; at first in the papers, then on television, and pretty soon on kilometer-high billboards in Taksim Square. You might have appeared on *Entertainment This Week* or half-naked on the cover of *Star* — but you weren't anyone until you and your mother glossed the back pages of an Özakin tabloid, holding Teletürk phones to your ears.

"The whole campaign was Yusuf's idea," the Mayor remembered. "He milked his connections, but gave Erdan all the credit.

It was simple: everyone loves a celebrity's mother. It made Erdan's name in the industry. He's still riding off that success, the great sloth. But really, it was all your brother's doing."

Only when the initial ads had run for two months to some buzz did Yusuf approach Erdan and just happen to mention he was hunting for a vacation house, just happen to mention he had put a deposit on this or that one, but had always had his eye on the smaller of the Özakin's island *kiosks*. Any chance his father would part with it? Erdan reminded Yusuf that these Ottoman mansions were national treasures, and had been in the family for generations. His dad would never give it up. Still, he'd see what he could do. Yusuf urged his friend not to stick his neck out. He didn't want to cause friction between a father and son.

I found this laughable. "He didn't, did he?" We were walking now past the Clock Tower; and I was chuckling at the story.

"No," the Mayor insisted, biting his lips. "Yusuf played the game patiently, positioning his pieces like a backgammon master, waiting for the perfect roll of the dice. Erdan believed it was ridiculous for his father to own seven houses, and two here on the same island. He hadn't stayed in the Halim Pasha House since he was seven. No one lived in it. What a waste! Back in his heady Marxist days nothing would have made Erdan happier than for his father to sell off a few of these places. "We didn't need heirlooms," he'd tell me. "We didn't need surplus family museums.""

Despite the son's mediation, the father said no. Neither of his historic island mansions was for sale, not to anyone, not even to Elmas, whose ads Vehbi was proud to run in his papers, and whose life of resiliency filled him with admiration. When Erdan delivered the news, Yusuf merely grinned.

It was only late that summer after the Mommy Ads, as they'd become known in the industry, had caught on, after starlets began clamoring to appear in pages of the *Resim* with their mothers, after the ad revenue for Özakin's papers had risen for the first time in a decade, after Erdan was spotted dancing in the foam with some dire bulimic at the Halikarnas Club, and sipping Moet on the Ortaköy coast with Yusuf's buddy Mehmet Akyol (our first Turkish NBA player), only after paparazzi had caught the publisher's son plastered, shirt unbuttoned, disembarking Yusuf's yacht, one arm around a Dutch figure-skater, the other spilling an Aegean Mojito — only then did Yusuf speak directly to the father.

He met the old man alone this time, on the terrace of the Hilton Hotel, over three o'clock tea. He offered double the value of the house. Vehbi Özakin leaned forward in his wicker chair, veins pulsing on his bald head as if from a life of thinking too much. He patted the young CEO on the hand. He thanked him for the compliment, but the Halim Pasha House was a family treasure, one he wanted passed down to his grandchildren, and was simply not for sale. Yusuf ordered an Efes Dark for himself, poured a second glass of *rakı* for the frail tycoon, and suggested in passing ("Just a thought, just a thought, mind you, Vehbi Bey") that he might have to cut off advertising with Özakin's papers, and run ads instead in the *Radikal*. Vehbi's olive skin turned pale. He raised his cold glass to his lips. Yusuf said that he had been speaking to Erdan about joining Teletürk — as Senior Vice President of International Marketing (an offer he had not made; a position that did not exist). He and Vehbi's son had a lot in common — educationally, socially, politically, well, they went way back. Vehbi Özakin took a slow drink, and mid-sip fell into a fit of coughing. A rivulet of white *rakı* dribbled down the old man's wrinkled chin, and he snatched up a napkin to wipe it off, glaring. Yusuf held the publisher's eyes a long moment until he turned away, his ancient liver-spotted hands trembling.

"Vehbi Özakin was a business genius," the Mayor claimed. "His son was his undoing. The whole thing was sweet, actually. Very old fashioned and very fatherly and very stupid."

Yusuf paid 3.2 million U.S. dollars in cash for the Halim Pasha House — a ridiculous sum, but far less than his original offer. "He swindled you," the Mayor used to tell Erdan, laughing. He and Yusuf had remained good friends even later, when Erdan had moved to the States, where the former Marxist now lived in a Chicago duplex with a view of Lake Michigan, two floors beneath Oprah Winfrey. "Well, he swindled my father at least," Erdan would say. "I didn't care. My dad sold him the house for half what he'd first offered, on the sole condition Yusuf leave me alone. That historic mansion was an ancient rat hole. This whole island smells like horse-shit. I can barely stand five minutes here, never mind making it your home. How do you even live in a place where you can't drive a fucking car?"

4

No Renovations

IN THE EYES of the Mayor, my cough-ridden, scrawny little brother had become some ideal of our modern *ghazi*, embracing technology and tradition, the Western entrepreneurial drive and the Eastern spirit. He straddled the continents; he wrestled with power-brokers. And who was I to argue? True, he had overcome the limitations of a progressive disease, of fifty pills a day and a strict regimen of breathing exercises and two brushes with life-threatening pneumonia. True, he had lifted himself up from the struggling middle-class roots of our family — from a hypochondriac mother obsessed by the latest herbal remedies, from an introverted father in love with watch parts — to the very heights of achievement. Monthly, despite myself, I used to stare at the photos I found of him dining with diplomats on some mega-yacht in the straits, of his evenings at glittering balls over the Golden Horn, of the epic operas at the National Cultural Center, of the publicized dates with ballerinas and fashionistas. I had long consoled myself that his life was devoid of substance. But to people like the Mayor he had been authentic, necessary

— if foolhardy, then heroically so. He'd played a hand in modernizing our country, in breaking the monopoly of the state telecommunications industry, in developing the very network of cellular telephone services used by school children on service buses and parliamentarians rushing down the streets of the capital. Teletürk Holdings. It was everywhere, its billboards in every backwater of our nation, its commercials on every network, its jingles on every radio station. *No matter how big you get, she still needs to hear from you.*

We'd arrived now back at the mansion, but standing outside the gate, taking in the Halim Pasha House, the Mayor wouldn't leave. With an air of determined nostalgia he was recalling for me the cool fall day Yusuf had moved in. "The ferry didn't dock at the public *iskele*," the Mayor recalled, "but back there." He waved his hand out to the private pier behind the property. My brother had chartered the boat from Bostancı, stuffed it with his furniture and appliances and collections of antique kilims and fine copperware, as well as twenty muscular Kurdish laborers from Edirnekapı. Village children lined the wrought iron gates around the gardens to catch glimpses of tireless Kurds hauling modern Bosch refrigerators, stereos, televisions, lush divans, teak desks, and ergonomic mattresses up the bobbing wooden pier and squeezing it all in through the French windows. Everyone had fully expected this to mark the beginning of a winter of noisy, intrusive renovations. Everyone expected the obligatory scaffolding to cloak the building's façade. The desecration of the Halim Pasha House had begun.

"But nothing happened," the mayor said, laughing. "No renovations. Yusuf moved in that same day, and lived right here, alone in his creaking island mansion, through the coldest winter months." The mayor jabbed a finger into my shoulder. "Just as he'd once promised you he would."

"That's right," I said, stepping back and taking in the old place, seeing it again for the first time. "Just like he'd once promised me."

With my training I found it bewildering. He had never overhauled his own structurally-questionable property. He did not update the 70-year-old indoor plumbing. I'd spotted frayed cloth-covered copper wiring still in use in some of the closet lighting fixtures — clearly a fire hazard. He'd stuck with the original creaking sea-shutters and paper-thin glass rather than thermal treatments and double-glazed windows that would have closed out the winter winds. He did not raise two slightly-sunken floors in the upstairs guest bedrooms, nor did he replace failing floor-joists, as any first-year Materials and Methods student would have advised. In the municipal property records I would never find evidence that my brother had hired, say, a timber-frame engineer to assess the framing, or that he'd sought recommendations for restoring structural integrity to the building. Yusuf had added only a few basic amenities to update the turn-of-the-century kitchen. He did not reroute the heating pipes or replace the ancient system of radiators with central air. And Nılay Gören, his maid, assured me that he spent his last decade without air-conditioning, or wireless internet, or even a fax machine.

It was exasperating. That a forward-looking technocrat interested only in modernizing our backward nation, one who had led a public charge to reinforce the stock of island homes, could be so willfully negligent. That a man of his standing inhabited this aging mansion fully aware of, and seemingly embracing, its structural faults, living more like a 19th century merchant than a 21st century mogul.

But why should any of it surprise me? Yusuf had always possessed this unique ability to mess with time — as if it bent to accommodate his whims.

"*Haydi*. I'll leave you now to it," the Mayor said. "You'll take care of this place. It's been an eyesore long enough. We'd like it not to stand out any more. Clean it up quickly."

"I'll do my best."

"Quickly, as I say." The Mayor's face had flattened; his voice had taken on an official tone. I only now realized he was giving me an order. He bit his lip, and nodded back over to the house. "Whatever you're going to do here, get to it. As I say, my work is always the law first, the law second, and then justice, etcetera, and all that. It took a long time for things to settle after your brother's madness. It was a massive headache for me, for the island. The whole world doesn't need to know what we're up to here, Avram. Let's be discreet. No one needs to be poking around, dredging up old memories. Less uncomfortable for me. Safer for you. Understand?"

5

Rolled Dough

Even the largest mistakes eventually blend into the landscape of your years. They become a thing you've looked at so often you no longer see. Eventually you trust in the permanency of that illusion. It works the same way in architecture. One of the tricks of the mind an architect learns is to accept that compromises made to some original vision were fundamentally necessary. But they were never necessary. They were compromises. They got the building built, and when it is standing before you, at some height of the ground, modifications, defects, and trade-offs staring you in the face, what are you supposed to do? Tear it all down? Begin again? The return to the island provided a much needed chance to step clear of my mistakes and survey damages done.

For as long as I could remember Mother had rolled her own *yufka*, a leisurely task that consumed most of a Sunday afternoon. Her pastries were famous at the synagogue for their lightness and crunch. Equally loved were her *boreka de handrajo* (grated eggplant, tomatoes and squash, cheese and yoghurt, wrapped in dough) as well as the sweet walnut-filled *borekas* she served every *Pesa*. Father, in his dauntless pursuit of stability, had spoken to friends and bankers and had scoured our Şisli neighborhood to see what it lacked. The production of thin dough for *börek* and *baklava* was a business that, in our community of aging women, could not fail. Mother had a reputation, there was a need; and out went the final boxes of pens and notebooks, in went the brick ovens, the sinks, and the industrial blenders, down went the calligraphied sign that said **Kardeşler Kırtasiye** and up went, in blazing orange letters, **Benezra Yufkası**. In this way we had used the money from the sale of our summer cottage to invest in a grueling business that would drive Mother to her grave.

What Father had not considered was the intensive labor required. Mother's *yufka* were praised for their water absorption, perfect color, and sponginess. But it was back-breaking work, making *yufka* in the hot storefront all morning, the floor covered in flour, the rolling pin like a barbell going back and forth, back and forth, over the counter. Mother had spent the early years of our childhood at home frantically seeing to Yusuf's medical needs, but now she was absent from us. I had to spend my own lunch hour in the grade school nurse's office running Yusuf through an abbreviated midday chest-clearing therapy. Clap clap clap — clap clap! Before we scarfed down lunch the school nurse would administer Yusuf's medications. At night, sitting next to Mother as she read her Zohar, or hugging her before we went to bed, we noticed the changes. We could smell the hot bricks on her skin and make out the white particles lodged in the wrinkles at her eyes. Her fingers had swollen, she wore her wedding ring on a chain around her neck, and rarely could she muster the energy to help Yusuf in the evenings. My brother, sick of having me straddling him three times a day, had begun complaining that I clapped him too often in the same spot, that I caused soreness by hitting seams on his shirt, that I lost concentration and didn't cup my hands so they properly conformed to his chest — in short, that I couldn't loosen his phlegm as well as Mother always had.

"If you're going to complain," I'd tell him, more sick of it than he was, "do it your own damn self."

Meanwhile Father had finally calculated correctly. The business did well enough. We would not have to move to Israel. "You see," our father liked to remind us, "There's no misfortune that's not for some good." And he promised we would one day purchase an even larger summer house on the islands to replace what had been a necessary sacrifice.

That day never came. After the 1980 military coup, after unforeseen devaluations of the lira and the vertiginous inflation rates that marked our lives, after we'd saved for Yusuf's clinical visits and antibiotics and private school tuition, the purchase of an island home through the sales of rolled dough was never a realistic prospect.

Yusuf, consumed by his own obstacles, ruthless in his blame, would forgive Father none of it. Noble intentions meant nothing to my brother. He was blind to the pressures of other people's lives.

While he blamed Father for the mess our lives had become, I was older, and could see things with a wider perspective. In my eyes our brave parents fought on. Their boys would not be deprived. Mother insisted on us wearing braces, for instance, a status symbol in those years reserved for the wealthy Robert College or Galatasaray kids. She hauled us to the orthodontist offices at the American Hospital (reluctantly we went, though with a secret pride) where we were outfitted with silver smiles. A hundred U.S dollars for each trip every month for three years. How many sheets of *yufka* had Mother rolled out, bending across the table, pushing down the heavy pin, swinging her tired arms back and forth, twisting the dough, and swinging them again, for the sake of her sons' straight teeth? And when Yusuf passed the entrance exam and was accepted into Üsküdar Amerikan Lise as a preparatory student somehow our parents came up with the money — six thousand dollars a year — to send him. (I went to the Ulus Jewish School on a partial scholarship supported by community donations.) Our parents paid, as well, for private tutoring to prepare us for the university exams. It was all a test of survival, not merely to put food on the table and enzyme tablets in my brother's stomach, but to retain the trappings of a middle-class family. They fought on so we would never know what we'd lost.

Only we did know. It was clear in a hundred ways. Previously, when those shots of the cannons booming over the straits announced the festive month of Ramadan, we'd return neighbors' late night *iftar* invitations with our own. Now those friendly dinners were turned down with quiet excuses. "Those are not our holidays," Mother muttered if we complained. Sometimes bills could not be paid, and we endured nights when the electricity was cut off, weeks without the use of the telephone. We'd once been accustomed to fine picnics of *pastelicos* and *yaprakes* on spring Sundays at Yildiz Park. No more. "Your mother's tired," Father explained. "Even the Lord has his day of rest."

Dinners became vegetarian affairs. "Okra and eggplant, okra

and eggplant," Yusuf would mumble, eyeing me over the glass-topped table. "Every night okra and eggplant."

"*Sus!*" I'd whisper. "Don't complain. It makes it worse."

"How does it get worse than okra and eggplant!"

Age was pulling us apart, and football didn't help. The family had always been devoted Fenerbahçe fans. It went back generations. Each season we'd attended at least one Fenerbahçe football match at the historic stadium in Kadıköy. I remembered the passion of Father singing the fight songs, the vitriol with which he cursed the opposing team's players, and how he protected us, clutching each of our hands as we fled the stadium, post-game, amid the crunch and surge of humanity. It had been three years since we had been to a match. Worse still, after Fenerbahçe lost a critical game in the 1982 season, Yusuf declared he would no longer root for the family's team. He was switching to Beşiktaş, who was leading the league at the time. Off his side of our bedroom's privacy wall he tore down a decade's worth of triumphant headlines and action photographs. The family teased him about his disloyalty; but what was a joke to them was apostasy to me. Unimaginable.

So Yusuf and I watched our separate teams only on television, at separate times, no better off than the nation of unemployed men around us who stared at the games in the damp card-houses, heating their hands above the wood-stoves, cursing opposing fans. What thin border separated us from our countrymen! The fate of our family was the fate of the nation: we too were growing up poor, uncertain of our loyalties.

6

Cleanliness of the Soul

KEEPING A SICK Yusuf out of the city's broiling summer smog remained the priority for Mother; and as a result for three summers Yusuf and I continued to pass a month of our holidays on the islands, hopping week to week, sometimes night to night, between our great uncle Haim and our father's cousin Yilda.

"They don't even want us here," Yusuf told me, lugging our bags off the ferry that last summer. He complained because there was nowhere to sleep, because we always wound up cramped together on our cousins' bedroom floors. To Yusuf we were not simply welcome guests, we were burdens to be distributed among the relations.

"Of course they want us," I assured him, dragging my own bag off the gangplank and up along the concrete pier. "Idiot, they wouldn't invite us if they didn't want us." But I felt it too: there was charity involved in these arrangements, not simply the close bonds of a large Jewish family. The relatives were purposefully taking us off our struggling parents' hands so that they might remain behind in the burning city to work. "For now, go!" Father had said. "Be with your cousins." One day, he promised us, we'd have a place to ourselves again. "But for now, where would you rather be? A summer on the islands!"

We did as we were told. During those holidays Mother visited us every Saturday. We would meet her at the two-o'clock ferry. She hugged and kissed Yusuf first, and I would wait my turn for my own two pecks on the cheek. She was becoming a heavy woman in those days, with steel-grey hair tied tightly into a bun, or a straw hat tied tightly beneath her chin. She had mysterious pains in her feet, and walked with something of a waddle. It was rare to see her exiting the ferry terminal without a cigarette between her fingers, so that her kisses on those occasions left not only wet lipstick on our cheeks, but the lingering smell of cheap Anatolian tobacco. She rolled behind her a floral-printed valise, which I quickly relieved her of, hoisting it above my head like a strong-man and lugging it through the village up the hill to whichever home we happened to be staying. Along the pier the afternoon sun would be heavy on our faces, but through the streets the branches of Judas trees would pattern the uneven sidewalks in shade, so that every few steps we'd be covered by alternating curtains of warmth and cold.

Mother loved the sea, it seemed her only solace, and it wasn't long after we picked her up that she had changed into her brilliant white linen suit and was hurrying to Seferoğlu Beach. In summers past she used to lead us both along the seaside road, her strong hand clasped around our wrists so that we would not plunge to our deaths over the sea walls. Now though, after we'd greeted her at the ferry and deposited her at one or another house, I would charge back outside to meet friends, to search out the next football match, to spy on girls I insisted I did not like, or to play in the largest game of *uzun eşek* — long donkey — the nation had ever known. Yusuf accompanied Mother to the beach alone.

At nights in those island cottages we slept in cramped quarters, with up to seven cousins, male and female, stuffed into the same room. The carpets retained the mildew smell from long wet winters in which the houses were boarded up. When I drank water the sour scent of the glasses pressed to my nose was curiously different from the glasses in our city apartment. The routine of washing varied with the house: Uncle Haim insisted our swimming in the Marmara was bath enough; while Aunt Yilda checked the dirt behind our ears nightly with a vicious military inspection, muttering, "Cleanliness of the body, cleanliness of the soul." The laws of bedtime hours, table etiquette, and the number of after-dinner *lokum* allowed varied as well, but we accepted these changes of regime — one adult's strictness versus another's laxities — with the bemusement of children at peace with the mysteries of grown-ups. In reality, in both houses we came and went as we pleased, the island was a safe place, everybody knew each other, and we understood that even when Uncle Haim was fast asleep on the front porch wicker chair, the weekly sports paper draped over his lap like a blanket, that the entire adult population was keeping perfect track of us. Those summers without our parents were a time of supervised adventure. On the island we were learning more about life, and learning it better, than we ever did in the stuffy confines of our winter classrooms.

Afternoons my friends and I engaged in raucous, no-holds-barred football matches. Our pitch (which the Elmas Foundation would one day repave with artificial turf, light with eight state-of-the-art towers, and erect a scoreboard over) was then just a fenced-in patch of concrete, broken glass, and thistles. On land I was a far greater athlete than Yusuf. I was faster, healthier, and always had a larger social circle at the Golf Park, where girls watched us play football, table tennis, and snooker. If Yusuf played we stuck him as goalie. He hated the position — we all did — for it offered no glory, only humiliation. My brother enjoyed the statistics and fanatical arguments of football more than playing it. Just by asking him to join us each afternoon, however, I felt I was looking out for him, as an older brother with absent parents must. Even when he was tired I would force him to put down his Isaac Asimov and volumes of *Life Encyclopedia* and drag him out of the house to get some exercise. It depressed me, in the island sunshine, the cool sea breeze wafting across the streets, for Yusuf to be inside, lying on the carpet, reading and wheezing and wasting the day. I didn't want him to be lonely; I wanted him to socialize and to be popular. Also, we needed a body in goal.

Then Yusuf had turned fifteen. I noticed he was growing tall. He was becoming a dedicated swimmer, and to keep in shape for the Adalar Kulübü he swam alone each morning, further and further out to sea, so that his arms and legs, his slightly hunched back and barrel-chest, had grown well-developed. He had no fat on him — I could see the definition in his tanned shoulders when he dove for a football shot. "You might not remember, Avram," our older cousin Canu later reminded me, "but from the time he was a teenager your brother was beautiful. He had those long fair eyelashes and a deep voice that made all my friends melt. While you and your buddies were cat-calling and playing pranks on

us, we were falling in love with Yusuf. You thought he was awkward. We thought he was precious. So stupid you boys were — to
think a girl can care if some hairy man slide-tackles someone to
the ground. Yusuf was quiet and shy and smart even back then.
We all felt sorry for him. He suffered so bravely. If he wasn't my
cousin I would have fought to sit behind him at the Lale Sinema
like the other girls did."

I'd been aware of none of this. My little brother fidgeted; he
coughed; he farted bombs. He sometimes stuttered. We teased
him; we razzed him. We stuck him in goal.

On one blazing July afternoon the other team had spent the
better part of an hour bashing a worn, flat football into Yusuf's
chest. His best saves came accidentally, when he was gazing up
at the sky or bent over tying his shoes or coughing into his forearm. The other team's shots would career off his knee or the side
of his head. "Great save, Yusuf!" we'd yell.

In the day's last game our team had been lucky: only a few
balls had managed to slip by my brother between the two orange
cones. Late in the second half the score was tied at four. Yusuf
caught a ball awkwardly with both arms and his chest, and
rolled it towards me on the line. I faked left, dribbled powerfully
through two of the defensemen, centered to our second-cous-
in Mert, who skimmed the rebound in two hops through the
opposing keeper's legs for the winning goal. Our team engaged
in the obligatory celebration: the pile on, the mad somersaults,
the removal of T-shirts and, twirling them above our heads, the
three victory laps around the pitch. Then we all stopped, our
eyes locked.

She was long legged, with bobbed red hair. Her sleeveless

blouse revealed constellations of freckles on her shoulders. She was walking self-consciously past us, so at first she seemed embarrassed to be running the gauntlet of shirtless, gawking teenage boys. But with a grin she looked up, weighed each of us with a bold glance, and one by one dropped us. Her eyes met Yusuf's, the color in her cheeks deepened, and she raised a hand.

"Hello Yusuf," she called in English.

"Hello," he said, also in English, scratching his elbow.

We were flummoxed. Our goalie! We watched her walk away, step by wondrous step, until she stopped, and slowly bent over to remove something stuck in her sandal — her tight orange pants hugging the curve of her behind, her blouse riding up and revealing a strip of pale lower back — and slowly she stood, adjusted her shirt with a twist, and disappeared past the swaying hyacinth bushes at the Bahar Pastry House.

We were all over him. We pressed him for answers: How did he know her? Where had they met? Where was she from? With his hands to his head Yusuf called out: "From England. Stop!"

My friends crowded him, grabbing his arms, driving knuckles into his forehead.

"Have you kissed her tangerines Yusuf?"

"Yusuf, have you walked with her in the woods?"

"Has she touched your cucumber Yusuf? How many times?"

He squatted low in the center our sweating pubescent scrum. We got out of him that she was an au-pair, charged with watching the son of one of the island's textile magnates; that last week he had sat next to her at an open-air performance of a traveling Greek percussion troupe; that a few nights ago he'd walked her home from the cinema through the park. Explaining this in clipped, embarrassed sentences, he stood and raised himself to his full height. For the first time my brother seemed as tall as any of us.

"You walked her home and not even a kiss?" someone yelled.

Our cousin Mert chimed in, "You know what he did in the bathroom that night?" and followed this with a furious round of coarse gestures. I tried not to laugh. Yusuf was calm. And then he spoke, and when I later considered the long months that followed, all the ways we lost each other, I wondered if these were the words that started it:

"Shitheads! She didn't just touch my cucumber. She tasted it."

It was a remarkable revelation on many levels: for its brazenness, for his ability to accept our abuse and to fight back, for the image he set in our minds of that forbidden act, for the off chance, as he stood there with a nervous smile, that it could even have been true. With an uproar my friends staggered outwards, laughing, and two of them massaged Yusuf on the shoulders.

"He's all right, this one."

"Your brother's a playboy."

"Yusuf Benezra, lady killer!"

"His head's up in the clouds," I muttered, peeling away from the circle and with a brutal kick smashing the ball against the rusted, rattling fence. "Don't even listen to him."

7

Love Bite

Our cousin Mert, these days a feature editor of the newspaper *Shalom*, remembered the redhead as well as any of us. "I asked Yusuf about her a few years later at a Bar Mitzvah. *Yürü be*! The way he went on about her, I knew he wasn't making the story up. Think of your own first kiss, Avram. The first time you held a girl's hand and she squeezed back. He had no reason to lie about any of it. At least to me."

The truth was I hadn't been keeping a close-enough eye on my brother. My group of friends would be out late those nights, coming and going as we pleased, stomping into one another's homes, perching on the picnic tables near the clock tower, flirting, whistling, trying to catch a girl's eye with staged fights and practical jokes. According to Mert, the funny thing was that Yusuf was so young, and wasn't even openly interested in girls. The red-head was eighteen. She'd finished high school in England, and a London agency promised her the romance of a summer in our enchanted country — but here she was, stuck on the hot tiny island, caring for some snotty four-year-old kid. She knew no one. She could barely mutter hello and thank you in Turkish. Yusuf needed only smile at her once, and ask in English what her name was to spark the slightest friendship. It was the summer of *Terminator* and Yusuf said he and the au pair went to the film four times in a single week. By the second night they were holding hands and sharing a bag of roasted pumpkin seeds, and in the back corner of the open air theater only the Lord knew what she was doing to him. He told us afterwards he would walk her home, and they took the long way up the hill by the ruins of the Greek Orphanage. On some nights they sat under the pines, and Yusuf pointed out the lights of the navy ships dotting the black water, the lights of airplanes and satellites arcing above, the lights of Bostancı high-rises marking the horizon. This is what he remembered to our cousin Mert. "All of us idiots dying to know about sex, what it felt like to reach under a woman's skirt," Mert said. "Yusuf remembered the lights. I mean, it was a summer fling and the girl must have been bored, but at the same time it was all opening up to him, you know? You remember that first time, smelling the girl's hair, wrapping your arm around her waist, touching her living flesh."

That summer I didn't want to imagine anything about Yusuf and the English redhead — whose name, I soon learned, was Rainbow Jacobson. Rainbow! What made the story more troubling was my brother's complete lack of insistence. If nobody wanted to believe him nobody had to.

And all summer long there was the disturbing evidence. I saw Rainbow waving to him. I noted my brother's disappearances. The kid who would spend entire evenings on the porch alone with a comic book, who had needed me to clap his back for an hour three times a day, was suddenly, mysteriously, absent from my life. Yusuf asked me to lend him money for a film he was taking her to. I handed over the coins. He told me he had helped Rainbow watch the four-year-old on the beach; that he was teaching the boy to snorkel. "You're unbelievable," I chided him with a forced smile. On Rainbow's day off they hiked to St. George's monastery, the highest point on the island, where Yusuf said they'd had a picnic lunch on the cliffs. She'd snuck white wine with her, and they'd polished off the whole bottle. "Must have been a blast," I replied.

It was early evening, and sharing the upstairs bathroom of Aunt Yilda's house, we'd begun arguing as usual about football. I'd already bathed, and had begun to shave in the steamed up mirror, which I wiped in circles every few moments with my wrist. Yusuf had run a bath for himself and had settled into the tub. We shared the bathroom like this in order to speed things up for the line of cousins, Aunt Yilda's five children, who were awaiting their own forced regimen of bathing, an eleventh commandment we had to fulfill if we planned to sleep under her roof.

"What good is it to root for a team that wins every year?" Yusuf was yelling over the spraying water. "Where's the thrill? When Beşiktaş wins, it's one for the ages."

I wet the razor. "Why don't you give up on them already, brother? Your team sucked this year, and they'll suck next year. Show yourself some mercy." Of the three storied teams in our city, Beşiktaş held the fewest championships, and their blue-collar fans were long suffering. The last time they'd won the cup was before Yusuf had even been born. Fenerbahçe was the best team in the country, a team looked upon favorably in the eyes of God, with the highest average attendance in the First League, which had resulted in nineteen national championships, two in the last two years. Despite his club's inadequacies, even in its worst seasons Yusuf could list off ways Beşiktaş was the superior team. If this shot had not hit the post, if they had been awarded the offside call in the Ankaraspor game, if Galatasaray had trounced Trabzonspor like they were supposed to… If this, if that. His team would have won the cup every year if the planets simply aligned.

I rinsed off the razor again and answered him with my stock phrase — "19-7" — the number of Fenerbahçe championships versus Beşiktaş's. It was the coup de grâce — enough to silence him.

Yusuf soaped his hair more vehemently, and I laughed, pulling the straight-edge across my cheeks. This had been a gift from Father, who'd grown tired of my borrowing his razor once a week. Yusuf didn't yet need a razor: he'd inherited Mother's Baltic fairness, and his blonde facial hair showed only as fuzz on his lip. The previous week, though, he claimed he wanted a clean face for Rainbow, and had asked me to teach him how to shave with Uncle Haim's safety blade. "A real man doesn't use that plastic junk," I advised him, and offered him the straight-edge. Yusuf lacked coordination, cut himself, and when I took up the razor to show him how to better use it I succeeded only in butchering his neck and chin further. It was a massacre. His face had bled for an hour. Initially amused, I grew somewhat concerned, and had finally torn pieces of a paper bag to patch him up the best I could. His cheeks pocked with bloody brown paper, he'd been as upset as I'd ever seen him.

Now I wiped the mirror with my wrist, and in the reflection I could see Yusuf, kneeling in the misty tub, spraying the soap out of his hair with the showerhead. He let out a disgusting cough and hacked into the drain. I was so used to these violent expectorations that I no longer noticed them. Still I thought: how can any woman *stand* this? A shaft of evening sunlight fell into the room by the single high window and faded through the steam into an orange glow. Pearls of soap rolled down Yusuf's lower neck as he rinsed. On the skin now revealed, I spotted the violet patch.

I turned, and pointing with the wet razor asked, "What'd you do to yourself this time?"

Yusuf felt around his neck, and covered it up.

I stepped over to him and pulled his hand away. "You're bleeding again?"

He grimaced, stood, and reached for the thin towel draped over the rack beside the tub. Water was dripping across Yusuf's face, dripping down his waist and bright white buttocks, dripping through his curly red pubic hair.

Now I saw the mark on his neck looked more like a burn. It was the size of a fifty lira coin and bulbous in shape, like the tattoo of a rose. I pulled the towel away from his neck.

"She kissed me," he said.

"Who kissed you?"

"Rainbow. The au pair."

"You got that from a kiss?"

"She kisses kind of hard."

"Is she some kind of animal?"

"It's called a *love bite*."

He used the English words, and I was caught off guard. "Of course. That's right." *Love bite?*

Yusuf shut the shower and the pipes snapped. "I gave her one too," he whispered.

"Did you?"

He blushed. "You kiss real long, almost bite down with your lips."

"Sure." I'd gone back to shaving. "Your first one, eh?"

"It hurts sort of," he said with an uneasy grin.

I pulled the razor up across my already-shaven chin. Yusuf dried himself off with the towel, flicking water from his shoulders. Our cousin Canu was pounding on the door and yelling, "*Bu ne ya*, assholes! You done in there yet?" Yusuf wrapped the towel around his bony hips, and hurried out of the room. I ran my hand down my smooth cheeks, my fingers across my own stinging neck.

8

The Arts of Deception

I ADMIT IT: I grew distraught. I had yet to kiss anyone (and would not until university), but here was my little brother, quietly running through a summer affair on the windswept island with an older, foreign woman. I should have known then that, whatever his limitations, great things were in store for him. Was it really possible something so small, a simple bruise, could spark twenty years of internecine warfare?

The next morning at breakfast Yusuf was wearing a collared shirt, and in the kitchen I pointed this out to my aunt, who shrugged it off. Yilda thought he was dressing to impress someone. "Let him have his fun. We've all been in love at that age."

"She's older," I said, dipping my vanilla biscuit into my tea. "She's foreign, from Britain. Some kind of hippy. Her name's Rainbow Jacobson." I pronounced it with a sneer. "Check out his neck."

Aunt Yilda raised her eyebrows.

I murmured into my cup, "And she's not Jewish."

My aunt held my stare until a look of fright clouded her face.

She marched into the dining room and yanked down Yusuf's collar, then slapped him on the side of the head. She looked up at the ceiling and raising one finger, speaking to a higher authority, claimed she would not be held responsible for the sins of her vagrant nephews. With thunder in her eyes she looked back down at Yusuf. "*Hadi ya*! You're going to get yourself into serious trouble. Or worse. And it won't be on my conscience. You hear me! Look at me!" But Yusuf was silent. He cranked his head in my direction. Standing behind my aunt with crossed arms, I couldn't hold his gaze.

That Saturday Aunt Yilda complained to our mother, who promptly spoke to Yusuf, asking him to stop seeing this Rainbow whatever-her-name-was. Yusuf, still unschooled in the arts of deception, told her he was sorry, but could promise her nothing. Mother was beaten down by work, and didn't have it in her to take on her fragile, sensitive son. Father, duly summoned, ferried out that very afternoon — his first appearance on the island all season. I relished what I had set in motion. When I came home I found the two of them arguing on Yilda's whitewashed porch: Father leaning against the low wall; and Yusuf, barefoot, swinging manically on the wicker rocking chair. They didn't acknowledge me. I was as invisible in this drama as I would be in larger dramas to come. Just inside the door I stopped and listened. I could hear Father forbidding Yusuf from seeing this English *orospu*. Yusuf, assuming a chivalric air, defended Rainbow from the insult. Father threatened to retract every privilege he could summon — Yusuf's part-time job at the cinema, his evenings out, his football magazine subscriptions, his stereo-set, any future summer on the island.

"Take it all away," Yusuf said. "I don't care."

"If you were me, here, in this situation, Yusuf, what would you do? What would you tell your son?"

"I'd trust him to do what was right."

"And if you knew this was a mistake? That somebody might be hurt?"

"There's no misfortune that's not for some good."

"You know what we've sacrificed for you, Yusuf? For this? For you to pull this… stunt?"

"I never asked for half of it."

"You don't know half of it."

"I keep track to the lira better than you do."

"Enough. I'm the father here. That's something you can't change. Understand? Look at me. You're not to see her again."

"Rainbow's an adult. You can't tell her what to do."

"I'll do my best."

"And what good has that done you up to now?"

"Enough Yusuf. I said enough! You'll speak to me as your father."

That night, before he returned to the city, Father donned his felt hat and paid a visit to Rainbow Jacobson's employer, the textile magnate, in an ancient *konak* on Nisan Caddesi, just above the Splendid Palas Hotel. The meeting lasted all of fifteen minutes. Father cited Yusuf's fragile condition, the dangers this kind of thing could pose to his son's fraught health, the age difference, the issue of religion, the inappropriateness of the relationship.

They shipped Rainbow Jacobson the next morning off the island to the city, where she would spend a night at the Star Hostel near the Aya Sofya before being tossed on a plane back to London. From a bench on the promenade it had given me some satisfaction to watch her: the somber, pale, long-legged foreigner wheeling her luggage down the pier, shadowed by her employer, an older man in a sports jacket and Panama hat, following step by ominous step behind her. Rainbow Jacobson stared with resolution into the ground. I sensed somewhere in the seaside crowd, all jostling and waiting for the 8:45 ferry, that Yusuf was watching too. I mentally urged Rainbow to look up and wave to someone, to show me where he was. She never did. She sauntered through the mayhem, across the gangplank, and out of our lives. The finality of it all, the grace and simplicity of Father's solution, unnerved me.

I could not have predicted how hard Yusuf would take it. That evening my brother never returned for dinner. We didn't know where he slept that night. Mother and Yilda were worried for him, worried that he had missed an evening of therapy and medications. Months later I learned that he'd ferried back to the city, and had spent two nights on the street, combing the hippy hotels of Beyoğlu and Sultanahmet, looking for Rainbow Jacobson at first in the wrong places, and then in the right place, when she was already gone.

Could he have actually been in love with her? Mert later theorized that in Yusuf those events triggered a vital force, a desperate need for female affection that diminished little in the remaining years of his compacted life. "You and me, Avram, we're busy with families and jobs and a hundred responsibilities, and we've forgotten what it felt like at that age. But Yusuf, I think, always remembered. He kept that feeling close to him. Back then we would have swum through a sea of vomit, either one of us, just to touch a girl's tits. Your brother was already on the other shore."

With the trouble Rainbow had caused, that summer would be our last on the island. For my brother it was a second exile — he blamed Father first, and me second — and it remained permanent until that day, twelve years and four months later, when he made his triumphant return. By then, with the economy sliding up to the '94 military coup, nearly all of our relations had sold their island houses. Uncle Haim had moved to Sweden, where he repaired shoes. Aunt Yilda had been committed to a home for the mentally incapacitated — where she spent her last years washing her care-worn hands, every twenty minutes, every hour, night and day. Cleanliness of the body, cleanliness of the soul.

9

A Great Passion

In my second week on the island I received at the mansion two unexpected visits.

The first was an old acquaintance: Yusuf's friend, Dr. Murat Baykan, the famous urologist. The doctor kept a villa here too, and had caught wind that I was cleaning up my brother's place. He claimed he only wanted to say hello, though it seemed to me he had come primarily to snoop around. I remembered last meeting him in graduate school. He still had the same round gut and the same drooping mustache, and he still wore the same silk dress shirts, open now to reveal tangles of graying chest hair — coordinated, it seemed, with the silvery mane on his head. On the porch I went to shake his hand and the doctor embraced me in an awkward bear hug, an affection I wasn't expecting, disproportionate to the degree we'd known one another. But memories did that to a person, I reasoned, stiffening in his grasp. Memories and death.

We walked outside the mansion, around the tangled statue garden. "What a shame," the doctor kept repeating, pointing out

the brown hedges, the dried out mimosa. He kicked at an overturned marble bird-bath, which rolled over and crushed the only
living groundcover in the plot. "Yes, such a shame," he said. I
didn't want to force on him the difficult subject of my brother, but
the doctor drew a cigarette from a pack of Marlboro Lights, seated
himself on a shaky stone bench, and rocking it with his heels,
dove right in.

"What can I say, Avram? What can I say? Nobody knew him.
Everyone always got him wrong." He was pointing with his cigarette out to sea, towards the city.

"How exactly, Doctor, did we always get him wrong?"

"For instance, people thought your brother had simply been
lucky in his fortune. But they didn't understand that he'd fit the
work of two men into a day that included nebulizers, enzyme
tablets, inhalers, and crucial breathing sessions. I've never met a
man so driven. You remember?"

"Of course I do."

"Everyone said Yusuf was a socialite, a partier, a heavy drink-
er. He created that myth! I went out with him every week. He
drank very little, with precise control. He sipped. He tasted. He
knew his limits."

"I believe you if you say so. I hadn't seen him in fourteen years."

Dr. Baykan claimed Yusuf cultivated a reputation as a womanizer, but he challenged me to name a single celebrity or super-
model with whom my brother had ever launched an actual affair.
I said I couldn't.

"Of course not. Of course not. But he could have had any
woman he'd wanted. That's my point. And here's another. Yusuf
would talk up the helicopter he sometimes commuted to the

city in. A refurbished Sikorsky. He once told a magazine that he'd trained to fly it himself, with his own private pilot. He did no such thing! Your brother hated flying in that helicopter. Five mornings a week he commuted on the slow ferry to Kabataş, like the other island commuters did. Tsk! You didn't know that either I bet. That's the kind of man he really was."

"Maybe he never got used to the money? We never had much. It had to have been — well, an adjustment."

"Ha!" the doctor exclaimed, jabbing his cigarette towards me. "He got used to it!"

Yusuf, he told me, had hired 35 full-time workers to crew his 120 meter yacht — refurbished with fifteen private suites, sun decks, fitness center, Turkish bath, swimming pool, and movie theater. But he never took it down to the Mediterranean, or to Bodrum, or to any jet-setting place for that matter. The yacht remained docked in Arnavutköy. Socialites rented it for weddings. The crew fished off its side into the straits. "Eventually," the doctor claimed, "they grew so bored, half of them quit. Only a skeleton crew was left."

"Why keep a yacht then?"

"What's a billionaire without his accouterments? Believe me Avram, Yusuf knew how to part with his money!"

Dr. Baykan admitted that Yusuf spent more time on his smaller ship, the *Bosphorus Princess*, that V-bottom powerboat which he moored behind the mansion on the private pier, and which he raced around the archipelago, often alone, on summer weekends. Dr. Baykan had never seen anything like that fated vehicle, and his eyes gleamed as he described it. It was a twin engine, thirteen meter Lightning, with a carpeted cabin, two enclosed heads, a fully equipped bedroom, a second guest room, and a stand-up galley, with built in refrigerator and seating for ten: "Perfect for gourmet dining!" Its double, one-thousand liter engine was capable of speeds in excess of 150 kilometers an hour. In the cockpit were hydraulic drop seats, console buttons for the spun-brass eight-trumpet musical air horn, and a Bluetooth stereo with four marine speakers. The doctor himself had helped Yusuf purchase it on a vacation they took together to Miami, in a place called Thunderboat Alley, a kind of bazaar, as I understood it, for offshore speed craft. Yusuf had it imported that same month.

The doctor rose from the bench, crushed his Marlboro with his heel, and started downhill towards the water. The wind off the sea was brisk and sour. I followed a step behind until we were standing together before the mansion's floating pier. Its timbers, rotting and splintered, had begun bleaching a silvery gray. Dr. Murat Baykan blinked at me, laughing, his shoulders shaking, as he recalled what Yusuf would do with that boat. "It was his home away from home, you see. On the weekends, after we'd go out, if he wanted a little privacy he could just as well have taken his reserved suite at the Cırağan Palace. But he used to spend nights moored in the boat. The motion of the water helped him sleep. He claimed it cleared his lungs. Tsk! As if he slept there! He was never alone."

"Never alone? You just said he was no womanizer."

"Not the womanizer people claimed. Not in a conventional sense. Yusuf's affairs weren't meant for public consumption. They came from a great *passion*."

Wide-eyed with nostalgia, Dr. Murat Baykan launched into

the random musings of a thousand random evenings. But the more the doctor remembered the more he slowed down, pausing between disconnected phrases. His own wounds were still raw, and after a few minutes he cut himself off, staring out at the darkening waters. Finally he shook me roughly by the arm, and invited me to join him for dinner in the city. "For old time's sake, Avram," he said. "For the memory of your brother."

10

Please Do Not Come Back

I wasn't yet allowing myself any caution. I was still hungry for the information, not discriminating, or guessing where it might lead me. So I dined with the famous urologist two nights later just off Istiklal Caddesi, in a raucous *meyhane* overflowing with music and shouting and drink — the very restaurant where the doctor had eaten the night before Yusuf drowned. A *fasıl* band headed by a gypsy on the *ud* and two improvisational *klarnet* players was grinding away. The diners packed in at the long linen-covered tables, picking at eggplant and lamb, raising toasts of *rakı* and spilling wine as they clanked glasses. By ten o'clock everyone was swaying and singing along. Murat put his arm around me, and we too swayed to the music. "Yusuf liked to be surrounded by people when he ate," the doctor bellowed in my ear. "Maybe it was living all alone, in the winter, on that island, in that empty house. 'Why don't you spend weeknights in the city?' I used to ask him. He was so stubborn. Yusuf! What a slug! He never listened to the advice of others. He had his own plans. He was my great friend. I called him as often as possible.

To get him off that damn island, you know. If he had met me that evening like he was supposed to —"

He began recounting for me details of that final night. Murat had saved a seat for Yusuf at the championship football match, in the German Hospital's private box, and had expected a late night of hell-raising to follow when their team won. But Yusuf had declined at the last minute, citing the next morning's pilgrimage to St. George — which in all his years on the island he'd never missed. "Pilgrimage! What do you mean, pilgrimage?" Dr. Baykan remembered exclaiming, "You're not Greek or Armenian. You're a Jew! And the only religion you follow is football!"

Now the lead gypsy was strumming his oud, his fingers moving in a flourish faster than my eyes could follow; the horns were blaring; and the doctor was weeping on my right shoulder. "He was a good man, your brother. My great friend. I knew I'd lose him eventually. I just didn't know how soon."

Looking around me, suddenly self-conscious, I searched for a way to subdue Murat. I remembered that I was supposed to phone Naomi; the twins had received their report cards, and I'd meant to check in. It had been days — how many? — since I'd spoken to them. I was neglecting my sacred duties as a father. But Dr. Baykan poured another glass of *rakı*. "Passions. Wait wait," he blubbered, "I've shown you nothing yet."

"*Tamam, tamam*," I pleaded, prying his claw of a hand off my arm. "Let me step outside, make a quick phone call."

Out on the street a few early winter snowflakes hit my cheeks like wet kisses. I dialed home on my pocket phone. Naomi's voice was distant and cold; I'd woken her. She asked me, sleepily, if I might make it home for the holiday. It was December 18th, a day before Hanukah, and I hadn't seen the twins since October.

"No, no." I found myself immediately defensive, striking the wrong note. "I won't be able to make it. Not this weekend."

"*Canım*, dear, it's gone on long enough. You've helped your father. The girls, they miss their dad."

"And you?"

A silence fell over the line, and I was reminded, holding the phone, of my confusion that night, nearly five years ago, when Yusuf had called. I switched the refurbished Teletürk K-122 to my other hand and leaned against the damp wall of the *meyhane*. Graffiti had been etched low on the bricks: "*NE OLUR GERI DÖNME!*" Please do not come back.

"Naomi."

"I'm here."

"Say something."

A deep exhalation of breath. "My parents have been looking into places."

"Places."

"They've found a rental for me. I've put a deposit down. I wanted to tell you this in person."

"What kind of rental? You mean an apartment?"

"Furnished." Her voice broke at the word. "One of us has to take a step, if we're not going to do this together."

For a moment I let what she was saying sink in. "This wasn't what I agreed to, coming out here. I didn't want this. I wasn't giving you license—"

"Avram, Avram." It was all she needed to say. After nineteen years of marriage who needed complete sentences? I imagined what a visit home now would feel like — the self-conscious hugs, the stilted conversation, the weighted smiles in front of the girls. The twins by now had to know what was happening. Our distance was plying us all apart. Maybe, I told myself, I'd visit home for New Years and try to change her mind. I could take the girls shopping at Armada, let them finally have their ears pierced, make the missing weeks up to them. Then I saw Dr. Baykan through the steamed window, shoulders hunched, eyes closed, rocking to the music.

Naomi was quiet. Five weeks absent, I understood her even at this distance, even in her sharp silence. I was encyclopedic in my knowledge of her: how her voice lilted when she grew upset, how even now she would be pressing her temples with two fingers and biting the corner of her upper lip, how the smooth lines on her forehead would be deepening with the emotional strain of talking to me. I understood her tacit recognition that our life together had unraveled. She was leaving me, not for another man, but for another country. The fact of it hit me in the chest.

She asked softly, "What's next?"

"Do you want to talk to a lawyer?"

"We'll have to work out support."

My pulse beat hard. "You won't have to worry. Omer's promised me work in his Levent office. He's waiting for a new round of contracts from the *Milli Eğitim*."

She digested this. "I'm not worried for myself. I'm thinking of Estela and Sara. Have you even thought of them?"

"They are all I've thought of. Look, this isn't something —"

"Don't Avram." She took another extended breath, and I imagined she might leave it there. But she went on. "Don't wade into your self-pity with me."

"Naomi, these last few months —"

"Don't you start talking to me about regrets. Not in the middle of the night. Nineteen years is love, Avram. We could have gotten through this together if you'd wanted to. It doesn't matter where we live. But you've been determined to just sling it away. Crumple up the years together and toss them in the trash. No answer's good enough for you. And we can't even settle this face to face. A late night phone call, that's what I get. I'll wake up in the morning and won't even know if I was *dreaming* this. I've given you my *life*, Avram. Two beautiful daughters. You are family to my family. None of this ever quieted your doubts." Her voice was unsteady.

"Shh, Naomi. *Tamam, tamam.* We can talk more tomorrow. Why don't you get some sleep? We'll talk more in the morning." I shivered. Through the window I saw the urologist, in the warm light of our table, refilling my glass with *rakı* until it overflowed.

"Talk? Am I keeping you from someone? Where are you?"

"Outside my father's apartment," I lied.

"You're not outside his apartment. Where *are* you Avram?"

Let there be drama. For nineteen years I had all but avoided drama, and it had led me only here, against this cold brick wall. "I'm on Istiklal. Having dinner with Murat Baykan."

"Yusuf's old friend?" A painful pause, followed by strained laughter. "Don't make up stories, Avram."

"Listen. I'm telling you where I am. He wanted to talk about my brother."

"This is the most ridiculous thing I've heard."

"I've wanted to talk too."

"Who's there with you? Really." Her voice flattened with

suspicions. "Be honest with me. What are you getting us into?"

And I was frightfully honest with her. I told her about inspecting the house, talking with the islanders, hiring on my brother's former help to clear the mansion.

"You can't let it go," she said. "You simply cannot let it go. What is it now? You want a piece of what your brother had? Is that what this house is all about? Do you think he ever knew love? Pop singers and ballet dancers and boys in midnight parks. Tabloid affairs. You think Yusuf knew love? I asked you not to get involved. A simple request. That was too much. Well, go ahead: live like him, and you'll die like him. Unloved by anyone — and alone." With that, the final threatening lilt to her voice, she hung up. I stared at the phone in my hand: a small device, smaller than my palm, capable of undoing the world. I pressed the red button, once, twice, until the damn thing sang off. Opening the door to the *meyhane* my fingers tingled on the frozen knob. Music rushed out; the doctor waved me in; and the swampy heat, the pulsing music, and the scent of fried cheese washed over me like some bitter salve.

11

The Second Visitor

Two hours and two bottles later, holding each other up, Dr. Murat Baykan and I staggered out of the *meyhane* into the damp air of the streets. A light wet snow was still falling. Everyone in the city seemed to have their arms around each other. I stumbled downhill with Yusuf's old friend, past the jazz clubs and gated music shops, towards the Galata Bridge. In tandem we shot vapors of *rakı* ahead of our faces. We were in no condition to walk these icy steps. I pictured Sara and Estela, sleeping the sleep of angels in their yellow-tinted bedroom, pink butterflies painted by their mother fluttering across the walls. I pictured my wife alone in our king-sized bed, wrenching the sheets around herself, wringing her hands. At the Karaköy Iskele the doctor hailed us a cab and against my weak protests directed the driver across the Atatürk Bridge into the infamous Sulukule neighborhood.

The taxi followed an unlit avenue along the Byzantine city walls, passing to our left two story makeshift wooden bungalows cramped side by side. Outside one dark nondescript house a horse was tied to the doorpost. The doctor ordered the driver to stop. An old gypsy on a wooden stool warmed himself by the fire of a rusted garbage can. He stood and greeted us, and directed us inside, turning on the foyer lights. I heard a scuttling from the floor above. A dog barked from a room to our left. We waited a moment until the noise upstairs stopped, a woman's voice rang out, and then we were led up to a bare room furnished only with plastic chairs and a card table. The floor's linoleum was scarred with cigarette burns. The doctor haggled with the old man for ten minutes, and when they finally settled, a young bongo player — the gypsy's son? — wiping sleep from his eyes, entered the room. He was followed by an elderly man with a banjo. The men played and sang, but I couldn't make out the tune of the banjo over the cacophony of the drums. At last a dancer, wearing an embroidered pink bikini-top over her heavy breasts and a bottom of long loose strings barely covering her powerful thighs, came writhing through the doorway, dancing in long slow steps her dark hips thrusting as she raised the castanets over her head. She recognized the doctor, let out a high pitched cry of joy, and Murat rose and danced in place beside her, his arms stretched wide, his fingers snapping. The old man — the woman's father? — poured more glasses of *rakı* in plastic cups, opened a tub of yogurt on the table, and dipped two spoons inside it. At the song's end the dancer flung back her dark hair, dashed over to the table, spooned out a dollop of yogurt and, leaning her perfumed chest over me, pushed my head back. I opened my mouth and she thrust the rancid yogurt in and slid the spoon out. Her other hand clenched my knee-cap and gave it two quick squeezes. I swallowed, slid to my feet, and all three of us now circled, dancing the next song together with arms raised. The rhythm picked up and I was growing dizzy. More shots of *rakı*, and another girl entered, this one only a teenager, but wearing a blue sequined top, the honeyed skin of her stomach lighter than the older woman's, who might have been her sister. And then a third girl, in a state of similar undress. We danced clumsily, we laughed, we sat and watched, twisting hundreds of lira into bikini tops, and by early-morning two more bottles stood empty on the table, the musicians were still playing, and a different kind of haggling had begun. I discouraged the doctor, but he wouldn't listen, and as the sun came up I little knew how I found myself outside a two-star hotel in Aksaray, the younger dancers in short fur jackets and bare legs each shivering on the doctor's elbows, the older gypsy woman, holding mine, asking if I, too, had been friends with the billionaire, Yusuf Elmas.

"I never knew the man," I said. I'd stopped myself at the revolving door.

"*Ne yapıyorsun?*" the doctor asked, pulling me by my free elbow. "What? Aren't you coming in? For old time's sake. We'll share." He patted the younger dancer on the bottom. "For the memory of your brother's… passions."

I was an imposter, an understudy who did not yet know my lines. Dizzy with grief, I shook my head. I considered the two young girls. "Enjoy yourself, Doctor."

"No? Really, no? How can you say no? Look at them! *Maşallah*! Look at what I'm offering!" He wagged a finger at me, laughing. "A do-gooder! Tsk! Yusuf always said you were too good for him! Now I know what he had to contend with. Last chance? No?" I held my ground, and watched the famous urologist maneuver through the gilded, spinning doors, a woman on each arm, their heads thrown back in laughter. Dawn had come early, and shivering now, hands deep in my pockets, I shuffled through the sloppy streets back down to the ferry terminal.

By the time I arrived back on the island it was nearly 9 am. I walked the empty Sunday morning streets like a zombie, senseless with exhaustion. My ears rang, my throat was scratched dry. Officer Ceber was patrolling my brother's street, coming downhill towards me. It seemed I'd hardly been able to walk to the hardware store or Municipal Offices, or even the ferry, without running into him. Recently the Governor's Mansion had rejected a simple application to replace the railing of the floating pier. The Mayor's office wanted a date for the completion of renovations. They were also asking for full compensation on "increased patrols" over the last four years. I wouldn't bow to such pressure.

Ceber lifted his *Polis* cap and ran his hand over his smooth bald head — his now established greeting to me. I pretended to laugh.

"*Merhaba*," he called from across the street.

"*Kolay gelsin.*"

"You have a visitor," he said, pointing behind him with his thumb.

Up the street at the Halim Pasha House I saw a strange figure, wrapped in a dark jacket, crouching on a chair on the porch, arms crossed, hands warming under her armpits. She stood as I approached, and I recognized Flora Demirkan, my brother's former cook. I hadn't spoken to or seen her since my first day on the island.

156

"Where've you been," she asked, as if we'd had an understanding. "I've been waiting here over an hour."

"It's good to see you again, Flora." I fumbled for my keys, dropped them on the floor, and when I bent to retrieve them my head swerved with vertigo. "You've changed your mind?"

"I came last night. You weren't around."

"Business," I said, pushing myself up from my unsteady squat. "In the city."

"*Hadi ya*! It looks like you had business. All night business, I'd say. You could still use a hand here? Cleaning and what-not?"

"It was an open invitation." I thrust the keys in the door, and shoved it with my shoulder and heel, as I'd learned to do. "Something's changed your mind, Flora?"

"That's my affair. I'll start this morning. What do you pay?"

My temples throbbed; my head felt swollen and enormous. I held the heavy door open and ushered Flora Demirkan into the mansion. She examined me as she brushed past across the threshold. "You look nothing even like your brother."

12

Playing the Trombone

I WAS THE ONE who discovered our mother's dead body, but for many years I had a difficult time convincing myself she was gone. I would open the door of our apartment and expect to spot her down the hall, hunched over the kitchen table and crushing out a guilty cigarette. During my army service I addressed my weekly letters home to Father, but often felt I was writing Mother too, and that only she would pore over my epic narratives of complaint with the attention they deserved. When I proposed to Naomi, my late mother was still the first person I wanted to tell. When my twins were newborns, I had the irrational thought that every miracle the girls pulled off — lifting their heads, smiling their gaseous smiles, holding the other's hand — could not fully be appreciated until she saw it too; and I had to remind myself that my children would never meet their grandmother. In these ways and others the momentum of her existence propelled her, like a sprinter, long past the finish line of her years. It was only when I learned of Yusuf's boating accident, and realized that he was forever out of the picture, that Mother too finally died for me. It had come down to a trick of the subconscious. For two decades I could never imagine my brother alive in this world without Mother looking out for him.

In her last years it was only her industry and forbearance that kept us afloat. The winter after Rainbow Jacobson Father made a concession: *Benezra Yufkası* was finally earning enough to employ a full-time baker. Mother would now only have to man the register and oversee the preparations of the dough. Father teased her that hiring an assistant would prove the best Hanukah present he'd ever given her.

She never saw the end of the holiday. On a Saturday in December I was filling in at the bakery so that Father could have a new suit (his own gift) fitted and pressed in time for New Years. Mother took lunch first, leaving me alone in the shop. On weekends she liked to meet Yusuf at home to gently nag him about his afternoon breathing exercises, which at that age he was sometimes skipping. A half-hour later than expected she had not returned to the *yufkası*. The place was quiet that day; I'd spent the extra time sweeping flour drifts out from under the counter and stacking crisp piles of *helva* up on the highest shelves in the storefront. I was perched on a footstool when Mother at last returned. Below me her face was greenish and she was gripping the back of her hair. My first thought was of Yusuf. I climbed down, asking if everything was all right.

"Fine, fine. I don't understand — I'm just so slow today." She stared out the window at the street where the perpetual winter drizzle of our city was falling. She stifled a yawn, rubbing circles into her temples. "Your brother never came home." She looked beaten down. I thought she'd simply had another bad night.

Father snored too much, honking and whistling through a deviated septum; and lately the two of them slept in separate rooms. Sometimes Yusuf or I would wake early and discover Mother sprawled on the living room couch beside the clanking radiator, one arm draped dramatically over her eyes. She would tell us Father was "playing the trombone" in his sleep. She called him "Omar Burunçi" — the famous jazz artist. It became their running shorthand. This very morning she had complained, "Your father was blowing like Omar Burunçi again." So in the shop I assumed another restless night on the couch was showing its effects. That was the way I would forever rationalize it.

She looked me in the eye. "Go! Have your lunch. There's soup on the stove I've left for you. Your favorite. Don't overheat it. And you don't need to come back. If your dad ever decides to return from the tailor — I don't know what's holding him — then I'll call it a day too. Go! Use your feet!" She understood why I was preoccupied. I had plans that afternoon with Naomi, a sandy-haired friend of our cousin Byanka's on whom I'd come to have a disabling crush. I hadn't told Mother about my feelings. There'd be time for that, should it become anything serious.

I left her bending for the low cabinet where she kept the sacks of flour and salt. Our apartment was a five minute walk past the Armenian Church up the street. On the kitchen stove I found the yoghurt soup still steaming. I added mint and melted butter and ate a bowl of it, listening to Brahms on the stereo, a fuzzy classical station Father insisted on tuning to, though it never came in clearly during the day. If any of us touched the dial we were threatened with our lives. I'd just ladled a second bowl when, remembering the exhaustion on Mother's face, I was overcome with a frightening premonition. Without rinsing the dishes I rushed out the door and down the street, sneakers slopping through the puddles, back to *Benezra Yufkası.*

The door, strangely, was locked; the windows slightly steamed over. I knocked, pounded the glass with the heel of my palm, then rattled the handles. I fumbled for my keys, and finally pulling open the glass door, I stepped inside. It was stiflingly warm, but the cold of the open door swept in behind me, clearing the air of its sweet burnt smell. At the other end of the counter, her back to me, Mother was slumped on all fours like a Muslim praying. I thought for an irrational moment that, in the middle of rolling what must have been the day's hundredth circle of dough, she had dropped something. Then I realized she had not looked up. I hurried around the counter, past the blazing oven, and knelt beside her. I touched her cold neck. The rolling pin, covered in flour, was still stuck in her tightened fist.

13

The Tearing of Clothes

YUSUF HAD BEEN working that afternoon at his part-time job as an usher at the Atlas Cinema, and had not come home for lunch as he had promised Mother he would. In those first few days I believed I took it harder than my brother did. We all should have known, I said. We all should have watched out for her, relieved her of more of life's burdens. I could have completely taken over Yusuf's physiotherapy. I could have rolled the dough myself on the weekends. My brother said little. Later I understood I only wore my grief more openly than he did. Yusuf suffered in his own way, pulling back inside himself where none of us could reach him.

Pulmoner embolizm– a massive blood clot — was the term the doctor's used. It had traveled from her legs to her lungs, and was caused, the doctors said, by too many hours on her feet, standing in the same position.

Father wouldn't acknowledge that. Instead he told everyone it was simply her heart. That was his innocuous story. We had to stick with it, and we were meant to spread it. He went over his official details with us, replaying the years of chest pains, the shortness of breath, the swollen ankles, the blood-thinning medicine on the kitchen counter, how she had seemed to slow down year after year in an accelerated process of aging, so that she had looked like an old woman when she was forty-eight. If she had taken better care of her heart. If she had stopped smoking. If she had eaten fewer sweets, worried less. Pressing his details upon us, he killed her over and over again in every way but the way it really happened. It could easily have been her heart. It was a story people would understand, a story we all had to agree upon. *If this, if that.*

After we had thrown grass in the grave, after we had performed the *kriah*, the tearing of clothes, our apartment grew crowded with neighbors and relatives coming to sit the first night's *siete*. I cast my eyes around the room. Byanka's friend Naomi had kindly come. Even Tobya and Abud and Grazya on our mother's side had shown up — crouching now, repentantly solemn, in a tense circle. The smoke from cigarettes collected in a haze below the ceiling. Across the kitchen counter shiva candles on paisley shawls wagged their lights. Many of the guests were sitting on pillows on the floor. We read the psalms with the rabbi. The table was laden with rose-petal jam and hard boiled eggs and foil-covered dishes of *presa koftesi* and *bumuelos*, all of her favorite foods, brought to see us through the thirty days of mourning. Nobody was crying. At seventeen, I felt stuck somewhere between manhood and childhood; I felt that I'd be pinned there forever by the loss of my mother too soon. Everyone should have been weeping; something more dramatic and painful should have been on display — scenes from some Homeric

Epic, the women tearing at their hair and beating their chests
— something more than these rote recitations and the muted
small-talk of wedding plans and the Israeli peace process, something commensurate to my suffering.

"Poor Avram," I'd heard friends and neighbors murmuring in
conversations around the room. I measured my complex guilt,
the strange pride, as if it had taken courage to stumble upon her
body, as if I were the only one who dared to have found her. It
was all somehow more tragic for me. My father said he wouldn't
have been able to handle it, had it been him. I was taking it
well, the rabbi assured me. Like a man beyond my years. "Poor
Avram," people whispered.

"She was too young...."

"Years of happiness ahead, with these two talented sons..."

"She gave too much..."

"Generous to a fault..."

Yusuf sat in a corner beside the piano, bent low over his knees.
His wheezing had been bad for two days now, this cigarette
smoke in the apartment didn't help, and I noticed he was not
eating anything. With a weight in my throat I watched Byanka
head over to him to introduce her friend Naomi. Naomi was
wearing a starched white blouse and a black skirt that fell con-
servatively to her ankles. Yusuf looked up at them, nodding, his
eyes worlds away, until they finally gave up and left him. Other
people tried to speak to him. An hour into the *siete* the rabbi
himself approached and offered Yusuf a plate of *börek*.

"You're going to have to eat, son," the rabbi insisted. He gestured permission to leave the plate on Yusuf's lap. "You, of all
people, have to keep your strength up." *Of all people* — a veiled

reference to his condition, something Yusuf loathed more than anything.

He looked up. "It shouldn't have happened this way, Rabbi."

"No, no," the rabbi whispered, bending to his knees. "But it was her time." He massaged the back of Yusuf's neck with long hairy-knuckled fingers. "May you be comforted from Heaven."

"She shouldn't have been working this hard," Yusuf repeated, louder. "And for what? All that work, then dying poor, like this, with nothing?" He gestured around our haphazardly furnished apartment, then looked at our father. Father stared back, eyes swollen. A friend was leaning over and talking at him, so it wasn't clear what he'd heard.

"Death," the rabbi said, "doesn't know the difference between rich and poor."

"But it does. It does. He worked her too hard," my brother continued, indicating Father with his chin.

"Her peace has come now, see?" The rabbi raised himself from his knees as if to shield the others in the room from Yusuf. "Yes, yes. She was much loved, and she's resting peacefully with the Lord." Three of my youngest cousins were crashing Yusuf's old toy cars down the wooden hallway to our bedroom. Our father continued nodding at his friend, but around the obstruction of the rabbi he was watching Yusuf warily.

"She wasn't a workhorse."

My brother's voice was too loud. Yilda, perched on the piano stool, hissed, "Yusuf!"

He turned to our aunt, then back to the rabbi. "He worked her like a mule, Aunt Yilda. How long would *you* have put up with that?"

Across the room Father cleared his throat. "Son," he said, shaking his head. "Son. Go take a walk outside. Some fresh air. Some exercise. Avram, do us all a favor and take care of your brother." He looked at me and indicated Yusuf with his chin. I was the wrong person to do it; but I strode over, gripped my brother's arm and tried to hoist him off the ground from the shoulder. Thick with grief, Yusuf was surprisingly heavy — dead weight. I was conscious of the room's eyes: Abud, Grazya, Tobya, Mert, all taking in the scene. On the couch Naomi was chewing her lips.

Yusuf windmilled an arm, grimacing. He stood without help, circled the room with his eyes, and directed his words at our father. "He knows what he did."

The rabbi stepped between them. "Yusuf Benezra. This has been a difficult three days for you. But grief has to be borne. You have to take it like the rest of us. We're all with you in your sorrow. No more of this."

"With me in my sorrow! You hardly knew her." Yusuf walked from the room. The front door squealed open and crashed shut. The guests cringed, lowering their heads as one.

"A teenager," the women whispered.

"…time. He needs time."

"…he doesn't know what will happen now."

"…like a nurse, she did everything for that one. Massages three times a day."

Silence clouded the room. Our eyes drifted to Father, then fell back to the floor. One of Mother's synagogue friends had a hand on his knee. Father's head was bent, his beard pressed against his chest. The damage was done. I realized only now that we'd have to live like this, together, without her. Father glanced at me, and returned his slow gaze to his lap. The rabbi was pulling at his own tangled brown beard, as if determined to unknot that mess of strings and curls. He eyed me, and after a moment said, "Go! Find your brother and bring him back. You can't live like this in a house of mourning."

I looked down at my nail-bitten fingers, then up at Naomi, who wouldn't meet my eyes, and back to the rabbi. "I've barely spoken to him since this summer. He doesn't want to see me. It'll just make him angrier."

"*Öyle mi?* Brothers. So close. Fighting? Over what?"

"Some girl he met this summer," I said, shrugging. I knew Yusuf had tracked down Rainbow's address in England, and for months had been writing her. I'd seen him late at night, at his desk across the bedroom, scribbling love notes when he should have been working on his English essays. As far as I could tell he'd never heard back from her, and the longer he went without a response the more often he wrote. Letters and letters, each longer than the last. I'd caught him twice emerging from the post office on his way home from school, hands deep in his pockets. He told me nothing, and his silence I took as proof. He would have gloated if they were back in touch.

"Go," the rabbi said. "This is no time for childish games."

I shook my head, but I couldn't defy the rabbi as Yusuf had. The room was watching. Naomi was fiddling with her paper plate on her knees, folding up the edges. Tobya and Aunt Grazya and Uncle Abud and all these unwelcome people only made it worse. A wave of emotion rose in me; I tightened my lips against it.

"Avram! Listen to the rabbi." It was Father's voice: an order.

My only urgency was not to cry in front of Naomi. I pushed the heavy cane chair out of my way back under the dining room table. "I don't even know where he went." It came out as a pathetic whisper.

The rabbi said, "You know better than any of us."

I shook my head. No one had any idea where Yusuf spent his time. Since summer he'd grown more distant, more secretive and vindictive. I knew he worked at the Atlas Theater. I knew, too, that over autumn he'd skipped tutoring appointments Mother's sweat and blood had gone to pay for. I slipped my arms into my leather jacket and shoved the door open — too fast. It swung and hit the wall. There were gasps. I stepped out into the hall, clicked the door softly behind me and stood in the darkness, gathering my breath.

14

My Little Lahmacun

I CLOPPED DOWN THE three flights of stairs, and once outside hustled around the corner, arms swinging, asking myself where he would go in the state he was in. I made my way through the graveyard of concrete and billboards that was Taksim Square, and then plunged down into Cihangir. The quarter mile of cobblestone stairs that led to the waterfront were crowded, and I dodged the covered women laboring a step at a time up the hill. Down at the straits I hoped that Yusuf could be taking a somber walk along the water — perhaps past his beloved Inönü Stadium to Dolmabahçe Palace. A few months ago I had spotted him eating a sesame roll on the rocks by the Naval Museum, next to the bobbing caiques of old fishermen and the seaside benches covered in pigeon shit. I rushed there, now jogging, now walking, but at the jetty I found only gypsy children in rags, screaming and splashing in the freezing currents.

Grief pressed down on me; I felt it pulsing in my neck and ears. I feared Yusuf might hurt himself — that he was exactly like those sensitive, misunderstood youths who had recently been leaping to sensational deaths off the Bosphorus Bridge. Yusuf had not eaten in three days, and I didn't know if he was skipping his medications entirely.

I was jogging back from the Beşiktaş ferry pier, working myself into a frenzy, when I spotted him at last. He was seated at the window of the Günaydın Cafe, with three small *lahmacun* piled on his plate. He was sprinkling the Arabic pizzas one by one with shaved lettuce. I hesitated at the door. He was fine; my little brother, for all his drama, was fine.

I understood why he had come here. Years ago, on days when Mother worked late at the jewelry store, she used to give us three lira each for an after-school snack. The school service bus dropped us off at this corner, and over *lahmacun* and tea we would wait 45 minutes in the restaurant until she picked us up. We would spread textbooks on the table and finish our homework as quickly as possible in order to free our evenings for football and martial arts movies. Yusuf was never much good at spelling, and if he had a test the next day I used to quiz him on the words. He would in turn check my math answers, spotting numerical patterns I was always blind to. He'd tell me which problems I'd gotten wrong so I could rework them without checking the answers in the back of the book. Mother would eventually appear in the doorway and come lay a hand on each of our shoulders. "My little *lahmacun*," she'd tease us. She'd kiss the top of each of our heads, help us pack up our books, wave to the cashier (our unpaid babysitter), and lead us uphill back home to the apartment.

Now my throat burned, my heart was still racing. I had overreacted: Yusuf wasn't out over the Bosphorus, wheezing, half-starved, hanging off the steel ledge sixty meters above the churning water. He was here, a few blocks from our house, at his once-favorite hole-in-the wall. I entered the cramped restaurant and the owner greeted me with a bow and a *"Buyurun!"* My brother had just finished sprinkling spiced onion over the first pizza. The clinical way he prepared this simple food, bit by bit, as if he were performing some grave surgical procedure, had always amused me. His hand went for the red pepper and finding it nearly empty he looked up and grimaced.

Hands clenched, I stood in front of the table for a moment until my breath came easier. The cook behind the counter was slamming his fists into balls of dough, sending puffs of flour into the air. His hairy, muscled arms seemed capable of strangling someone. With the wood oven blazing the humid heat of the restaurant was intense. An overpowering smell of burnt dough and raw onions stung the nose. From outside the open door floated the calls of the roasted chickpea seller.

I watched Yusuf reach over to a cigarette in the ash tray. He took a long drag, imitating — consciously or not — our mother's secret habit. The smoke came pouring out the left side of his mouth; he blew it away from his plate. I resisted the urge to tear the cigarette from his fingers. This, despite his *KF*, was what he'd taken up. It would kill him — his own private Bosphorus Bridge.

I motioned to the *lahmacun*. "Good today?"

"The same every day."

I pulled out a chair. "Let me have a piece."

"Order your own."

I called *"Abey!"* to the cook, raised two fingers, and sat down. Yusuf's table was cast in shadow. Above it two of the yellow fluorescent bulbs were missing. We had not sat alone at a table like this since Rainbow Jacobson had been kicked off the island. Now he didn't speak. When the waiter brought over the *lahmacun* I folded them up with lettuce, no onions, as Father had always done, and ate the first one in four excessive bites. He was right: this fast food tasted so different, and better, than the mournful meals we'd been having courtesy of the relatives coming for the *siete*. I realized now what had probably already occurred to my brother: we didn't need their sympathy. Better to be left alone. We could take only so much foil-wrapped food. Eating out in a fast-food joint felt more appropriate to her memory. It was something we would have done before she was gone.

Yusuf eyed me preparing the second piece. "You don't put any red pepper on it."

"It's spicy enough the way they make it."

"What, you can't take some spice?"

"It burns your mouth." I shook my head, chewing. "Plus then your breath's disgusting."

"Priss!" Yusuf laughed. He leaned back in his chair. "Have they gone yet, you think?"

"A few of them were leaving. His friends will stay another few hours."

"The rabbi?"

In the last year the rabbi and Father had ramped up a campaign to get Yusuf to attend the yeshiva in Hasköy. The two of them had been sowing the seeds in his head since Yusuf's Bar Mitzvah. The hope was that an intense study of the Torah might help him better deal with his disease, better deal with the fate of a foreshortened life — or at least accept the terms dictated by God. Yusuf didn't want to hear about God's terms. Back then I weighed the scales. If I had been so cursed, the disease would have consumed me; I would have been able to talk of nothing else; and I didn't imagine I could so bravely face the days of life leaking, drip by drip, that swiftly away. Religion might have helped — though secretly I admired my brother's refusal of the spiritual medicine the rabbi offered.

"He was still there when I left," I said.

"I hate that man."

For a moment I thought he meant the rabbi; then I realized Yusuf was talking about our father.

"He's a weak man. I've always known it. And now look what he's done. The lies! I tell myself," — he shook his head — "I tell myself, that's not who you'll become."

I almost laughed at this. The kid would be dead if it wasn't for Father's sacrifices. A strange light, the moment between dusk and evening, fell outside the window. I dug into my second piece. Down the street the workers were disassembling the stalls of the Monday street market with an uproar of hammering and cursing. Despite his extensive preparations Yusuf was not eating. He reached for the remains of the Bulgarian cigarette and took two quick pulls, then suppressed a cough with his pale wrist. "You're being unfair," I told him, chewing, "You shouldn't have said what you did."

"Somebody needed to say it."

"Think of what he's lost, Yusuf. It's hardest on him."

"No, I don't think it is."

I was sick of his self-righteousness. "Who are you to embarrass him on a day like this? You have to make it worse? Who are you?"

"All these years, he wasn't even thinking about what he was doing to her."

"Why do you think she worked so hard? For us! Not for him."

"She worked twice as hard as he ever did. He's been a fool. And now he expects us to lie for him? He can't face what he's done."

I lay down my food. "She put up with us as long as she could. She never complained. She would have seen this differently."

"What do you know how she felt? She was entitled to a life too. To catch her breath once in a while."

His inability to see the simple truth here exasperated me, and I finally broke. "Who consumed her life? Have you considered that? Who worried her every minute of her waking life?" I swallowed another large bite and stood to leave. "He sent me out to find you. Can you understand what it means to worry for someone else? Can you conceive of that?"

Yusuf seemed momentarily struck by this, readjusting his thoughts into a new line of defensiveness. "Then go home and relieve him of his worries," he said. "You always do. The reliable one. Father can count on you." He leaned forward, grasping the edge of the table, and lowered his voice to a whisper. "Go and make up stories with him."

I bent towards Yusuf and whispered back. "Why does everything turn into a goddamned fight with you lately? I'm your brother. I've always helped you out."

He lifted his cigarette, then smushed it into the ash tray. He looked hard at me, and I felt in my chest the cold block of guilt I'd hauled around since the summer, since the *love bite*.

"I can't take this," Yusuf said. He leaned back in his chair away from me as if he was finished, but then another thought seized him. "This summer everything was shaping up." He shook his head. "I'm through. I can't take this."

I stared down at the nearly empty jar of red-pepper flakes, a few individual seeds of red and yellow crusted to the glass. I could eat no more *lahmacun.*

Yusuf said. "You'll see. Take my word for it. I'm through caring."

"You're through. *Haydi,* I'm getting out of here."

I stood and paid for us both; and to my surprise Yusuf followed me out of the restaurant. On the walk home suddenly he was smiling and talking and, one arm over my shoulder, hugging me so close he had me scared. More scared then when I couldn't find him. I could smell his salty skin, I could feel the boniness of his chest pressing against my side. Something in him had come unhinged. The brother who had hardly spoken a full sentence to me in four months was now prattling on about Beşiktaş's assistant manager and swimming and some new girl he worked with at the movie theater, as if all this chatter had been stored in a jar under pressure and the cap had finally been twisted off. He had a wild misty look in his eyes.

15

Prisoners

WHEN HE SAID he was through, I hadn't understood what he'd meant.

He dropped swimming first. Three weeks earlier at the try-outs for the All-City team, Yusuf had swum the best time of his life in the breaststroke. In the months after the funeral, however, he refused the invitations to try out for the national junior team, despite two personal phone-calls by the coach from the National Sports Center in Galatasaray. For all of Father's urging, Yusuf simply would not swim. Then he quit the Anadolu Club team without any notice. The coaches assumed it was all connected to our mother's death. Time, he needed time, they said. He would come back stronger by summer. After an appropriate interval, at Father's urging, a coach from the National Sports Center came by our apartment to speak to Yusuf. In our living room Yusuf sat, stone silent, his hands folded between his legs, and stared at the man. He refused to discuss a return to the sport. He was embarrassing Father on purpose: a silent declaration of war.

"That was a mistake, for me to invite that coach to the house,"

Father later recalled. "All the training, the sacrifices, the obstacles he'd overcome to reach that level. Swimming was his lifeline. I asked him what he thought his mother would want him to do. The coach and I assumed he was struggling with the decision, but Yusuf had already made up his mind. He was forever five moves ahead of me. He liked our pleading. It amused him to watch his old man and this important coach discuss his fate, when he'd already decided it himself."

Hebrew lessons, presidency of the Kardeşlik Derneği Youth Club, and treasurer of the temple newsletter came next. He jettisoned them all. Our rabbi tracked Yusuf down, sat him in a café, and dispensed the wisdom of Maimonides, trying to speak some sense into him. Yusuf nodded, lowered his eyes, drank his medium-sweet tea; but when the rabbi left he pulled out his Bulgarian cigarettes. He never went back to the synagogue.

That spring, lashing out in the only way he knew how, Yusuf engaged in a reckless campaign to kill himself. He would be gone weekend nights, and come home Sunday mornings reeking of Beyoğlu back alleys, his shirt soaked with sweat and stained with unknowable filth. He stopped attending tutoring entirely. His grades plummeted. With his boundless memory my brother could have earned fives in his *lise* classes; but he took home two's all semester — a purposeful grade, enough to pass so that he wouldn't be burdened with having to repeat a year, but also enough to protest what he'd started calling "the uselessness of education in this dead-end country." He could go for days without a bath. The director of Üsküdar Amerikan Lise complained to Father about Yusuf's hygiene and threatened to have him expelled. Against school regulations Yusuf grew his hair long — he hadn't cut it since Mother's death, refused to cut it until the unveiling. He did this, I knew, to spite Father, who was not supposed to shave for the year of mourning, but had already done so for business reasons. Yusuf had given up his breathing exercises; and at night in our room he'd fall into extended hacking fits that unnerved me. He refused my offers of therapy, refused if I cajoled him to let me clap his back when the coughing was thick. The doctors gave Father dire warnings, and through the evenings he and Yusuf partook in operatic battles that would rage until the downstairs neighbors pounded the ceiling with a broom. I escaped to the street. Father's litanies over haircuts and swimming and phone-calls from the school evolved into tearful supplications concerning Yusuf's health. It was a clash of wills. He'd grown sick with the notion that his gifted son was wasting an enormous potential, tossing away his hard-earned health. Yusuf was doing his best never to please the man again.

Father's hair went white. "I threatened to throw him out of the house. Week after week I threatened it. I couldn't live like that, you see." What had finally broken him was that Yusuf had begun stealing money from Father's wallet to support his carousing. Once we came home (our apartment had become a reeking, dusty disaster by then) and found Yusuf had taken Mother's wedding ring — a ring Father had designed and sized with his own hands. Accused, Yusuf said that he of all people should sympathize with the occasional need to steal jewelry from one's own family. Father hid the rest of Mother's jewelry at Aunt Yilda's house, hid his watch at night, packed away our set of antique silverware. He was afraid to leave home when Yusuf was there. "A prisoner in our own apartment," he recalled.

One Saturday night around this time Beşiktaş had lost yet another close qualifying match for the championship cup. I'd returned home from watching the game with Naomi and Byanka at Uncle Haim's, only to find a body sprawled unconscious on the first floor cement stairwell. When I flicked on the timer for the lights I saw that it was Yusuf. I thought, simply and clearly: my brother is dead. He was emanating the anise fumes of *rakı* and his bottom lip was swollen. He had a gash from his chin halfway up his right cheek. I slapped his other cheek to see if he would wake up. "Brother," I whispered. After thirty seconds the lights flicked off and, cursing, I had to flick them on again. Twice this happened. Yusuf was breathing, but I couldn't get him to open his eyes. In a panic I rushed up three flights to the apartment and woke Father.

I wouldn't go back down with him. I was honestly too frightened. Father paced the front foyer twice, and then threw on his slippers and flung himself out the door.

"At that point we resented everything about each other," Father remembered. "He knew I had a forgiving nature, and he was pushing as far as it would go. But what can you do? Just let your son die? Just abandon him? I found him in a puddle of vomit, gasping for air. I've never been so scared."

Upstairs I had caved into my own fears and called an ambulance. Yusuf was in the hospital for two days with alcohol poisoning. They purged his body. In the months that followed it became a familiar routine. He had stopped taking his antibiotics. He suffered a broken collarbone from a roll down a flight of steps in Tünel. He nearly died experimenting with heroine procured from a street hippy in a Teşvikiye alley. For the rest of the semester my brother was in and out of the German Hospital for infections and airway clearance and flare ups. The hospital's pale blue waiting room became Father's second home, its doting nurses the closest things he had in those days to a family. He resigned himself to suffering for his son, and filled his days with it. For my part I visited only twice, only when the nightly guilt loomed so dark and large I couldn't live with myself.

Father was never overly devout, but now he started going to synagogue daily in the mornings to pray for Yusuf. He met with the Head Rabbi for counseling. It was clear to everyone he had run out of options. That fall, at the rabbi's suggestion, Father shipped Yusuf four hours south, to the Amerikan Collegiate Institute in Izmir, a sister-school of Üsküdar's. Yusuf packed and left without saying goodbye to me. At the Institute he lived in a boarding house and wore the stiff woolen school uniform. We saw him once in those eight months. He had shaved his hair to his scalp. He resumed his medical regimen; the school nurses and two student volunteers helped administer his physiotherapy. His first semester he received perfect scores on his report card.

His graduation yearbook, which Father always kept half-hidden on a top shelf in the apartment, declared that over the next two years Yusuf had won seven academic prizes, had become president of the Honor Society, had composed the class poem, and had co-founded the student Barakuda scuba-diving club. He had enthusiastically swum for the Institute, was nicknamed "The Bullet" by his teammates, and led them both years to the regional championships. Away from home, he'd achieved the only perfect grade point average in the school's fifty-year history. He graduated in the rigorous Science track, two springs later, first in his class, and gave one of the graduation speeches. He had not let Father or me come see him on the podium, receiving his well-earned applause.

Book III

1

Always On Guard

I FOUND MYSELF WATCHING Flora Demirkan dipping her brush into a can of faux-granite paint, and stirring in long contemplative strokes.

Yusuf's former cook had suggested practical ways she'd always hoped his kitchen might be modernized. She had worked in any number of kitchens on the island and possessed strong opinions on the matter. At her recommendation I'd already replaced the ancient dishwasher with an Aristan, and this afternoon a man from the city was scheduled to deliver a hanging convection microwave, which I'd install under the oak cabinet above the range. In the meantime she was helping me lay the first coat of paint on the wooden pedestal table. On my first inspection three weeks ago I'd found the initials of two lovers — *E.M. + Z.A. 2006 Gerçekten çok seviyorum*!! — scratched multiple times with a knife across the surface. Hoping to restore an authentic look of rust-colored granite I'd scrubbed and sanded the antique table down, and this morning Flora helped spread cloth tarps across the hardwood floor. Both of us were now crouching on stools over the table's edge. The granite paint was thick, cumbersome. I'd demonstrated how to work in slow strokes to prevent flecking — a technique I'd once learned from Naomi. Flora, ignoring me, painted in broad, quick, overly-determined lines.

I paid my three laborers fair but paltry wages for their work, and wished I could offer more. But that was the way it went. Until Omer took me on I was being careful: renovations were going to be costly, and I needed to budget for unexpected expenses. I was willing to use my severance package for salaries. For supplies, when necessary, I could dip into the money we'd earned from the sale of Father's apartment. Meanwhile I was settling terms with Fortis Bank on a personal installment loan.

And clearly I could have done better than Yusuf's old help. Nılay Gören spent most of her time drinking tea, and Mustafa Faik, though spirited, tired quickly. I might have found a couple of younger cleaning women — industrious teenagers perhaps — who would have been less inclined towards incessant gossip and leisurely lunches. But I was intrigued by the idea of bringing the former staff back to the mansion, their chatter suited my purpose, and despite the Mayor's pressure I was in no particular hurry to be finished with this project.

Nılay and Mustafa had accepted the offer of winter employment for the wages, but it seemed to me Flora Demirkan had returned as a kind of penance. For a week now I'd watched her closely. Here among these rooms she too felt the loss of someone vital to who she was — though I still did not understand the scope. Flora, always on guard, was not yet speaking to me of her daughter. Too many others had come; too many others had pressed their questions upon her. Five years on, hers was still a stubborn secrecy.

Over these drawn-out days I'd watched her cleaning, moving from uncertainty to resignation to obsessive excavation, like a woman afraid of heights edging closer to a cliff. I saw her sorting with Nılay Gören through linens and detergents in a useless search for what might be salvaged. I saw her dumping out the old frayed mops, the torn dust rags, the pots filthy in their grooves with grime. I saw her sniffing through the fetid spices of the very kitchen cupboards she herself had organized. I saw her tossing away the cartons of garbage bags nibbled at by mice, and the roach traps whose poisonous glue had long ago dried. I saw her sweeping the dust of footprints from who knew what visitors — police or vandals, treasure-seekers or lovers, burglars or the simply curious — off the scratched kitchen tiles. I saw her scrubbing the bathtubs where the grout had grayed and cracked, scrubbing ferociously at the radiator pipes, rusted where they met the hardwood floors. In the laundry room I found her coaxing with whispered prayers one of the industrial-sized washing machines gently back to life. She cursed at the lint never emptied from the bowels of the enormous electric drier, and opening the lid, released the stale odor of dead fashion trapped in its lungs. The birdcages, warped and swollen, I watched her carry to the statue garden one by one, where Mustafa Faik sprayed them down with the garden hose. The hard water stains at the bottom of a leaking sink Flora attacked unsuccessfully with Hydro, bleach, and a rough sponge. I watched her and Nılay Gören begin remaking the bedrooms, where important guests must have once slept beneath ironed sheets. Now those sheets were freckled with mildew. Snowlike dust balls covered the headboards and had drifted beneath the beds and into the ransacked armoires. Dust had accumulated everywhere, and by the end of our days our eyes itched with it. I spotted Flora in the upstairs bathroom prying off the syrupy bottles that stuck with great determination to medicine cabinet shelves, and examining the boxes of long-expired pills, and pinching the herbal soaps caked in scum off the sinks. I noticed that in the master bedroom, in Yusuf's cavernous closet, amid other numinous scents, traces of my brother's colognes still floated, and that Flora avoided that room entirely.

Three weeks in, and for all the work it seemed like we had made little progress. Still, I wasn't a finicky man, and the house was finally bearable enough for me to sleep here while the renovations continued. That would spare me the expense of the Hotel Saydam Planet, and the claustrophobia of Father's dank basement apartment.

Once the first coat of paint was laid I suggested to Flora we break for lunch to let the table dry. We left the house together and I walked her back to the village in search of an ATM. I needed cash to pay her for the week's work. Outside the mansion, in public, she walked tentatively now with me; and at the ATM when I handed her salary over she crumpled the bills into a wad and thrust it into her purse without counting. I prepared myself for her abrupt goodbye. Each day now Flora had gone home to see to her kids' lunch, while I'd settled for a *durum* of *döner* meat and soggy French-fries at the Different Kebaps Restaurant, whose garrulous owner I was getting to know a bit too well. But at the bank this time Flora lingered. She was staring over my shoulder, at someone coming up behind us.

"*Nasılsınız!*" boomed a gruff voice. Officer Ceber was taking off his cap and rubbing his hand over his bald head. "Flora, out for a walk?"

She'd gone stiff in his presence. "Avram and I were just grabbing a drink. Come Officer. Join us."

"Where are you going?"

She didn't hesitate. "The Culture House."

"A bit cold for a patio, no?" He lay a hand over his heart. "If only I had the time, Flora. You know how it is. Enjoy your drink." He turned to me with a half smile, nodded to Flora more seriously, and walked on in the direction of the clock tower. I'd become accustomed to running into him, but I wasn't clear why Flora had lied.

"Come," she said now, itching at her throat. She led me a few blocks up, past the clock tower, until we found ourselves climbing the steps to the lush courtyard of the Touring and Automobile Club's Culture House. We sat on its sunny patio café — the only customers on this blustery winter day. I ordered us each an apricot juice and we sipped from the sweating cans with our straws. Between two houses across the street I could make out, in the distance, the rocky shoreline of the city. Flora sat drinking meditatively, looking past me. She wore too much makeup — far too much, I decided now — layers of blush and eyeliner and lipstick glossing over the scuffs and chinks in her complexion.

I attempted some chit-chat, pointing out where my family used to picnic on the island, and where we used to swim, and off in the distance the spot where, sixty years ago, my grandmother's boat had nearly washed ashore. I was describing for Flora how my grandmother was saved, but how my great-grandparents had drowned fleeing the fires to come in Europe. Flora was only half-listening, her eyes directionless. I cut myself off mid-sentence.

"Drowning in the Marmara," she murmured, and bent her straw.

I'd made a large mistake, but smiled through it. "My great-grandparent's boat, the *Salvador*, had no working engine. It was tossed around in a winter storm. That's what they've always said."

"What *they've* always said. Avram Bey, listen. I long ago got sick of what *they've* always said. You're not the only one with such stories. We have our own family tragedies, remember."

"I apologize. I wasn't thinking."

She looked around to see if anyone was listening. The breeze was rattling the Coca-Cola umbrellas over the tables, flapping the leaves of potted carnations and acacias. There were no other customers on the patio, but she lowered her voice anyway. "I wish I could tell you. You'd forgive me more."

"There's nothing to forgive."

"For your brother, I mean."

"Is there something I should forgive you for?"

"The way I treated him. I wasn't kind. What happened to him — I wished it here." She was pointing to her heart. "It all came back to haunt me."

"Wishes don't kill people, Flora."

"You might not think so. What I'm saying is, I wished him ill and I was punished for it. I was forever impatient with him. I should have been more understanding of who he'd become. That he too had his limits. I shouldn't have hoped he could be more than what he was."

"It was hard to be sympathetic when it came to Yusuf. I'm sure you took your share of abuse. He must have been impossible to work for."

"Impossible, yes. But I mean I could have been more understanding of his history. Of what he carried."

To this I had no reply. Five centuries of Jewish history in our city was baggage Yusuf had thought could be left behind, tossed aside. Our past caused him only pain. He'd jettisoned it. He was burdened, as far as I knew, by none of it.

"I could have been more trusting," she said. "Less suspicious. I might have forgiven him the constant meddling." Flora looked over her shoulder to where the lone waiter was leaning up against the outdoor bar. The teenager had white speaker buds from an MP3 player dangling vinelike from of his ears. She turned back. "What he was doing with my daughter." Her voice was sunken when she pronounced these words, with a desperate pitch to it, like the humming of a machine whose batteries were running low.

"He did what he pleased, Flora. Nobody could stop him, once he put his mind to something."

"That's true."

"But why come back to the mansion then?"

Flora looked away. "Nılay told me you were a good man. My curiosity got the best of me. I wanted to see for myself what kind of person could tolerate such a brother."

"I couldn't tolerate him."

Now she looked up. "Then why come back yourself?"

I'd felt something changing in me these last weeks, with these glimpses into our missing years. Yet how could I explain precisely what that change was? How could I explain that my return to the island had shaken me out of what felt like a twenty-year stupor? I took a hesitant sip of my apricot juice. "Well, you wind up in a place without knowing how you got there," I said. "You know that feeling?"

"That's my life, Avram!"

We laughed together, and I felt an opening here. "But tell me why…I mean your daughter, that is, Yasemin — why she was on his boat that morning? How exactly was he meddling?"

I'd stepped too quickly. A pain clouded Flora's eyes, and she bent down to the table and found her straw with her mouth. She sipped, and looked to her right, out to sea. I looked where she was looking, but there was nothing there, just the bobbing waves. A moment later, as if summoned by our talk, a lone figure appeared again — Officer Ceber, in his black padded jacket, black American baseball cap, black boots — coming up the road. Twenty yards away I saw him walk past the garden walls, his full figure framed momentarily, mid-stride, in the wrought iron gate. He didn't look in; he simply passed on again, but something in his gait unnerved me.

"It's getting cold," Flora finally said, indicating the waiter with her chin.

2

The Battering Ram

I WAS BACK AT the Halim Pasha House only a few minutes, set to work alone that afternoon on a second coat of paint for the pedestal table, when a raucous banging sounded at the front door. Opening it with a rush, I found standing there a large-eared boy of about eight. His eyes were red-rimmed, swollen and moist, and his foot, lifted mid-kick, was poised to strike the door again. I'd startled him. He gaped up at me and lowered his foot.

"Son, what's the problem?"

"Where's my mother?" he asked, mumbling unintelligibly about some injustice he'd just suffered at the park. He was clenching his groin. "My mother," he repeated. "Is she here?"

"Flora?"

He nodded.

"She went home for the day. You checked your house?"

The boy's eyes sank. A curl of hair was plastered in dry sweat across his forehead.

"Come in here, son. Come in."

I settled the boy down in the kitchen beside the still-wet table and offered him a bottle of water. Through tears he was stifling he explained that he'd had an argument with his classmates on the football pitch.

"An argument? What kind of argument?"

"They were making fun of my team."

With no working television in the mansion, I hadn't seen last night's matches, or heard the results.

"Which team?"

"Beşiktaş."

"They lost?"

He grimaced. "To Karabükspor."

It was a pathetic side to lose to. "Bad?" I asked. He swung his head around indeterminately. "How bad?"

"Four-nil."

I had to stop myself from laughing. "How can you root for that team?"

He shrugged. "My brothers all root for them, so I root for them."

Another doomed Beşiktaş follower. In a city where organized mobs commanded the actions of fans, where rival football supporters could hardly walk down the same street without knifing each other, Flora's son might have chosen his team more wisely. I looked into his dark wet eyes and pitied the kid. You couldn't change your football genes.

His name was Sarp and he was the second-youngest of Flora's sons. Amid his starts and stops I was able to make out what had happened in the park. The boys had been mocking him, and when he lashed back at one, they'd yelled as a group, "Get the infidel! Battering Ram!"

There was no need to explain from there; it had happened

to me too. I could see it clearly enough: the kids wrestling Sarp down to the turf, then lifting him up squirming, two on each of his legs, two more at his shoulders, and then charging him, legs open, into the spiky trunk of a pine tree. According to Sarp, three times they swung him into the tree, yelling "Circumcise him! Infidel! Battering Ram!" and erupting in laughter before they dropped him into the dirt. It was an old cruel antic I remembered from my army hazing days (the pain still vivid between my thighs.) It brought with it memories of chili pepper up my anus, the officers threatening me with a second circumcision, then a third, until I'd finally know how it felt to be a man.

"Sarp," I said, "Don't worry about it. It's over now. They were just joking, right? These are friends of yours?"

He nodded.

"Really great friends, heh?"

"They're all from out East," Sarp snorted, and clicked his tongue, as if that explained everything. He was echoing an adult complaint — one I'd heard murmured around the village — that the island was changing too quickly. It was being taken over like the rest of the city by poor Muslims from the sticks. It was no longer the peaceful insular haven of Jews and Christians it had been in my childhood.

Sarp's brown hair still had a few stalks of straw and grass tangled among the curls. He continued to massage his groin.

"You bleeding down there?"

"I don't think so."

I explained how, in the army, they'd done it so hard to me that I was unable to pee for two days. I crossed my legs in an exaggeration of pain.

Sarp looked up with glassy eyes and grinned.

"You'll get them back. You will. Everyone gets the Battering Ram at some point in his life. You can't avoid it, see?"

"The whole week at school they've been calling me a *son of a whore infidel.* Akın's the worst. His father's Mayor, so the teachers hear him and don't say anything."

I sat silently.

"I don't even know what it means," he said.

I reached for an explanation. Could I honestly tell him it would get any better with age? That he should brush the insult off and forget it? "They're just throwing out curses they hear their parents use. Look," I said, "I have a proposition. Your mother's done here for the day. Let's wash you up and I'll walk you back. We'll find her together."

"I'll find her myself," he insisted. The raised chin — I recognized in it the stubborn pride of the mother.

I told him I needed some air anyway, that these paint fumes were getting to me. At the kitchen sink I offered him a dishtowel to clean his face. While he was scrubbing his skin, he told me Yusuf Bey had once shown his brothers a framed Beşiktaş jersey, signed by the entire 2004 team. Was it still in the mansion? His eyes widened. I assured him it wasn't. I pulled the grass from his hair, and one arm over his shoulder led the boy out onto the porch, through the overgrown garden, and back the half-kilometer down the hill into the village. *Son of a whore infidel.* Where did kids come up with such things? Sarp walked tenderly, but with the overcompensating gait of a child pretending he wasn't hurt. Beneath my arm his rough woolen sweater, unwashed, had the texture of horse-blanketing. At the shuttered hovel we found

Flora just returning from the market, two clear plastic bags of eggplants and cucumbers dangling from her wrists. She hurried over to us and bent down on a knee towards her son's face, then glanced up at me in mild fear. "What's happened?"

"Nothing, nothing. Some rough-housing at the park."

Sarp blushed, brushing off her ministrations, and walked past her. A man! Opening the gate for his mother, he looked back.

"Stay well, Sarp," I called. "They'll win next week. I guarantee you."

"*Güle güle.*"

"Win?" Flora seized her son by the wrist, slid her packages into his hands, and entered her yard. "Win what? What trouble are you causing?" She offered him a kick on his behind as he walked ahead of her. "And I told you to stay away from that mansion!" Sarp ducked his head at another swipe and scuttled towards the house. Flora cast a baleful look back at me before the darkness of the front door swallowed her whole.

I raised a hand farewell, and made my slow way back up the alley.

3

Flora's Chorus of Mistakes

AFTER THAT I found myself keeping better track of Flora Demirkan's herd of children, recognizing them in the grocer's and at the Reks Internet cafe. In between Feride, now her oldest, and Saim, her youngest, there were four other Demirkans still running loose across the island: the younger girl (Adalet) and three boys (Jelal, Doruk, and Sarp), whose names and ages I couldn't yet keep straight. Flora never let on, to me or to anyone I'd spoken to, who their fathers were; and when I asked once, seeking clarification between two of the boys, she waved me off and said, "They're my chorus of mistakes, Avram Bey. You know the song."

They were clean, well-scrubbed, ruddy children, recognizable now by their mother's large, opaque Eastern eyes. The girls had vile mouths, which people said they also got from their mother. The boys had a reputation for stealing and getting away with it. In less than a month on the island I'd already spotted them in unlikely places: playing football in the courtyard of the new mosque, or stomping up on an Algida ice cream cart, or scaling the sun-stroked roofs of the Yörük Ali Vacation Villa. I heard a rumor that Jelal, at nine, had once gone up to the bartender at the Moon Club and asked for a martini — "shaken, not stirred." I didn't believe that rumor. To the consternation of the police the older boys made a habit of sneaking onto the ferries, hiding like stowaways until the ships departed, then cannonballing off the highest deck and swimming ashore.

"Watch out for them," Mustafa Faik, the old security guard, warned me when I mentioned Sarp's visit. "I wouldn't let them in the house. We used to advise your brother against it. Sticky fingers, you know."

From all accounts Flora's pack of children had once formed a kind of café club in the kitchen of Yusuf's mansion, and during the afternoons on his orders the staff had given them reign to play in the pool and the statue garden, as long as they came and went through the French doors at the back patio. Flora claimed Yusuf had enjoyed the noise and play her children brought into his home. A whirlwind when you saw them in a group, laughing at their own private jokes, elbowing each other, cursing and yanking each others' arms, alone the children were extremely polite. I once found Adalet chastising Saim at a tea stall for accepting a pastry and not saying thank you. I brought this up one afternoon at the Different Kebaps Restaurant with Elif Bozkaya, who had been teaching at the island's *ilk öğretmen* for the last twenty-five years, and who had seen each of the seven children pass through the boot camp of a kindergarten class she ran. "That's the way it's always been," she said. "They raised themselves. They ran the household themselves. They helped each other with their home-work. They shopped for food at the market themselves. Selma

Nasim gave Adalet a line of credit at her pickle shop. The girl was only eleven!" At this, the teacher shrugged. "So we've adopted the little terrors? The entire island. What could we do? Their mother popped them out and forgot she had them. At least we could make sure no harm came to them. They'd grow up, we figured, cook in the restaurants, clean houses, drive the horses."

Many around the island agreed with Elif Bozkaya's contention that the children had been abandoned by Fate, and everyone I spoke to claimed to have helped look out for the kids over the years in their own separate ways; though it occurred to me that the villagers enjoyed attaching themselves, even tangentially, to the scandal of a billionaire. From what I could make out it was all exaggeration. I had a hard time believing that Flora Demirkan truly let her children run wild. She called them her 'mistakes' but spoke of them with affection. "Mom's strict," Sarp told me on our walk home after the Battering Ram incident. "If I'm not in bed by nine, she beats me. But soon I'll be big enough to beat her back!"

I learned too from Elif Bozkaya how Flora had come to be stranded on the island with all these kids. She had grown up in Kurtuluş, on the European side of the city, a neighborhood not far from our own. She had lost both parents at an early age, and had been raised, one of two girls, by doting grandparents. Originally she had worked in a cafeteria in a private Armenian school in Karaköy. When she was twenty-one she took a job as a year-round cook for a natural gas tycoon, Aristeides Demopoulous, who summered here on the high slopes of the island in an ancient *konak* he had restored by hand. But the Greek would visit his young cook in the house, even in the off-season when his wife resided in Nişantası; and the subsequent birth of Flora's first daughter, Yasemin, had broken up his marriage.

The businessman promised to take care of them both, but with the affair unveiled he sold his sun-filled home and disappeared. Word reached the island that he had moved to Vienna, where he took a job with Coca Cola. Marooned, Flora pieced together a living for herself and her growing herd of children (the products, I gathered, of later misbegotten love) in the steaming kitchens of the fish restaurants along the pier, until she was hired nine years later by my brother.

She had raised the children alone, without support. Her oldest kids were changing diapers and warming bottles from the time they were eight. Flora mentioned to me how she had bestowed upon Feride spanking rights. In their small house the girls shared a room with their mother if she was in a mood to allow it, or joined the boys in the second, smaller bedroom, where three beds could be lined up against each other — like berths, I imagined, in some lost ship's galley. The older children slept at friends' as often as they slept at home. I'd heard the police had once caught all four boys hibernating like bums in the ruins of the open air theater, beneath the Founder's memorial, in a makeshift tent fashioned out of sheets from the Princess Hotel. It had been a brutally hot night; and when the police rounded them up the boys claimed they were simply "camping." It was unclear for how long they'd been doing so.

The children all shared the ignominy of not knowing who their fathers were, though it was commonly accepted in the assorted features, in the range of skin and eye colors, in the varying heights and weights, in the extremes of dispositions, that none of them shared a father. For over a decade on the island Flora had squeezed out children with surprising regularity. "Another immaculate conception," the old carriage drivers used to joke. Between card games at the Dostlar Kıraathanesi, looking over the waves of the Marmara, a favorite topic of conversation was to guess who on the island — homeowner, laborer, dignitary — was which kid's father. For no one ever saw Flora leave. "We never saw her going to the city," Mustafa Faik claimed with a twinkle in his eye. "We never saw her entertaining a man in her home. She was just always pregnant." With a two bedroom house and her horde of children, how Flora Demirkan did what she did, and when she did it, and where, remained to this day a savory island mystery, to be enjoyed by the villagers with croissants and *simit* over tables at the Dolci Café.

I was scraping the weathered paint and graffiti off the front porch, with Flora sweeping the dust flakes into a bin, when I braved the question of her children's paternity for the second time. She'd been talking about Feride's dream of becoming a Hollywood actress — a silly dream she had appropriated from her older sister Yasemin. It was the first Flora had mentioned her lost daughter's name since her return. Smacking the broom against a wooden beam she said, "I tell Feride she's talented enough and pretty enough not to have to sleep her way to fame, like so many others." When I asked Flora what she meant she hesitated, and said, "You know, I saw them all parading in, one after another. Yusuf would bring these women back to the island for his dinner parties, and I'd have to serve them. Beautiful twenty-five year old girls with crystal wine glasses raised to their fake lips. They had brains, some of them. They could have done anything with themselves, but they could only think of one thing, and one way of getting somewhere. Soap operas. Game shows. Affairs with a rich man. I didn't raise my daughters to be that way. Yasemin was purer than pure. So innocent. But then, she also had her father's hot Greek temper. That's what got her into trouble. Not one of my children has ever stopped surprising me."

"They all have a bit of their father in them?" I asked.

Flora lifted her straw broom, and leaned her hand on her waist. "Don't beat around the bush, Avram Bey. You mean *fathers*." She smirked. "They have a little bit of their *fathers* in them. Every one of them, different blood. I'm not proud, I'll tell you that."

We worked again in silence. My mind was calculating. Yusuf would surely have been unable to father children: doctors had said, in no uncertain terms, he could never have a family of his own. Still, the thought occurred to me with sudden urgency that I should know if, by some off chance, I was related to one of these kids. If I bore any of them the responsibility of an uncle.

"Forgive me, Flora Hanım," I murmured, "but none of them are Yusuf's?" Against the scraping Flora pretended not to hear me. I stopped working over the wood and raised myself to my knees. "Did Yusuf have any children?"

Flora clicked her tongue, glaring at me with a sharpness that seemed part rage, part longing to tell. She continued her ferocious sweeping. I had broken an unstated agreement to let her control the flow of information. It looked like she was grinding her teeth. There was a tensing of her upper lips. The breeze was blowing her chestnut bangs over her forehead, and when she stood still to catch her breath — her eyes wet and scornful and gazing down at the porch — she appeared for a moment vulnerable, and much younger than her forty-six years. I watched until she looked up at me, then lowered my own gaze, blushing. Hesitating, I forced my gaze back up, along her waist, her neckline, and back to those startling Demirkan eyes.

"Flora, I'm only trying to understand."

She swept in silence. About her younger children, over multiple interruptions she would willingly pick up the threads of her own stories. Of my brother and Yasemin she still wouldn't budge. Could I blame her? In those first weeks the secrets had gone both ways. I told her little of myself, nothing about the looming divorce, nothing about the two daughters I was now guilty of abandoning, nothing about my wife's impending move out of the country. Flora, preserving our privacies, hadn't asked.

She stopped her sweeping. "Trying to understand what, exactly?"

"What there was between you and Yusuf."

"Between us? I was his cook. That was what we had between us."

"Why your daughter was on his boat that last morning."

"Do you have any daughters Avram?"

"Yes. Two."

"And do you know where they are at this moment?"

"Of course not."

"Daughters are slippery. Keep an eye on them."

She pulled herself up and dumped a final pan of paint flakes into the garbage, then retrieved the broom. "Look, sometimes I had to bring your brother special meals when he wasn't well. Sometimes he'd ask me to help him clear out his lungs. Or bide the time while he used his vest. We'd talk. It's what you do when you work for someone. You talk. Like this. There was never any child. Not from him. He spared me that gift, at least." She brushed off her hands violently. "Satisfied? Are you going to report this now — what? — to the tabloids?"

"I'd never do such a thing."

"I don't put it past you." She sucked in an enormous breath and went inside.

I was left standing alone, the putty knife dangling from my hand. Yusuf Elmas, a handsome, wealthy bachelor with an oversized reputation for flirtation. Flora Demirkan, his grateful servant, a provocative woman who, boasting a parade of bastard children, had long ago thrown morality to the wind. I did the math. Anyone who knew what he was capable of would quickly have seen where it must have led.

4

Wet Burgers

AT TWENTY-THREE I had returned to the city on the first furlough of my army service. We walked everywhere back then; it was a fifteen minute stroll from the apartment down to the straits, and going out with a group — in this case to a concert with old college friends — meant that we needed a central meeting point. We had chosen the Üsküdar Ferry Terminal. Standing that night at the *iskele*, the first to arrive, I found myself unnerved by the screaming of a one-armed man, dressed in many-colored rags, who held up tokens in front of the ticket booth and sold them for a fifteen *kuruş* profit. "Hurry hurry hurry!" he yelled. "It's leaving it's leaving! Last chance last chance!" On and on he bellowed, trying to incite a panic in our city's frenzied commuters, all terrified of missing the ferry and the twenty minutes of life that would be lost.

Naomi arrived at last. Her hair, which she'd always worn short in imitation of models in Parisian fashion magazines, now fell extravagantly to her shoulders. She wasn't wearing her glasses, and explained later that she could afford contact lenses for the first time. Otherwise, striding up to the ferry terminal she looked much the same as I'd imagined her — lively, studious, with her long black eyelashes blinking at me. I hadn't seen her since graduation the previous June, after which I had left for my military duty. She was now going to school while working part-time as a cashier at an Ak Bank branch on Bagdat Caddesi, handing out money to the privileged families on the Asian side, who strolled into the bank in their Italian blouses and English raincoats trailing French poodles on leashes. Naomi had smooth olive skin and a light straight figure and she held herself, as she had for the five years I had known her, with an air of steady irony. A constant half-smile rested on her lips. She was equally capable of ignoring the flirtatious teasing my classmates subjected her to — or of jabbing back with a quick rebuke. Seeing her at the ferry for the first time in six months I decided she could not have been more beautiful. She was, I imagined then, the woman of my life.

Those endless weeks, on the cold damp cot of the barracks, in the lonely base at Safranbölü, I had pictured her working in her bank, painting in her free time, always idealizing her in my memories. In reality such memories had so often set me up for disillusionment. With other women I'd worked so hard and so patiently for love, but it eluded me just as I'd grasp for it. With Naomi it was different: there was no one with whom I felt more at ease. She was fun-loving. Patient. Supportive. Now, as she took my right hand and kissed me on each cheek, her voice shimmered with excitement. "Avram! I've missed you." It was all I needed to hear.

In the five minutes before Mert and our friends joined us for the reunion we caught up quickly. There was none of the awkward reaching I felt with other women. During college we used to meet twice a week at a pudding shop. Opposite each other at a small, unbalanced table, we could study under the glare of the harsh light, hardly speaking, until I had polished off a chicken-breast pudding and our Liptons had long gone cold. I would walk her back through dark traffic to her dormitory at the Mimar Sinan Fine Arts University. I thought of her as my closest friend. The studying together was enough. It cemented the promise of something to come. What that was — a relationship? a future? — was never clear. I assumed the friendship, unforced, would ripen. I assumed once we had left the poverty of university behind, the regimented world of employment and adulthood would point us on our way.

My cousin arrived at the ferry terminal, and while we waited for the three others Mert pulled me by the shoulder to the fast food *büfe*. This was a replay of an old running joke we shared: eating questionable street food to the indignation of our female friends. Mert paid for the three soggiest, greasiest burgers. "You shouldn't eat that stuff," Naomi chided us, playing along. "They've been sitting in the sun all day. You're going to get sick at the concert." She was probably right. The street vendor drenched the burgers in un-refrigerated mayonnaise, stacked on some stringy pickles, and slopped it all with watery ketchup. He passed one to me through the window, and I held the burger out to Naomi. An offering.

"I'm keeping kosher."

"Since when?"

"Since now."

"Nobody will know."

Her lovely face twisted. "God would know."

"God would approve," Mert said, chomping an enormous bite out of his.

"You don't understand what you're missing," I explained. "It absorbs traffic fumes all day. Like a marinade." I swallowed mine in two overly-ambitious bites, and said with my mouth full, "We don't get food like this in the army."

Naomi acted appropriately disgusted. She spotted our three other friends, and leading us over to them she stopped, arms akimbo, at the ragged, one-armed man pawning tokens. "Hurry hurry. Last chance last chance. Hurry hurry. It's leaving." Naomi bought all six of our tokens from the beggar, and screamed over to the latecomers that we were going to miss the ferry.

On the upper deck I motioned to our friend Canu to sit on the last free seat. Instead, she pushed me down by the shoulder onto the plastic bench beside Naomi. "You sit," Canu said with a cryptic smile.

The cold mist had already dampened our hair. "A nasty night," I said, crushing in next to her.

Naomi placed her leather purse across her knees to make more room. "I like the rain in the winter time."

Above me Canu asked, "So you're bored in the army?"

I told her how awful it was.

"It's going fast though," Naomi added. "He's halfway through."

"A third," I corrected her, wondering how she could overestimate these critical calculations. "Twelve months more. It's like centuries. I go into town once in awhile when it gets too bad."

"Don't complain. School's no picnic either. I'm on my feet all day. At the easel the professors don't cut me a break. Look at what's happened to my hand." Naomi held up her fingers, and in the haze of the ferry bulbs and sea mist I could make out three thin red scabs. "Blisters!" she said. "From the paintbrush."

"You sacrifice your body for your art. Why don't you come visit me in Safranbölü? Take some time off. Give the fingers a rest. Have you been?"

"To Safranbölü? I've never been."

"Come then. You can paint the old caravansaries."

"I'd like that Avram. I really would. Maybe I can get Canu to ride with me." She looked up. "You want to entertain our troops in Safranbölü?"

Canu winced. "What a drag! If I'm taking a weekend away, I'm going somewhere south and warm. The coast. Bodrum." She swung her leg around the white metal pole she was holding, and gyrated her hips in imitation of some seductive dancer.

I goaded her. "I'll take a weekend's leave, Canu. We can drive up to Amasra. Home of the Amazon women. You'll fit right in."

Over a swell the ferry rocked beneath us, and Naomi's weight was pushed into my hip. She whispered in my ear. "I'll visit you myself. Are you learning anything at least, in the defense of our great nation?" She smiled her sweet ironic smile. In the wet lights of the ferry the air came alive with possibility.

I explained how I'd been assigned the anti-tank project. Every day, all afternoon, we drilled in teams of four. "Loading mortars. Firing ground missiles at the Black Sea hills. Enormously stimulating stuff. I pretend to like it." *Be like a fool*, my father had warned me, *so you can finish*. In the army I tried not to stand out.

"And when you're done?

"I'll find a job here."

"Shooting missiles?"

"That's right." I knew she was joking, but at the time it was all I wanted. A job. A home. A wife. Children. Architecture school was not something I'd even yet considered. I'd thought then that the secret to happiness was setting clear, attainable goals. I wanted a life with this woman — a purposeful life, bereft of drama.

5

Infidels

THE CONCERT WE were attending was scheduled for eight-o'clock in a Bosphorus University auditorium, a small venue for a performer of Sait Veysel's reputation. It was meant to be an intimate production. The exiled musician was slipping in and out of the country. This was the second time since the 1980 coup he had come back — a display of courage and patriotism meant to show he was not intimidated by our daft military rule, that he held so much love for his homeland he could not be deterred from returning.

We all knew Sait Veysel must be cautious. He would give his concert and flee once more, only to reappear in two or three years. It occurred to me that he might not be staying the night. The government was well aware of the concert, but wouldn't risk jailing a performer of his reputation and incurring international wrath. My brother — who during these years as a computer science major seemed to have uncommon access to politically banned events — was the one who had secured for me the six concert tickets for this weekend furlough. He claimed it was an early birthday present. I was grateful he'd thought of me. My army service, his university studies — the distance had proven good for us. We were experiencing a détente. I had forgiven him his adolescent offenses, and I'd hoped he'd forgiven me mine.

On the shore in Beşiktaş my friends all crowded into the cab. Naomi sat on my lap in the front seat. It was a straight shot up the coastal highway past the Çırağan Palace to the university, and though the driver could be ticketed for excessive passengers, he accepted our bribe. He began steering and eating a sesame roll at the same time. Naomi reached by the gear shift and grabbed the taxi's requisite bottle of lemon cologne. "Have some," she said, spraying an acrid squirt into my hair. She squirted some behind us, into the faces of our friends, all squashed in a pile of legs and arms in the back seat. "Enough! Nobody will want to sit next to us," Canu was screaming. They all shrieked, dodging another shot of the citrus scent.

"Have you ever seen Sait Veysel's group?" someone asked.

"They're wonderful," Mert said.

"He's supposed to bring an entire ensemble from Europe." I'd heard about a harpist from Copenhagen, two drummers from Cairo, and a Polish jazz-fusion guitarist. "They need to bring music like this to the army," I said. "Entertain the troops once in awhile."

"What *do* they do to keep you busy?" Naomi asked, her hand clenching my forearm.

"You know, the usual whores and belly dancers. It gets tiring, every night."

"Every night!" yelled Mert.

"Sometimes twice a night. So tiring!"

"Shut up Avram," Canu yelled. But I could feel Naomi laughing, her lower back pressed against my stomach, her easy weight a delight on my lap. Past the Ortaköy Synagogue the driver ran a red light, leaning on the horn and chewing his *simit*.

This was the longest I'd ever touched her, and we had never even kissed. One afternoon in her parents' living room we had been cramming for a physics exam together and she had fallen asleep against my arm on the couch. Feeling her against me I had closed my own eyes. Let her wake when she would, I thought. Only the racket of the door opening — Naomi's mother returning from work at a reference publisher's — roused us at last. Naomi smiled at me, wiping sleep from her face. She glanced down at her book, heard the footsteps, and her eyes registered panic. Just as her mother walked into the room Naomi pried me in a deliberately loud voice with a question about potential energy. Bolting up, I answered incorrectly, then stood and greeted her mom. The next day I had miserably failed that physics exam. I had never been happier.

The concert was to be held in a lecture hall in the university's Social Sciences building, a space that could seat just a few hundred people. The rows of bolted chairs meant there was no room to stand up and dance. We had difficulty finding seats together. Only through Naomi's relentless bartering and negotiating — asking grumbling couples to move here and to switch over to there — were we able to secure six adjoining seats.

The concert began to long grateful applause. Our exiled folk singer entered with a quick bow. He didn't even greet the full house — he simply launched into the music, and one by one his bandmates entered, dragged their folding chairs into a horseshoe, lifted their instruments, and joined in. A Balkan jazz-fusion drummer. A Lebanese clarinetist. A Czech who had learned the tabla in Benares. A Danish saz player. A Kurd who played the oud and kuma. They offered a few well-known traditional dances and then moved into whimsical jazz sets. At one point Veysel launched them into a heady Greek rebetiko. I wondered if it might be a political statement. What, in this overly-pressurized nation of ours, was not a political statement?

The concert lasted more than an hour. Sait Veysel did not speak between sets; he nodded as he played, as if he were saying, I'm here making music for you, it's enough. And it was. Unable to dance in the tight lecture hall we became joyously caged animals. But when the band rose and bowed and left the stage we stood as one in a roar of applause, calling out for the encore and clapping in unison. In less than a minute Veysel and his crew jogged back out, lifted their instruments, and one by one they improvised, riffing on the songs they had run through over the last hour. Now nobody in the audience would sit down. Naomi grabbed my arm and we hustled with a great many others into the aisles, linked fingers, and like Laz dancers began a steady swaying to the rising music.

We were on our feet, pinkies locked in a chain of strangers. This was joy: the brave musician playing on into the night, my fingers linked with Naomi's or Canu's or Mert's (I was hardly keeping track), our feet stepping and crossing, our heads rising and bending in a single coordinated wave as we shouted. Soft at first, the music grew louder and its pace quickened and we were dancing faster, for everything we were worth. This weekend would be a short one; the night would be over before it had begun. Sait Veysel would flee the country. I would return to my service, still an infidel charged with playing the fool in defense of our great nation. I would not see Naomi for another six months. Dancing! Dancing! In the sweating chaos of the frenzied stepping I realized my partner to the right had changed again, and looking up I found I was grasping my brother Yusuf's hand. He'd come to the concert himself! He hadn't told me he'd be here.

Yusuf gave me his terrific smile and we continued to dance, then he hugged my head and I slapped his back.

"Something else!" I yelled. "It's been something else! *Vallahi*! A great great concert. I can't thank you enough!" We were applauding Sait Veysel's bow. The crowd was chanting, urging him to play one final song. The room was shaking with the chorus of voices. I wiped my forehead and pointed my brother out to Naomi. "Look who came!"

"Yusuf!" she screamed.

"Told you I'd see you again!" Yusuf yelled.

Smiling, blushing, Naomi nodded. And then the musicians started playing the final song — the last song, in fact, that Sait Veysel would ever play in our city. He would die two months later, in exile, in Berlin, famously knifed on the street in a racist incident that went unprosecuted. But no one in that room knew then that his life had run its course. We listened to the clarinet's cascading notes and Veysel's rhythmic accompaniment on the *oud,* and we danced.

Arms at my sides now, I was working out when Yusuf might have told Naomi he'd see her again. They weren't friends; I couldn't remember having heard they'd run into each other. Yusuf grabbed for my hand, and I accepted it half-heartedly, and went through the motions of the Black Sea dance, forcing myself to smile. Yusuf danced effortlessly between me and Naomi. My own legs were growing tired, my chest pounding to keep up with them.

Halfway through the song Naomi ducked through my brother's arm in a nifty flourish, and they were both to my left, Naomi now dancing between us. I didn't know which was worse, having Yusuf separating us, or sharing her with him. Sait Veysel was strumming for his life and singing. We danced, Yusuf calling out at the height of each chorus. With the warmth of Naomi's grasp I was now better able to fake my enthusiasm. The players at last rose into the crescendo, blew out three unified beats, Veysel lifted the oud's handle, chopped it downward, and precisely at the same moment the whole band fell silent. They had given two extended encores. During the long bows the crowd, huffing and sweating, offered an applause that — at least in my memory — went on forever, as if we sensed it might be the last time. Amid the roar the musicians walked offstage, mortals again, suddenly diminished. The lights flickered on. The applause continued, but there would be no more encores. People dawdled in pairs, looked at their feet, grinned up at one another. No one wanted to leave. Was everyone as drained and as empty as I now felt?

"Drinks!" my brother yelled at last. "Drinks!" He had shoved his way through the hordes and found his own computer-science friends; and he was introducing them to Mert, trying to organize an outing. I recognized two of them, with their long unkempt hair and threadbare black T-shirts, as Yusuf's communist buddies. I'd heard they'd founded a student organization offering private tutoring in an illegal *gecekondu* in Ümraniye. To Yusuf it was a progressive grass-roots charity. But it was clearly controversial: their pupils were impoverished Kurds, fresh from the villages of the southeast. On weekends the group tutored them for the national university exam, and in between lessons of mathematics and the verses of Nazım Hikmet the tutors tossed in hardy doses of Marxist ideology. A million small gestures like this, Yusuf had once told me — that's what it would take to change this doomed country of ours.

"Come on out with us," my brother called to Naomi over the heads bobbing across the hall.

She glanced at me shyly and mouthed, "You'll come?"

"Where you going?" Mert called back over to Yusuf. "Tell us where. We'll meet you."

"Where?" Naomi relayed over my head.

"Where? Where?" people were calling through the crowd.

"Same as last time," Yusuf yelled back.

I thought: *last time?*

6

Pummeling My Brother

As we fought our way out of the lecture hall I asked Naomi when she had last seen Yusuf. Her face colored; she hesitated just slightly, but enough. "I ran into him at a café in Ortaköy," she said amid the jostling bodies. "We played some backgammon. I've gone out with them once or twice. As a group."

The *as a group* stung more than the confession. She had not written about seeing my brother. "As a group?" I asked. "With his *communists*?" Someone was pushing me in the lower back, stepping on my heels.

She shrugged. "Come on. They're fun."

"I've got to spend a year and a half in the army, making sure your country can defend itself from these communists. To you, they're fun."

She was now walking ahead of me, but cranking her head around to say, "It's not the same thing, Avram. These aren't militants. They're just students."

"No, you're right. It's not the same. These guys are frauds. Pseudo-Marxists. Trying to make a statement. A teenagers' game.

Wait until the time comes for them to shave their heads and serve. See what treatment they'll get."

She reached back and took hold of my hand. "You're angry at me."

I shook my head. "I'm not. Really I'm not. So you've gone out with Yusuf's friends a few times. I'm glad he's keeping an eye on you. Keeping you out of trouble." I tried to smile, but then I spotted my brother outside the open glass doors, his finger circling the air, giving Mert directions to some local bar.

"I have to call it a night."

"Call it a night?" Naomi stared at me, her lips pursed. "It's way too early, Avram."

"Been a packed weekend for me. I've got to catch an early morning bus back to base. I've hardly spent any time with my father."

She glanced down at the tiled floor. "Don't hate me for this, Avram."

"I couldn't hate you." I pressed my fingers into her palm and squeezed.

She released my hand, and I gave her a gentle kiss on each cheek. People were jostling past us, bumping our shoulders. Outside, Mert and Canu and the others stared at me when I said goodbye, then exchanged knowing looks with Naomi. Everyone knew more than I did. I shook hands with my brother.

"You won't come?" Yusuf yelled.

"An early morning." I motioned with a nod back to my friends. "Show them a good time."

"We will! We will! But come on, Sergeant! You're home one Saturday in six months. Just one drink. An early birthday drink! We're meeting Murat and his buddies. You like Murat.

Afterwards I'll come back home with you. For old time's sake. Naomi!" Yusuf called. "What in God's name did you say to him?"

She laughed, acknowledging a joke that wasn't there, and waved Yusuf off. Down the block I got in a taxi alone for the return trip to Şişli. The driver purposely forgot to reset the meter. The usual song and dance. I had to remind him with feigned anger to hit the button, he had to apologize with feigned sincerity, and as the vehicle lurched off we shot past my friends. Yusuf had one arm around Mert, the other around Naomi. They were sauntering forward in long musical steps, and they were laughing.

Back home I fell restlessly asleep on the green couch by the radiator until sometime in the night I heard Yusuf come through the front door. I kept my eyes closed. My brother walked over, took off his jacket, and shook me on the shoulder. Alcohol and smoke were heavy on his breath, the sweetness of marijuana lingered on his shirt. Let it go, I thought, let it go. He's done nothing to you this time.

His voice hoarse now and full of phlegm, Yusuf said, "Should have come out with us, Sergeant." His throat was raspier today than I remembered hearing it last we'd met, and I wondered to what extent he was keeping up with his *fizyoterapi*. He'd lost weight; the cleft in his chin seemed more pronounced than I remembered. In the light from the kitchen I examined now, close up, my brother's yellowish eyes, his slightly-clubbed fingers. You wouldn't guess he was sick, you had to look closely, but I knew next year he'd get a full clearance from his own Military Service.

"Fuck off. Let me sleep."

"She was disappointed." He was leaning over me on the couch, swaying. "She wanted you there. She told me."

"I've got a headache." I covered my eyes with my forearm. "You're making it worse."

"You don't know a single thing about women." Yusuf laughed, crouching over my face. And before I knew what he was doing, he'd given me a salty wet peck on the neck. "A love bite," he whispered with fake passion.

I throttled Yusuf. I grabbed him with both hands, both thumbs pressing into his Adam's apple, stood him up and swung his head violently left and right. At the moment this seemed the only worthwhile thing these months of basic training had prepared me for. My grip was strong from chin-ups; I'd never been in better shape. We did our special kind of dance. His light-heartedness, the hours he'd spent with Naomi, all of it was seeping up through my arms, down into my gut, charging my resentment. I imagined with perfect clarity the years of jail ahead, the liberation I'd feel, the clean slate that awaited me. I wanted sanity. I could do twenty years, I could do life, as long as Yusuf was out of this picture. He was gripping my hands, trying to pry them loose, but I was stronger — I'd always been stronger, pummeling him to keep him alive. His eyes had widened; he had stopped moaning; he couldn't gather enough breath to beg me off. With rigid shaking thumbs I was supporting him by the neck alone. Then something broke in me as it always did with my brother. My hands loosened and I released him.

Yusuf reeled. He took a step back, gasping, coughing, rubbing his neck, and started to speak again. I didn't want to hear it. I swung at his face. The blow was tempered by doubt, but still my knuckle felt the soft pressure of Yusuf's socket give in. For the rest of my life I would hold the physical memory of that softness, of the jelly-like give of my brother's eye. Yusuf didn't even call out. He collapsed onto the darkness of the floor with a gratifying thud, and in the morning I found him like that, eye swollen, breath scabrous, left hand curled against his reddened throat, his open lips crusty and rounded in a knowing grin.

He was still passed-out when Father found me in the living room sitting over him. I was considering what Mother would make of her two sons. At the sight of Yusuf Father grasped his stomach (by now he was dealing with an ulcer) but averted his eyes and refrained from examining the disaster that was my brother. We each stepped over Yusuf's sprawled legs and out of the apartment. We walked in silence, arm in arm, the five blocks to the Ulusoy bus terminal. There Father kissed me goodbye, wished me luck, begged me to be safe, and began to turn away. But at the last moment he turned back around. "He hasn't slept in the apartment in months. I have no idea where he usually sleeps. The dormitory maybe? With friends? Do you have any idea?"

"How would I have any idea? You think I'm his keeper?"

From the army base, my first letter to Naomi went unanswered. The second she answered in a friendly fashion, and mentioned in a single confessional line tutoring basic mathematics, on her Sundays off, at the Kurdish center in Ümraniye. *It would take a million small gestures like this,* she wrote, *to begin to change this doomed country.* The third and final letter asked if I'd be hurt if she told me she was in love with my brother.

All spring and summer I loaded the munitions, and we bombed the empty hills of the Black Sea coast.

7

Housewarming

Living full-time on the island would save me two hours a day commuting back and forth from the city — time I could devote to renovations. When I informed Father he seemed non-plussed, completely dismissive about what I was doing. I invited him out to help me relocate a bathroom light fixture and patch up its dry-wall — jobs he'd always enjoyed. But he had no interest in seeing the Halim Pasha House, little interest even in hearing me discuss its improvements.

A bull-headed man, my father! But I wouldn't argue with him or try to convince him to face what my brother had left behind. Not if he wasn't yet ready. Once he saw the villa, once he saw its expansive views and old-world charm, he'd change his tune.

Saturday morning I arrived with my two suitcases. Nılay Gören was already there, pretending to be working, though by now I knew she was doing nothing. I'd first met Yusuf's former maid at the Dolci Café, and when I'd offered her the job she complained that she'd just had surgery to remove her gallbladder. She'd placed her hand on her upper stomach. This was her excuse for spending most of the first week of her employment sitting on a stool in the kitchen. The second week she seemed to have forgotten the details of that recovery, and watching us work she complained instead about arthritis in both knees, both wrists, and one ankle (her left, she claimed, though sometimes it switched to her right.) In her fifties, Nılay was a sturdy battle-axe of a woman, with one cheek patched brown by an unfortunate birthmark — a blotch of fate she complained about whenever she noticed an attractive face in a magazine. Actually Nılay had fared better than the rest of Yusuf's staff, holding down a job every summer since the accident, but she complained she'd have to work until her dying day to make up the salary difference. These seasonal jobs paid far less than Yusuf's year-round employment once had. He'd spoiled the staff with his generosity. This was something to complain about as well.

Flora Demirkan came an hour after my arrival, lugging in plastic grocery bags filled with enough food to stock the refrigerator. "You can't live in a house without food," she announced. "You don't cook."

"I hold my own on a grill."

"I'll make you lunch today."

"Flora, really. We've got too much to do. That's not necessary."

"You might not think so. But I've seen what you've been eating. French fries!"

"Trust her," Nılay Gören chimed in from her perch on the stool, rubbing her ankle. "Flora knows when a man needs a good meal."

So I agreed to a housewarming luncheon. By late morning the cavernous kitchen was whirring with gas burners and fans and the new industrial convection oven. A talk program was playing through a miniature radio Nılay had propped by the sink. The announcer was railing against the European Council in Brussels, and the maid, listening from the table, agreed with everything he said. "What more do they want?" she kept yelling. "What more can they ask of us? Cultural rights! Let's send the PKK terrorists to Brussels. We'll see what they make of cultural rights then!"

Flora, unperturbed, had already sliced tomatoes and trimmed artichokes after soaking them in a glass bowl of lemon water. She had experience tuning out Nılay Gören, and was showing me how it was done. Now with her sleeves rolled up she was skewering chunks of white-wine-marinated swordfish between onions and tomatoes for the grill. I offered a hand. While Nılay watched, hard-eyed, sitting at the table and massaging her wrists, Flora set me to work on the *ezme salatası* — to accompany the swordfish — directing me to remove the seeds of the tomato, cucumbers, and peppers, to measure out the mint and the paprika, and then to chop it all down into extremely fine pieces. I worked, swatting away thoughts of Naomi, who back in the Capital would be hovering over the twins in similar Saturday lunch preparations. Flora finally pushed me aside with a good-natured shove and doused my efforts with olive oil. She folded the mixture over again with her broad wooden spoon, then dipped her pinky into my spread, tasted it, and added more wine vinegar. "Now I can say I made it," she joked.

Outside on the desolate patio I checked the slow charcoal fire. The coals were not yet red, so I sat alone by the grill facing into the cold wind. Mustafa Faik emerged from the back garden, where he'd been attacking the long weeds again with a dull scythe. I asked the old guard how his scything was going. He was inordinately proud of his scything skills; and I always made a point of complimenting him on his slow progress through the ruined gardens.

An energetic gray-headed, gray-mustached man, Mustafa Faik had been the longest serving security guard at the mansion. He had treated Yusuf like a son, and to this day overflowed with pride in having worked for a man of such worldly distinction. The death of my brother had hit him as hard as anyone: for five years now he had suffered, jobless, living off his meager state pension. I'd first found him sitting alone in the dank seaside cafeteria he now haunted, savoring an extra roll of crusty bread that came gratis with his soup. He'd accepted my offer of work without trying to hide his eagerness; and without a question he'd politely take on any job or errand. A good soul. As the weeks progressed I'd come to like him more and more.

Together now we watched the smoke curl up and around a tall cypress. From the branches above us two gulls squawked out in protest.

"Avram Bey," Mustafa asked, "what are you doing here?"

"Waiting for the coals to heat."

"I mean *here*. What are you doing *here*? Why move in here now, in the winter? It'll be too cold for you."

"But Mustafa, you live here all year long. Flora and Nılay too."

"And we freeze all winter!"

I stood and raised my hand over the grill. It was gaining heat.

He nodded, watching the coals, their corners now tinged grey, a slow orange spreading into the center of the stack. "But this place. Why fix up this place? You hadn't talked to him in years. Yusuf never even mentioned to me he had a brother."

I motioned across the patio to the covered pool, its tarpaulin sagging with green puddles. "You know what it does to an architect to see a property like this go to hell? The place has history, no?"

History. It was enough of a reason for Mustafa. The old man stood, one hand thrust deep into his worn trouser pockets where he kept his worry beads. He circled the pool nervously, contemplating exactly what history I might be referring to in those puddles of algae. With his other hand he flattened the spongy clumps of white hair outlining his smooth head. One lap around, he glanced down at his soiled dress shirt, making sure all of the buttons were in place, tight up to his neck, and in this I recognized the pride of the impeccably-dressed man he must once have been, the proud veteran of the Korean War who on weekends, in shirt and black tie, used to take his late wife dancing at the military club, where (he'd assured me several times) a six course dinner and the music of a brass band could be had for "less than the cost of a rice pudding at Saray."

Now the French doors swung open and Flora stalked out with a military air. "I don't want your first lunch here to turn into a total disaster," she said, inspecting the coals.

Mustafa Faik looked at me. I fought back a smile. Flora wouldn't trust us men with any of the food, not even the grill. She had her hands on her thick hips, calculating something. "Get the swordfish. I'm going to make sure you don't overcook it."

"*Hanımefendim*," I replied with a slight bow, and turned back to the kitchen. Pulling the door closed behind me I saw Flora and Mustafa standing in the smoke, half-frowns on their faces. Flora was rubbing her shoulders, and Mustafa, holding his palms out over the fire, was murmuring something to her.

8

Encouragements

It was too windy to eat outside, so we ate my welcome lunch that afternoon in the kitchen, the four of us seated around the freshly-painted pedestal table. Flora served the *mezes* of string beans and spiced bulgur and artichokes with olive oil and dill. She served me the *ezme salatası* that I had helped throw together. "*Afiyet olsun,*" she said. Good digestion. The swordfish she served over the fresh flat bread she'd left warming in the oven. "*Afiyet olsun,*" she repeated, dishing me something anew. You felt immediately the confidence and complexity of her cooking. The meal was the most satisfying I'd had in months. She ate little herself, but continued to replace whatever food we'd polished off as soon as it was gone. *Afiyet olsun. Afiyet olsun.* I was bursting, and trying to slow down, asked them to tell me what they remembered of my brother when he first came to the island.

Flora fell quiet, concentrating only on the table. She dug up another piece of swordfish and thrust it at me. I held up a hand, and she slid the filet onto Mustafa's plate instead.

"It was Yusuf's *encouragements* I remember most," said Mustafa, flush with food. The year Yusuf had hired him the village had funded construction of a new mosque, only a half kilometer down the hill from the Halim Pasha House. On its completion its young imam invited everyone in the neighborhood to visit. Mustafa had accompanied my brother. "He eyed the back balcony, which, Avram, is reserved only for women. He said he wanted to see that. I thought it was strange, but the imam allowed us up there. Yusuf inspected the mosque's fresh carpeting, the impressive wall tiles. They're probably already faded, but back then the new tiles were striking, all tangled blue flowers and tulips. Your brother asked what the imam was studying. Up on the women's balcony, right there, the young man belted out the *namaz* for us. Just the first few notes. Yusuf laughed and said he sounded like an old master. I'll never forget that. It was his curiosity, his open mind, I like to remember. Even an imam just starting out needs encouragement, you know. After that your brother would always wave when they passed each other on the streets."

The new mosque's call to prayer resounded in the dark mornings through the mansion's high windows that Yusuf left open — even a crack in the winter — because the salt air helped his breathing. According to his staff he slept in the Halim Pasha House most weekdays. That muezzin's call rarely woke him; he heard the earliest prayers only in his sleep, and it was often then, in the darkest moments of morning, that Yusuf's dreams would take a strange turn and he would let out his muffled screams. (Screams I remembered, too, from long ago in our bedroom.) Weekdays on the island he awoke at five-thirty-five to perform his hour of deep breathing exercises and electric vest, until he could at last cough up the night's heavy phlegm. Then he used his nebulizer and took his antibiotics, and with a clear chest he was ready to crush the world between his fists.

Contrary to my long-held assumptions, Mustafa assured me Yusuf's daily routine here had remained Spartan. He breakfasted on a single potato pastry and tea (he had little appetite in the morning), took his prescribed walk past the new mosque to İlhan Saracoğlu's *bakkal* to buy the financial and football papers, then caught the slow ferry to the mainland. After work, if he had no social obligations in the city he flew home by helicopter from his offices in the Teletürk Tower, arriving on the island before the evening call to prayer. Only on weekends, if his invitations to dinner and peregrinations around the tavernas of Beyoğlu lasted deep into the night, would he sleep in one of his apartments in the city: a two-story terraced loft on Bagdat Caddesi, or his penthouse on the European side.

Nılay Gören disputed these details. "How were we supposed to know where he slept?" she said, adding that he sometimes took a room in the Divan Hotel, across the street in Arnavutköy from where he moored his yacht. "We had no way of keeping track of him."

"That's not true," Flora chimed in.

"It's true enough. You'd complain yourself each time he didn't come back."

"Nılay," Mustafa murmured.

"We had to assume he'd be coming home, and I never knew about the dinner preparations," Flora explained.

"See?" Nilay added. "He had one life here, and many others off the island."

Nılay remembered how in her first year, even in the desolate winter months, weekend mornings Yusuf would strenuously hike the circumference of the island, ending up at the Monastery of Saint George. He was as full of encouragements for the Orthodox monks on the mountaintop as he had been with the imam. Back when our family had first vacationed here these monks used to bottle a supply of wine each year, sealing it with yellow candle wax. They sold it to the picnicking pilgrims, who drank it up on the cliffs, under the pergolas of woven straw, shaded by an ancient three-armed Mediterranean pine. But the rotation of caretaking priests sent from Greece had thinned as politics between our nations had worsened, and St. George's tradition of artisan viniculture had long dried up. Nılay remembered Yusuf petitioning each of the rotating priests to give it another try. "'This place was once paradise on earth,' your brother would say. 'The gulls, the bells, the stone walls, the rustic tables. It put you in the proper meditative state. Food, prayer, the icons, the sea. And a bottle of wine to complement it all.'"

Mustafa Faik added, "Your brother understood how special the island was. There's no place like it in the world. Yusuf was a soul prone to great happiness, given the proper ingredients. Forget what a mess he made of those last years. He never got down, even with the heavy burdens God placed on his shoulders." It delighted Mustafa to remember Yusuf's ritual exchange with the monks. "To those priests he used to say, 'Such a glorious morning. Do you have some wine for me, Father?' He wanted things just so. He never let you forget it." Eventually an anonymous donation to the monastery provided resources enough to bottle its first twenty cases of red and twenty cases of white in a decade. The wine sold out before summer; and since then the monastery had increased production each year.

Yusuf's solitary hikes had the forlorn air of nostalgia, as if he had lost something and was determined to hunt it down. His staff recalled that the first year he'd arrived, on his trek back down from the mountain he would stop to lunch alone at the Ali Baba Restaurant. In the fall he ate under its billowing seaside tarpaulin, but on winter days he came inside, and seated himself at the simple oak table near the wood stove. He'd become a regular. He claimed he liked Ali Baba's fried turbot, but it was obvious to everyone that he came for more than the turbot.

Flora Demirkan, in consternation at the lack of a full-time job, still struggling to support her precocious nine-year-old daughter and — at the time — four other wayward young children, worked as the cook in the restaurant. Over the slow winter months she also doubled as its waitress. I pictured her at the height of her distressing beauty. Yusuf, I imagined, could not have been immune — even with her white cook's apron on — to the swagger of Flora's hips, to her sandpaper voice, or to the way she brushed his shoulder when she leaned over to clear his plates.

"I began preparing special dishes for him," Flora explained, removing our own empty dishes from the lunch table. "I knew he was an important man, coming to eat after a long morning of exercise, and I wanted him to enjoy his meal. What? Was anything wrong with that?" Flora challenged first Mustafa, then Nılay, with a look. "What was I supposed to do?" she asked. "Not feed the man?"

Yusuf could eat enormous amounts, quantities that took your breath away, and never gain any weight — a fact that had consumed our mother to the end of her days. But gourmet food was lost on him; he always preferred simple street food and *lokantas* to fancy meals. Flora, too, had noticed this appetite, and had done her best to help in the only way she knew how. "Sunday mornings at the restaurant I made an anchovy pilaf, or a stewed shrimp. But he liked the stuffed grape leaves best. Once he told me he craved my *dolma* all week long. I was not surprised. It was my specialty — the family recipe."

By spring, on the weekend of the yearly pilgrimage to St. George, Yusuf had stolen her away from Ali Baba's and had hired her on full-time himself, in addition to the three rotating security guards, a butler, a caretaker, a gardener, a boatman, and Nılay Gören as his live-in maid.

9

Dishwater

I THANKED FLORA NOW for the extravagant housewarming lunch, and we helped clear the table and pile plates by the sink. Flora excused herself — she needed to get home to her kids. As our cook collected her shopping bags, Nılay assured her she would clean up. Clearly she hung around to gossip more freely once Flora left. These days Nılay lived alone in a yellow cottage high up the hill behind the village, where the donkeys roamed, braying into the night. Like Flora she had never been married, but unlike Flora she had no children waiting for her. "Only donkeys," she'd joked. I stood by the kitchen sink, drying the pans the maid washed, her arms elbow deep in dishwater snapping with suds. I wasn't about to discourage Nılay. Mustafa Faik had stayed too, apparently to referee. He was still sitting at the table, blowing into a cup of tea that had long gone cold.

"Let me tell you Avram," the maid was saying, "for the first year the two of them hardly spoke a full sentence to each other. Flora would serve her meals in dainty silence. Or she'd cook and leave the house before Yusuf had eaten. *I'd* have to serve and clear alone, just like now. I held a grudge about that a long time, let me tell you."

Nılay grumbled about how Flora had worked in the ancient kitchen with one or two children, whom she dragged everywhere, forever underfoot. She'd make holiday sweets like Noah's Pudding with her girls, which the kids would distribute to anyone who came to the kitchen. Eventually the kids got old enough to help set the table, or to assist Nılay polishing the silverware. "But they never did anything right. I'd have to redo the spoons every time. They spilled and broke everything they touched."

"Cut it out Nılay," Mustafa Faik said. "They were good kids. They *are* good kids. Flora does her best. It's all we can ask of anyone in her position."

"Her position! Exactly! That was always the problem, her position."

During those first two years Flora had purchased her small house in the village, had moved the children out of her rented home, and with the generous raises Yusuf offered the staff she paid off her debts. Mustafa Faik remembered seeing her smile, and hearing her sing Sezen Aksu songs as she stirred the lentil soup. "She was happy enough back then, Nılay."

"Yes, the happiest overworked cook in the world. She and her endless kids annoyed us all. Why Yusuf put up with their racket none of us understood. Praise to God, though, we loved her food."

On Sunday mornings Flora attended church, so Yusuf had requested that Nılay bring his brunch of muesli and black olives, bread, and honey up to his room, along with his enzyme medications. For no clear reason the arrangements shifted and Flora started working Sunday mornings. She carried the late breakfasts herself up the mansion's winding back staircase. On one occasion Yusuf had asked Flora to remove her apron before she brought him the food so that she would no longer carry the stench of the kitchen into his room. "He thinks he smells of rose-water, like the Prophet!" she'd grumbled, assuring the rest of the staff she would never capitulate to Yusuf's ridiculous demands.

But capitulate she did; and soon the cook's regular Sunday trips (apron removed) up those stairs to the master bedroom were lasting the length of the morning. The Turkish pine creaking beneath Flora's feet announced her journey to the entire house. She'd disappear until noon. If Nılay teased her, Flora adamantly claimed she was simply helping their boss with his *fizyoterapi*. "I'm not one to cast judgment," Nılay Gören told me. "So what if I worked in a brothel? So what? Everyone eventually gets what they deserve. God sees to that, not me. Who am I to judge?"

Nılay would press her for details of those *fizyoterapi* sessions. Flora insisted she'd been clapping his back that entire morning, as Yusuf contorted himself in practiced positions over the ottoman, coughing and hacking. She'd recall the airy room, the soft blue light streaming into the windows, the lines of inhalers and respiratory equipment positioned like chess pieces across the armoire. His skin smelled alarmingly salty; and it was this smell that aroused a disturbing pity in Flora, so much so that she used to slip and call him "that poor child." The maid mimed for me how Flora would have to cup her hands, and where on his back you'd have to pat him, and with what proper percussive rhythms. *Clap clap clap — clap clap.*

But these therapy sessions lasted longer than Nılay believed even the sickest man's chest would take to clear. And despite their Sunday intimacies, around the mansion it was all formality. They rarely made eye contact, and he never thanked Flora at the dinner table when she served him.

"But let me tell you, Avram, they were attached," Nilay contended. "That woman was tormented when Yusuf was away for business. Flora was always worried he'd forgotton his medicine. I'd find her in the foyer, rifling through the newspapers the security guards left in the bin, looking for news about him. Those publicity stunts to Asia, Africa, those daredevil boat races. Everywhere he flew off to. For my part I just hoped he didn't get himself killed jumping out of a helicopter. Because without Yusuf I'd have no job, you see?"

So Flora and I had shared that reluctant passion. It occurred to me that over those years we might even have thumbed the same articles, from the same late editions, in search of his name.

10

An Affair With No End

It was Flora who first put an end to those *fizyoterapi* sessions. One Sunday she told Nilay to bring Yusuf his breakfast. She wasn't going up there again, no matter what kind of coughing she heard. "He's a man just like every other man I've known. A complete shit. Believe me, Nılay Hanim."

What set her off was this: Yusuf had hired a new cleaning lady to augment the staff. She was a young plump Turkish-Bulgarian teen named Aybike, and she came three-times a week to work on the floors and windows, and she was also responsible for the laundry. In her white head scarf and loose black pants and terry-slippers she worked harder than any other domestics Yusuf had hired to that point. Vacuuming rugs, polishing the floors and the silverware, bundling the dirty laundry and drying it in the machine imported from Germany — the girl was everywhere.

"Flora wouldn't speak with that Pomak," Nılay remembered, laughing. "She was bitter, our cook. She could hold a grudge that would outlast time."

"Jealousy among the help," Mustafa responded with a shrug

from the table when I turned to him. "I'll never understand what Flora was thinking. Whatever people said about Yusuf, he wasn't interested in his own personal harem. I knew him best, like a son, and I can vouch for that. For crying out loud, Aybike was a *niece* of Orhan Veysel — the owner of the dry goods store where Yusuf bought his walnuts. Yusuf had done the old man a favor, hiring her on. We all knew that."

"The idea of that Aybike girl ironing Yusuf's pajamas upset the woman."

"*Baksana*, Nılay. Come on now. Yusuf couldn't even remember her name. She was just a child, passing through. Flora was seeing things that weren't there."

But she saw them anyway. Yusuf's instructions to the staff were pinned to the corkboard in the rear laundry room where the servants signed in, and where special notes for Aybike were written in a careful cursive, in his best handwriting. The orders he left the young laundress — to prepare his striped shirt for the opening night of the *Bienali*, or to make sure she had the tuxedo dry-cleaned for Tuesday's flight to Alma Ate — all read to Flora like coded secrets. He used the informal suffix. He signed with his first name only. And Flora Demirkan *was* the only person in the Halim Pasha House with firsthand knowledge of Yusuf's surreptitious love codes. Of my brother she seemed to know things others didn't know, to see things others didn't see.

Mustafa Faik believed she had lost it. "Your brother was casual with all the help, whatever their age. He didn't put on airs. He didn't hold us to formalities. If he used the informal with that Aybike — well, he used it with me too. And I never slept with the man."

Apparently it all struck a chord in Flora. It bothered her when she came to work early on Tuesday mornings and found Aybike had arrived even earlier. In the afternoons, when the mansion was empty, to hear the young woman padding down the noisy stairs from the main bedroom — where she might only have been fitting Yusuf's sheets — sent Flora to pulverizing the chicken with terrible whacks of the meat tenderizer.

Her suspicions boiled over one Sunday in March, a month after Aybike had been hired. Yusuf had ordered his breakfast in bed, and Flora had refused to send it up for him. "Let him come down for it himself, the lazy ape!" Soon enough Yusuf had done just that, and had confronted Flora in the kitchen. The cook had made him a garlicky *menemen*, a dish she knew he couldn't stomach, and she resolutely clattered the breakfast plate before him at the table. "*Afiyet olsun.*"

"What's this?"

"Breakfast!"

The entire staff had heard them arguing. They heard Flora, in an incandescent rage, accusing Yusuf of planning to release her. She rattled off his social dates and appointments, the fundraisers and balls he'd attended and never mentioned, the women who'd escorted him to dinner, the trip to Switzerland he'd gone on, all without telling her, everything without telling her. Flora's encyclopedic knowledge of their boss's movements was impressively disturbing. She quoted him from television programs he'd appeared on. She lobbed insults like grenades. His charities were empty-hearted. His hygiene reprehensible. She noted his selfishness and his public philandering. "I've played this game too many times, Yusuf. You've had your fill, and I'll be looking for work again by spring."

"You've never taken a word I've said seriously."

"So this is how you treat me? A new laundress?"

He was half-laughing, half-pleading with her simply to trust him. "For God's sake, Flora. Keep it down."

"You think you can take and take, whenever, whatever you want, like some sultan, like some prince, without a thought to anyone else's needs. Just chew us up and spit out the bones."

Now Yusuf burst into emphatic laughter, asking what she wanted of him. Where did this go?

"It can't go anywhere. It always goes right to the same damn place: To hell! Never again."

"Tell me what you want from me."

"Go on Yusuf. I've heard your talk before. You think I don't know the ring of empty promises?"

She wouldn't stand in that room and listen to him spout his lies. She hustled down the hallway. With his strafed voice he called after her, but she didn't look back. That night in the maid's quarters Flora had unburdened herself to Nılay. "He might pretend, but I *know* what he really thinks of us. It's easy to promise, but Yusuf's not a man to deliver. Not to me at least."

A year would pass, and then another, and the drama would repeat itself. The staff would hear them fighting in much the same way. For over a decade it became their disquieting pattern. Mustafa Faik believed that Flora, unable to accept her boss's affections, made a terrible mistake. "Your brother, for all his excesses, was an honest man when it came to love. He didn't care about appearances. He was smitten. We all knew it. But she treated him like a young boy. She'd lure him in and — snap! — push him away, pointing the fingers of blame. He'd order her not to come up to him anymore, and she'd come up anyway. She'd vow not to bring him his breakfasts, and next thing she was bringing them. They wouldn't speak for months, and suddenly they were speaking again. You know, he was devastated when it came to her. That laundry girl was gone after three months. But all those years Yusuf kept Flora employed, despite the abuses. And she stayed on, all those years. It was the worst kind of affair: an affair with no end. He should have let her go, washed his hands of that whole mess. That would have been the real charity. It would have been the merciful thing, considering what became of them both. Of course my own father used to say, "No good comes from a beautiful woman.'"

I couldn't tell if any of this was spinning on Faik's part. I'd found his loyalty to his boss blinded him to essential truths. Nılay Gören, after all, placed the blame squarely on Flora. "The thing is this. Flora couldn't commit to one man. Let me tell you, those years she watched him like a hawk, but *she* was the one who was seducing the millionaires and squeezing out children more times than we could count. She had endless passions, that one. Another immaculate conception! Allah Allah! He was right not to trust her. I have nothing against the woman. She's had her own hard knocks. But those of us who really knew her never harbored any sympathy. A rotten board won't hold nails."

So Flora's staunchness about Yusuf's capacity for deception remained a mystery. That winter I would be unable to sort out which came first: her eternal doubts, or my brother's late night carousing with the likes of Dr. Baykan and his young gypsy women. Had she known about those evenings? Or had she only guessed a man like Yusuf capable of them? I was still finding it difficult to believe that a single woman with no prospects, trapped on an island with a gaggle of children, could rebuff the advances of a wealthy man who might have promised her everything. Later I would have the opportunity to ask Flora where her perpetual doubts had come from. Had it been a simple matter of social class? Of Yusuf's illness? That he wouldn't be around into old age? Was it because he was Jewish? Maybe they just saw the world in different ways?"

She would bristle at this last suggestion. "We saw the world in *exactly* the same way, Avram Bey. That was forever our problem."

Flora insisted my brother never could have made a faithful partner, for her or for anyone else, and that he was more dangerous than anyone knew. In me she had found a sympathetic ear.

11

The Letter G

BEFORE I WAS even out of the army Yusuf had dumped Naomi. I hadn't spoken to either of them. For me it was a double loss, a sickness of the heart which during two years of graduate school had come to seem like a permanent condition.

And then, an invitation. My cousin Byanka, now a Masters student at the Mimar Sinan Fine Arts University, was showing her thesis paintings in an exhibition and had invited everyone she knew. It was the kind of extended family obligation I normally ducked if I had any reasonable excuse. But on my return home from my Building Construction lab that Friday, due to high winds, the private Beşiktaş ferries had stopped running. I had to take the municipal ferry instead to Karaköy. Now I would practically pass Byanka's exhibition on the walk home, and realized I may as well stop in. Later I understood the fingers of fate had given me a gentle nudge.

The university had set up its end-of-semester show in a former shipping warehouse along the Bosphorus. Inside only a few people were walking the enormous aisles, squinting at the incomprehensible paintings and bizarre statuary and freakish installations. In the ominous silence footsteps echoed off the high exposed ceilings. The cavernous space shot disembodied voices around like phantom shrieks. It was a dim affair; there was too little light to appreciate the earnest details of the art; and it occurred to me this might be a good thing. I searched for Byanka and didn't know if I had somehow missed her paintings. But when I turned the corner of the final row I spotted relatives and friends whispering around my cousin. Her work was hanging on a wall closest to the windows; and the late afternoon sun streaming in off the straits cast her minimalist paintings in an amber glow. Byanka was pointing to a framed drawing. Everyone was laughing at something. I saw that one of these people was Naomi, and I wished right then I hadn't come.

She wore black rimmed glasses so large I imagined a conscious effort must be needed to keep her head from falling forward. She had her arms crossed with authority, and she was smiling whimsically and nodding, as if she understood something about Byanka's paintings the rest of the world never would.

I nearly turned, but Byanka had already noticed me. "Avram! You made it!"

"I never miss an exhibit of a soon-to-be major artist," I said, striding up to her. My cousin rolled her eyes at me, and I exchanged kisses with her and our relations.

Naomi was wearing, beneath her long exposed calves, some kind of German clogs. She uncrossed her arms, stepped towards me, and with perfect poise held out her hand. "Avram."

I took her long fingers in mine. "How are you, Naomi?"

"I'm good. I'm exhibiting here, with Byanka. We're rooming together, this last semester." Her voice had never matched her looks, but it was higher than I remembered it, slightly grating, though I'd always found this distinctive rather than off-putting, as it might have been with other women.

"Well," I said, "then you can explain some of this stuff to me." I waved to a large red painting of the letter G and made a clownish show of whispering, "I don't know the first thing about the avant-garde."

Byanka stepped forward. "Avram's studying architecture, you know. He draws squares and rectangles."

"Structure and form," I explained, catching my cousin's glance. "With us it's only structure and form."

"I've heard, I've heard." Naomi examined my scuffed shoes and the beaten oversized leather portfolio I clutched in my left hand. I grew immediately self-conscious. Through those glasses she had the kind of piercing gaze that was never wasted. "You'll make a terrific architect, Avram. I'm sure you know more than you admit about the post-modern. Let me give you a tour of Byanka Casuto's masterpieces."

And for the next fifteen minutes she did just that. The crowd of seven of us gathered around Naomi. Byanka protested at first, then retreated. Like a docent her perfectly poised classmate explained the significance of each of my cousin's five large thesis paintings. Naomi knew Byanka and her oeuvre intimately. She spoke of the difficult artistic decisions her roommate had made, of the need for balance of shape and color, of the clear influence of the New York school, whatever that meant. She joked about the deceptive simplicity of the letter G. The idea was that the more you left out, the more you said. Naomi understood everything Byanka had poured into that painting: the angle on the canvas, the thickness of its line, the contrast of its off-white background, the fading color on the G's inside hook. I found myself strangely jealous of that letter G. I wanted to be known as affectionately in this woman's eyes.

One of my aunts asked Naomi where her own paintings were. She led us down to the end of the row. Our leather shoes, following the brazen clunking of Naomi's clogs, squeaked across the worn grey cement. We all fell silent when we approached her pieces, nodding as we took them in. Naomi was now working exclusively in watercolors, her thesis comprised of a series of very large fruit stand paintings. *Monday Market: Üsküdar. Tuesday Market: Kadıköy. Thursday Market: Beşiktaş.* The idea was trite, kitschy; but the more I stared the more the paintings took hold of me with their odd energy. They were different from anything I'd seen of hers, and better. The subject was the barest excuse for the work. The essence of these market paintings, I understood in my own slow way, was their colors and lines, the playful dance of all this jumbled fruit and wood and texture. There was vitality here, a vitality Byanka's overly conceptual work had lacked. With Naomi's paintings nobody asked for an explanation. The more I looked the more I loved them. I loved the colors and the light and their whimsy. I loved their utter uselessness. During these years of graduate school my own designs had been driven by purely practical impulses: loads and materials and the weights they could bear.

My Uncle Haim was impressed too. He had his hands thrust deep in his pockets, and he was smiling. "Cezanne?" he asked Naomi. "Or Van Gogh? The Post-Impressionists, right?"

"It's possible she just likes fruit," I whispered to myself.

At my side Naomi broke into laughter, her cheeks coloring as she looked at me. "Exactly, Avram. I *do* just like fruit. Pomegranates especially. See, you pretend you don't understand." She turned to Uncle Haim and winked at him. "I try not to be categorized."

As everyone shuffled back down the aisle I hung back, pretending to lose myself in the melons of *Tuesday Market: Kadıköy*. When I looked Naomi was still there, a few steps to my right.

"And how are you, Avram?"

"Good. Nothing changes."

"Graduating this year, then?"

"Yes."

"Any word from your brother?" she asked, in her disarmingly direct manner. She wanted me to know she didn't fear the subject.

Yusuf's company was earning a profit. He had been disqualified from military service, and had used those extra years granted him to co-found a computer start-up. Systems integration for international clients. While I was still living at home, post-army, with my father, safely ensconced in the cocoon of the familiar, my little brother could already afford his own apartment — sailing brazenly off on a life for himself. Our paths crossed at parties of relatives and at weddings, occasionally at *Pesa* or *Kipur* services, where we sat in separate rows. Yusuf would grace us with his presence at some bar mitzvah, reeking of confidence and mettle, his arm around this or that stilletoed young beauty, and two weeks later we'd spot him in Ortaköy, holding the elbow of some other former school-mate of mine, women I could barely recognize in the perfumed bloom of their adulthood.

Our community was small enough that Yusuf had run through nearly all of our attractive friends — and their friends as well. I heard whisperings that certain mothers in our congregation had forbidden their daughters from seeing him.

"He's fine. Getting around, you know."

Naomi was silent for a moment. I thought she was edging towards an apology, and I wanted to save us both from that. "You can sell some of these," I said, pointing up at her work. "They're very good. For watercolors, that is."

She laughed. "I wanted to see how far I could take a simple medium. But my stuff isn't commercial. It's more the kind of thing, I don't know, you'd hang in the bathroom or something."

"I'd buy it. This one. *Tuesday*. What are you charging?"

Naomi stood, urbane, straight-backed, on rigid legs. "I'm honored Avram. Let me think about it. You know how it is. It'd be difficult to part with, for any price."

She smiled and I turned to leave. She walked behind me a few steps; and before we reached my family she had taken my wrist and asked me to one of our old cafés.

12

A Fruity Haze

W E   H A D   T E A together in Tophane, a few blocks down from the university, among the seaside hookah stands we once frequented, back in our early college days. We sat on little wooden stools, a foot off the ground. I leaned my beaten portfolio against the low table. The water of the straits ran in silvery lines before us, and in its glinting current a plastic Gazoz bottle dragged itself by. Naomi drank her tea strong, a dark brown, without a single cube of sugar. Puffs of smoke from nearby *nargiles* dissolved around us in a fruity haze.

She asked me about school, exactly what kind of architect I was hoping to become. Crossing my elbows on the low table, I fumbled for an answer. I'd have my degree in six months, but I had yet to consider the question with any seriousness. Architecture, I told her, was just a career; and I'd half chosen it just to please my father. It would lead to something interesting, or lucrative — maybe both. What that might be was not entirely in my control. I had to see who would hire me, where I wound up, where my studies led. Naomi disagreed. Everything is in our control, she said. I could do whatever I wanted, wherever I wanted to do it. Didn't I have my own *aspirations*? Didn't I want a license for my own *private* practice? What kind of buildings did I dream of designing?

"Actually," I said, "I just like playing with the drafting tools. Twirling the compass around the paper. Dragging a pencil along a T-square. I forget myself in all that. Sweeping the rubber flecks off the paper with the duster brush. You know that sound?"

She did. Naomi adjusted her glasses and smirked at me. Her chin was delicate, pointed, a touch paler than the red in her face. I imagined touching my lips to it, and then to her cheeks. I watched that chin as she filled me in on her own plans. Once she had her Masters she was ready to head to the capital, where her parents had moved and her Father now managed a textile plant. They were overbearing, it had been nice to have had this distance, but with every year apart she missed them more. They didn't want her to work. They believed in her talents; at least they said they did. They'd be happy if she just lived with them and painted. It suited her too. She had projects in mind — a *world* of projects. There were too many subjects to fit into a single lifetime of painting. She might take a trip to Cappadocia. She was thinking of a series of paintings of the ancient caravans and cave churches. Down the road she'd have to support herself. For now, she could just be an artist. It might be the only time in her life she could call herself that. We had to make the most of the time we were given, hadn't we?

Over the second cup of tea she asked after my father. She'd been taking a jewelry design course last semester. "A little hobby. I'm no good at it at all. In fact, I stink. Oh, I have so many *questions* for him. You think he'd mind?"

I told her there was nothing in the world my father would rather talk about than jewelry.

I shook my head, returning her grin. To our left a wizened man with a long white beard sat down and, after examining his *nargile*, ordered a strawberry tobacco. Mangy dogs and cats were lounging beside the tables like sultans of the café. "I should go," I started.

Naomi stopped me, her palm on my wrist. "Forgive me Avram."

I was biting the inside of my bottom lip.

"Your brother — it was my biggest mistake."

I swirled the residue of tea and sugar in my empty glass.

"You know I tried once, to paint Yusuf's portrait. In oil. It came out very very ugly."

I forced a laugh. "I'm sure the painting was good."

"It was so bad he broke up with me just after."

"He breaks things off with everyone. It's his unique gift."

"I've promised myself I won't paint portraits. Fruit — at least it's safe."

I smiled into my tea glass. "So that's the new rule? No portraits, then?"

"Yes, the new rule. I refuse to do portraits."

"Not even mine?" I lifted my chin in profile.

She removed her glasses, brushed aside her sharp bangs, and tilted her lovely, out-of-focus eyes at me. "For you, Avram, I might make one last exception."

We saw each other once a week, then twice a week, and pretty soon nightly. Naomi had been attending Temple Tiferet Israel, but on Friday nights she now came to our smaller, family synagogue. Those nights she ate dinner with me and Father in our apartment; and at his insistence led us in the Shabat prayers. Hearing them sung once again, in a woman's voice, in our kitchen, touched me deeply. For one of her fine arts courses she was making an *ogadera*, an Ottoman Jewish marriage ornament, and she held long consultations with Father over the clasps and chains. He eventually took her half-formed pieces with him to a jeweler friend in the Covered Bazaar, where he had them adjusted so that the clasps would properly close. In less than two months Naomi would be graduating and moving to the capital. I had no idea, with her half a country away, how I'd make it through my final semester of graduate school.

On the day she was leaving, I proposed.

13

The Receiving Line

THE FIRST JOB I landed in the capital I took; and during our year-long engagement Naomi and I saw nothing of Yusuf. We were planning a modest affair: the civil ceremony at the state marriage house, followed one week later by a service at Naomi's family synagogue, then a dinner party at a fish restaurant called Yeni Hamsıköy. It would take us a year to save for it.

I'd been following through Father the rapid trajectory of Yusuf's career. Disqualified from military service, Yusuf had thrown his full weight into his computer start-up. Systems Integration, for international clients, a growing number of whom were seeking footholds in our emerging market. Yusuf and his partner Ali, a computer freak, were living in and working out of a dingy two-room apartment/office in Sirkeci. Yusuf once showed Father around. There was little more to see than four computers, and reams of paper spilling out of a grinding printer, and empty plastic Burger King cups, and half-eaten Whoppers fermenting in their cardboard containers. That was his Company. Father had held his breath at the stench. But supposedly there were two large accounts already under contract. They had been putting in twenty-hour workdays, seven days a week, for months.

So when Yusuf fell ill and had to be hospitalized, Father guessed he might have run himself down. "Until we started this thing I never had any real sense how much money's actually out there," he'd told Father in the hospital. "I'll be honest. I got a bit carried away."

It was pneumonia, and would turn out to be one of the more dangerous episodes in his life. I would not go see Yusuf myself. I held my ground through my brother's first precarious week in the hospital. I knew our estrangement was taking its emotional toll on Father — who wanted only that his sons be civil, if not close again, capable of sitting down to a dinner together and not, say, murdering each other. I no longer knew if that was possible. But Father could not give up on his son. He visited Yusuf in the German Hospital every day after work, and when we spoke he would urge me to join him, as if I might suddenly and dramatically hop on the overnight train. I tried to convince Father that he, too, had been taken advantage of. No one should put up with so many years of abuse, not even a parent. Father agreed but said that, when it comes to the responsibilities owed to a life one has tossed indiscriminately into this world, a parent must see it through to the end.

"If something happens to Yusuf now," he warned me, "if he doesn't make it through this spell — for the rest of your days you'll regret being so vindictive."

I said I doubted it.

"He's dying; it'll haunt you. You'll regret it. You will. Whatever you think of him, he's still your brother."

"He's always dying," I said. "Baba, he's been dying his whole life."

The second Tuesday Yusuf's prognosis had grown dire, and on the phone Father more forcefully insisted Naomi and I visit, and immediately. He didn't understand how we could stay away.

"It eats at me," I said. "It eats and eats away at me. I've decided I help Yusuf more by steering clear. It's the best thing for both of us. An unspoken arrangement we've settled on. I send him my prayers, for this life and the next. It's enough."

Two weeks after he'd been admitted Yusuf decided he would not yet be inconvenienced by death, and was released. His doctors warned him he was going to have to take it easy, if he didn't want to hurt himself.

When it came now to our approaching wedding, I told Father I'd leave Yusuf's invitation up to the bride. Despite his recent illness, Naomi wouldn't budge on the matter.

Nevertheless, during the service, beside the *hupa*, as Father and my in-laws were raising the prayer shawl over our heads, I spotted my brother in the back row sitting beside Uncle Haim. He'd come. Yusuf had his arms crossed on his chest, and he was smiling in a way that unnerved me. Naomi and I signed the marriage contract with slightly trembling hands; I presented the ring to her father; and after the blessings, side by side we turned our backs to the crowd and faced the Torah. Our families joined us: Naomi's to her left, Father to my right. Gazing beyond the marriage canopy, towards the door draped with the Star of David, opened something new in me: relief. The love of a beautiful woman had immunized me against all resentments. Let him be here. At this bittersweet moment, the most hopeful of my life, I couldn't bother worrying over him, way back there, behind me. Let him witness our joy. I considered the success of the wedding in moving me beyond the childhood spats, the games of brinksman-ship, the deeply entrenched grievances. Who had time for any of that now? I was docked at last in the safe harbor of marriage. Life pointed in one direction: forward.

He waited for us as we assembled for the *kortej*, and towards the end of the receiving line he approached. Startled at the sight of him, Naomi stiffened beside me, but she bravely smiled and accepted his hand. He held it in his double grasp and spoke pas-sionately for a moment about how he wished Mother could be there with us that day, to experience the happiness of her son. "My noble brother," he called me, turning to Naomi's parents, but still not releasing her hand. "A good man. A loyal man. The kind of man you'd want to marry. A man any mother would be glad to call her son." In his gravelly, breaking voice, his words brought tears to my in-laws' eyes.

Naomi was attempting a smile that I alone understood was a scowl. Finally releasing her hand, he leaned in to kiss her. In her brilliant white wedding dress she ducked her chin shyly for a good-natured moment, then glanced at me. My face was stone. To be done with it she leaned slightly forward and succumbed. My brother pressed his lips to my wife's cheek.

It might have only been a peck, but it seemed to linger. I watched it with astonishment. "Enough!" I called out — I couldn't help myself by now — and separated them. I raised a bit of a scene, and shoving Yusuf at the chest backwards away from the *kortej* I found myself whispering, "Who do you think you are, coming here like this? Who the hell do you think you are?" Around me the celebratory chatter collapsed.

For months afterwards, the first months of my marriage, I

would be stuck in the strait-jacket of that moment. I could not stop replaying in my mind: his nerve showing up, his unrelenting grasp, the kiss, the struggle, the image of my brother in his silk Italian suit, his arms splayed, a bewildered smile on his tanned, wet, hawkish face. I worried that in the depths of Naomi's heart that kiss might long resonate. That despite her denials she might have felt something, might have been moved in ways she would never admit. I worried Naomi would always wonder what kind of life she might have led if it had worked out with the other Benezra. I told myself I was being ridiculous. But Naomi's hatred of Yusuf always ran a touch too deep, as if she too worried what wild regrets might consume her were we to have anything more to do with the man.

Our Blue Cruise honeymoon along the Turquoise Coast had been disastrous. I grew ineffectual, incapable of love. Naomi was distraught, and accused me of obsessing; but I knew she felt the insult as deeply as I had.

"Forget him," she pleaded. "Cut him out. He's dead to us. Can we leave it at that?"

14

Doubly Blessed

WE WERE NOT the famous artist and successful architect my wife had assured me we would become. We were hacks. We struggled with money back then. And we were childless: the years of my first job and our first apartment stretched across a barren, dusty Anatolian plain. We would not be blessed with children for seven years — and for each of those years we believed more emphatically and with greater resignation they might never come. So we sank ourselves into work and let it consume us. Naomi taught after-school art lessons to diplomats' kids, until the commissions from the sales of her paintings freed her. Unencumbered by the responsibilities of family, capable of longer hours than my co-workers, I moved steadily from my first job as a drafting assistant to project leader with a new firm, where I would stay on for the next seventeen years, designing jails.

So when children did come — two at once — it was a joyous surprise, a reprieve, and I thanked the Lord for saving us from the dreary routine life had been reduced to. Naomi's art was put on hiatus. She had a new project. In those exhausting first weeks she nursed and cared for the babies with an intensity and passion I'd rarely seen. Reenergized, I followed her lead. As newborns the girls took their bottles from me half the time, and when they did I saw the yellow flecks in their eyes as if dipped from Naomi's brush. When they reached and kicked I admired the strange angles and post-modern curves of their arms and legs. It thrilled me to hold them together on my knees, to ponder the pair of them, to understand that beneath these lives we had created lurked mysteries the study of painting and architecture had ill-prepared us for. Art that squirmed and hungered. Naomi's masterpiece, I thought.

They were fraternal, but looked so much alike people thought they were identical. Straight from the womb they had lots of hair: Estela's were thin strands of short gold, Sara's slightly darker and longer, with streaks that lightened in the central Anatolian sun. Those first weeks when I was alone with them I used to brush this hair up and down, across and back, with a soft-bristled plastic brush the hospital had provided. I had never imagined I would do such a thing. In one sudden rush, like spilled cement, the twins had filled the rough holes of our existence.

We were doubly blessed: they were perfect. And as a father I felt every little thing that threatened this perfection had to be dealt with swiftly but with measured care. For I now better understood what my own father had endured with Yusuf, and the reasons why.

Three weeks after Sara and Estela were born the crying began, and for three months it did not stop. The doctor told Naomi it was colic. The girls' cries — violent, end-of-the-world shrieks

— tore at my gut. Our apartment became a madhouse: crying in every direction, in stereo, at all hours day and night. We found out by chance the only thing that would quiet the girls were rides up and down the elevator. When I could no longer handle the screaming I would take one of the twins. "What floor?" some kind neighbor would ask me. "Ground floor please." Down we'd go, but when the elevator slowed and its door lurched open I would not get out. The neighbor would squint at me. I'd press fifteen, and ride it up again, then down again, until Sara or Estela calmed. It was the only peace I knew.

With me on that elevator I eventually took an *AutoCAD Quick Reference Guide* I'd long needed to memorize. I brought along a folding stool. When I returned home from the job, up and down I would ride, sitting, reading, bouncing the baby in my arm, until whichever twin I was holding finally nodded off. At the apartment door Naomi would pass me the other screaming child. Praying one would not wake the other, I'd pull the quick switch, and I'd ride the elevator again, swinging, burping, singing like a lunatic at all hours of the night. I got to know the intimate routines and secret habits of many of our neighbors. They'd praise to the hilt the baby girl in my arms, then add a hearty "*Maşallah!*" to protect her from the evil eye. Sometimes it took up to an hour before a child fell off — especially Estela, forever the stubborn one. If we were lucky, back in the apartment we'd have fifteen minutes. Sprawled on the bed in the same sour milk-stained pajamas she'd been wearing for two straight months, Naomi would try to shut her eyes. And then one of the girls would wake; and the pressure inside my head would build once more.

In the elevator late one night somewhere in those delirious months I had a vision of my brother as an infant. I was too young when Yusuf was born for any of it to be accurate; but still, I was certain I could recall his staccato cough as a baby, and how it must have been so worrying, for so long, for our poor mother. How had she managed? She might have told herself — as I now did, in the elevator, during the breaths between every bracing scream — that when Yusuf finally quieted they were over the worst of it. That maybe this was the last attack and there would be stillness to come. That maybe he would sleep through this night, breathing freely on his own. I now understood, stricken child or not, every parent prays for this and this alone.

Through the days and nights of elevator rides and diapers and crawling and cruising and first steps Naomi praised me as a dutiful father. Endlessly patient, she bragged to friends. Caring. Empathetic. Dedicated. But I felt none of that. I felt panicked. I felt the urgency of getting the twins through the day safely, not run over by shared-taxis, not electrocuted by lamp wires, not choked by a lethal mouthful of squash or chicken *kebap*. Even when we moved beyond the incessant crying, the nightly satisfaction of closing my eyes to sleep meant only that we had conquered a single day.

For everything needed ceaseless attention. During the Age of Colic, crying so much and so fiercely, the girls would scratch their faces. Naomi and I bickered about the cause. It seemed to me their nails were always too long. Estela was the worst. She'd slit disturbing lines of red from cheek to eye. I worried these cuts would scar — but really, by the next day you could hardly see the scratch. An infant's skin healed that quickly. Once, rushing out to work, I reminded Naomi to take care of the twins' nails, and that night I found she had resorted to socks on their hands. Squeamish, she couldn't cut fingernails with a scissors, afraid the child would jerk away and she'd take off a finger.

So keeping the nails short was my responsibility. I grew to enjoy it actually, and became quite skillful. Estela was a power-house. How she squirmed! I'd have to wrestle her down, wrap her on my lap in a contortion that immobilized her arms or legs. Sara was the obedient one — so much so that by the time she turned three she was helping me cut her own toenails. I'd snip an edge, and she would tug it off with her little finger and hand me the lint-like shaving. "One more, Baba! Cut one more!"

Caught in the hurricane swirl of fatherhood, I had no time to think of Yusuf. Then, before I knew it, word reached me from home: my brother was no longer merely doing well — he was now officially a multi-millionaire. He and his Whopper-breathed partner had just sold their start-up for 25 million dollars to a British venture capitalist. With his share of the money Yusuf had taken a leap into telecommunications, laying the groundwork for what would become the upstart behemoth Teletürk.

This apparently had all happened while I was cutting toenails.

And with the news Father informed me of one last thing con-cerning my brother. His wealth firmly established, his celebrity growing, Yusuf had changed his surname.

"He no longer goes by Benezra in the magazines," Father was yelling into the phone, his voice catching. "He goes by Elmas."

"Elmas?"

"Look it up. Yusuf Elmas, CEO and founder of Teletürk Holdings. That's his name now. It's what he calls himself."

"Ridiculous."

"It's very sad. He won't return my calls."

"Yusuf Elmas." I tasted the bitter words on my lips. I swallowed them down, and said nothing more. What else was there to say? I found myself laughing a disengaged laugh.

Let him try it! I thought. If discarding the past was as simple as crossing out a name and writing in a new one, let him try. The gesture was futile. The press praised him as a self-made man. No such thing existed. *We* made Yusuf the man he'd become. He might have changed what people called him; but how could he rewrite the hours and days he had lived among us? He might have dismissed his ancestry; but how could he deny the long waves of lineage and tragedy that had settled him here, in this country that enabled his fortune? He might have risen above his disease; but how could he rid himself of the two mutated genes lodged in every cell of his person? And how could he forget the ill-will he had stoked in exchange for our care? How could he erase the thousand missteps of his youthful pride? Let him change his name. Let him deny that for ten years his mother and his brother had clapped his back, morning and night, to clear his lungs. Let him deny that his father had sacrificed every extra lira to the altar of his good health. We'd be with him to the end, whatever he chose to call himself.

On the phone I sensed the immense sadness in Father's voice, a tone I hadn't heard since the year of Mother's passing. He was clearly struggling with it. Analyzing motives. Rationalizing defenses. Trying to imagine how the exigencies of business in Eastern Europe might necessitate such a gesture. A Jewish name after all helped nobody. No, Yusuf's petty act did not reflect a complete turning away from us. It was just a pretense. It's what famous people did these days. Someone probably talked him into it, perhaps for legal reasons. I said nothing to convince Father otherwise. I knew the truth. It would take him months to admit it, but eventually he, too, understood.

"How could he do this to me?" he asked.

And this, the final rejection, was more than our steadfast father could bear. He never spoke to my brother again.

Book IV

1

Tectonic Instability

At nights now the villa was silent, harboring its age-old secrets. Alone in the mansion I took the measure of the shadowed rooms. It had been a tumultuous century for the Halim Pasha House: a collapsed Ottoman empire, a resurgent Republic, two world wars, three revolutions, a massive earthquake, then five years of complete neglect. Around its empty hallways I felt the sadness of the place, its isolation, in my joints.

After a day of work I crashed now, in a calcified sweat, on a sofa in the mansion's frigid office, pulling one of the ancient velvet pillows beneath my head. I'd found I couldn't get to sleep up in my brother's bedroom, up on Yusuf's sour-smelling mattress. Downstairs, alone with the ghosts in the echoing villa, I'd turn over in my head what to do with this place. The possibility of selling the mansion and returning a new man to Naomi still hung in the back of my mind: a fallback option, should I be unable to get Father to move out here. I would get in touch with a real estate lawyer, talk to my bank about an appraisement.

But the mansion would be difficult to part with, at any price.

All the tinkering and scouring was leading to thoughts of larger renovations. One sleepless evening I was overcome by a sudden urge to sketch out the blueprints of the house. Forget patches and tiny repairs. Forget its long history. Forget 19th Century architectural integrity. The place could clearly be modernized, enhanced, updated. In the stale light of Yusuf's office I found a notebook of graph paper, settled myself at the escritoire, and began drafting a new open-design concept for the downstairs. The late hours passed, the pencil sweaty in my hand, the eraser worn down to a nub. My first large-scale project, I decided, would be to remove a slice of nonbearing wall to replace the two cramped sea-facing rooms — this office and the maid's quarter — with one extended bedroom, carving out a place where my father might comfortably live on the first floor. As I now sketched it the single room would have fourteen windows, ten facing the sea and two each to the east and west — an impressive space, light and airy, easily accessible through sliding glass doors to the outdoor living area, and larger than the basement apartment I had forced him into. In summers it would benefit from the natural ventilation of the ground floor. Additional windows would bring light deeper into the house, make the open space feel larger from the inside than its footprint would suggest. We could use roll-down rain screens for inclement weather. Father, I thought, would like these. I drew them in.

Bleary-eyed, I placed the pencil down, returned to the couch and stretched out. I found myself mentally lining everyone in the family up in their proper places, like wooden soldiers conforming to a revised martial strategy. Father would live without complaint in these updated rooms I'd designed for him. Naomi would visit, taking my hand as I gave her the grand tour, won over by the work I had performed as a loyal son and inspired architect. My daughters would come crashing through the French doors, shouting for their grandfather, tracking water from the pool onto the expensive kilims, eliciting only our laughter. We'd sit out in the evenings on the back patio as a family, the sports pages on my lap, a sketch pad on Naomi's, listening to our daughters enjoying on the radio the latest hits of some god-awful British boy band.

Now I gave up on any attempt at sleep and pulled out from under the couch, where I kept it, the box of dead letters the postman had given me on my first week on the island. Yet again I found myself flipping through those dire warnings. *Tectonic and Geological Instability. Excessive seismicity of the Marmara Region…One of the most seismically active zones of the world… The sea itself formed by tectonic shifts 2.5 million years ago…. Dangers of strike-slip faulting…. Remaining fault strain to be released by some future seismic event….Grabens, fault offsets, and structural topomorphological features at the bottom of the Marmara confirm branch movement of the North Anatolian fault…. Government programs must undertake extensive review…. Necessary steps to mitigate the effects of large-scale tsunamis…*

Why had he left father, in his will, this doomed island home? How to reconcile the glorified public image of my brother with the private man who had lived here, between these cracking walls, soliciting such reports? The technocrat addressed in these letters — *Monsieur Elmas, Herrn Elmas, Honorable Yusuf Elmas* — had been touted as forward looking, ahead of his time, predicting the winds of technology. Everything could be improved, reformulated, recast. A newer version of Teletürk's premium cellular phones appeared every six months, pumped full of fresh features — texting, voice dialing, built-in cameras. Broadband speeds increased faster than customers could sign up for new plans. Entire blocks of the city were transformed into Teletürk wireless zones. Even here, on the island, the stock of antique mansions could be secured against an earthquake. Forward, forward, forward! A necessary optimism, in the face of what he knew.

Yet at the same time he'd been completely reckless. In the end someone or something had spun him back around, back towards us, his past, and he had wanted me in on it. *A word, just a word.*

Nearly 3 AM, on the edge of sleep. Letters scattered on my chest, letters on the cushions, letters on the floor, useless letters all around me. I collected them into the box, and kicked it back under the couch with my heel. I turned to the desk, and willed the phone to ring. I imagined talking to him this time very rationally, very patiently, giving him a moment, giving him his word, and having my answers. We'd talk like brothers should.

2

Nothing Leaves this House

THROUGH A SUNNY January now with the help of my time-worn crew I had spent six weeks clearing the detritus. Mustafa Faik did his best to tackle the ruins of the gardens, but by late morning the old man would tire of his scything. Nılay Gören, resolutely avoiding any task too physical, offered us generous criticism and moral support. We all put up with it. Flora Demirkan, unflappable, was the only one still pouring herself into the work. Scrubbing the window panes. Dragging rugs outside to the patio to beat them with spatulas. Working with rags on her hands and knees to scrape caked dirt from behind the radiators. Whatever memories may have been settling now for five years amid the dust balls and mouse droppings of these rooms she attacked with renewed zeal.

Every renovation has its challenges. For my part, I'd had a frustrating accident. I'd hired three men to help repair and weather-proof the floating dock, and when I was inspecting their work the first day one of the rotting, splintered boards had given out beneath me. My foot went straight through to the water, tearing open my pants and slicing a gash from shin to knee. At the small island clinic a pretty nurse removed three ugly wooden splinters with oversized tweezers and then, haphazardly, stitched up my leg. The nurse warned me not to bathe until the wound closed, and that I could shower only if I covered the lesion with plastic bags and rubber bands. I couldn't be bothered. I stopped bathing for the time being — then I stopped shaving too. Who did I have to impress?

Forced to take on less physical work, I'd settled on repairing the stenciling of the faded master bedroom walls, retracing their repeating patterns of lavender floral sprays. The job would be meditative, I reasoned, but even this simple task turned out to be difficult. By the second day it was painful to climb the step ladder, painful to stand on it in a prolonged fixed position. And each repair of the stenciling only suggested another; each improvement revealed how far I still had to go.

Now, limping around the mansion, wincing with each step, I wondered if I'd taken on too much. The novelty of the work had worn thin. The truth seized upon me: I was doing here only what I'd always done, cleaning up some enormous mess my brother had left behind.

By mid-afternoon I gave up on the stenciling, and went back downstairs.

In the foyer I nearly ran into Flora, who was rushing back upstairs with a folded stack of clean-smelling sheets. We exchanged tired smiles. The far window up the stairs was cracked open, so a cold refreshing draft chilled the damp space. I wiped my forehead and slouched down against the teak door in an exaggerated gesture of exhaustion, taking the weight off my leg. To my surprise Flora slid down too, plopped the pile of sheets to her side, and sat across the hall from me, knees drawn to her chest.

"How's the leg?" she asked. "Infected, I bet. You're limping worse today."

"No, it's better," I lied.

"You shouldn't be climbing ladders and stairs. Let me take a look at it."

"I'm fine."

We sat for a few moments, catching our breaths.

"It's so damn quiet when we're working here," Flora said. The collar of her loose cleaning robe sagged damply against her neck.

"Yes, very quiet."

"Today I realized what it is. The birds." She indicated the antique birdcages with her chin. The empty cages had been lined up with martial precision in the far corner of the hallway, waiting for me to decide what to do with them. "They were Yusuf's gifts to her, you know."

"Gifts?" She nodded. Cautiously I asked, "But why keep the birds here...in the mansion? If they were gifts...for her...why didn't she keep them herself?"

Flora swung her hands out towards the bird cages. "He bought her too many," she said, grimacing. "I was fed up caring for so many birds in our little house. They were tormenting my cats, those songbirds. I ordered Yusuf to take them back, every single one of them, every bird. From then on he kept rows and rows of cages here. In the foyer. Over in his office. Even in the kitchen. Stinking birds everywhere. Just to torture me!"

I swiped my palm across the sharp stubble of my chin.

Flora's eyes were tired. She sat rubbing a finger along the sole of her cheap slippers.

I'd noticed the bitter strain in her voice, remembering my reflexive assumptions when I'd first learned of Yusuf's partner-in-death. *So he had taken down with him some desperate whore of his, half his age, one of his toys, a daughter of a Greek Coca Cola magnate. Such a disgrace! The shamelessness!* The news had been clear affirmation of the man he'd become. It had fit the vision of my brother I'd formed in his absence. I remembered Father, on hearing it, had remained steady. "*Tabii.* How like him. One who is born a donkey dies a donkey." Yusuf's name was rife with scandal. We were wholly prepared to accept the worst.

Now I saw that her daughter's real connection to my brother remained a gap in the official accounts of Yusuf's last days. Yasemin Demopoulous might not have been the starry-eyed hanger-on, the aspiring celebutante that the press had led us to believe.

Casually I passed the back of my hand over the recently waxed floor, cool to the touch. I bent my bad leg up to my chest, stretched it down to the floor, then up again, testing the wound. Flora watched me for a moment. I'd learned to wait out these silences. I was determined not to drive her away with the wrong questions. In truth, I'd become fearful of losing her company. I focused on my leg: bent it again, stretched it, flexed it again, winced.

"I was always upset by his relationship with the kids," Flora said. "If the man had wanted a family, he could have had one."

I sighed, hauled myself up, turned my back on her, and walked over to ponder the collection of birdcages. I twisted open one of the miniature gates, closed it, locked it, and opened it again, testing the spring mechanism.

"He didn't need to be messing around all the time with mine."

I reached inside a different cage and adjusted the porcelain water dish.

"Nothing he did for my daughter, for any one of them, was going to change my mind about him."

I gave her a moment, examining this cage. It was made not of rattan, but of cheap hollow bamboo which had been spray-painted white. I ran my hand along the outside, along the hidden cracks covered by paint. The knots where the twisted rattan connected were deceptively sharp.

"Are you listening to me?" she asked.

"If you have something you need to tell me, Flora, then say it. If you don't trust me, then don't. You can leave any time." I limped back over to her, and slid down beside her against the wall, our shoulders nearly touching now. "I understand how hard it's been."

And I promised her. Nothing would leave this house.

3

Yasemin's Songbirds

"Wʜᴀᴛ ʏᴏᴜ ʜᴀᴠᴇ to understand, Avram, was that, from the start, she was his favorite. He spoiled the girl."

Yasemin was nine when Flora had taken the job. She'd become a fixture in the mansion. Visiting business associates assumed the girl was related to the billionaire. Yusuf treated her as if she were. He would give Yasemin money to take her brothers and sisters to the open air summer movies, where they gorged themselves on melon seeds. He bought her a Carrefour army tent for the class camping trip to Şile. He spent a month of Sunday afternoons teaching the older children how to swim, and when they mastered the breast stroke and the butterfly he bought Yasemin diving equipment and registered her for weekend Bubblemakers Diving classes in Ataköy. The girl invited him once to the Feast of St. George, and it became their yearly tradition to meet at the peak before the dawn mass. She had celebrated her thirteenth birthday at the mansion's pool — back then a fragrant oasis surrounded by blooming wisteria and lit by hanging lanterns. It had been the grandest pool party the island kids had ever known.

The entire staff was there, plus Flora's children, as well as eighteen of Yasemin's girlfriends from the village. Yusuf himself grilled the *sucuk* and corn for the children.

As a gift that day he'd bought Yasemin her first two bulbuls from the pet bazaar in Kadıköy; and he continued to buy her a different bird for each birthday and New Year: an African Grey who bit its own toenails, two Military Macaws who ruffled their chest feathers in waves, a pair of baby lovebirds that yawned when you rubbed beneath their ears, and a Lemon Crested Cockatoo that repeated the muezzin's call to prayer. These were the gifts Flora later insisted her daughter return. So the Halim Pasha House became filled with the music of Yasemin's songbirds.

"They were everywhere," Flora said, "those stupid birds. Twittering. Screeching. Stinking up the foyer. You couldn't escape them."

I'd struck a new vein in the story. Now that I started asking around the island, I was treated to elegiac memories of the girl, which I could piece together to form a half-finished mosaic: Yasemin wearing her long dark ponytail braided straight back through her Nike baseball caps. Yasemin riding behind her little brother Sarp on a bicycle built for two, screaming at him to pedal faster. Yasemin carrying groceries home from the Thursday Bazaar, an array of plastic bags dangling from her wrists to her elbows: bags full of Frosties and Ciokella for her brothers, bags full of *börek* with cream for her mother.

Everyone recalled the lost girl with affection. Many islanders remembered the perpetual fox smile on Yasemin's bright young face. The constant cry of exasperation — "Uff yah!" — that she had learned from Flora. The waiters at Ali Baba remembered greeting her on the pier with a slight punch on the shoulders, which even as a young child she didn't hesitate to return. Mustafa Faik recalled her fetching the guards the Sunday newspapers and refusing to accept their tips. "A smart girl doesn't need a dowry," she'd chide him.

Yasemin as a five-year-old with her nails already painted. Running around in sneakers without socks, pushing her little bothers and sisters in their makeshift strollers past the İnci Pastanesi and the PTT. Stopping to pet every stray island cat that crossed her path, and feeding cookies to the horses pulling the flower seller's cart. Directing the movers, who rolled appliances off the ferries on hand-carts, to this or to that mansion — and keeping perfect track of the gleaming washers and driers, the stainless steel refrigerators and flat-screen televisions, the water heaters and Jacuzzi baths, so that by the age of eleven the girl had an exhaustive knowledge of every island villa and the make of its bathroom sink.

Who on the island didn't know her well? And knowing her, who could *refrain* from spoiling her? The baker at Büyükada Fırını sneaking an extra *poğaca* into her school bag. The Yunus Ice Cream vendor sculpting her ices into a double rose. Her haggling the Bostan vegetable seller down on his artichokes until he'd swing up his palms in frustration and tell Yasemin to leave him alone for once in his life. "We all loved her like a daughter," the vendor remembered, showing me the back of his hand. "Like a daughter you needed to slap."

The skip in her step when she was late and in a hurry. Her flip flops with the pink plastic flowers clapping down the wet pavement. The way she hung her hand at the wrist when she was lost or confused. The Different Kebabs Restaurant owner always screaming at her during the winter rains to put on a jacket. "As children, the other Demirkan kids were brats," the *kebabci* recalled. "It was like they weren't even from the same planet."

One warm morning later that week I stopped by Flora's house to pay her, and she sat me at her little patio table amid the hanging laundry and mewing cats and insisted I drink some herbal tea with her. Along with the tea she brought out first a bowl of roasted pumpkin seeds, and then a wooden box, inlaid with mother of pearl, full of loose papers.

"Here," she said, "I don't have it in me to look at these any more."

The box was filled with the scattered debris of parenthood: Polaroids, certificates, report cards, Children's Day awards. (In our house Naomi kept such papers in a manila folder labeled "Important Junk!") I found among the papers loose photographs of Flora's children across the years. Sipping from my fluted glass, I flipped silently through a pile of the curling, yellowing prints. Among shots of children I saw Yasemin as a honey-skinned five-year-old with her *Need a Hug?* T-shirt, her pink Barbie Backpack, her denim skirts and puff-ball socks. I saw the young girl brushing out her mother's courtyard with a pail of water and a straw broom. I saw her sipping on a sour cherry juice, up at the Monastery of St. George, from a glass she held with two hands. There was a picture of her — she must have been eight, in her blue school vest, navy skirt, and long socks pulled up to her knees — outside the Erinç Pet Shop, letting a parrot kiss her fingernails. In another shot she was posing with the repairman at the Sektor Bike Shop.

"He used to let the kids test his rentals," Flora explained, tapping the photo with a finger, "to make sure the brakes worked down the hills."

"And if they didn't?"

"Didn't what?"

"If the brakes didn't work?"

"I don't know. She'd hop off, I guess."

And there was the requisite picture of the girl, around the age of my own daughters, after the FON Kuaför hairstylist had given her a disastrous permanent. When Yasemin had appeared at the Halim Pasha House with this adult haircut Yusuf had affectionately dubbed her "The Little Princess." This sounded to me like a teasing nickname, but Flora seemed to be suggesting he doted on her eldest daughter a bit too much.

Glancing through these photos in Flora's courtyard I could see my own girls growing up; I could taste my own youthful, short-lived summers on the island. After her chores in the morning — feeding the army of cats, dressing her siblings, fetching milk from the *bakkal* — Yasemin would wander off to school, books pressed to her chest, greeting the men in the shop-fronts by name. By her mother's account Yasemin displayed a sharp intelligence but was not one to give herself over to classwork. Life was too much fun. With each year she grew less studious and more mischievous: spreading false gossip, changing her seats without letting the teacher know, giggling during the national anthem I'd seen the school children sing, as one, on the cracking cement courtyard every Monday morning. "And her mouth!" Flora remembered. "That girl could make the whores of Galata blush. Don't ask me where she got such a mouth from."

Nonetheless, her teachers were won over by the girl's good nature, by her ready smile, and by the focused attention of her eyes when they lectured. They rewarded Yasemin with fives on her report cards. With every year she brought them home, though, she raised further her mother's hopes that this first mistake of a daughter might one day amount to something. Flora could now admit that Yasemin hadn't deserved those grades. She did only what she needed to get by, her highest achievement not Biology or Religion or The History of the Republic but the realization that she could get whatever she wanted by blinking long eyelashes and flashing timely smiles.

In those years Flora's long hours of work and the uninterrupted emergencies of single parenting were beginning to take their toll. By the time Yasemin was fourteen she was coming to the Halim Pasha House after school to help prepare the dinners. Flora had taught her the family recipes, and the girl had long been cooking at home. "To this day Sarp and Feride still tell me they liked their sister's stuffed vegetables better," Flora claimed. "Her cooking is what they remember best. Do you know what it does to me every time they say that? I don't make those dishes any more. I can't compete with her."

Yasemin's help became a welcome relief. On holidays like Şeker Bayram or Kurban Bayram she would join her mother preparing feasts for the mansion's visiting dignitaries and powerbrokers. While the guests ate, mother and daughter waited in the kitchen for the final dishes to be brought back to clean. They played backgammon at the pedestal table to pass the time. Flora could never beat her oldest daughter. She claimed Yasemin had learned how to cheat from her wily brothers. At the end of

the long nights the teenager would sometimes send her mother
home after those games and finish the dishes herself.

"Such a helper. And don't get me wrong. Yasemin had this infectious energy with everyone. Yusuf's eyes would light up when
he saw her. You would have felt exactly the same way about her,
Avram Bey. She was charming. My oldest girl was charming."

"So he treated her like a daughter?" I asked, flipping through
the pictures in Flora's courtyard. It moved me to imagine Yusuf
playing the role of a surrogate father.

"That's what always bothered me. He kept far too much track
of her. He let her do stuff I never would have allowed."

Closely he'd followed Yasemin's test scores and report cards.
When he learned she was struggling with eighth-form algebra, he
rearranged his social calendar and met with her every weeknight
for a month to tutor her. "She has a good mind for math," he'd tell
Flora. "But she says she's going to be a cook, and that she'll be perfectly happy that way, thank you very much." He'd tell Yasemin not
to play a fool. When she said she didn't understand the math, he'd
accuse her of faking. She understood all right. Why should a girl
pretend to be stupid? Where was the ambition in that?"

It wasn't clear whose idea it was for her to take the national private high school entrance exam. Flora seemed to remember pushing her daughter into it. Mustafa Faik recalled the cook
bragging that Yasemin's teachers had signed her up without
asking. "There are scholarships," Flora would remind everyone.
In reality the scholarships were limited and highly competi-
tive; and bright as Yasemin was, for all her self-possession and
steely pride, after seven years of the island's second-rate grammar school she had little shot at winning one. Still, Yasemin

performed well on the exam, if not well enough to secure a place in a top-tier high school.

So when word got out that Flora's oldest daughter had won herself a spot at the Amerikan Collegiate Institute — one of the nation's elite private schools — no one was under any illusion how that slot had materialized. The Institute was Yusuf's alma mater. But tuition cost upward of 16 million lira a year, far out of the range of a single cook, supporting six children, who lived in a backstreet hovel. Soon it was announced that Yasemin Demopoulous had also won the Anadolu Adalar Prize: a scholarship given to a single student from the islands' public schools to attend a high school of his or her choice. A ridiculously generous award — life-changing for a kid from that village — an award that, as far as anyone knew, had never existed before.

While Yasemin was boarding at the Institute, the islanders saw her less and less; and she visited home only on holidays. Yusuf rarely spent holiday nights on the island, and by all accounts had hardly seen Flora's daughter. The girl he'd known for seven years, scuttling in and out of the kitchen, at foot under the servants or repairmen, playing with her myna birds in the grand foyer, making herself perfectly at home in a mansion that was not hers — this girl existed now only as an absence in the creaking memory of the house.

"Who even cared?" Nilay Gören told me. "Yasemin had no time for us anymore. Girls that age — they can hardly put up with an older generation's ramblings long enough to say *merhaba*. When she did stop in she was more formal and studious than we'd ever seen her. It was that snooty school, turning her into something she wasn't. If you ask me she was quickly becoming a snob.

All those English, French, German words. Too big for the island, she probably thought. We had enough snobs bossing us around. We didn't need another one."

Yasemin did return though for the entire second summer, and it was clear to everyone that Flora's daughter was now a young woman in full bloom. In the mansion Yusuf greeted her perfunctorily, with a harrumph and a quick nod and barely a word. He never enquired about her private life in Izmir, her grades, her after-school activities, her roommates. By then Yasemin was earning notoriety in the Institute's Drama Branch, and had joined the Barakuda Scuba Club — the very club my brother had once co-founded. She'd received her diving certification off the Karaburun peninsula. If accomplishments of this kind delighted Yusuf, he didn't show it. It was as if he'd forgotten who was funding her scholarship, or was pretending he didn't know.

"We were servants in the house," Flora explained. "I was perfectly okay with that. But I didn't need him *reminding* my daughter like he did. I mean, suddenly he was treating us so formally. He was treating us like shit."

Mustafa Faik disagreed. "Yusuf Bey had to set some limits. He never said this to me himself. But these women *worked* for him. He couldn't go inviting them to sit at his dinner table with — what? — the Swedish ambassador, could he? He had to establish a firmer line. If Flora blames him now for it, it's out of bitterness. His wasn't charity he liked publicized. Yusuf was a very private man when it came to helping people." Mustafa Faik blinked twice, considering what he'd just said, and flashed me his broken-tooth smile. "He may have already blurred that line a few times, if you know what I mean."

The growing distance perplexed Flora. Yusuf called her daughter *hanımefendim*, no longer using her casual nickname. He returned dishes Yasemin brought him uneaten, and did not express the familiar complaints he'd always used, ("This thing is swimming in red pepper Yasemin!" or "Stir the yogurt, Yasemin. Unstirred yogurt causes heartburn!") He didn't invite Yasemin to sit beside him to chat, as he once had when she was in grammar school. Their relationship had taken a business turn. He was her benefactor, the sponsor of her scholarship, her mother's employer, nothing more.

Flora denied any of it ever bothered her by then, and insisted that she was completely blind to where all of this was leading. "Yasemin was growing up, Avram! She had a million pressures from that private school — making friends, clubs, academics, the university exam that is the state's curse on all our youth. Don't misunderstand: I was grateful for his generosity, but I never asked Yusuf for one single lira. He hardly talked to us anymore. Shit, I was grateful not to have to be constantly thanking him. I don't know what I could have said. 'You've paid a small fortune for my daughter's education, *beyefendim*, and here's some olive oil eggplant?' And at that Amerikan Institute all Yasemin managed were three's on her report card. She couldn't measure up in that school. After that first year she would have been perfectly content to crawl back onto the island without any more of those pressures. I was her mother, and I knew she didn't belong there. Instead Yusuf tossed her out into the big world, away from us. He thought he was doing her some kind of favor. It would have been best if he hadn't picked up the tab. I never, never should have accepted that scholarship. We raised everyone's hopes for the poor girl. It was a lot of pressure. That's not who she was. She wasn't up for it."

I assured Flora all of this was typical of my brother. "To bludgeon someone like that, even when he meant well. But if you were troubled by what was happening, why didn't you just pull her out of that private school?"

"It was prestigious, Avram Bey! But I should have. Absolutely. I should have stood up to Yusuf more. You're right. I should have kept her close to home. Nobody should let a kid that age move half a country away. See, someone like you would have made a good father to the girl. Someone like you would have understood her. Not him. He never did. She was just a charity case, another project for him. He played with my daughter's life."

4

No Fairy Tale Ending

I SOMETIMES USED TO wonder if Mother was disappointed not to have had a daughter. I teased her about this once, on a morning in the *yufkası* when she'd seemed especially low, and she insisted with a weary smile that, no, she'd never wished for such a thing. But I heard the hesitation in her voice. Ours was a household dominated by men and by men's problems. A little girl might have helped restore some balance. I couldn't help thinking later that a daughter might have taken the edge off her grief, provided camaraderie enough to have saved her.

For instance, Mother used to tell us stories from a book she liked to read, the *Oseh Pele*. These were Jewish fairy tales that had made their far-flung way from Spain, had spread throughout the Balkans and into the Ottoman Empire, where they remained firmly lodged all these years in our community. Mother was a good storyteller, and could mimic the voices of knights and princesses with her cigarette-raspy voice. But Yusuf and I never paid much attention, and as an adult I remembered only pieces. There was one strange tale of a young maiden who fell

down a well, then spouted pearls from her mouth and left footprints of gold. There was another story of a great eagle that had
flown out of the clouds and snatched up the son of a rabbi, then
dropped him into the garden of the King of Spain — where he
met his future bride, the King's daughter. Naomi later informed
me that these folktales were meant to prepare adolescents for
married life. If so they were wasted on us, two sons who cared
more about football, martial arts, and lewd comics than about
how luck and destiny drove a marriage.

On the island now I wished I had paid attention to those tales
of my mother. I might not have lost sight of my family, or accepted my daughters slipping so rapidly from my life. I might
have gleaned some ancient wisdom that would have helped put
the brakes on these private disasters, redirected the course of a
marriage cursed from its first moments. As it were, there was no
fairy tale ending here.

Naomi and the twins were finally moving to Tel Aviv. I'd
been away from them for three months, and I no longer had the
power, at this distance, to stop them. They would be staying at
my in-laws' condominium until the furnished rental Naomi had
located became available. We'd keep the apartment in the capital
for the time being. There was some security in that concession
for me, as I imagined there was for Naomi. So I could at least see
the girls before they left the country, she arranged their connecting flight through TAV Airport, and agreed to spend the night.

They arrived on a wet Friday evening. Father and I picked
them up at the airport. In the taxi the twins were slightly shy and
subdued; but maybe they were just echoing the mood of their
parents. Their hair was longer than I remembered it; their jeans

tighter, their black frilled blouses more fashionable — no longer the soft, brightly colored clothing worn by little girls. On our way home we took them to the Pizza Hut on Istiklal for dinner. Sara and Estela shared a salad; and they insisted with complete conviction that we order the *Vejetaryen Spesiyal*, no meat, absolutely no meat. I obliged, but when the meatless pizza came neither twin would touch it. I looked at them each in turn. They looked at their mother for support.

"They're watching their figures," Naomi explained to me, shrugging.

"They're ten years old!"

"It starts now," Naomi said. "What country have you been living in?"

I turned to my father. He was laughing and rubbing his eyes, only half-hearing all this, delighting in his granddaughters and ignorant of the larger implications of this visit. At that moment what he had endured with Yusuf seemed utterly heroic to me. What similar claims of steadfastness could I make as a parent?

I piled three slices of the vegetarian pizza on my plate. Naomi wasn't eating any either. She was leveraging her fork with her long fingers, digging into lettuce leaves and flipping them over, spearing and flipping them back again. Her ring finger, I saw now, was bare.

I ate the tasteless pizza with abandon, far more than I should have, until I'd nearly made myself ill.

At the basement apartment Naomi said kind things about Father's new home and the ways we had appointed it. But her eyes were lowered and she spoke quietly, holding back the suggestions about the half-empty walls and bare bulbs I knew she was formulating. I understood the pity in her tone, borne of regret that she had not been here to properly see to Father's move, to lend the place the comfort of a woman's touch. She loved my father; in moving to Tel Aviv she was abandoning him too, and in refusing to proffer advice, I saw, she was trying to let go.

That night we slept one last time as a family, crammed together in the guest bedroom like some demented pajama party. Naomi and I lay up on the bed, immobile, arms across our chests, while the twins (after some bickering) crashed on the floor around us on puffy piles of blankets. I was awake all night, considering the prospect of living alone, of seeing my daughters in strained circumstances like this once or twice a year. On Yusuf's island, exhausting myself with work on the mansion, speaking to the villagers, living close to my brother's life, none of it yet had seemed to be happening. But now, as I lay in the unfamiliar bedroom, listening to the lovelorn cats wailing outside the window, to the sweet familiar breaths of my sleeping daughters, to the rocky silence of my wife across the demilitarized zone of the bed, the reality settled in. A weight of panic and regret.

I was considering her bare finger that evening. It hurt to remember how I myself had struggled, just out of graduate school, to buy Naomi the largest diamond I could afford, a stone commensurate with my feelings for her. There was no way I could pay for both size and quality. I'd chosen size. It was not huge, but large enough to draw the requisite oohs and ahs from her girlfriends. On more than one occasion I had been with Naomi when she had pressed her fingers together, curled them slightly back, and cooed, "Have you seen the ring my fiancé bought me? A little thing. A little thing." And the person would say, "Wow! Not a little thing at all." And my future wife, this woman of confident charm, this woman nineteen years later I could no longer hold on to, would wink at me and joke, "He'll do better next time."

In the morning I loaded their ridiculously heavy suitcases back into the taxi, and rode with them to the airport. The twins were in a festive mood. They'd been to Israel once before. They associated the place with sunshine, the beach, their grandparents, and pop music in foreign languages. For them it was a holiday, not a life-changing exodus to a nation whose very existence was still imperiled. The flight, of course, was delayed, and in the cavernous International Terminal I was relieved to have a few more moments. I suggested we sit together at the Gloria Jean's coffee stand, but Sara dragged us in the direction of the duty-free stores.

At passport control the guard, checking for boarding passes, held me up and told me I could go no further. I asked if he could make an exception. "I'm the girls' father," I explained. "They need some help with their bags. They want to look in the shops. Just over there. I'd like a few more minutes with them." My voice was dry. "Please," I whispered. The guard inflated his chest and tsked his tongue and flicked his head back: no exceptions could be made to airport security. So in a confusing rush I kissed my daughters there and then, each on the forehead, and waited for them to pass with Naomi through the checkpoint. Estela turned and waved once. Sara, in her excitement, skipping into the Hermes shop, never looked back.

5

Bashing in Walls

ALONE IN THE villa that evening I was not in a reasonable state
of mind. I attempted to sleep once again up in the master bedroom, on my brother's bed. The night was long. I told myself to
go back to the capital, back to the apartment that I owned. It was
time to start piecing together my own life — not his.

But I couldn't face an abandoned home, the twins' room empty,
my empty bed, the hallway photographs of school-posed smiles.
I asked myself if I might pack it all up, ditch this ruined mansion,
head to Israel to be with the girls, let Naomi win this Battle of the
Wills. "Avram," I told myself, "you can't succumb to loneliness so
quickly. What you are doing is not unreasonable. You are an architect, on a perfectly just mission to reclaim property that rightfully
belongs to the family. Whatever happens between you and Naomi,
you've earned your daughters' love with credit to spare. In time
they'll forgive you, as all children eventually do."

An hour later I was still awake, still picturing Sara skipping
into the Hermes store. I gave up on Yusuf's bedroom, and retreated downstairs to the office, armed with a pillow.

I tossed it on the couch. Forget sleep: what I felt like doing was bashing in walls. I examined a section I'd need to knock out in order to open this space into Father's first-floor bedroom. I'd have a go at it in the morning with some kind of sledgehammer. Before I could do that the wall's bookshelves would need to be emptied and disassembled. I found three boxes in the hallway, taped them together, and in an insomniac rage tossed, shoved, and stomped in Yusuf's books, one useless, unread tome after another.

I was working this way, half dazed, when I found I was holding, for the second time, Yusuf's *haftora*. Something seized up in me. I ran my hand over the gold inscribed leather binding. Father would want it; I should be careful it wouldn't be lost. I placed it gently, reasonably, on the writing desk. The next book on the shelf gave me pause as well. It was a green and red hardback, with a bit of yellow paper peeking from its pages.

To Kill A Mockingbird. An English edition. A fat over-arching oak tree sketched across the worn cover. The novel had been required reading in the second-year English courses of our private high schools. I'd struggled with it in the original, in this same edition, and hadn't enjoyed it at all. Years later I read it in Turkish and liked it much better. Yusuf, I remembered, had refused to read it back in Lise 2 — he was busy getting himself thrown out of school at the time. So it was strange to find it still, all these years later, among his possessions.

I flipped through the Harper Lee. Across its brown tea stains, through its smudged dog ears, so many passages had been underlined by so many generations that it seemed most of the text was highlighted. The yellow sheets of legal paper were folded thin, in thirds, at the very back of the ragged pages. Unfolding them, I found the draft of the old English essay I'd glanced at on my first day here, when I'd perused these dusty shelves with Flora at my side. Only now did I look it over more carefully.

On the first lines the student had copied the assignment: *"What are the faults of Atticus Finch in "To Kill A Mockingbird? Does he himself display any prejudices that blind him to certain truths in his community?"*

It was written in a girl's heartbreakingly neat handwriting, in bright purple gel-pen. The kind of pens my daughters squabbled over. Pens unavailable to Yusuf and me back in high school. And the lined yellow legal paper did not feel thirty years old. It was too crisp, the ink too fresh.

As an epigraph she'd written: *"Who, after all, speaks today of the annihilation of the Armenians?" Adolf Hitler — 1942*

There was no name on the front of the draft. Words had been crossed out in blue pencil, sentences scribbled in the margins around what looked like blotches of dried up water stains. I pored over the three pages, translating small sections. *"My great-grandfather had his head crushed with a stone by our gendarmes, and they raped my great-aunt and stole her away too... Back then they took everything they had from us. They took our religion. My family knows this is true...If I were there, should I have loved those people with my generous heart? I'd hate them. We're bound to hate them. Forgiveness isn't strength."*

I turned over the sheets, once, twice, searching for a name on the draft. Nothing.

I didn't need a name. Calmer now than I'd been all night, I folded it back up, tucked it into the book, closed it firmly, and brought it to the kitchen.

6

In the Apricot Orchard

THE FOLLOWING MORNING Flora was making us tea at the kitchen table. As she poured mine out, leaning over me, I could smell the strawberry scent lingering in her hair. I watched without self-consciousness her slow grace with the kettle, her pouting lips, her startling dark eyes. "Avram Bey," she asked, handing me the cup and saucer, "what's troubling you this morning?"

"Daughters."

"You saw your family then? Your girls?"

"Their names are Sarah and Estela," I said. "Twins."

Flora needed no more than that. She nodded.

I sipped my tea, considering. I had always over-thought parenthood. I would analyze every twist and turn of the girls' education. Their manners. Their sensitivities. How far up the happiness scale their temperaments registered at any given moment. "You know how it is," I explained to Flora. "You spend all these years teaching them how to walk. How to hold a spoon. How to zip their jackets and write their cursive letters and wipe their little behinds." I held out my hands with a bemused shrug.

Flora was looking at me strangely, her head tilted. "I'm sure they're good girls," she said warily. "You've been a real father to them. That's more than my own ever had."

"Good girls, maybe. Who knows? You fail your kids in a thousand ways."

"You're just figuring this out now?" She dropped another cube of sugar into her glass and stirred. Her eyes bore into me.

"I used to dream about their successes. The future glories. Brilliant careers. Public service. Such contributions my own flesh and blood would one day offer this great nation of ours. In the arts. Maybe the sciences. Business women. Modern women. A new generation, to right the wrongs of the world. Every year you trim back. None of it matters. You want them happy. That's it."

"Allah! Allah! Do I need this today?" She blew on her tea, eyeing me over her glass.

"That's it. I mean happy now. Every second. It's a kind of intensity. You feel that physically for them." I thumped my heart with a closed fist.

"Get over it, Avram. That's what I say. Everything you want for them is a mistake."

"It's wrong to want a thing so out of your control."

"Get over it. You're lucky," Flora whispered, "if they even make it to twenty."

I sipped my own scalding tea. Yes, what was happiness to this woman, or to her pack of island kids? She had dropped them indiscriminately into this world, with no regard for what little control she'd have over their fates. She had let an unforgiving nation do with her bastard children what it would. It was instructive. I could learn from Flora.

I stood, rattled my glass and saucer over to the sink, and lifted out from under a pile of architecture magazines the hardcover book. I removed the yellow paper, walked back over to the table, and unfolded the essay. Before I could explain Flora had snatched it up and was holding it by a finger and a thumb, squinting at the script. "Where'd you find this?"

"You recognize it?"

"Where'd you find this Avram?" Her voice was rising. She'd recognized the handwriting.

I offered her the hardcover and rustled the pages with my thumb. "Why would he have a copy of this?"

Her face blanched. She pushed *To Kill a Mockingbird* away from her. "I don't know. It's all foreign to me. I can't read English. Maybe he helped her with it. He was always helping her. Things wind up places. You lose them, you find them."

"Part of this essay's about your family."

"Certainly not," she said, but she was flattening the paper out against the table with her palm.

"So he helped her with this, Flora?"

"Some help, your brother was!"

"Then you remember her writing it?"

"Really, Avram, it was nothing. The usual frustrations, with the two of them."

She looked it over another long moment and then folded the essay as if she would keep it, but I snatched the pages back from her. She rose from her seat, her eyes now defiantly alive. I'd gone too far. I expected her to leave, but she went to the stove and violently filled her tea cup a second time, came back, rattled it into its saucer, and settled down opposite me at the pedestal table, arms crossed, skewering me with a look.

"Listen," Flora told me after a moment, checking the kitchen doorway to be certain we were alone. "You know as well as I do what happened in this country in 1915."

"I've only heard what we've all heard. Second hand. Third hand."

She pointed a finger at me. "What they've let you hear. My grandmother Silva, you understand, was raised out East, in a village near Van."

"What kind of village?"

"Out East, I said. Are you listening? She was only seven when the war began. This was when the Ottomans were invading Russia and Persia. Taking heavy losses. Armenians in that region, they said, were helping the enemies. As if these poor villagers could help anyone! Nonsense. I mean, I don't know what truth you believe, Avram, but it was nonsense. For revenge, the government was nailing horseshoes on the feet of Armenians. Literally. That's what we've always known, no matter what *they've* said. That's how cruel a time it was. That's the kind of country we lived in then. An order had come to the subgovernor to kill all the Armenians. Exterminate them. Wipe them out."

I lowered my eyes as Flora explained. In the spring the gendarmes broke into her great grandparents' house, looking for rope. Her grandmother Silva and two sisters, just children at the time, were so frightened they started shouting "Gendarmes! Gendarmes!" The soldiers had bayonets on their rifles. They collected all the rope in the village and tied up the men, and when Silva's father resisted the soldiers dragged him out to the courtyard.

"In front of the family they crushed his head with a big stone.

Pop! We all know this happened, whatever it is *they've* said. He was gone. Families don't make up such stories."

They led the rest of the village men, hands tied behind their backs, to the *meydan* and slaughtered all thirty of them. Cutting throats like cattle. Slicing heads off like chickens. Tossing them into the river. "You understand, Avram Bey? The boys of the village, even Silva's little brother, were thrown into a pile, and the gendarmes attacked that pile with axes, scythes, rakes, whatever they had. We all know this happened too."

Silva and her sisters fled with their mother. For six days and six nights they walked without food or water, so hungry they ate grass, until they heard about a nearby church where a few hundred Christians had supposedly taken refuge. Trekking to it, half-starved, they found an orchard and stopped to look for scraps of fruit. Just to rest their bleeding feet, just for a moment. It was there in the orchard hunting for fruit that Silva's oldest sister was caught by two Kurds. She was dragged away on a horse into the forest.

"One of the last things my grandmother ever told me was this — how she always remembered her sister looking back through the apricot trees. She was crying, "Mama djan! Mama djan!" It was the last they ever saw of her. Imagine, Avram Bey, living the rest of your life, remembering such a scene?"

In a village nearby a family of Muslims warned Silva's mother not to go to the church they were seeking. The army was planning to burn it down with everyone inside. This family seemed sympathetic, even kind. Silva's mother didn't know what to do. Her girls were starving. She gave Silva and her sister to this Muslim family, so that they could live with them. "You're *musulman*," she instructed the girls. "You're a Muslim from now on." The family offered the mother a donkey and sent her into hiding in a cave in the nearby mountains. Generosity like that was risky for them, too. They were taking a chance with their own lives. They told her to stay there in the daytime and to come back only at night. The next day the girls waited. And the next.

"This is how my great-grandmother was lost. This is no story up for debate. We know this. It's in our blood. My grandmother and her sister became servants to that family, but they had to pretend they were their daughters. With all the violence, they had to pretend to be Muslims. The family that risked taking them in — may God show them mercy — had seen Armenians slaughtered. Beheaded. Forced to flee naked. Our women had their fingernails torn out. Pregnant girls were attacked with these long knives. Mothers were throwing their babies into rivers. The family had seen corpses of children in piles. Rotting bodies filled the streams and creeks where they went to fetch drinking water. They'd *seen* this."

So it was only by this family's brave kindness that her grandmother survived at that house. The girls grew up and became cooks and worked at the local hospital. Later, when they married, both moved west, here, to the city, and started new lives. But they were always hiding who they were. Flora's grandmother had met her grandfather, a convert too. He, too, was pretending to be Muslim.

"They tried to bury those memories, see. It only hurts to remember, and my grandmother Silva confessed this all to me only before she died. They didn't want to look back. They were afraid what would happen to them if they became Christians again. You know the pressure, the intimidation. So our family continued on this way. It's the only reason we're still here. I'd see my grandmother cross herself on the forehead and shoulders before we ate, like this, but until I was older I never knew what this — this thing she did — even *meant*."

Through Flora's hoarse whisper I'd been flattening her daughter's essay against the table. Now I watched her demonstrate her grandmother's sign of the cross. I stared past her out the window at the ruined herb gardens. Reflexively Flora checked back over her shoulder down the dark hallway, as if Nilay or Officer Ceber would show up any moment and accuse her of something terrible. She said between her teeth, "All those years, all those years, Silva never spoke of these things. She believed if she were silent God would see to justice. What justice! Where is there justice, Avram? Only when I was an adult did she whisper these stories to me. Only then did I find out who I was. You understand me? A *muhtedi*! A convert! She told me we are not allowed to talk about it because certain people *want* us to forget." She looked again across her shoulder down the hall and lowered her voice further. "But now I can't forget. Those stories are branded on my brain. I feel them in my blood. Your brother listened to me. We traded stories. Here, I thought, is a man who could understand me."

"So my brother knew all this?"

"We used to talk about it right here, or upstairs, in his room. I wanted someone important to know what my family had been through. Yusuf was an important man, see, but like me he was *azınlık*. He wasn't of this country. He was free to listen and believe."

"He believed everything?"

"There's only one truth, Avram. What I used to tell Yusuf was we're the children of survivors too. We had that in common. When he'd tell me about the *Salvador*, about your grandmother's boat, I'd say, "You at least know where it went down. I'm not even so lucky. This whole country is a grave to me."

"And his speeches then? The…activism? His life took a sudden turn, and I never understood what drove him."

"Don't look at me, Avram. I never asked Yusuf to say a word. If he did any of that out of knowing us, then I admit it: I'm honored. He was brave and foolish, your brother. When you have money and an international reputation and two private jets, you can afford to be a bit braver and a bit more foolish than the rest of us."

"So this?" I turned the essay on the table and ran the side of my hand across its creases. I was thinking of her youngest son, Sarp, facing the Battering Ram. *Son of a whore infidel.* "Your children know everything?"

"I made sure my children knew exactly who they were from the first day they were born. I told them the real family name, Kalustyan. Not Demirkan. Kalustyan. I'd take them to the pilgrimage twice a year, to honor who we are. They know."

"You've kept your name, though."

"Would you want the word 'convert' on your birth certificate? I didn't want them to suffer that fate. To have that shame." She clicked her tongue. "One way or the other, everything you want for them is a mistake. I should have simply let them grow up here, happy and innocent Muslims, forgetting all that. See? I've come down, like my grandmother, against remembering. She never should have told me, and I never should have told them."

"No, no. Look at me, Flora. Of course you needed to tell them the truth."

"You don't see it, Avram. If I had held back these stories, I'd still have my daughter."

$$7$$

A Practical Guide to Critical Thinking

THE BASIC DRAMA behind the *Mockingbird* essay was this: In writing that paper Yasemin had managed, in her second year of *lise*, to get herself tossed out of the Amerikan Collegiate Institute.

"I'd sewn her a dress for the Junior Dance," Flora remembered. "Black satin! Sleeveless. Such a dress! And she had come home to the island the weekend before to pick it up. I had only just heard how badly she was struggling that semester. It was because of all of her extracurricular activities. She couldn't make it in the classroom, but I figured at least she was doing well around school, making a name for herself." Yasemin had won the lead role in the Drama Branch's production of "The Seagull." She had been scuba diving for the Barakuda Club, and dancing for the Folkloric Society. "In our phone calls every week she told me about all of it, but what she never told me were her grades. I'd just gotten a call from the Director. I didn't know until then how serious it was: that Yasemin was in danger of flunking English for the second straight time. And if she did, even with her scholarship she'd be asked to leave. It was an English school, that stuck-up director explained to me. All of the courses were taught in English. If she couldn't keep up with what the teachers were saying, how could she stay?"

Yasemin had returned for her dress on the weekend of the Feast to St. George, and had spent two days defending her efforts. She was doing better than her first term, she promised her mother. In all of her other classes, at least. Only the English coursework had been difficult. "They take off for spelling and grammar," she'd said. "All my classmates had seven years of prep! With native speakers! I can't catch up. I mean, *Annem*, I still have to look up every other word in the damn dictionary!"

She had a midterm essay to write for Monday, based on a textbook they were using: *A Practical Guide to Critical Thinking*. She knew she needed a solid grade to pass the course. She'd already begun a draft and was having difficulty. Flora asked what the essay was about and Yasemin explained it was on this American novel. A classic. "At one point," she said, "this man Atticus tells his daughter Scout, "It's not okay to hate anyone." Not even Hitler. He says it's not even okay to hate *Hitler*. So, in the paper, I'm disagreeing. I cite other examples. *Yani*, it's okay to hate the people who murdered Armenians in your grandmother's village. The people who stole your home after the Wealth Taxes. The people who stoned houses in the Greek Riots. All the people responsible for the deaths of our family."

Hearing her daughter talk about writing an essay so charged, in a foreign language, unnerved Flora. "You'll get yourself in trouble, writing these things in a big shot school like yours." At this point, she wanted the girl only to make good on Yusuf's scholarship, not to draw attention to herself.

Yasemin explained that her teacher was Canadian, and that he encouraged them to speak their minds. They talked about big themes like this all the time. Deeper, he'd always say, slapping his hand on their textbook. Go deeper, beneath the surface. Think for yourself.

"Maybe," Flora said, "a foreigner should show some sensitivity where he's teaching such thinking. And to whom."

Yasemin insisted she had brought it up on her own. During class they were talking about Atticus's statement — that it's not okay to even hate such an evil man as Hitler. Everyone was going along with it. So noble, Atticus was. Such a hero. "What about the people who killed my relatives?" Yasemin asked. The class fell quiet. "My great-grandfather was murdered. They raped his daughter. They took everything they had from us. If I were there, should I have loved those people with my generous heart?" The class was looking at her; her teacher was looking at her. "Forget Atticus," she said. "We have to be honest." Nobody in the class would say anything. The teacher quickly changed the subject. There and then she'd decided if they wouldn't talk about it, she'd write about it in her critical thinking essay.

"Have you even read the Mockingbird book?" Flora had asked.

Yasemin swung her head back and forth. "Mostly." She admitted that she had read only ten pages or so. It took her forever to read English novels. She was getting by just listening to class discussions. Flora reminded Yasemin that she needed this grade to pass, that she had to be realistic here and think of her future.

That night, sprawled on the floor of their cold cramped

bedroom, with her two sisters sleeping on the bed above her, Yasemin tried to finish the assignment. Flora woke a number of times to find the girl, with her Redman's Dictionary propped on her pillow, scribbling feverishly on a legal pad and slashing out words. A cold dread flooded through her. Her daughter needed better direction than she could give.

Loath to do it, the next morning she dragged Yasemin back to the Halim Pasha House. Yusuf and Flora were in the midst of one of their strained silent periods, but she was hoping he would at least convince her daughter not to write anything stupid. In the kitchen she'd begun preparations for a gala Children's Day luncheon with the director of the Foundation for Culture and the Arts — but while she cooked she observed Yusuf reading Yasemin's draft. Over coffee he read the four pages the same way he read the weekend newspapers, spreading them carelessly out on the still damp kitchen counter so that they grew splotched with water stains. His eyes wandered from the first page to the second to the third, back to the first, and then he read a few sentences aloud. To Flora his English accent seemed confident and studied. Hearing her daughter's foreign words given life in the rich man's voice stirred in her a pride she'd admit to neither of them.

Yusuf was gentle in his criticism. "Yasemin, you've got a lot here," he'd said, collecting his thoughts. "A great deal of potential, but no organization. This wouldn't fly at university. Not with the teachers I used to have, anyway."

"I was having trouble figuring out how to put things."

"You're making connections here. But which direction is it going? It leaps forward and back on itself. It's like you spit it out half-asleep."

The essay's flawed structure must have been the one component my brother, with his highly technical mind, felt comfortable criticizing. He ordered Yasemin to grab an empty notebook and together they retreated to the breakfast table Flora had now cleared. In the light from the bronze chandelier they spread the essay out again, and on a blank page he had Yasemin break down her themes into three manageable categories, encouraging her to quote directly and liberally from the novel itself. "In a school like this it doesn't matter what you say. Just get the grammar down. That's all your teacher's looking for."

He was tiptoeing around an honest response to the writing, trying to nudge her daughter in safer directions. Flora was relieved he'd taken the reins. He made Yasemin outline her paragraphs and list supporting evidence. She reminded him how she needed an introduction and a conclusion; and while she drafted yet another outline, he thumbed through her copy of *Mockingbird*. Yasemin had put the final touches on the second outline and finally let him have a look. Yusuf murmured the English aloud. He seemed concerned over one particular heading: **Forgiveness**. "*That*," Yasemin had written, "*is soft philosophical nonsense. Forgiveness isn't strength.*" She supported this by outlining her great-grandmother Silva's escape from their village in eastern Anatolia, and the hidden life the girl had made for herself posing as a Muslim servant.

Yusuf glanced up at Flora. Flora suggested her daughter just cut the entire paragraph.

"That's the heart of my argument," Yasemin cried.

Waving her carving knife, Flora had told her that she couldn't say things like this. Not on paper. Maybe she didn't understand

what kind of trouble she could get into. And not just herself —
her teacher too. "I told her to trust me, to stay out of it. It took us
three generations to melt back into this city. As if things weren't
still bad enough."

Yasemin wanted to know what the point of a private foreign
language school was if she couldn't write an essay like this. "And
you'd be surprised, *Annem*, by what I understand. I understand
you were lied to. You didn't even know who you *were*."

"What difference does all that make now? We know the truth.
God won't forget."

Yusuf, trying to referee, was thrumming the paper on the
table with his fingertips. "They're her words," he finally said to
Flora. "Let her keep them."

"People go to prison for writing quieter stuff than this.
Journalists get shot."

"So the girl should clam up? That's what you want to teach her?"

"The girl should put her head down, graduate, and head to
university. The girl should make good on the scholarship you've
handed her. The girl should be realistic, and write a simple essay
about the mockingbirds. That's what the girl should do."

"Maybe your mother's right?"

"*Annem*!" Yasemin said, "you spend half my childhood telling me these stories. What are we supposed to do, whisper these
things the rest of our lives? My whole class just sits there, silent.
They won't admit that horrible things have been done to us."

Flora reminded her that rice doesn't get cooked with words.
She should get used to it. She'd be a guest here to the end of her
days. An infidel. A convert's spawn. She should know her place
and keep her head down and make something better of herself,

as Yusuf had done. "Success — that will be your statement. My grandmother used to say, "May those days go, and may they never return." A bright girl like you has a future. That's what my grandmother wanted. That's why she was silent."

"If your grandmother wanted us to forget, she never would have told you." Yasemin turned to Yusuf for support. "You see! Just ignore it. That's just what my classmates think. A million people, maybe two million, wiped out. They had futures too! My class sits there. Robots! That's the kind of prestige school you've sent me to."

"It's not up to me to tell you what to write." Yusuf raised both hands in the air, walked back from the table, and began to leave.

"I didn't ask for your help. My mother did."

He spun around. "They're your words. You'll deal with the fallout. Not me. Not your mother. It won't be on us."

With that, he left. Flora had been hoping for more from him. Incensed at them both, she'd jabbed the knife into the marinated lamb.

8

A Woman Dependent on No One

Yasemin's English teacher returned the essay ungraded, with the ominous note scrawled in red ink at the top: UNACCEPTABLE. SEE ME ABOUT THIS. After the lesson, alone in the classroom, he had asked Yasemin how she expected him to grade such a paper. Yes, he was sympathetic to her family's difficult history, but he couldn't accept this kind of half-formed ungrammatical tirade in lieu of a polished essay about *To Kill a Mockingbird.* How could he pass her? He gave her another week to turn in a revised copy, focusing on the question, and only the question, of what prejudices blind Atticus Finch to the truths in his community.

One week later Yasemin handed in her revised essay. It was now an impassioned plea for the nation to come to terms with the murders of Armenians at the hands of the Ottoman Empire, and to admit to the ways minorities were intimidated since then under the auspices of National Unity. There was no mention of *To Kill a Mockingbird.*

It took all of an afternoon for the paper to make its way from English teacher, to Academic Dean, to the American Principal, and finally to the Director, whose job it was to negotiate matters of this kind with the Ministry of Education. Under these unique circumstances the Director felt a meeting with Yusuf Elmas, sponsor of her scholarship, respected member of the Alumni Board, was in order.

Yusuf was flown down to Izmir that very Friday in his helicopter. As he'd later recount to Flora, he expected to clear this misunderstanding up in a matter of minutes, but the meeting with the headmaster lasted nearly an hour. It grew more and more tense. The Director was a Secularist blowhard, and the two of them had never gotten along. Yusuf was the school's most famous graduate, he'd donated money for the academy's new swimming facility (the pool remains, to the this day, the *Elmas Yüzme Havuzu)* but even with the weight of his influence he couldn't convince the man to overlook the contents of an essay written off topic, by a student the school had gone out of its way to admit. If they allowed this kind of defiance, what next? Students wearing head-scarves? Demanding cultural autonomy to the Kurds? The *Milli Eğitim* would be all over them.

Yusuf had tried to laugh, tried to downplay the entire episode. They were making a big deal out of a misspelled essay. Defiance? How was it defiant? She was just a young woman expressing her views, challenging a bit of history. An idealistic teenager.

The Director said what she'd written was an insult to the nation.

"Come on now," Yusuf had said. "I helped her with this myself. This paper's as dangerous as your little toe."

The Director stared into the expanse of his desk.

Yusuf said they should be *encouraging* a student like this. They should be proud of her independent mind. She was serving as a strong example for her fellow students.

The Director told Yusuf he could take his pride and independence elsewhere. This was questionable history Yasemin was raising, everyone knew that. Even the essay's epigram — he snapped his fingers at the top of the page. "From Hitler? We all know Hitler never said such a thing."

Yusuf wouldn't dignify this with a debate, and tried to steer the conversation back to Yasemin's future. The Director reminded him the institution had done Yusuf a favor, accepting the girl, and they were doing her a favor by not reporting this. There were pressures on him, too. What would the Regional Inspector of Schools do to them? Out of respect for Yusuf, in gratitude for his many generosities, they wouldn't pursue this further. He himself wasn't expecting a thank you. But he wished Yusuf would at least acknowledge favors had been done. He raised himself and stood at his desk.

Never a person to acknowledge favors, Yusuf stood as well. He was seething, and it took everything he had not to hurl the volley of expletives rising in his mind. He left the office without shaking the Director's hand, and met Yasemin outside the girls' dormitory, where he ordered her to pack her things.

"For the moment I've done everything I can," Yusuf told Flora after dinner that night, back on the island. He had called her to the front porch, where he'd taken her arm into his own and recounted all this. It was the only time Flora could remember him apologizing to her for anything. "That school doesn't deserve a student like her. I'm sorry, Flora Hanım. I want only the best for the girl. You know that. Let's let it cool off, for now."

"The girl's impossible."

"Maybe I should have fought a bit harder. With her? With the Director?"

"No, no, no. She did this to herself."

"And here she is, punished. A few words — things we all know are true — scribbled on a paper. All the potential, and this is her undoing?"

"Her attitude's her undoing. You warned her."

Yusuf was silent, gazing out through the shadows at a *fayton* driver who was walking his horse past the iron gate, beneath the linden trees, its harness bells jingling.

"You warned her many times," Flora said.

"I can pursue this. Legally, if you want."

"For love of God, Yusuf! We don't live in a place where you get away with stunts like this. If she learned nothing else at that school she learned that. It's an important lesson."

"It's no lesson at all."

What Flora didn't tell Yusuf on the porch was she was certain Yasemin had failed out on purpose. "She always blamed her poor grades on not going to the after school cram courses, like the rich kids did. But I saw it: she wanted off that assembly line as soon as possible. Kids that age, you'll see how they are. Every one of them a rebel. Figuring life is just magically going to work out for them, no matter how many times they screw it up. Turning in that essay was a ridiculous thing to do once, never mind twice. Yasemin was too smart not to understand. I'm sure she regretted it later. Shit, she could have gone to a Fine Arts school. She could have had a real career. In the theater…a biologist…a lawyer maybe. There would have been options."

So Flora's oldest child returned, triumphant in her own mutinous way, to the island. She graduated the next year from its lousy public school, and impressively flunked both the Science and Literature components of the university exam. If Yusuf said nothing, everyone understood his disappointment, not to mention his buried anger that his alma mater, the object of his generous donations, had refused to turn a blind eye.

Yasemin was back to helping run Flora's chaotic household. Possessed of a maternal instinct she'd been born with, she would get all of the children off to school in the morning, buy them clothes in the Kadıköy Tuesday bazaar, make sure they were bathed and fed at night. In the absence of paid work she took over Flora's dinners at the Halim Pasha House. On weekends she covered for Nılay Gören, who liked to visit her nieces in İstiniye. Nobody in the mansion stated the obvious: What was the point of Yusuf's attentions — the tutoring, the private education, the scholarship, the language courses, all the hope the young woman had come to represent? For this? To work as a simple domestic?

Her mother, immune to shame, did not dwell on the disappointment. She still remembered with gratitude Yasemin's help. "Twenty years, on your feet, every day, at 5 AM, in addition running after the kids. It wears on you, Avram Bey. In the early years, maybe I'd felt burdened, but now I saw what a blessing a daughter was. I didn't want Yasemin helping me forever, you understand. Never mind the Amerikan Collegiate Institute. She could always retake the university exam. I wanted her to consider a trade school down the road. Secretary work. Teaching — maybe here on the island. A woman dependent on no one. We had our own small dreams, you see. I wanted my daughter happy, Avram. Not challenging the world. Just happy. I trimmed my dreams down too. You're not alone in that."

9

Don't You Have Anything To Wear?

YASEMIN'S HIGH SCHOOL troubles overlapped those years following the Marmara Earthquake, when everyone in the city knew someone who had been killed. Amid the civic mourning and national paralysis my brother, according to his staff, seemed a different man. In the wake of the tragedy he'd quietly attended every Teletürk employee funeral. Weekends would pass without the islanders hearing his helicopter land behind the house or his powerboat raging out across the surf. That year he stopped frequenting social functions at the Governor's Mansion, and would be gone weeks at a time, traveling exclusively for his charity work in support of quake victims. The Elmas Foundation funded three expansive tent-cities in Yalova, and the company's Izmit steel joist plant issued an employment initiative to hire those left jobless in the tragedy. Teletürk offered undisclosed relocation and compensation packages to affected families. Long after his fellow billionaires had stopped, Yusuf continued campaigning, at home and abroad, for emergency and redevelopment aid. His staff remembered him returning to the island harried and forlorn, seeking privacy and isolation. He took few personal calls and spoke little to the help. He had entered a new stage of his life: more contemplative, less social.

"People thought he was taking all that suffering harder than most," Mustafa Faik told me. "But I understood your brother. That's the responsibility of people with power. He'd internalized it all. Twenty thousand people dead. Maybe — what? — forty thousand? This was a national catastrophe, but he was a man of the nation. To Yusuf it was a personal disaster."

Death was everywhere, all around him, and surrounded by it he must have realized there were limits even to his own expansive energies. He had worked himself too hard and abused himself too long. His own aging body and scarring lungs could no longer take the full-time punishment. In the summer after Yasemin graduated Yusuf had caught a dangerous *grip*, and what followed from all accounts was the kind of drama I'd once been all too familiar with. There were high risks of complications; he had to be hospitalized for a month. Doctors were afraid the flu would heighten his lung damage and lead to severe pulmonary exacerbations. They warned him once again he'd have to limit himself.

On his return from the hospital Yusuf went on bed-rest for two weeks. Nılay Gören brought up his meals. Flora wouldn't bring them herself unless he specifically asked for her, and that year he no longer did. She would never inquire directly about her boss's health, though she received continuous updates through the staff. From September on he slowly returned to working a few hours in the mornings on the telephone out of his downstairs office. In the kitchen Flora could hear his murmuring down the hall, punctuated by lung-bruising coughs, and she'd resist the urge to stop in to see if he needed anything.

She was about to turn forty. For weeks the villa had been mournfully quiet — all voices subdued — so that on the Monday of Flora's birthday she was startled when, in the radiant late afternoon the kitchen windows began rattling, the floor tiles vibrating. She grabbed hold of the counter, still unnerved by the widespread fear of a follow-up earthquake that would sink the island forever. Then she realized it was only Yusuf's helicopter, landing down the hill once again, shattering the weeks of recuperative silence. The trees outside the French doors bent in the wind; metallic reflections speckled sunlight onto the walls. Her boss appeared a moment later, framed in the doorway of the kitchen, healthier than he'd looked in months, gaunt but lively in his full tuxedo, his normally unkempt-hair brushed and oiled back.

"Flora, I've been stood up." Hands on his hips, he took her in for a moment, then strode towards her in a rush, carrying into the kitchen the golden scent of some frighteningly expensive cologne. "Nobody to go out with tonight. I was thinking you'll join me for dinner. In town. It's important."

She already had plans to take the children for *kebaps* — a modest fortieth birthday celebration she wasn't about to let him ruin. She dismissed him with a laugh and stepped back to her work at the counter.

"Important business," Yusuf repeated.

Now it was more an order than invitation. But such an order! How could she refuse? The only thing that bothered her was that phrase. *Important business.* She'd have to dine with some foreign luminary. Benjamin Netanyahu. The Prime Minister of Slovakia.

She'd die of shyness or say something ridiculous or cause an international incident. "Where do you have to be?" she asked. "You could have given me a few hours notice, at least."

He glanced down at her stained apron. "Don't you have anything to wear?"

She ran home and fetched the only thing she could think of: the sleeveless satin dress she had sewn three years ago, for the Amerikan Institute's Junior Dance, which Yasemin had never worn, and into which Flora would just have to squeeze. Breathlessly she canceled her plans with the children and hurried back to the mansion. To avoid the prying eyes of the staff Yusuf had suggested she change in the rear cabin of the helicopter. Captain Metin Dede, decorated Air Force sergeant and newly-hired pilot, met her there, welcoming her with a half bow. From the cockpit a doorway opened to a wide cabin with four bucket seats. With practiced formality the pilot pointed out where the television and VCR, the mini-fridge, the satellite phones, and the stereo had each been installed, should she need them. He showed her the sliding closet, where he instructed Flora she could hang her clothes. The captain left her to change, dragging the curtain across the doorway. Beneath her still bare feet, just as she finished tugging down the dress, the engines came to life.

It was her first time flying, her first glimpse for that matter into Yusuf's off-island existence. In the rear cabin he fitted her with a headset to block out the ungodly noise. They lifted over the Marmara, the island tilted below, her stomach leapt, and they set out, churning the surface of the water white beneath them. Flora refused to be impressed. Actually she was terrified, her stomach twisting somersaults. She was fully convinced they would plummet into the speeding waters below and it would be over for her at last. Such a way to go, she tried to tell herself, such a way to go. They finally landed at the Naval Museum beside Dolmabahçe Palace. A Peugeot limousine awaited them. Sliding into its cavernous interior Flora tore a seam in her daughter's dress, just slightly, and cursed God's tricks beneath her breath. They were driven uphill to Nişantası, where they were to meet whomever they were meeting in the downstairs room at Meze Luna. They had the low-ceilinged room, all beige and brown paneling, entirely to themselves. Yusuf ordered without the aid of a menu. The waiters disappeared, and all at once they were alone. In the silence Flora fumbled with her fingers, looking left and right, waiting. She had imagined to that point that Yusuf had been left without an escort for some critical business negotiation, that she was substituting for someone. She hadn't understood until halfway through the second course that her fortieth birthday *was* the occasion.

"He laughed when I asked what gnocchi was!" Flora recalled. "The jerk! I'd never even eaten Italian before." Yusuf ate disturbingly little himself, but watched her move with pleasure through her bruschetta and antipasti and gnocchi and pork gorgonzola and a scoop each of raspberry and chocolate gelato. "It was way too much food, and I'd eaten more than I could carry in that dress. But I thought this birthday meal might be a one-time thing, and I wasn't going to waste a bite."

Flora needn't have worried. Each Sunday through the autumn, at Yusuf's request, she would leave the island to meet him. She would sneak off to Fenerbahçe Yacht Club, where he would pick her up in his Lightning speedboat. They'd cruise out north of the islands and afterwards eat seafood in Bostancı or walk together down Baghdad Street, dodging the restaurant hosts thrusting menus in their faces. Sometimes less formally they had *lahmacun* on the terrace at Günaydın, where they watched the silent vessels plying their way once again from the earthquake-ravaged shipyards of Yalova out into the straits.

With Flora Yusuf would launch into tirades about the city, tirades she'd never heard, the kind of complaints she'd expect of an old and restless man. "Look at this place! This is why we live on an island! Look at the traffic, jammed over the Bosphorus Bridge, all hours, day and night? And always those fishermen, damn them, casting from the sidewalks. No regard if they're going to swing a hook into your eye. *Bak*! Look at them! What is there to miss about living here, Flora? What's there to miss?" Everything bothered Yusuf now: The AyGas truck tormenting him with its ridiculous twelve-note jingle. The garbage collector crying out for trash to sell on his broken down cart. Women fishing their woven baskets out of four-story windows for bread deliveries. "Have you ever seen such a thing?" he'd ask her. "Cell phones in every pocket, the entire countryside wired, but it's still the Dark Ages here Flora! The Dark Ages!" The tragedy for him seemed to be that even a man of his vision could not better direct the course of this nation. Gypsy women on every corner, bent over, selling their flowers. The fish sandwich boats still importing "fresh local catch" from Canada. The air unbreathable, the sidewalks unwalkable, the seaside palaces with priceless views unsold, uninhabited, crumbling to the ground. The Municipality using plastic bags as garbage bins for fear of bombs. The park fountains all leaking and dribbling. Not a single cab driver with enough money to break a fifty lira bill. "The Dark Ages, I tell you Flora! That's why we live on an island."

Sailing her back to Fenerbahçe, just past Borgazada, with the wind and salt spray beating into their faces, Yusuf would point to a spot off the coast of the city. "And down there, the *Salvador*." She knew by now that it was our grandmother's boat. She understood that Yusuf had begun seeking permission for a research dive, to locate it once and for all. "A simple dive! In the interests of history. Yet they won't permit it. *Bıktım!* We live in a backwards nation, Flora. My heart bleeds for this country. I won't be sorry to leave it."

At the time it seemed to her no more than a single complaint in a long litany of grievances with a country that would never accommodate his oversized expectations. "You've told me," she would call from her perch beside him at the wheel. "You've told me a hundred times. Let it go, Yusuf. You can't let everything weigh on you like you do."

"You're absolutely right. Let the little things go. Let it all go." He'd say that, but then in a furious rush he'd turn the wheel and circle back against the scalloped waves.

10

Controllability Maneuvers

So Flora had kept him company in those waning days of his final autumn. "He could have been living anywhere in the world, with any woman he snapped his fingers at. But he was having seven-lira *lahmacun* with me. I never understood it."

For three years Yusuf had been bribing city officials to clear way for the construction of a high rise Ritz Carlton hotel. Teletürk Holdings Limited was building it on the hill just above his beloved Inönü Stadium, home to his Beşiktaş football *kulübü*. Many in the city had opposed the plans, which broke municipal ordinances banning high rises in view of historic Ottoman monuments. But Yusuf knew the people to whom such ordinances meant nothing. His architects arranged for a private sushi club to be built in the penthouse, with an unobstructed view forty-seven stories below to the stadium. That fall, with the skyscraper nearing completion, against all regulations he invited Flora to the still unfinished top floor, from which they'd watch an early-season football match.

The room that has since become our city's finest Japanese

restaurant was then dusty and uncarpeted, with piles of drywall and empty bottles of paint lying around exposed wires. Amid that mess Yusuf's office staff had set up folding chairs and a table with hors d'oeuvres. Looking down for the first time, Flora leaned her forehead against the cool window and dizzily watched the tiny *dolmuşes* plying the traffic circles, the taxis curling around the football stadium in a whorl of red brake lights. Yusuf turned on the construction crew's paint-splattered radio for the play by play. Perched on folding chairs, they passed a pair of opera binoculars back and forth, and in that way safely watched the mayhem below.

The shouts of thirty thousand Beşiktaş fanatics were vibrating the reflective glass windows — half the stadium calling "Black!" and the other half responding, "White!" Flora had murmured along laughing, and Yusuf, in his scratchy but still sonorous voice, joined the crowd's fist-pumping chants:

I realized that other loves are nothing but lies,

The prettiest love is yours.

If I die before being champion,

Let my shroud be black and white.

Flora confessed to me, "He'd made me wear the striped team scarf. It was the most fun I'd had in twenty years. And let me tell you, Avram, one thing I never admitted to him. Until then I'd always rooted for Galatasaray!"

Beşiktaş took a 2-0 lead; and on the second score, caught up in the bedlam, as the radio announcer chanted "Goal! Goal!" Flora had raised her fists and leapt from her seat and clasped my brother's shoulder. Yusuf stood and put his own arm around her. Hip to hip they watched the crowd beneath them erupt, completely berserk, into dancing waves of undulating black and white flags.

Flora turned to him. It was an awkward hug, a reflexive response to the excitement of the goal, and in it she could feel the lightness of his bones. For a second she looked at his slightly curved white teeth, at his sensitive and calculating yellowed eyes, at what little color was left in his face. Bemused, their foreheads touched. Below them the crowd had begun chanting, "Lai lai lai — lai lai lai! Oh Beşiktaş!" Holding her breath she listened and watched, until the press of his arms around her suddenly loosened.

"Another?" He stepped away, staring down at her midsection. "Flora, you're kidding me. Another one still? At your age?" The crowd was still cheering the goal, but he held her at arms length by the shoulders and met her eyes for a long moment, then his gaze fell to her belt.

She nodded. She'd honestly forgotten until that moment. In that hug Yusuf had felt the muscular firmness of her stomach, the slight bulge pressing against him.

"How long?"

Three months, she admitted. Or maybe it was four.

He seemed for a moment completely thrown off, his face went paler. Was it anyone's he knew. A friend of his? Some guest, say, of the mansion?

She lowered her head; her own face burning. "It's the way it is with me. You've always known that." The child would be a boy: Saim Demirkan, her last.

Yusuf was struggling to smile for her but couldn't manage it. She felt his grip ease; he released her shoulders. "Congratulations," he said. "*Aferin*. May it come easy." He returned to the folding seat, crossed his legs firmly, then his arms. She sat, angled away from him, and they watched the rest of the game from those heights in silence.

All those years together in the Halim Pasha House, and only now, at this late date, were they even getting to know each other. Off the island, out of the mansion, it had been completely innocent. Long talks about nothing. They had found they actually liked being together. They might have done that to the end, if she hadn't been so careless. Now Yusuf would shut her out again — and he had every right to — but it upset her more than ever, for she was finally seeing the man he could have been.

Beneath them the crowd chanted their songs: *Eagle Goal Goal Goal!* and *We Love Much Like a Lunatic!* and *Don't Bury Us Alive!* It was only an exhibition match, but in typical form Beşiktaş collapsed in the second half, gave up the lead, and managed to eke out the win, through luck alone, on penalty kicks.

The flight back that evening in the helicopter was interminable. Captain Metin Dede had lifted off up along the Bosphorus, following the coastline at two thousand meters, over the bridges connecting the continents, then out to the Black Sea, a purple mass outlined by the scraggly white beaches of Asia. The captain's voice came over the headphones, "Congratulations, Yusuf Bey. A celebratory lap for the team?" Sullen now, lost in his head, Yusuf didn't answer, but stared out at the coastline of the city. The dark purple of the Black Sea spread before them, a bruise without end. Captain Metin Dede flew on, circling up over the Belgrade Forest where Yusuf owned property, then out along the ancient Roman Aqueducts and towards the mirrored skyscrapers of Levent.

It was here on the roof of the Teletürk Tower Yusuf often landed for weeknight business and social appointments. "Shall I land?" the captain called now. "Change of plans," Yusuf answered, "Fly on!" They wheeled southwest against the sunset, lower now, out over the mosques of Sultanahmet. It should have been a spectacular sight: the Aya Sofya glowing its reddish orange, the Blue Mosque's minarets thrusting heavenward, the imperial gray of Suleyman Mosque bearing eternal witness to the ebb and flow of empire. But to Flora the city had never looked so frighteningly large. She had never understood its size, the extent of it all, all that churning desperation, all those miserable lives down there, the swinish multitude locked together in some collective struggle. To what end? They orbited the seven hills of the old city, cast in shadows from the passing clouds. She didn't want to look down any more. She was sick with herself, sick of the years of this back and forth, of the lack of commitment, of never knowing where she stood or who she even was. She locked her hands on her stomach, wanting only to be done with him and back on her island.

The captain flew out over the Marmara, and still not picking up on the somber mood emanating from the rear cabin, entertained them, as he sometimes had, with controllability maneuvers he'd excelled at in military flight training. He performed, just briefly, just to show off, an aggressive forward pitched dive. The entire windshield turned black with the Sea of Marmara. Then he started a steep, cyclic climb. Flora was going to be ill. Through his headphones Yusuf cursed at the pilot to cut it out. Leveling, Captain Metin Dede aimed them directly home to the island. After the skids settled onto the concrete with a scrape and a final thud Yusuf jerked the curtains open and gestured to Flora to make her way out through the flight deck. He whipped the curtains shut behind her. She heard him cursing at the pilot with a brutality she didn't know he possessed. He ordered Metin Dede to park the helicopter there on the island for the night, and when the captain asked how he should get home, Yusuf barked, "Don't fuck with me, Metin. Sleep like a dog on the streets. What's it to me?"

11

The Annihilator

ARCHITECTS RARELY GET dirty. We wear a collared shirt and tie, and our work is done primarily on paper, in an office, under strong clean lights. So I'd never had the opportunity to tear down Ottoman-era walls with my own hands, or to cap pipes, or to finish trim, and I was only now learning how limited my first-hand knowledge of construction had always been.

The messiest job I undertook that winter was the partial removal of the office wall adjoining the maid's quarters. I wound up finding a carpenter from the village to help. I'd never worked with horsehair plaster and lathe walls before, and would have unwisely taken a sledgehammer to the whole thing without first thinking it through. The carpenter insisted we staple and hang plastic sheets off the ceiling to create a sealed-off space. Despite this he warned me to send the rest of the staff home for the day. We were in for a dust storm of Biblical proportions. When it came time to bash the wall down we donned particle masks, and he demonstrated how to use the wide end of the sledgehammer, how to drive it low into the wall, how to knock the plaster off in larger chunks so that with any luck the lathe remained in place. Only then, taking turns, did we have at it with a hammer and wrecking bar.

This wrecking bar he wielded with inordinate pride. It was a heavy black iron device called *The Annihilator*, with a thick rubber handle and vicious stainless steel point. You felt immediately stronger holding that bar in your hands. In taking brutal whacks at my brother's house, in marking each blow with a guttural grunt, in sending up clouds of white dust, something long pent up came out in me. I got carried away. I could have knocked the whole wall down, the furniture in the room, the entire mansion, if the carpenter hadn't intervened. But he wanted his turn with his prized wrecking bar. Once the hole was large enough we spent the bulk of the afternoon sweeping and shoveling plaster, which is heavier than it looks. With the large pass-through opening complete, I had hours of work ahead of me fixing irregularities and finishing with paint.

I knew Nılay and Flora would be disgusted when they saw the dust that had, despite the plastic sheeting, drifted in clouds across the house. The next morning the office still looked like it had suffered a kind of nuclear winter, and I was taking a broom to it once again when I heard Flora arriving in the kitchen. I finished another pass, lay down the broom, and went down the hall, expecting some kind of reproach.

She didn't notice me. She was absorbed at the pedestal table, rifling through the shoebox of Yusuf's old correspondence, which I'd moved here to keep out of the dust. For the first time I felt a proprietorial sense of violation, of Flora overstepping her bounds. She was already unsorting letters and reports I'd sorted.

"Can I help you find something?" I asked, trying to blunt the sharpness in my voice.

Flora glanced up, but said nothing about the mess of the house, didn't acknowledge her employer was covered in a ghostly white dust. Preoccupied, she returned to the envelopes, peering at the addresses. "They're foreign," she said, taking up another envelope and removing its report.

"I think that was the point."

"He was hiding something." She unfolded the page. "What's this mean? This, here: *Dangers of strike-slip faulting*?"

For three months now, late at night when I couldn't sleep I'd pored over the findings in this box, one dire warning at a time. It never occurred to me that Flora would have any interest in these technical studies. "Maybe he wanted to expose the government's mishandling of the earthquake?" I asked. "Embarrass them into action."

"No." She was puzzling over a letter written in English, only half-listening. "Narrow beam echo sounder system," she murmured.

I snapped my finger at the envelope she was holding, postmarked from Cairns, Australia. "There's another like that, from the same address. He was offering to fund an underwater seismic monitoring station. Do you have any idea why the Coast Guard denied these scientists diving permits?"

"I know this, Avram," Flora said, folding the paper. "Your brother didn't care a thing about fault lines, or even historic island neighborhoods."

"He'd thrown a lot of money at it," I said, shaking the box, "for a man who didn't care."

"I steered clear of his private stunts. My daughter was the one who got caught up in it." She stopped herself, and looked blankly past me at a spot on the wall. "If you really want to know, there's someone you can talk to. Ayda Subaşı. She was the one Yusuf was seeing when his troubles began. She was here all the time in those months. I had to serve them dinner in the kitchen. Just the two of them. By candle light. They hardly ate. They'd fall silent when I came in the room. You understand me." Her voice broke. "Were there any letters here in this box from her?"

"Come on, Flora. He wouldn't have done that to you. Not here. Not in the mansion."

"You say he wouldn't. You're forgetting your brother."

Ayda Subaşı, Ph.D., was a name I recognized once I located her online biography at the Reks Internet Café later that afternoon. She was a maritime archaeologist, currently director of the Ak Bank Museum and Cultural Foundation, which housed an art gallery, library, and publishing press back in the city, across the square from Galatasaray High School. Subaşı had known my brother at the Amerikan Collegiate Institute, where the two of them had co-founded the Barakuda Scuba Diving Club. She had been diving since the age of 16, and after graduating had gone on to pursue marine archeology. Trained in the use of side-scan sonar and proton magnometers, she had joined the famous dive team that had salvaged the steamboat *Liman 2* from the Golden Horn, eventually restoring the vessel to seaworthiness. She had achieved further notoriety through the identification of three German U-boats, sunk in the Black Sea during World War II. On the Web I saw that Subaşı had just delivered a speech about her findings at the International

Shipwreck Conference at Plymouth University. Recently she had appeared on television, reporting on efforts to locate the wreckage of an Australian World War I submarine 73 meters beneath the Marmara. There had been some controversy about whether or not the ship should be pulled from those depths, restored, and placed in a museum in Gallipoli. "I'm not interested in pulling up actual boats and disturbing old resting sites," Subaşı had argued in the video stream. "We're not trying to resurrect painful memories here. With wrecks, we only want to know what happened to them. Why they sank. How they got to lie where they did. That's my life's work."

None of this was the reason her name had struck a chord with me. I returned to her online CV on the Museum's website, and scrolling further down came upon the familiar outlines of an entirely different expedition. I remembered now. She'd been on the crew, and was interviewed in Sunday magazine sections, about the frustrated search for the *Struma*.

Everyone in our community knew about this boat, though we rarely spoke of it. It was the refugee steamer that had fled Romania in a doomed effort to get to Palestine, nearly a year after my grandmother's cattle boat had attempted the same voyage. On the Black Sea the *Struma's* engines had failed, and during the war the boat had sat in our harbor for ten excruciating weeks, tied up in a bureaucratic limbo. Nobody knew what to do with a disabled ship full of Jewish refugees. Nobody wanted them on their shores. The British, the Turks, the Americans all balked. For no apparent reason it was tugged again out to the Black Sea, and set adrift without working engines. Within hours it was bombed by a Russian torpedo. Nearly 800 people died.

Only one person survived the wreck. That disaster officially put an end to those journeys, closing off that route of escape from the coming genocide.

Ayda Subaşı, Ph.D., was no marine geologist. If my brother had worked with her, then he'd been interested in more than underwater seismicity. He'd taken on something else entirely.

I returned to the home page of the Ak Bank Museum and Cultural Foundation, and searched for an e-mail address.

12

Wrecks On Top Of Wrecks

Dr. Subaşı was a busy woman, but agreed to meet for a cup of coffee at the Ada Café, across the street from the cultural center she now directed. It was a sleek café, with low leather divans and a large open window facing the parade of pedestrians on Istiklal. Dr. Subaşı was late, and for nearly twenty minutes I sat alone, watching the vendors passing by, one wheeling his cart of grilled corn ("Milky Corn! Milky Corn!"), another lugging plates of green almonds on ice. My attention was drawn across the street, where a beggar dressed in rags kept, on a plastic crate, a fortune-telling rabbit. If you paid a lira and told the rodent your name the rabbit picked your fortune with its teeth, in the form of wadded up bits of paper jammed into plywood. Next door the clowning ice cream man had just rung his bells with his spatula. This scared the hell out of some baby who, carried past by her laughing mother, was wailing uncontrollably. Wistfully I remembered my own daughters crying, in chorus, every time one of those obnoxious vendors clanged his bell. When they were older we'd let them buy their ice cream themselves. You tried to grab the cone, and the vendor slipped it away from you, right through your fingers. He offered it to you again; you'd end up with a handful of napkins. He'd press the ice cream with the spatula, offer it a third time, and you'd end up with an empty cone; the ice cream stuck to the spatula. It was an act of impossible prestidigitation. How my girls used to grow frustrated! *Uff ya!* they'd wail. *Bu ne!* How Naomi and I would laugh at them!

Finished with my cola, I glanced at my watch, and just when I was reaching for my wallet a woman came rushing in, panicked, looking this way and that. She was shorter, more petite than I would have imagined from the online video, her arms thin and muscular, her hair shaven nearly to a crew cut. I stood and waved her over. "Avram Benezra?" she asked, out of breath. "I'm quite sorry. I didn't forget you. Traffic was horrible. The Jazz Festival."

I smiled. "Traffic is always horrible, Jazz Festival or no. Join me." I held an open palm out to the leather divan and the low ivory-inlaid table.

"Sometimes this city does me in!" She smiled, sat down, called out *"Bakar mısınız!"* with a high snap of the fingers, and asked the waiter how large their teas were.

"Big," he promised.

"How big?"

"Extra large glasses," he promised, stretching his thumb and forefinger.

She squinted at him for a moment. "Cappuccino then." She wheeled around to me. "So! Yusuf's brother!" she announced, shaking her head, grinning as she slung her enormous laptop bag up over her neck and off her back. She had a broad determined forehead, her close cropped hair brown but still tinged with red henna. "Older or younger?"

"I was the older one. There were just the two of us."

"Ah! I have a younger brother too! A complete pain in the ass. Did you and Yusuf get along?"

"Did we get along?" I laughed. "Look, Dr. Subaşı, I don't mean to take up your valuable time."

"Ayda. Call me Ayda. No, no, no. I'm *happy* to talk to a relative of Yusuf's."

I showed her three of the geological reports I'd brought along, laying them out one by one on the table for her to peruse. "Yusuf had apparently taken an interest in earthquakes in his final months. Did you know anything about this?"

"Well, we all had, back then, if you remember." She was half-distracted. Her cappuccino had come, and dousing it with sugar in a rush, Dr. Subaşı spilled some granules on the old correspondence, and sweeping these off, splattered half her whipped cream on the table, splotching the papers. "I'm sorry!" She dabbed them with a napkin. "Look at this mess. Were these important?"

I clicked my tongue, rescuing the letters from the puddles of froth. "I heard you were working together with him. Closely."

She took a large swallow of cream, licked off her lips, and with an exaggerated gulp said, "Yes, for a short time, yes."

"You'd known my brother since school?" I was already laughing to myself at Flora's suspicions. This woman cared little about Yusuf. There was no hint of emotion here.

"We hadn't seen each other in twenty years! I ran into him on a boat, up in the Black Sea, during the whole *Struma* fiasco."

"The Jew Boat," I said, using the blunt name Black Sea fisher-men still called it.

"You know it then."

"And that's where you'd reconnected?"

"Yes, reconnected. I'd been brought on to try new tactics."

"Why new tactics?"

"It was a frustrated search. Remember, no one had any luck locating the *Struma*. The National Underwater Research Society claimed they had found the wreck site; but evidence was hardly conclusive. Four years later, a diver from Britain had searched possible sinking locations. He brought families from Europe, Israel, the U.S., to a memorial service, rented a boat up in the Black Sea. But they never identified it either. Nobody could pin it down. They asked me to get involved."

"How so?"

She ran her fingers through the bristles of her hair. "There were always two problems looking for the *Struma*: limited funding, and resistance from the powers above. 20,000 Jewish refugees passing through our borders, Avram. You'd think it's a legacy we could be proud of. But this was the war's heaviest naval civilian disaster. Our paranoid government can't admit to mistakes of such scale. For those British divers it had been one bureaucratic maze after another. I'd gained some notoriety by then. They'd brought me on to try to steer through government objections."

"And how was my brother involved?"

"Money. The team knew Yusuf's sympathies. They'd applied for grants from the Elmas Foundation. Your brother sponsored three rounds of those dives. He put up the money for the filming of a documentary on the most promising search. He was invited out on the boat, out on the Black Sea, to watch with the film crews, in real time. That's when we met up again, after all those years. On the day we sent the submersibles down."

"A documentary on a failed search? Not much of a film then."

"When it didn't pan out they turned it into something broader. The frustrations locating the *Struma*, the interviews with the only survivor, the family reunions, the memorial, all that. A Canadian director, I believe. *The Struma: Only a Survivor Can Tell.* You haven't seen it?"

"It's not something they'd show prime-time on TRT1." I clicked my tongue.

"What a shame." She looked around and said, "I'll burn you a copy." She removed a small notebook from her bag and jotted my address. "But you're right. Our Generals couldn't have been happy someone of Yusuf's reputation was involved. He was a provocative man, your brother. Actually he was quite fearless. Out on the platform, coughing, breathing heavy, his chest laboring, he joked with me he'd like to make the dive; that he should be down there himself. He used to be a real swimmer when he had better health. Not many people remember that."

"I remember." Her description of meeting Yusuf, on a boat, out at sea, had brought another excursion to mind. Two young men, shoulder to shoulder, in the rain and mist at the back of a ferry. "We learned to swim together. Our dad taught us."

She looked at me. I stared down beside the table at a piece of café kitsch: an enormous wine-bottle-shaped vase perched on the hardwood floor. It was a translucent green, and inside it held hundreds, maybe thousands, of used corks.

Ayda said, "So in the General's eyes it was a controversial

thing your brother was starting all over again, a year or two later, forming a new team."

"To look for the *Salvador* this time?"

"Yes, the *Salvador*." She smiled. "You know this too?"

I recalled sitting on the rocks with Yusuf, on Seferoğlu beach, two sons on either side of their father, basking in the evening sunshine. I recalled Father telling us the story of that boat going down, urging us to learn how to swim, swim for our lives.

"The *Struma* was one thing," she was saying. "Yusuf could let that puzzle go. The *Salvador* — that was something very personal. He told you all this, of course."

"He told me none of it."

"But this was your family's history, buried under those waves. How to locate it was — well, a private obsession for Yusuf, even up to those last weeks."

I sat there in the café, ankles crossed beneath the table, listening to Dr. Subaşı chronicling my brothers' private obsessions, astonished by the steady flow of revelations. The words *your family's history* excited in me the old feelings. The legacy of the *Salvador* didn't belong to the brother who'd left us, to the celebrated billionaire. It belonged to the brother I'd once known, whose room I'd shared, whose back I'd clapped, tapping out all six positions for five minutes each with a firm, steady five-beat count. Clap clap clap — clap clap!

"Money was clearly not the problem," Ayda Subaşı was saying. "The Generals were the issue. He was risking his reputation, his connections. He was waging all of it. He hired me on as his logistics manager. We had the plans drawn up. He commissioned the dive boat — an Australian crew he had once met out on some

Heli-diving stunt. I got together for him the survey crew and the film crew. A diving safety officer who owns a shop in Karaköy. Two hyperbaric physicians. Two computer engineers. We set up the details with a Naval liaison officer. Yusuf had had drop cameras specially engineered for the dive. He was looking into robotic arms to use for recovering evidence. He gave me no budget. I was simply amazed, Avram, at the resources he was willing to spend. On a single dive! It's not the way it usually works."

"And what'd you find?"

"No, no, you're jumping ahead of me. Listen. It never got off. We had trouble getting the submersible, brought up from Australia, through customs. The Institute of Nautical Archaeology finally helped us with that, but it wasn't the real issue."

"What was the real issue then?"

She glanced around. "Look," Ayda continued, "I used to explain to your brother that the shores around the Marmara have been littered with shipwrecks since 14 BC. Just because something's down there, close to the coastline, doesn't make it any easier to find. Money isn't the answer. It's especially tough diving. The wrecks are pounded by dangerous currents, covered in tangles of fishing nets, slammed into by anchors and trawlers. Sometimes the sunken boats crash into each other. Wrecks on top of wrecks. The history is sensitive here. You do as much damage as good to these sites, trying to search one out. Plus, you know regulations in our city, Avram. Every civic improvement brought to a standstill by the discovery of some Byzantine ruin. They're tunneling now under the straits, and look what a disaster that's been. Out there you're in the middle of shipping lanes. It's a complicated process, diving in the Marmara. We needed a few weeks to troll with the sonar sled, to create a logical map grid that way. If we located a promising wreck, we'd have to start with a photomosaic to verify the ship. This before we could even *touch* anything. Yusuf was out ahead of himself. He was an impatient man."

"In what ways?"

She smiled. "Listen, I'm telling you. So we applied for diving permits from the Regional Coast Guard Headquarters to search out likely sites. I was doubtful. Let's just say this. The government was not inclined to grant permission to photograph a ship full of dead Jews, sunken just off our city's coastline. Excuse my coarseness Avram."

"Please."

"And then, imagine, maybe recover pieces for the world to behold: these refugees that had died this close to us, fleeing the Nazis, just off our shores. Personally, I wasn't in favor of that either. I was trying to convince your brother, *if* we were granted permissions, and *if* we found it, to set up a small buoy, memorialize the site. Something quiet and respectful."

"Quiet was not who my brother was."

"Or respectful. Then I started hearing rumors from my diving friends that the government was taking notice. Understand Avram, in the middle of the whole EU mess, this wasn't publicity they wanted on the front pages of the papers. Before we could even start the pre-disturbance survey, we needed diving permissions. The Coast Guard would give us their word, a verbal green light. But they'd toss one bureaucratic hurdle in front of us, then another, never giving us the permissions in writing. It seemed to me — and I told Yusuf this — they were trying to frustrate him. They were hoping, I think, he'd just tire of it all and give up. They would never outright deny the diving licenses. But they wouldn't grant them either.

"So we waited. I knew the *Struma* divers had been through all this, so I was patient. I got the support of some of my connections at the Ministry of Culture. I asked General Headquarters of the Monuments Museum to exert some pressure. We applied again. Waited again. Nothing. The permits were always in the works — they just never came."

"There was no other way?" I found it impossible to believe Yusuf would have been stifled in so obvious a manner.

"It was a clear enough message they were sending. I'm afraid I had to pull out then. I told your brother that I had my own projects to consider. I had an archeology career to think of. I couldn't risk my reputation on something as foolish as diving without permission in restricted waters."

"If you knew my brother," I said, "you knew restricted waters didn't matter."

Dr. Subaşı nodded with a sad grin and ran a finger along the base of her coffee mug. Beneath the chatter and jazz of the cafe she leaned over the low table and murmured, "It was a month after I'd quit that I heard Yusuf was retiring, as CEO of Teletürk. He had turned his foundation's attention to privately financing earthquake research. Projects charting locations for potential monitoring stations. The fault-lines beneath the sea. The grinding of tectonic plates. Mapping offshore seismicity. Do you understand what I mean?" She locked me in a stare. "After the Marmara Earthquake, those were studies in the national interest. Underwater research the government needed to promote. Expedited grants a philanthropist like Yusuf could readily finance."

"Then these reports?" I asked, fingering the envelopes. She nodded, and I saw it. Yusuf's high-profile charity arm for the restoration of historic homes had been a side-step, a feint, an elaborate front. "He was sending divers down looking for the *Salvador*?"

"Seismic surveys." Dr. Subaşı leaned back and smiled. "But if you happen to find a wreck offshore, document it, measure it, photograph it. So typical of your brother. He enjoyed these games."

A chill from the open window closed over me. If I had been so blind to his interests in the family history, how many other ways had I misunderstood him? For so long I had thought he had turned his back on us, but he could have been facing us all those years, arms outstretched. Who'd been the culprit here?

"Please," I asked Dr. Subaşı, with the fervor of sudden regret, "tell me then, in all these surveys, did they find the wreckage? Did anyone ever identify the *Salvador*, to your knowledge?"

"I'm not sure. I'm not sure."

"You see, Doctor Subaşı –"

"Ayda. Please."

"You see, Ayda, we hadn't spoken in fourteen years. Suddenly I'm sick over that." The dogged optimism of a young boy, hunched between his father and brother, skimming rocks into the Marmara. He'd kept that faith, across all those years. If I had understood any of this, I would have taken that final phone call of his, even in the middle of the night.

Ayda Subaşı was staring at me strangely, pity in her eyes. "For fourteen years you hadn't spoken? To your own brother? But why?"

"It was ridiculous." I circled my palm in the air. "Too long to go into now. You don't know if he had news then?"

Dr. Subaşı nodded; her eyes widened. "Rumors, down in the diving shops in Karaköy. The week of his accident, they'd mapped a promising site. But something went wrong."

"They? Who were they?"

"Honestly, Avram, I don't know. I was gone by then, and it was all hushed gossip. He was using foreign crews at that point. A team of Romanian geologists, I believe. The research vessel was disguised as an old fishing boat. When I was working for him, we used to do the planning on his yacht. We'd stay aboard overnight. Our team met there in the galley. You know, playing with the computer models, mapping possible sinking locations. It was a private place, under tight wraps. We had Yusuf's crew waiting on us. It felt more like a cruise than a scientific expedition. He used to bring that young friend of his from the island. The one on the boat with him, the morning he went down. I didn't know her myself. Yelda? Yildiz? Yağmur?"

"Yasemin?"

Dr. Subaşı gulped the last of her cappuccino and clattered her mug into its saucer. "Yasemin. Right. A pretty girl. Sweet."

"She came with him out to his yacht?"

"She was always with him, from what I saw. I'd first met her at the filming for the *Struma* documentary, two years before. He pestered me to tutor her on the magnometers. I never found the chance."

"Yasemin Demopoulous? You're sure?"

"That's right."

I digested this fact for a few moments. If he'd taken her out to the *Struma* filming…then she'd been out to sea with him for a year or two at least, since she'd graduated and failed her exams. Flora didn't know this.

Outside the window the historic Beyoğlu trolley rattled by, clanging its bell, five dark urchins hanging off the back in their flip flops. Dr. Subaşı was swiping her lips with her napkin. I asked, "Do you think the government knew?"

This brought a bemused smile. "Are you kidding me? Avram, of course they knew! Allah Allah! They were following his boats from the start. From the air, from the sea. They'd held our submersible in customs. The MIT had him under complete surveillance. He wasn't fooling anyone. On his last morning he was probably heading to the yacht to meet up with the fishing vessel. One chance too many. That's what I've always guessed. The question for the Generals was how to quietly put a stop to him, without it blowing up in public, in their faces. It had become a battle of wills. Your brother, you know, was very good at those."

Book V

1

A Foolhardy Speech

The editorialist Hakan Bozbey, the *Büyük Baba* of the Sunday columns, had called him a "Disgrace to the Nation. A half-Turk. An embarrassment." Alper Karasu, an oversized Kemalist known for his raunchy and biting tongue, dubbed him 'The Narcissist.' Six months before his boat went down Yusuf's name was appearing daily in the opinion pieces of the ultranationalist papers, but I hadn't known why. Only back on the island, with the perspective of years, could I finally reconcile what I'd then read with what I now knew.

Half a country away, overwhelmed with the schedules of twin preschoolers, I'd been slow to keep up with events precipitating the disaster. I'd seen the wire a full week after the news had already broken. Over a lunch of börek at a neighborhood cafe I was flipping through an old copy of the *Çevap* when I stumbled upon:

CEO of Teletürk Calls It Quits after 12 Years

Saturday, October 21st *— Yusuf Elmas, the chief executive officer of Teletürk Telecommunications Ltd, the nation's largest private phone company, said yesterday he was resigning immediately,* *but gave no reason for the abrupt decision. The announcement, which came on a Friday night after the stock market had closed, caught investors by surprise. It is certain to cause shock-waves across the telecommunications industry.*

"It's absolutely a surprise. It's not something he'd been hinting at," said Omer Saydel, managing director at Saydel Asset Management. He added that "an inevitable reflex reaction would likely be seen in Teletürk's share price" once the market reopens on Monday.

Elmas has been Chief Executive Officer of the country's tenth largest listed holding since May 1993. His resignation would take effect Monday, leaving the company in the hands of his management team until a replacement is found. The news was delivered through a prepared statement read by Hamit Bilgili, the company's chairman. Elmas was vague about his motivation for stepping down. "It's hard to find one reason only," he wrote. "At some point you decide that you have been working in a role for too long, and need to look for change. Ask any head of a large holding. Twelve years is a long time for any CEO, in any company."

"I have completely enjoyed my ride here. It's been rewarding — both a challenge and tremendous fun."

Well known for his daredevil public relations stunts, Elmas, 38, co-founded his first company as a systems integration start-up, and has since expanded his holdings to include management and majority stakes of discount airlines, real estate ventures, online banking, energy suppliers, and the manufacturing of steel joists. He also personally chairs the company's high-profile charitable arm.

Speculation will certainly follow. Senior executives, speaking off the record, indicated that the resignation may be connected to health concerns. The Teletürk CEO has lived with cystic fibrosis since childhood. Close associates have been uncertain how many more years he would be strong enough to meet the demands of the position. Elmas has never spoken publicly about his lifelong battle with the disease.

His written statement gave limited insight into how he came to the decision. "It seemed to me it might be now or never. I have since day one informed the board that I would not hold the position forever. There's currently a powerful management team in place. Teletürk is strongly positioned for continued growth. The board has a wealth of highly qualified internal candidates to consider, but I welcome a search for external candidates as well. To lead a company of this breadth and vitality — it's a marvelous opportunity. A privilege."

Chairman Bilgili said the board had not yet begun discussing the process of searching for Elmas's successor. "We're shaken. We're in a bit of a crunch now, as Yusuf knows. His will be horribly difficult shoes to fill. We'll look for the best technical and business minds, in and out of the organization. We'll rebound. I can guarantee investors that. The best companies weather changes of this sort. Teletürk is such a company."

In his statement Elmas emphasized he has given no thought about what comes next for him personally. "At this point I have neither solicited nor received any offers." He hoped to continue to serve the public good, but politics was not on the horizon. "Yusuf has told me many times that he was not suited for office," Bilgili said. "He has zero interest in pursuing a political career, at the city or at the national level."

Teletürk shares, which made their debut on the local market on Nov 8, 1994, have traded below the price of TL5.60, at which they were sold to institutional investors over six years. The stock closed at TL 4.73 yesterday...

I'd scooped up the rest of that week's papers. Commentary in the business pages surmised that Yusuf was cashing out, yielding his controlling shares and accepting a buyout of his holdings without properly alerting investors. By Monday, to quell these rumors and calm shareholders' nerves, Teletürk staff had issued invitations to select press and dignitaries for a farewell black-tie dinner in two weeks' time, when further details would be offered. So our raucous news media reeled in its assumptions, and now everyone figured Yusuf Elmas was simply retiring, like all good billionaires did, to focus on his charitable work.

The well-documented retirement celebration was held on the second Saturday of November, on the tiled roof of the Armada Hotel, just behind the Blue Mosque. All reports confirmed it was a velvet-smooth evening, with a breeze rolling across the Marmara churning up green waves. In the waning sun the straits were alive with speckled light. To the west the cupolas of the Aya Sofya loomed in their bulbous splendor, and in the opposite direction, out to sea, the staunch grey humps of the Princes' Islands propped up the sky. Fourteen round tables were draped in white, a string quartet played on stools beneath a covered pavilion, and the waiters served the grilled squid mezes and salt-crusted bluefish with efficiency and grace. The wind picked up after the sun finally set, and couples danced on a small parquet floor as the nightly touristic light show blared over the landmark mosques behind them. Across the straits sounded distant wedding fireworks. The air was laden with anticipation. Yusuf Elmas, CEO, known to come to a party in high spirits and dance with every woman present, had sat alone at his table, his chin in his palm, watching the couples gliding in ovals around one another. In the press accounts some guests later acknowledged his pensiveness, but most understood it as a simple matter of pride. The man was saddened to be relinquishing power over his holdings — eleven companies employing over 15,000 people. Others argued: if he was so sad, why on earth had he made this rash decision to step down without warning? In the months to come I personally liked to imagine this reported melancholy stemming from wistfulness — from regret that he could not share this moment, this celebration of the heights of his achievements, with those who had once mattered most to him.

The sky had darkened and it had begun to drizzle, but the quartet played intrepidly on until precisely 9:30 when, with a raised finger, Yusuf signaled the company's Vice President that he was ready. A light wooden podium was hauled up on stage and Yusuf strode towards it, took a hand from the cellist stepping up, and adjusted the microphone and his bowtie. He glanced around; perhaps he had not counted on as many news agencies covering the event, or as full a spectrum of politicians and dignitaries in attendance. Dr. Murat Baykan was there, as were Erdan Özakin, and the Mayor of the Islands, and three high-ranking members of the *Meclis*, who'd flown directly from the capital following a parliamentary victory. In televised news briefs Yusuf would appear thin and haggard. He cleared his throat into his closed fist, blinked, and without any written notes spoke too close to the microphone.

The speech took an immediate and unexpected turn from business. He used the occasion to talk at length about his expectations for a speedy acceptance of the country into the

European Union. About his respect for his beloved homeland, which had given his own family — "Jews, as everyone here knows" — refuge over the past five centuries. It was his first public acknowledgement since he had changed his surname of his minority background. He spoke of historical identity, of our distant relatives who'd fled the inquisition and Queen Isabella's rule and, wandering Northern Africa and Southern Europe, found a haven here as artisans among the Muslims of the Ottoman empire. He spoke of closer relations still, of our mother's father, who had rushed to these shores, "only a few hundred meters from this hotel rooftop where I now address you," to drag our grandmother from the freezing waters. He mentioned his humble upbringing, his father a jeweler and shopkeeper, his mother a baker of *yufka*. He spoke of historical guilt. "I look at Germany today, a nation whose people perpetrated the genocide my grandmother fled. A nation where many of our own brothers and sisters now seek work. I see a free and open nation, struggling to come to terms with its own unutterable crimes. It's no easy task. It will never be finished. But who could have predicted this fifty years ago? So it is possible to begin. It's possible. When Europe asks us to do the same, I say it's possible. I'm suggesting dignity. We're a proud nation of tolerance, but one that refuses still to come to terms with our mistakes. The Armenians in 1915. Today, the Kurds. We talk of none of it. A nation that won't acknowledge its crimes is no nation anyone should accept into its club of brothers. It makes us poorer in every way."

The Mayor of the Islands had told me he was sitting less than ten meters away, picking the onions out of his shepherd's salad with his fork, when Yusuf had uttered the word. "For a moment, as it slipped from your brother's mouth, I closed my eyes, wishing myself he had not said it. Could he have been unaware of what he'd just done? Equating the tragedy of the Jews with that of the Armenians? I felt the insult myself. But he went on with his speech, without missing a note."

Yusuf spoke of his gratitude for the economic opportunities this country had given a man of his background, of his hopes for its golden future, of its central role in world affairs. He called us a "a crucial secular model for the region."

Finally he announced the resignation of his position. In answer to the question on everyone's mind — why now? — he alluded only to a vague motivation "to pursue private matters." He smiled and bowed his head, and to uncertain applause thanked the guests for attending. He hopped off the stage, landed on both feet, but stumbled slightly and had to be helped up from a crouch by a stylish young woman standing off to the side. He quickly recovered; and at his slashing signal the quartet struck up again. From the heavens what had begun as a misty drizzle now sped into a rousing downpour. Women, hitching their gowns, escaped to the indoor bar. Television crews scurried to cover their equipment. At his table Yusuf shook hands all around, then excused himself for the restroom. He did not return. Even his closest friends had no idea where he'd gone. Guests of honor, crouching beneath umbrellas the waiters were hastily assembling, left in confusion before the crème brûlée was served.

"We were all in shock, full of dread," Dr. Murat Baykan had recalled for me. "Hell, this was no hushed dinner conversation over a beer on Nevizade Street. This was a public function, with television cameras whirring and journalists taking notes. A fool-hardy speech!"

Naomi and I had stayed up for the 11:00 news on NTV that night. In a thirty-second clip, the first I would see, the retirement speech was covered, the speech reported, the word "genocide" quoted and replayed. For weeks to come I scoured four papers a day for coverage of my brother. Everyone expected the guillotine to descend in the form of charges brought by some lackey of the state. The rumors circulated, but the much-expected fallout never fell. Could my brother have clout enough, connections enough, to openly challenge the presiding powers in such a way? Surely not.

2

A Bottle of 1907 Heidsieck

PERHAPS THE GOOD will of our Generals might have successfully been tested a single time. Recent courageous artists and journalists had proven it was possible. But what got my brother into trouble were continual references to events in our history that, for all the trappings of our democracy, we're not at liberty to speak of. Yusuf might have any time stopped alluding to them; he knew the dangers. Speech by speech he kept it up. Over a four-month period following his abrupt resignation Yusuf traveled through Europe and North America on a well-publicized schedule. He spoke at the Economic Summit of Developing Nations in Milan. He gave the inaugural address for the First Congress of Russian Rabbis in St. Petersburg, broke ground for new synagogues in Warsaw and Montreal, attended the Nobel Peace Prize ceremonies, as well as the Venice Biennale. He appeared on panels at Davos with Silicon Valley technocrats and former U.S. Secretary of State Warren Christopher. He pledged twenty-million dollars to Bill Clinton's Aids foundation. He was interviewed on English and German news television shows: on the VOA, on the ARD, and most notably on CNN's Worldview, hashing things out with the international editor of Time Magazine. Attention to his politics had grown acute.

Over and over Yusuf was offering a more detailed version of the retirement speech he'd delivered that fall at the Armada Hotel. What he seemed to be doing (and I only appreciated the strategy after my astonishment faded) was embracing his role as a public face of our nation's entry into the European Union, while using that cover to criticize our hard-headed leaders. To me, at first, it had seemed brilliant and brave. He touted again and again the great social and economic progress our once-backward nation had in so short a time made. He appealed to Europe to open its doors to the riches our entry as co-equal members of the union would ensure. He held us up as a singularly tolerant Muslim nation, a close ally of Israel and the United States, the essential link between East and West. But Yusuf's liberal instincts were difficult to pin down, and he remained an iconoclast to the end. I hated one stance in particular: unlike ninety percent of the country he supported the war in Iraq, thanking America for providing accountability towards the tyrants of the world, chiding our public for its willing appeasement of terrorists. Our geography, he said, had blessed us strategically while cursing us with threats from every direction. We had "no choice but to eliminate such cancers before they metastasized." It seemed to me that Yusuf's blind love for all things Western, plus a life-long willingness to overturn the chessboard, had led him to support the misadventure, when anyone with sense denounced America's bullying of our politicians.

Into a closed mouth a fly doesn't enter. Of course, any stance a person takes in this overly politicized country is going to be problematic to someone. Surely Yusuf had insulted large segments of the population. But none of it would have incited death threats and calls for his imprisonment. It would all have passed quickly enough. The Pope was visiting. Iraq was in tatters. As a nation we had great things preoccupying us. I see now that if my brother had simply shut his mouth, he might have bought himself a bit more time.

Speech by speech he further challenged our nation's intractability towards its own recent past. He denounced the Greek repatriation of 1923 and the government-induced riots of 1955. He mentioned, in a single sentence, that upwards of a million Armenians were murdered in 1915, and over the last few decades tens of thousands of Kurds. "But who in my country is willing to talk about this?" he was quoted in the *Milliyet* as asking. "A silent donkey is taken to be a sage." And then, infamously: "Our leaders are in the doomed business of muffling history. It'll come back to haunt us. It always does. My heart bleeds for this gagged nation of ours."

By then Yusuf's melancholy had settled into something like mania. He must have known death was tracking him, if not in the form of the National Intelligence Organization, then disguised as some ultranationalist loony or socialist iconoclast or vicious anti-Semite or military idealist. In one editorial Alper Karasu, keeping count, claimed Elmas had used the term "genocide" eighteen times over a period of four months. The press attacked: They misquoted him. They misrepresented the thrust of his pro-nationalist, pro-secularist stances. Very few people I knew would have argued with his words, but very few of us doubted repercussions would come.

Our nation waited, some with eagerness, for the other shoe to drop. The social papers were gleefully noting his absence from his usual charity functions. Many of Yusuf's remaining friends had stopped defending him to the press. High level executives at Teletürk were resigning at a furious pace. By that March he was not to be seen, and there were whisperings on television that he had gone into hiding. "Let's just say it wouldn't have been a stupid thing to do," the journalist Koreli Ahmetöğlü, who'd covered Yusuf's story for the *Hurriyet*, had written on his weekly blog. "I myself would never have resurfaced."

Yusuf, it turned out, was not in hiding, but was simply vacationing in Miami, Florida, following his beloved speedboat poker races in Thunderboat Alley. At the end of the festival he was photographed there, in a South Beach lounge, partying with his NBA basketball friend Mehmet Aykol and advertising mogul Erdan Özakin. The grainy photograph had been taken on a mobile phone. It showed Aykol pouring champagne with his impossibly long, outstretched arm, into a glass Yusuf was holding, at an angle, from a cushioned couch. The caption claimed it was a $275,000 bottle of 1907 Heidsieck, salvaged from a shipwreck off the coast of Finland.

Not even two weeks after that photograph was splattered across tabloid websites, inflaming passions further, Yusuf had flown back home.

3

The Solitary Prince

"He came in on a trans-Atlantic red-eye," Koreli Ahmetöğlü had written, reporting on Yusuf's infamous return to TAV Airport, "With an economy class ticket he had purchased himself online. I was among the press that greeted him, and asked if he thought he would somehow slide in under the radar by traveling on the cheap. Denying it, Elmas joked he simply wanted to see how well his old Princess.com website was holding up. It didn't seem to torment him that he was at the center of attention and speculation. He wheeled his own luggage to passport control, where he waited calmly in line with his fellow passengers."

The circus began. Yusuf was held at the customs gate by armed gendarmes, escorted to the airport police station, and served notice of the first charges against him. Article 301 of the Penal Code. He was accused on multiple counts of "insulting the state" and "betraying the nation" and "denigrating national identity." The night of his return, press cameras flashing, his lawyer announced Yusuf Elmas had been indicted with up to three years of jail for each offense: prison as far as the eye could see.

"It's come to this," Naomi remarked with pity in her voice, on hearing the news. "Your idiot brother's finally getting his due."

The pending trial, as covered in the international headlines, put him in an awkward position I can't believe he'd foreseen. Yusuf had become a symbol, a shuttlecock to be swatted back and forth over the mahogany tables of five-star hotel conference rooms across Europe. Secularists said by referencing the Armenian Genocide he was denigrating the nation. French officials cited the upcoming trial as an example of human rights abuses and the lack of free speech that made them hesitate to embrace our country. E.U. spokespersons warned our Prime Minister that prosecution of intellectuals (Intellectuals! My brother!) was harmful to our membership bid. Then the Left chimed in, saying the sheer publicity of Yusuf's international campaign had backfired, that the Elmas Trial would hold the nation back from achieving its dream of Westernization. The paranoid among us claimed it was all a ruse devised by ultra-nationalist lawyers to take the country back fifty years, and that Yusuf himself was in on it all — that he too was a member of the Deep State. My billionaire brother was arraigned panoramically. During that time I searched his name on Google News, and over 1,400 articles referencing him — each vitriolic headline worse than the next — had appeared in the previous three weeks.

"And what did Elmas do to defend himself?" Koreli Ahmetöğlü later wrote in his best-selling, state-sanctioned, smear of a biography, *The Solitary Prince: The Death and Life of Yusuf Elmas*. "He continued to toss the word into every public appearance he held. Just one word. As an aside. Squeezed in, always, by definitive statements of his love for the state, for his homeland, for this place of refuge, this nation that had allowed his great fortune. But nothing else mattered: the word was like that single thin ingredient spread into a *tost* sandwich, a tiny bit of flavoring beneath mounds of meat and cheese and salads, all pressed and melted together. Yet it was the only ingredient you tasted. It stuck in the throat."

The hungry vortex of our national media had eaten it up. Newspaper columnists, following the lead of the publisher Vehbi Özakin (whose house Yusuf had once swindled) launched relentless online campaigns urging boycotts of Teletürk cellular phone contracts and Princess Airlines flights. At weekend demonstrations in Taksim Square banners of Teletürk logos were burned by throngs of stomping university students. The company's Internet advertising campaigns had been cut off. Teletürk commercials were banned — even on private television channels, and even though Yusuf had relinquished control of the company. Now we all better understood the merciful timing of his resignation. What none of us yet understood was the provocative urge that had gripped him. It came to me only months later, after he was gone, that this had been the driving force of his life: not to be limited by fear, or by others' definitions of him. Forever the combative mentality of the outsider.

And it wasn't simply jail time my brother had to worry about. His island home had become a fortress, with fingerprint recognition added to beef up the programmable key cards needed for entry, and a full-time security boat patrolling the dock.

These heightened security measures seemed providential when, two Sundays after his return from Miami, Yusuf was found sprawled unconscious behind a bench in the park above Taksim

Square, his dress shirt torn, his face bloodied, his chest caved in with broken ribs, his thigh slashed open by two knife gashes.

Police had reportedly 'discovered' him in this state, although there were questions raised in the international press over who had actually found him and where. Some news accounts said it had been a random mugging. Talk-show pundits surmised political retaliation. Columnists suggested: fair warning. Bloggers wondered what a man of Yusuf's standing was doing in one of the more infamous parks of the city, where in the darkest hours sex tourists and heroin addicts and transvestites cruised for one score or another. Yusuf had been out with his friend Murat until two that morning. According to police transcripts leaked to the press my brother testified that, searching for a taxi to Arnavutköy (where he planned to spend the night in his yacht) he had been attacked, beaten unconscious, and dragged into the park. It was an entirely plausible story. Nobody believed it. The park had too dark a reputation, Yusuf was too wide a target for the press to resist letting loose with a flurry of cruel speculation.

Later, in the weeks after his death, our fake television news investigations would spend prime-time hours rehashing the lurid possibilities of that evening, mining the event for some hidden connection to his final disappearance at sea one month later. As the narrator ran through the possibilities, actors with blurred faces portrayed Yusuf sharing needles with heroin addicts, propositioning a man in a flowery pink dress, stroking the faces of school boys in the shadows behind the McDonalds. The voice-over asked with grave seriousness: Was Elmas caught at last in the organized drug rings he was suspected to be running? Had he been using black money to force school boys to submit to his will? For weeks programs of this kind panned over the same official police photo, the handsome playboy with one eye swollen shut, a five o-clock shadow peppering his cheeks, hair tangled about his forehead, neck splotched in violet black bruises: a mess of a man who had let fortune go to his head and believed, in the words of one television special, that he was "beyond any moral considerations." Half a country away I'd watch these shows, unable to avert my eyes. Naomi would beg me to change the channel, and when I couldn't she'd corral the twins into their room and read them their Winnie the Pooh books. Alone, I'd turn up the volume.

4

A Friend in Cyprus

I HAD AN APPOINTMENT, at last, to discuss work with my old drafting buddy Omer, back in the city. On the way to the ferry I went to drop off two checks in the PTT. Waiting in line, I turned to find the Mayor waiting as well, just behind me. "This old man," he whispered too loudly, indicating the postmaster, "moves like a sloth. I sometimes think he personally holds up the entire progress of these islands." The words echoed around the dingy wood-paneled room. The mayor laughed. The postmaster looked up. He was helping a scarved retiree two customers ahead of us search out a letter that had never come.

"Dr. Ayda Subaşi?" the mayor said with a soft whistle. I turned to find him nodding his head at me. "Heard you had a little meeting with Yusuf's old friend."

"You know her?"

"I know of her. Professionally."

"She mentioned we met?"

"News makes its way. In my office, Avram, you hear of such things. Listen, please, I'm going to give you some advice, as a close friend of your brother's, listen to me. I'm worried for you."

"I appreciate it."

"Please Avram, watch your back. It's one thing to be asking questions here on the island. It's another…entirely… Listen to me, I worry."

"Thank you sir. I appreciate it. I do." I was fingering the envelopes I needed to mail. We waited another minute in frustrated silence. The old lady at the desk wasn't taking no for an answer.

"Tell me how the house is coming."

I turned again. The Mayor knew, I guessed, perfectly well how the house was coming. Last week the Municipality had rejected my application to replace a railing on the floating pier, claiming "aesthetic conflicts" with the Monuments Council's regulations and citing the "historical authenticity" of the rotting wooden rails I wanted to replace. I'd received a bill demanding back-payments to property taxes I'd already made. The Governor's Mansion wouldn't help me; they said my Land Owner's ID Card had not been properly signed, and then claimed to have no record of my payments. Two days later I was cited for submitting the improper *Declaration Form on Plumbing Work*, then again for not bothering with the property's *Soil Survey Report*, which I'd been assured wasn't needed. Yesterday a secretary from Zoning and City Planning had come to the mansion, asking when renovations "intrusive to the peacefulness of a culturally significant neighborhood" would be completed.

"I could use some help actually," I told the mayor. While we waited some more I explained the hold-up with the floating pier, the confusion on the property taxes.

"This is progress, I tell you." He clicked his tongue and said he'd see what he could do to expedite the situation. "None of it surprises me, honestly. They expect us to govern the municipality on ten-year old computer systems. A single fax machine. Dot matrix printers. These things happen constantly. Let them beg me to run again, I say. I've had it to here."

When it was my turn at the desk I stepped aside to let the worked-up Mayor receive his package before me.

"*Beyefendim*, it hasn't come yet, I'm afraid," the postmaster told him.

"Nothing?" He'd raised his voice, as if the postmaster was to blame.

The poor man checked again and clicked his tongue. The Mayor turned on his heels. "Take it easy then, Avram," he said, walking out of the post office, a hand on his heart. "And let's be careful, please. I worry." The postmaster's eyes followed the mayor out the door until we were alone.

"He's in Famagusta," he murmured, his face twisted, handing me my own mail. "Cyprus."

"I'm sorry?"

"Your friend. In Cyprus." He was mumbling into his desk now; he wouldn't look at me.

"I have no friends in Cyprus." I wondered if he was losing it, confusing me with someone. I smiled and handed him ten lira for a book of stamps.

"Sometimes people do and don't recall." With his deformed left hand — one finger, one thumb — slowly he counted out my change, made a mistake, and slowly counted again. I saw what the Mayor had meant now about the old man. I was going to miss the ferry, and then my appointment with Omer, if he didn't hurry. Slowly handing over my last lira, slowly the book of stamps, he said, "Strange country. We all have a friend in Cyprus, Avram Benezra, whether we'll admit it or not." I thanked him, hardly processing his senile nonsense, and rushing down to the pier I made the ferry with seconds to spare.

In the city an hour later I found Omer's office just off Taksim, on Cumhuriyet Caddesi, in a five-story complex he shared with the Consulate of India. The elevator doors opened but wouldn't shut, so I had to climb to the fifth floor through a half-lit staircase that smelled strongly of curry. Omer greeted me warmly, but he was all business, and didn't even ask after my family. Perhaps my old co-worker had heard where I stood with Naomi, and was sparing me. He said he'd start me off shadowing one of his consulting teams until I learned the ropes. His civil engineers were still surveying municipal buildings — courts, hospitals, marriage houses — for any residual earthquake damage and potential vulnerabilities. Crack patterns, leans, buckled walls, shear failures, foundational movement. I'd write up recommendations for retrofitting and de-scriptions of basic construction inadequacies. When it came to the material quality and non-engineered design of the oldest buildings, a certain level of hazard was allowable. "We can't expect the entire city be rebuilt, can we?" Omer asked with a loud barking laugh. I now remembered how this laugh had always annoyed me. There was a lot of rubber-stamping involved, he warned. Occasionally one had to turn a blind eye to what one found. Omer needed me comfortable with the scope of the firm's billable hours before he'd send me out supervising my own teams. He used the term *flexible billing options* — as if it was a special service he offered the govern-ment, and not a clear gouging of public funds.

He was testing me, concerned I might not play ball. It all seemed one step removed from architectural design and a few pegs below even drafting jails. After these months of hands-on restorations I didn't know if I could put on a suit and tie — in service of what? Omer's wallet? False certifications? TOKI covering up for its historic lack of public housing oversight? But what choice did I have? I stood, accepted, and thanking Omer profusely, shook his single hand with two of mine.

As easy as that, I was employed again.

Out in the hallway the elevator, summoned, never came. After a few moments I trudged down the five flights of stairs.

5

The Ten-Year March

I WAS STOPPING BY to check in with my father, and would have to pass the German Hospital on my way down Siraselviler. Dr. Murat Baykan had an office around here. My time playing at restorations was now running out; my schedule would soon be full. From what I'd learned about Yusuf over these last months I couldn't help feeling his best friend had known more than he'd let on.

I found the doctor's phone number on my mobile, but couldn't reach him. A few moments later, while I was schlepping my way through Taksim Square, he called back. "Avram Benezra, you've caught me at a bad time. What do you need?" Apparently Murat was still miffed with me for abandoning him with his three young gypsies on our outing back in December. Now he'd stepped out of some kind of testicular surgery to return my call. What was so urgent?

I ignored the put-upon tone, and sat down on a low white fence by the Republic Monument. I asked him if he knew anything about what Yusuf was doing with his cook in the Halim Pasha House.

Murat went quiet on the phone. "Whatever Yusuf did on that

island of his was his own business. I tried not to get involved."

"So you knew. And you knew Yasemin, the girl who went down with him, was this woman's daughter? But that you didn't explain either."

"Avram, listen."

"What about the *Salvador*? Did you know he was looking for our grandmother's boat?"

"Yes, I knew."

"Tell me if he found it. *Haydi*, that's all I want."

"Even from me, his closest friend, he had his secrets. He told me so little of what he was doing. To protect me, see. How do you think that makes me feel?"

My breath came evenly, slowly. "How does it make you feel, Murat?"

"Shitty. It was never easy being loyal to your brother, and it still isn't. What would you like me to say, Avram? You have to understand where he was in those last months. I was his one true friend. I tiptoed around his schemes. He had nobody. "

"Look, I'm close by in Taksim. Can you meet? We'll talk face to face." I suggested I'd come up to his office if he had the time.

"Why don't I meet you on the island? This weekend?"

"The island's no longer a good place to talk Murat."

"Why's that?"

How to explain my fears without sounding paranoid? All this week I'd been unable to walk to the ferry or hardware store without running into the balding Officer Ceber, or spotting him a block or two behind me.

"Murat," I said, "they're sending me signals. You don't need to be seen with me there."

He hesitated. "Better if I come down. Give me thirty minutes. Where are you?"

I waited for the doctor by walking halfway up Istiklal, then back down past the French Consulate, and across the tram tracks of Taksim Square. All around me the place was being cleaned up, Europeanized, the casinos and pornographic cinemas that had once sparked my teenage fantasies were gone, the *kokoreç* stands — grilled innards with a delectable smell — gone. A metro stop gutted the center of the square, our city's useless attempt to relieve traffic. Across the street, on a kiosk at the National Cultural Center, I examined the week's schedule. A tribute to our Founding Father was on the bill: The Ten Year March, The Black Sea March. Eminently missable. The children's program this coming weekend listed some production called *The Happy Prince*. It was the only show I'd pay to see.

When I spotted the doctor he was shuffling across the uneven gray cobblestones of the square. I waved for him to wait, and dodged my way across the Formula 1 Racetrack this traffic circle had become. Murat was patting his face with a handkerchief and undoing the second button of his dress shirt, revealing silver tufts of hair.

"Long day?"

He was out of breath. "Tsk! You spared me another surgery. A colleague's stepping in. Simple vasectomy. I do them with my eyes closed. Believe me, my young colleague can use the practice."

Past the lines of idling buses we found a seat on the steps at the cement base of an empty flagpole, where our conversation could be drowned by the rush and swirl of traffic. I was filling him in on what Ayda Subaşı had told me.

"See, it wasn't only me, Avram. He offered himself fully to nobody. Everyone who knew him got only part of the story."

"A month before he died," I said, "there were rumors he was lying low in the U.S. In Miami? Is that even true?"

"He was supposed to be vacationing, following the races in Thunderboat Alley. That's what we told people. That's what he wanted people to know."

The real story, according to the Doctor, was this: Yusuf had spent three weeks at the Cystic Fibrosis Center in Miami's St. Mary's Hospital, submitting to CT scans and pulmonary function tests, then to an experimental hypertonic saline solution treatment. Murat had learned about the procedure from a former medical school colleague, and had convinced Yusuf he might be eligible for the clinical trial.

"He knew — the end stages were approaching. There was certainly denial there. Even with treatment for scarring and lung inflammation, Yusuf would be lucky to see forty. *Vallahi*! He was in so deep, in so much trouble everywhere. I figured it would be good for him to step out of the limelight. Let things quiet down. For a few weeks at least. I hoped longer."

"Why didn't he stay in Miami?"

"He wasn't a candidate for the extended treatment, Avram. His lungs were too far gone. The doctors couldn't help. They gave him less than a year."

"They told him that?"

"One year, at most."

"I didn't know." I looked at my brother's friend. It hit me hard now, as if it still mattered.

The doctor clicked his tongue, raised his eyebrows, and

swung up his arms. "No one did. I found this out in confidence from my colleague at St. Mary's."

The light had changed, and taxis were cutting off an ambulance blaring its siren. I held my breath through a cloud of exhaust a *dolmuş* spit past us. A bus lurched to the left, taking the circle too quickly. Seeing it nearly too late, a herd of white-clad Arab tourists scuttled like frightened sheep back to the safety of the median by the Marmara Hotel.

"How had he taken the news?"

"How had he always taken it? In Miami they'd cleared his lungs and he was released. By that time his visa had nearly expired. There were a hundred simple ways he could have extended it, Avram. Instead of remaining close to the best medical care available, he returns to our city. He steps right into the storm. He comes back and before he even picks up his bags, he's officially charged at the airport. Article 301. He knew exactly what he was returning to. Listen, I wanted him only to rest. He insisted nothing change. Weekdays, weekends, one woman, three women, old girlfriends, new, what did it matter now? He'd call me up, I'd go. How could I say no to a dead man?"

Awaiting his sham of a trial they had frequented with renewed energies the *meyhanes* of Beyoğlu, the tavernas of Aksaray, the oriental clubs of Teşvikiye, the open air sea bars of Ortaköy. I pictured them in the gypsy houses of Sulukule, dancing with the angels of love, or in the hotel lobbies of Floralı, admiring *Natashas* from Moldova and Kazakhstan, dark women blowing double trails of smoke from their nostrils, casting lurid glances at the well-dressed men.

"But it was risky for you, too, wasn't it?" I asked the doctor.

"I'm not trying to sound brave here. I was always looking over my shoulder. We'd leave these Beyoğlu *meyhanes*, and for blocks and blocks I'd hear footsteps. I wasn't his goddamned bodyguard. We should have been in a limousine. We could have been in a penthouse in London. Strolling the streets of Paris. We could have holed ourselves up at the Oriental in Bangkok, listening to jazz and drinking Mekong Whiskey. None of this posturing was necessary. On principle he wasn't willing to give up any of this grand life he'd built for himself. "Principle," I told him, "is going to get you killed." I'm ashamed, but I dreaded going out with him." The doctor had begun making excuses, cutting their evenings short. "Even inviting him to our box for the Super League Cup, it took nerve on my part. I was honestly afraid to sit next to the man in public."

I told him he was right to be afraid.

The doctor flung his hand out towards Taksim Park. "Then he gets found over there. Cut up, beaten, mauled."

"You were with him that night?"

Murat's shoulders tensed; he was glowering at me. "What do you take me for, Avram? Yes, I was with him. I'd been out with him until two that morning. We'd said our goodbyes. I left him with a taxi, just over there. My story doesn't change. The truth doesn't change. You can believe it or choose not to. Am I suddenly a suspect?"

"So he was attacked after you left him then?"

"Attacked in the park, attacked in the press. On TV, online, on the radio. Tsk! What those bastards did to him, once he was gone, I've never seen anything like it."

"And did you see him at the hospital while he was recovering?"

"*I* was the one who made him *come* to the German Hospital. It was me. You're not getting it, Avram. Even beaten to bloody pulp he wouldn't have rested. God knows what would have happened. I flew in nurses from Munich. We stationed security guards outside his room."

"Men you trusted?"

"I trusted them, I trusted them. I was honestly more worried they'd let him out of bed, out of the hospital, than let anyone in. Yusuf was determined to get out before he was ready. He would have pulled the IV's and strolled right out himself if we weren't watching him. I slipped his guards *bahşiş* to keep him there."

At this I smiled. "My brother — your prisoner."

"You're the jail expert, Avram." The doctor bent over, rubbing his knees, falling silent while a man wheeling a handcart past us nearly ran over our toes. On the handcart was a beat-up produce box. In the produce box was a young boy, sleeping.

"Yes, until he recovered, he was my prisoner in the hospital. We practically had to tie him down on that bed. He only wanted out of there. His days, he felt, were falling away fast, and he told me he had work to do. I was trying to get him to slow down, take care of arrangements. Catch his breath. Between you and me, I just wanted the man to shut his mouth for a week or two. Let things settle. "So much I've missed, Murat," he'd say to me in the hospital. I assured him he'd missed nothing. He owed nobody apologies."

"What kind of arrangements were you trying to get him to see to?"

"His personal affairs were a disaster. Power of attorney. Do not resuscitate orders. He hadn't revised his will. For all he was concerned, the world would lurch to a halt once he was gone. He had to take care of his legacy. Tsk! Legacy! He didn't want to hear about any legacy. So we struck a deal: he'd get his affairs in order, and I'd arrange his release home."

"You're telling me he saw to his final effects from the hospital?"

"We had his lawyers summoned to his room. He dictated changes to his last will and testament from his bed, into a digital tape recorder. When they brought the printed copy back, the security guards served as witnesses."

I was trying to imagine the scene. "Were you in the room with him, Murat? Did he speak to you about any of this? About leaving my father his villa — did he give any reason?"

The doctor rolled his eyes. "No, no, no, they wouldn't permit it. If Yusuf wanted to leave me anything, I couldn't be there. I told his lawyers I didn't care if Yusuf left me a single Euro. But conflict of interest. His lawyers tossed me out of there."

"And did Yusuf — in the end — leave you anything?"

"Me?" At the doctor's feet two pigeons were tugging on opposite ends of a juice box straw. The doctor, watching them, had a wistful look in his eye. "Yes. His one true possession. A thing I coveted above all else. He knew I loved it more than I loved anything — or anyone, even him."

"What was that?"

Dr. Baykan put a hand on my shoulder and swung himself up off the concrete steps, turned to face me and help me up. "Your brother left me his speedboat, the *Bosphorus Princess*."

6

Releasing the Staff

THE OUTSIDE PORCH had been painted, the kitchen updated, the furnace replaced, the garden fully weeded and readied for replanting. We had scrubbed the age out of the villa, removing mote by mote its five years and 500 square meters of accumulated dust and mold and grime. I had sealed leaking pipes, straightened sagging gutters, refinished the opened wall and refurnished the office into a spacious bedroom with access to a bath and the back door — more than enough room for an old man to live comfortably on the first floor alone. I was employed again. I could take the Governor's Office's hints; I hadn't come here to raise any trouble. After four months of steady restorations it was finally time to get my father out here, to look at the mansion.

Only loose ends to tie before his visit. I'd been waiting for a kitchen gas delivery, fighting with a stubborn manager who didn't seem to want my business. I'd paid for the delivery two weeks ago, but at the Ay Gas station in the village the manager told me, "I sent the boy myself — you weren't at home."

"When?"

"Yesterday."

"Look, I'll take one now."

"How will you carry it, *beyefendim*?"

"I'll hire a *fayton*. Let me go around the block and talk to a driver. Put the *tüp* out front."

"But installation."

"I've done this a million times."

"You have a new oven, an Aristan. I couldn't let you do such a thing."

I was sick of him already. "My father's visiting. We won't be able to cook in a day or two. Bring it by tomorrow or I'll take my business down the street."

"Yes, *beyefendim*."

Meanwhile I had disassembled Yusuf's cast-iron bed, and Mustafa Faik had helped me move it piece by piece downstairs to the new first-floor bedroom. Its king-sized mattress, however, proved too unwieldy for the old man; and in our attempt to lift it I'd discovered the source of its sour smell: the mattress had grown moldy with peppered spots.

I asked Nılay and Flora which of them had made the bed, whether either of them had noticed the state of the mattress. They claimed they hadn't. I had no time for this. Nılay defensively suggested a Katibim showroom that had always supplied Yusuf's bedroom furnishings. Flora offered to come with me shopping in the city, to show me where it was. I told her that wasn't necessary, but she insisted.

In the Bostanci store there had been an awkwardness picking out that replacement mattress together. "You'll never sleep better," the salesman assured us. "It's Swedish! Lie down and try. I dare you. I dare you." With Flora watching on I had lowered myself onto the mattress, trying to assess what Father would make of it. "Soft?" the salesman insisted. "Soft? It's a pillow-top, see. Lie down. All the way back. That's it. It's Swedish, see?"

Swedish, pillow-top, or not, I couldn't tell how it might feel without the plastic packaging creased beneath my back. I stared up at the fluorescent lights, examining the ceiling HVAC system, thinking Naomi and I had lived for nineteen years with the same old mattress — full of lumpy creaking springs, worn down by the accumulated years of our aging bodies — and neither of us had ever complained. Would Father even care about a pillow-top?

All at once at the salesman's insistence Flora flopped down next to me. "Tell him," he was saying. "Tell your husband how comfortable you are in this new bed. Tell him you're sick of your crappy old bed!"

We were lying shoulder to shoulder. Flora hesitated. Instead of correcting him, she cranked her head towards me and whispered, "I'm sick of my crappy old bed."

I stared at the merciless fluorescent lights. I shifted. The mattress at that moment seemed firmer and more luxurious than anything I'd ever slept on myself. In the mad scheme of renovations I had overextended myself in countless ways. Now, with a job in sight, what were another thousand Euros spent on a top-quality mattress? Let the old man have a pillow-top.

It was delivered on the same ferry we rode to the island, and when I made it back to the house I found the Ay Gas delivery had also come. That night I tried Yusuf's bed once again, now on the side of the room that had previously been the maid's quarters. I still couldn't sleep on it. The villa's pipes slamming, the floorboards moaning, seemed suddenly loud enough to wake the dead. I noticed drafts I hadn't noticed before from the opposite side of the room, and even fully turned up the radiators could hardly warm the enlarged open space. I hibernated under three woolen blankets. I heard strange noises. Was it the wind? The calls of distant ships? Or him still? When I closed my eyes I could feel Yusuf's presence watching me, weighing my feeble grounds for existence in this world. I was convinced I might open my eyes and find my brother staring up at me from the foot of his bed, hands on his hips.

Nice mattress, he'd say. *Swedish?*

We were finished, but it felt strange breaking the news to the staff. The following morning when I attempted, with the utmost tact, to release Nılay Gören, the maid accused me of not keeping my word. She claimed I'd promised her work straight through summer. I had clearly never made such a promise. With arms raised heavenward Nılay accused me of being as "unreliable as your goddamned brother," and then stormed from the house (taking with her, I later found, a set of antique silver serving spoons).

Mustafa Faik handled the news more calmly — too calmly, in fact. The old guard did not seem to process what I was telling him, and though I warned him twice that I could no longer pay his salary, he continued to hang around that day, and would do so for two weeks to come, just to "keep an eye on things."

Flora I found later that morning bending over the cast iron sink in the washroom, scrubbing it out after soaking it in bleach for the fourth day in a row, still trying, and still failing, to remove the rusted shadows of hard water stains. When I told her this was the last day I'd need her she turned from me and leaned further into the sink, scrubbing for all she was worth.

"You want me gone. Is that what you're saying?"

"If there was more to do, I'd keep you on. Stop with the stains already. It's as clean as we need it. Stop."

She rested for a second, propping herself by both arms on the rim of the sink. Her breath came fast and tight. "What now for this place?"

"My father might move in."

"And if he doesn't?"

"We'll have to sell it for him."

On this she was ready to pounce. She turned and thrust an accusing finger at me. "A property like this, and you'll just pass it on to the next bidder. Whatever happened here, it all means nothing to you."

"That's not true."

"Don't make me laugh, Avram Bey. I know your kind. I've known it since I met you. I was right from the very beginning. You'll be glad to wash your hands of our sob stories once and for all. You've come and now you're gone, while we're stuck with it."

"I have work waiting in the city, Flora. I'll be leaving. We're done cleaning. What would you like from me?"

"Nothing. I'm yours to hire or release, as you wish. I float in the wind. That's the way it's always been with you brothers."

Her extreme sensitivity to my leaving took me aback. She was a woman whose depths I would never know. We had spoken for hours; she'd been honest about my brother, honest about her daughter, honest about her Armenian background; but she remained an enigma. Why would she still want to be reminded day after day of all she had suffered in this house?

I stood beside her at the sink. "You miss him?"

Her eyes filled, but she gave me a look of horror. "He was an asshole."

"Exactly."

"A man like every other man."

"But you loved him, Flora."

She wagged her head and set back to work, unleashing a blast of water from the faucet and rinsing out the sink again. I regarded her at my side, perched against the counter, shapely and urgent even in her loose white work clothes. Flora understood what I'd endured with my brother better than anyone. Ours was a strange connection. She felt it as strongly as I did, had felt it since we'd first met, from the moment she had thrust her Armenian butter cookies upon me. For a few seconds I imagined living comfortably with her here in the mansion we'd repaired. An architecture office on the island. Renovations of other historic villas. Fish dinners every week at Ali Baba. A few lazy laps in the Watersports Club swimming pool. A life lived on a grand scale, with my brother's former lover at my side. Who would blame me? Only a sleazy job and the prospects of a divorce awaited me on the mainland. Suddenly there could not have been a more alluring woman in all of Anatolia than Yusuf's amorous cook, stuck in this washroom, unable to get the stains out of the sink, and unwilling to let it go.

"Uff-ya. Go ahead Avram, pawn this place off," Flora said, pushing herself away from the sink. "You try to forget. I don't even try anymore." She dried her hands on a towel, and in two quick jabs of her fingers shoved her loose hair back under her kerchief. "I have to pass this house every time I walk up this shitty street."

With that she left for the kitchen to gather her jacket. I walked through the foyer to the front window, drew aside the tulle curtains, and caught Flora, a cloth shopping bag half-tangled across her shoulder, making her determined way through the statue garden and out the front gate.

7

I Was A Fool To Believe You

ON THE SLOW ferry from Kabataş I tried to sell Father, one last time, on the advantages of living on the island. It seemed a straight-forward choice to me: either he could ride out his remaining days in that dank basement apartment — or enjoy the luxury of an historic villa, with spacious rooms and a garden and fresh breezes, old friends to play cards with at the *Belediye Gazinosu,* and a synagogue only three blocks away. It didn't seem straight-forward to Father. At the mansion he came up the porch grumbling about the lack of a mezuzah on the outside gate. Once I got him inside he hobbled silently among the first floor rooms and hallways. Squinting in the kitchen, he ran his hand across the polished pedestal table and asked what kind of paint I had used. It was, to his mind, the wrong kind. He refused to admire the down-stairs bedroom I had remodeled out of the office, but stood there, opening and closing the drawers of the writing desk, trying to assess how smoothly the dovetailed joints shut. I showed him the bed, pressing down on the mattress. "It's a pillow-top, see? You'll never sleep better." He offered no comment, not a word, and made his way out into the foyer, where he stepped in one direction, hesitated, and stepped back in another. He'd gotten turned around.

"Where do you want to see? Come, I'll show you the second floor."

He had no interest, but I led him by the arm. "It's far too big for me," he said as we climbed the two flights. He was taking a break on each step, one rigid arm locked in mine. "What would I do in such a place?"

It took us two long minutes to make it up the staircase, and as soon as we stepped onto the hardwood of the landing Father said, "Even I can hear that creaking." In the emptied master bedroom he bent down to his knees and ran his hands over the slightly warped floor. Water must have gotten in and the boards were beginning to buckle — a problem only noticeable with the bed removed, and one I'd been willing to ignore for the time being, priorities elsewhere. "You know what this would cost to fix?" Father asked. "We'd have to remove the whole floor. I don't even know how they'd do that!"

"Baba, you're being ridiculous. We wouldn't have to fix it. Not any time soon. There are plenty of other rooms to live in. Have your pick! There's the bedroom downstairs now for you. It's more spacious than anything up here."

"How can you just pretend something's not broken?"

I stepped towards the window, admiring the framed maps of ancient neighborhoods, the early photographs, the panoramas and watercolors of the Marmara and Golden Horn that Yusuf had hung on these bedroom walls. An engraving from the eighteenth century whose glass had cracked still needed to be reframed. With all the neglect it was amazing that anything had survived. What had made it this far had done so barely on a thread. Why couldn't Father accept it on these terms?

I took a deep breath and turned to him. "OK. OK. Let's see. It's the moisture. We'd have to pull up the floorboards, put some kind of damp-proof membrane beneath it. We might have to remove that skirting over there, some of that plaster. You're right," I laughed, "a lot of work."

"I'm seventy-four years old. The last thing I need to be doing is pulling up floorboards."

"We'd do it together. You'd retire here. Enjoy yourself. You've earned it. A house on the island, after all these years. Where would you rather be?"

"Don't you have anything better to do than hanging out with your old man, repairing floors?"

"I'd enjoy it." I bent to help him up by the elbow and shoulder.

"Pathetic, the state it's in." I saw his eyes swell. He wasn't chastising me. He was somewhere else, with another son, the one who had let it all go to hell.

I steered him slowly back down the wooden stairs, around the foyer, and parking him at the kitchen table, found him a diet cola in the refrigerator.

"Look Avram, I don't know why you took this on."

"I did it for you." I poured half the cola into his glass and plonked it too loudly on the table.

"It's time you went home already."

I was staring out the window, past my ghostly reflection, across the late morning fog of the Islamic garden. "Home? What home?" Home for me was a state of longing for some life I'd completely missed.

"You have a wife and daughters."

"Who have left the country."

"Go to them. Do you even know how lucky you are, to have a wife and children like that? So beautiful. Kids that adore you. Go to them. Be with Sara and Estela. Eat their vegetarian pizza. Help Naomi get settled down there. That's what you need to fix. What's a family without a father? This place isn't important to anyone anymore."

"It's historic."

"Should that mean something to us? What's this to us?"

"This is the house your own son left to you." I was yelling to make sure he heard me properly. "He knew it was what you'd always wanted — a house on the Princes' Islands."

"Your brother left me a rotting house with sinking floors to curse me. *Allah kahretsin!* It was his last chance to spit in my face. He blamed *me* for your mother. He blamed *me* for those difficult years."

"You have it wrong, Baba." I lowered my voice. "He was a different man in those last days. He hadn't forgotten us. He thought of you."

"Bah! I know my son. About me he never changed his mind. He blamed *me* for what became of the family. You never forget the hatred of a son. You never forget that blame."

I hadn't understood the house would affect Father so much. I should have seen this coming. "Stop it, Baba. That was all thirty years ago. You're over-thinking this."

"About everything, Yusuf was always right. That's what's so sad."

"Certainly not. Just forget it."

"He knew I'd stolen the money from the shop."

"You didn't steal any money. Forget it already, Baba."

"Doctor's bills. Treatments!"

"Forget it Baba."

"He knew what every procedure and every medication and every clinical visit was costing us. Yusuf knew the equipment. He read our accounts. A perfect mind for numbers, your brother. He knew what we owed down to the lira. Look at me, Avram. Are you listening to me? I couldn't afford to help him any other way."

"You didn't take that money. Uncle Abud took it to frame you. We've always known that." Father was misremembering. Too much life confuses a man. "It was your own jewelry store, Baba. Abud ruined everything for us."

"You don't understand, Avram." He patted his chest. "I took it. Me. I had no choice. Your brother always knew."

I sat across from him at the table, watching an old man shifting arthritically in his chair. I had once wondered what the use of it was, turning over the past, digging deeper and deeper in an attempt to figure out where one's life had gone wrong. I saw Father working for three decades in his closet of a jewelry repair shop, suffering amid that noise this secret of what he'd done, dismantling Mother's death again and again, the way he'd take apart a stopped watch or a bracelet he couldn't fix. Here he was, handing the truth off to me. I didn't want it.

"Baba, that was all so long ago. Who even cares any more?"

His eyes pointed up at the ceiling. "For years I lied to your mother. But she always knew. She could read right through me. With God's help she's forgiven me."

"Yes."

"But you believed. You were the only one."

"Yes."

"You trusted your good father."

"Yes."

He reached for the back of my neck, clasped it with one hand, and drew my head towards his chest. I leaned into his warm old-man's scent and felt his heart beating against my ears, his chest rising and falling beneath his yellowed linen shirt.

"I was a fool to believe you."

"You were a good son."

He let go of my neck and set his elbows on the table, chewing the inside of his mouth. His translucent hands — blue veins, swollen knuckles — were wrapped round his glass of cola, fingers interwoven, still working, always working. "You see now, Avram? I could never live in this house. It's a torment knowing it's here." He pulled from the inside pocket of his wool sports jacket a sealed envelope. "One lifetime of abuse is enough. Take this. I don't want it. Something more your brother left me. Just afterwards this came." He slid it at me. "Take it."

The return address: *Y. Elmas, H.M. Pasha House, Yilmaztürk Caddesi No: 25, Büyükada.* I recognized my brother's florid handwriting. The envelope, stamped 22-04-2005, one day before his accident, was unopened.

8

A Heavenly Piece of Property

THE BROKER FROM the Prinkipos Agency, a squat, thick-wristed, hard-breathing man, perspired climbing the steep stairs of the front porch. I walked him twice around the mansion, pointing out the salon and bathroom on each floor, the six bedrooms with their poster beds, the wide basement for storage, the music room, the renovated office, the waxed cedar floors, the baroque furniture and antique birdcages that would be included with a hypothetical sale, then I led him out through the Islamic garden to show off the refinished pier. All the time the broker snapped random photos with his slim pink digital camera. He took notes on a clipboard, writing with his left hand and nodding, and I had to resist the architect's urge to look over his shoulder and see if he'd written precisely what I'd described.

Near the pier he stopped and turned to view the house across the dry sloping gardens.

"A heavenly piece of property," I suggested. "No? Don't you think? The potential here. Imagine!"

"Well…" he started, but hesitated, chewing over his words with a bovine patience. "These days — the market for antique island property — how to put it? — it's gone." He re-framed his thought, and started again. "Fault lines directly beneath the archipelago," he explained with a weak smile. The pity in his voice hit me hard. Slowly, gesturing towards the house, he explained that two similar estates on this same side of the village had remained vacant for the last five years — properties waiting like the rest of the island for the long predicted follow-up earthquake, which any year now might swallow the archipelago whole. In his first estimation, the house might be worth over two million Euros. But it would be a bear to sell, for that price or even a quarter of it. "Seismic risk. I assume it's at least been structurally renovated to code?" the broker asked.

"No," I admitted. "It's never been reinforced. Intrusive renovations would ruin the historical authenticity, don't you think? That's what Yusuf believed."

He blinked into the glare from the twenty-four north-facing windows, now aflame with the sun. "Foolish. But you said you're an architect. You should have talked your brother into the necessary precautions."

"I should have. I absolutely should have."

We were alone, but the broker glanced left and right before he whispered, "Nobody with any sense would invest under these circumstances. In Yusuf Elmas's house, of all places. You'd have to be mad." With his enormous nicotine-stained fingers he patted his pen against the clipboard. "You might lure a foreigner to take it off your hands. As a second or third home, perhaps. That's the only way I see this going. It might take years to find someone. And foreigners need military clearance to buy property. Didn't you know that?"

"I know now."

"You'll have all those bureaucratic hacks questioning why someone would want to purchase Yusuf Elmas's former mansion. Do you really want to be involved in that? Look Avram, what your brother's left behind is an impressive 500 square meter nightmare. Let me talk to my manager, but I won't promise you anything. I can't recommend our agency getting involved here. You're free to try others."

At the Ali Baba Restaurant that night I ate alone, sipping through an entire bottle of *rakı*. The endive and rocket salad was bitter, the grilled bluefish tasteless — its lone eye staring up at me in accusation. The sun fell behind the archipelago, the sky darkening over the shoreline villas. I was out a lot of money: my severance spent; loans up to my neck. Naomi had been right about the house. A man should listen to his wife or suffer the consequences. I pictured her in Tel Aviv, standing before the Sabbath table this Friday evening, blessing the candles, then blessing my daughters. A cloud passed over me. I poured myself another drink. In the thin light of dusk I noticed the water to my left was filmed with oil from some godforsaken tanker. Against the concrete pier it glistened with green algae and bubbled over in a polluted effervescence. This place of exile, an island where once banished princes could see the Queen City but never return — it was no longer the idyll of our youth. Who in their right mind would want to own a home here anyway? I nursed my final sips of lion's milk and was just considering another bottle when I felt a hand on my shoulder, offering two gentle squeezes.

"*Afiyet olsun.*"

Clumsily I swung my head left, then right, and found Flora

Demirkan standing behind me. She was wearing a scarf tied European-style around a black sweater, and a long full butterfly-print skirt that fell to her ankles. I wasn't used to seeing her dressed so elegantly, without her loose cleaning clothes. She must have been coming from an island party, maybe a school concert.

"*Kalamar*? I thought you didn't even like *kalamar*?" She reached around my neck and helped herself to a piece of my left-over squid. "Too much batter," she said, assessing the crisp, golden skin. "Not enough salt."

"A drink? Join me." I shuffled my chair back from the table.

She clicked her tongue. "So much at home to do. I've let everything slide these weeks." Reaching for some firmer excuse, she failed to find one, and dragged out a chair opposite me. "Just one," she said. When the waiter came over he greeted Flora by name with a high pitched shout and bent to kiss her on each cheek. I ordered a half-bottle of *rakı* and another bucket of ice.

We clinked cubes one by one into our glasses, and sipped together from our cups of sorrows.

"I heard you were showing the house. Buyers already?"

"Where'd you hear that?"

She fluttered her hand. "The wind."

"That was just my father," I said. "He's not buying."

"You're asking too much then. You, Avram, always drive too hard a bargain."

I laughed at this, and told Flora about my father's reaction to the mansion, then about the dim appraisal of the house. The waiter brought us nuts and roasted chickpeas to nibble on, and a plate of his 'special' stuffed mussels for Flora to try, though we hadn't asked for any of it. Fifteen years on, Ali Baba's owner was still eager to win his former cook's approval. When it came to seafood Flora's was the only opinion on the island that mattered. A group of four policemen walked past us and waved, Officer Ceber among them. I saluted him with two fingers. He removed his cap and rubbed his bald head at me. Flora fell silent until they passed. A few minutes later the Mayor of the Islands walked by with a friend. "Romantic evening, Flora?" he asked by way of greeting. "Avram. May it come easy." I hoped like the policemen they would walk on, but the two men parked themselves at the very next restaurant. Beneath the tarpaulin, hung like fruit with lanterns, the Mayor loudly angled his chair to face us.

Flora grew sullen, and sprinkled salt on the mussels. "You look so beat," she said, picking at a few grains of rice and pine nuts with her nails. "Aren't you sleeping?"

"I sleep. I sleep."

"How's the new mattress? Too soft, after all? You should have gone with something firmer." She pointed the salt-shaker at me. "I warned you."

"You never warned me."

Chewing, swallowing, she said beneath her breath, "I meant to."

"And that's supposed to be good enough?"

"Avram, Avram." She reached around the plate of mussels and, taking my open hand, turned it over onto her open palm, clenching and unclenching my fingers in hers. I hesitated, then ran my thumb along her rough wrist. Her own hand was solid, the skin calloused and heavily lined. We sat together like that for a few moments, ignoring the eyes of the Mayor. Flora's chewing slowed, then stopped, and with her other hand she set the salt-shaker down. She was staring very seriously at me, clicking her tongue in sympathy.

"How can I help you, Avram? What can I do?"

"You can tell me where he was that final night, when he called me."

She shook her head. "It hurts too much to talk about that night."

I sat in silence, squeezing her hand tighter. She took my other hand in hers as well, glanced once behind her, and lowered her voice further. "It won't do any good. You'll judge me."

"I won't judge you."

"But I simply don't know. Nobody knows."

"You can tell me, then, what you remember."

From my jacket packet I removed the envelope my Father had given me and passed it to her. I watched as she slid out its single sheet, watched her beautiful dark eyes scanning it over. A photocopy, slightly grainy. The three-dimensional image of underwater wreckage, with numbered measurements and white, computer-generated labels marking its features. Engine. Pilot House. The bow pointing 300 degrees northwest. Ribs and decking clearly visible. At the bottom, the simple title: Shipwreck *Salvador*, circa 1941.

Head lowered, Flora read it over until her eyes flashed back up at me, then at the Mayor. "Come," she said, patting my hand. She lifted her chin. "We'll find a better place to talk."

I stood and paid. I hadn't understood what she meant by a better place until she was leading me closely by the arm past the Mayor — tense-necked, biting his upper lip — back up the hill in the direction of the mansion.

Book VI

1

The Evil Eye

On the Friday night before the accident, thirteen hours before his boat would flip over, Flora had gone looking for Yusuf. Eight months pregnant by then, she could walk only with a determined waddle, leaning back to support the lead balloon of her belly. Beşiktaş and Fenerbahçe were playing for the Super League Cup that night, and she'd learned from the guards that Yusuf had tickets in his doctor friend's private box, so she'd made him an early dinner.

She found him on the back patio, sitting alone, facing the Islamic garden, shivering on a metal chair beside the tarpaulin-covered pool. He had just been out at the pier fiddling with the *Bosphorus Princess* — fueling it up, he'd told her. The boat mechanic Hakan Öztürk was still down by the water, cleaning up in the tool shed. Yusuf was watching the pier closely for something.

"I'd made him stuffed grape leaves — his favorite. I was trying to get him to come inside and eat. It was going to rain and I always worried about his lungs more than he did. He brushed me off. I couldn't take his ignoring me any more, Avram Bey. Your brother could scratch someone out of his life like that."

Flora had snapped her fingers at me. It was an unnecessary gesture. I knew perfectly well what he was capable of scratching from his life.

She'd gone back inside and found an umbrella in the foyer leaning up against one of the bird cages. When she returned Yusuf's gaze was no longer focused on the pier, but on the clouds gathering out over Camlica Mountain beyond the city. He had on a pilled cotton sweater. His hair, usually soft and light, had not been washed in days. His eye was still bruised a yellowish-blue, and a shadow of bristle surrounded his goatee.

"You're not going to eat anything?"

"Yasemin made me a big lunch."

"I thought she wasn't around."

"She came in for Nılay, I think."

"Strange she didn't tell me." Flora sat in a chair a few feet from him and faced it out to sea. "What'd she make?"

"I can't remember. Turbot. Striped Bass, maybe." He turned to her. "She's actually a very decent cook, your daughter."

Flora found his pointing this out unsettling. "Are you waiting for someone?" she asked. His knee was tapping, and he kept glancing down at the pier in the direction of the boat mechanic.

"With him, I'm always waiting. Good help, Flora — I still haven't found it." She placed the umbrella on the chair to his left, and he looked at it, grimaced, then stared back out across the somber waters. Fifty meters down the hill Hakan Öztürk was coming down off the *Bosphorus Princess*.

"Finished?" Yusuf had called.

"Finished, *beyefendim!*" He saluted, and carried his toolbox and a tangle of black hose round the pool towards the larger storage shed on the eastern end of the grounds.

"Storm," Flora said. The sky was darkening. She found she had unconsciously placed her hands on the convenient shelf of her belly, a late-term habit of hers acquired now through seven pregnancies; but she quickly drew them back up to the armrests: she didn't want Yusuf to think she was covering her stomach. She only wanted to be there if he needed to talk. She herself felt a growing hunger for his conversation. She watched him until his eyes tightened; then looking out to sea, saw what he saw. A helicopter, approaching from the city. Only when it was close enough could she make out that it was green and vaguely military looking — not the same vehicle they had once ridden together. It flew rapidly at a wasp-like tilt, coming in low enough over the pier that she waited for Yusuf to rise and take cover inside. His heavy eyes stared straight forward even as the crisp swipe of the blades cracked the air above them. The trees and shrubs bowed. The tarp covering the pool whipped in violent depressions. The helicopter hovered for a thunderous moment, spun once, and sailed with a rush straight behind the mansion.

"Friends of yours?" she asked when the noise faded.

He crossed and recrossed his legs. The hollows under his eyes had darkened.

"Where is any of this going to get you?"

He met her gaze for the first time. "What are you worried for?"

The moronic confidence grated on her. "You know perfectly well. You've spoken and you've spoken. There's nothing new to say."

"Empty threats. Gamesmanship."

"You'll take it too far."

He was coughing into his hand. "Such is the freedom of the unattached man."

She glared at him. From her blouse pocket she drew out the security card for the mansion he had recently issued the staff. "You won't think of yourself, Yusuf, but think of us."

Angered letters had been piling up at the PTT — so many that the postmaster had a boy special-deliver them in a cardboard box each afternoon. The home telephone had been ringing late and often at all hours of the night. Hysterical voices left threatening messages. Already three times that winter the Halim Pasha House's unpublished numbers had to be changed. A security company had installed a system of cameras and locks on the front gate and doors, which could now be opened only by sliding an ID card, so that even Flora's children needed the guards' permission to enter the grounds. The rotating security staff had doubled in size to twelve, and at all times two armed guards manned the front gates and another patrolled the rear by the pool and the dock. "This business," she said, flashing him the card. "This is what I mean."

"If security's an inconvenience, you can find work elsewhere Flora."

The rhythmic thumping returned, growing louder. The helicopter was back, scratching the wind, circling out over the inlet and then, directly above them, over the house. She covered her ears. Hovering, the chopper descended in a slow taunting spin. She waited for Yusuf to make a move. The hydrangea bushes crouched to the ground. Two unoccupied wicker chairs slid against the garden wall as if fleeing for cover. Her hair flapped wildly. Finally the helicopter lifted, spun briefly out of sight, then buzzed the mansion one last time before making its way out to sea, back out over Kinali Island. Together they watched it disappear into the gloom of the city.

"Yusuf," she pleaded.

"They want me silent, but they don't have the nerve." He looked at her seriously. "Do you believe in the evil eye, Flora? The *nazar*?"

"I was never any good as a Muslim. You know that."

"It's not just Muslims. People in my family used to believe it too. My mother used to tell us these recipes for the cures our relatives once used. The most powerful was isolation. *Enseredura*. What us Jews used to do was this. They'd lock you up in a room alone towards the end of the month, and just after midnight you'd have to name the person who'd cursed you. The healer would have to find that person's house, wash the front steps, bring the washwater back. You'd drink a few sips. This potion freed you."

"Disgusting."

"No, no. A powerful cure! *Enseredura*!" He gestured off into the distance. "Scrub the whole city, Flora. Bring me wash water from the entire nation's front steps."

She stood, heaving up the weight of her middle. "You've done this to yourself. No one's casting the evil eye on you." Blood rushed to her head and she leaned a moment on the arm-rests to catch her balance. "If it's come to this, leave then."

"Where would I go, Flora?"

"Anywhere!" She turned towards the kitchen doors. "Nobody's keeping you here. You're not sentenced yet."

"Flora!"

And she turned back — too eagerly, she realized.

She could see him struggling. "*El amojado no se espanta de la luvia.*" He lifted the umbrella. "The one who's wet isn't afraid of the rain." He waved the umbrella at her with a grave smile. "I appreciate it. I do." The umbrella snapped open over his head and he held out his palm, testing for rain that hadn't yet come. She nodded, and returned to the kitchen more upset than she'd been before. Inside she collapsed onto a chair in her usual state: exhausted by him. Now he needed her, and he wouldn't let himself admit it. She settled her hands on her belly. The child was sliding lengthwise across her middle, kicking fiercely.

2

She'd Never Get Off This Island

By the time the uneaten dinner had been packed away she assumed Yusuf had already left for the match. Yet the *Bosphorus Princess* was still moored, his helicopter had not been summoned, and nobody on the staff could tell her what his plans for breakfast were the next morning. On her walk home she had stopped in at the Saydam Planet to say hello to Feride, who had begun her first job as the hotel's weekend overnight clerk. Yasemin was there too, playing on the hotel's computer, taking advantage of the free Internet connection, something Flora had warned her girls against. She had no strength now to argue. She sat with them, letting Feride stroke her belly. All of her girls delighted in feeling the child's steady roll across her insides. She had over three weeks to term, but the false contractions had begun, and she knew she could go any day now.

At the computer Yasemin was confiding a typically ridiculous plan she'd been hatching. She wanted to travel to Los Angeles on a tourist visa and try to find work there as an actress, maybe an extra. She'd been grumbling recently that she wanted off this island, away from this country, this dead-end place that still hated Armenians, as far away as possible. She'd heard Los Angeles was the place to go. Her younger sister was helping her search the Internet for the cheapest tickets. By now Yasemin was frustrated at the round-trip prices, and after threatening the computer she began looking for one-way fares. Even these were too expensive. Flora, always suspicious of this Internet thing, watched on. She told Yasemin to be realistic: it would take months of saving to afford a ticket to Los Angeles. And the cost of rent in America? This wasn't a plan, this was idiocy. Flora found herself laughing at her daughter's feverish scheming.

"I knew none of this would ever happen," she remembered. "I knew in my heart she'd never get off this island. I saw it even then, with perfect clarity."

Feride helped her sister check the Princess Airlines web-site for discount rates to Los Angeles. An animated image of an idealized Yusuf Elmas — goatee, sharp nose, flowing mane of sandy hair — still welcomed visitors to the site in five lan-guages. Every time you clicked on him he opened his arms wide and said "*Merhaba*" in a deep baritone. Feride was making fun of the cartoon Yusuf, and they were laughing as a group when Flora looked up and found the man himself, in the flesh, push-ing through the hotel's heavy wooden doors, as if summoned by some wickedness of the computer. Yasemin bolted up and Feride flicked off the monitor before Yusuf came over and leaned onto the desk with both elbows.

"*Merhaba*," he said.

"*Merhaba*," all three women replied at once, and broke into uncontrollable laughter.

Flora had been surprised and embarrassed. She'd assumed to that moment that Yusuf was at his football match. No force on earth could have kept him away from that game.

Apparently she was wrong. Yusuf greeted each of the women with a close-lipped grin; and as he waited out their private laughter fell into a fit of spasmodic coughing. Feride offered him a glass of tea; but he ducked his chin into his chest and held up a hand. He had on dark glasses despite the early evening mist. His hair was now combed back — no longer the wild shoulder length tresses of his younger tabloid days. He was wearing, in casual billionaire style, a light brown sports jacket with a loose tie, the shirt open at the collar. Violently he coughed into his fist again; and removing his sunglasses he glanced at Yasemin with his dark bruised eye and asked, between coughs, if he couldn't speak with her alone. The daughters exchanged knowing looks.

"Well what's this about?" Flora asked, her smile fading. "What can't a mother hear?"

Yusuf thrummed his fingers on the wooden desk. "Just a small favor."

"A secret favor?"

"*Annem!*" Yasemin cried.

"What are you keeping from me?" Flora asked.

"Let the girl off her chain now and then, Flora Hanım. It wouldn't hurt her." Yusuf's voice seemed thinner, raspier now, more strained than earlier in the evening. Behind him, over his head, the Founder of the Republic's portrait glared down at them all.

"Suddenly you're the father. Go then. Both of you. What do your little secrets matter to me? Go on! Don't forget, tomorrow's an early morning." She'd had to remind both daughters that tomorrow was the Feast of St. George. The girls moaned. The annual pilgrimage meant a pre-dawn barefoot climb up the mountain, and in recent years Flora had struggled to rouse her older children for the effort.

"She'll be there," Yusuf said. "Has she ever missed it? You'll be there, Yasemin? Promise your mother."

With his bony arms Yusuf held the door open for the girl, and through the lobby windows Flora watched them walk out together to the pier, where they turned up in the direction of the clock tower. Straight-backed and regal, Yusuf was excited about something, his chest heaving and straining as he spoke. He took her daughter's elbow and, as if to some pressing engagement, led Yasemin faster up the hill and out of sight.

"I could have put a stop to it right then," Flora remembered. "I could have said no. But I didn't understand what he needed from her. I waited in the hotel for an hour for them to come back. Then I got worried. Suddenly I had a bad feeling about this favor. I didn't want to think the thoughts that were occurring to me. I had moved past all this with your brother. But the thoughts came anyway. They always did. With Yusuf I couldn't help myself. I started calculating. What was he? 38? Practically twice her age?"

Flora trudged home through the village, one hand on her lower back. She had settled her youngest sons down to sleep, and was just retiring, prostrate in bed, humming to the *sanat* music on the radio and brushing her long hair — plucking out the grays — when Yasemin herself burst into the room like some lunatic. The girl's face was flushed; she had run home from somewhere.

On the edge of the bed she tossed herself at her mother's feet. "*Annem*," she began, "I'm sorry what happened at the hotel. I haven't meant to keep secrets from you. *Üzülüyorum!*"

"What's this? What's wrong?"

"He needs me to come out with him tomorrow morning, on his boat."

And she listened to her daughter's breathless confessions. Flora took it in — all in — in complete silence. Sometimes she shifted in bed, or sat up to relieve the stinging pressure on her back, or pulled her feet beneath her as she digested the news. This wasn't the first time he needed help. For months now Yasemin had been quietly sailing off with Yusuf to observe some kind of diving expedition in the Marmara. He'd been picking her up on the next island over in the *Bosphorus Princess*, shuttling her to his yacht to meet a foreign marine crew.

The *sanat* music hummed on. Flora sat up. "But diving for what?"

Yasemin, shrugging, was defiantly vague. "Some are scientists."

"And he'd expect me to give you permission to do this? With foreign men!"

"They're not all men. And when you're nearly twenty you don't need your mother's permission to do anything."

"Nearly twenty! Oh Yasemin! *Canım!* What are you doing with him?"

"Doing?" Caught in her mother's web of suspicions Yasemin took a sharp breath and confessed more. Yusuf's team was convinced they'd located the wreckage of his grandmother's ship. They were trying to confirm the identity of the vessel. Under the guise of a fishing expedition the crews had spent the last six weeks scanning promising sites in restricted waters. This evening they'd captured a high-frequency image off the sea bottom that matched the dimensions of the *Salvador*. Yusuf had just now shown her the printout. Tomorrow afternoon the divers were going down for it. They might be able to video the wreckage. He needed a hand navigating the speedboat — difficult to steer alone — and getting the sonar and equipment lines in the water, assembling weight-belts for the divers. He'd promised her she could help monitor the radio. Yusuf hoped they'd make a quick strike, get the video they needed to confirm the vessel, and wrap things up quickly. "I want to be there for the confirmation. Such an opportunity, *Annem*, to witness something historical like this."

Flora had heard too much. She lifted herself up off the bed and stood. "Why would he involve you?" She clenched the collar of her nightgown and began pacing. "The *Salvador*! So what? So he knows where a boat sank half a century ago? I won't have it. Don't you see why he wouldn't tell *me* any of this?"

"Because you're afraid."

"Because he's a charged man. Do you even understand what that means?"

"I understand it's a farce."

"You're not stepping foot on that boat with him. Promise me that."

"I've told him I'm coming."

"Promise me."

"It's the only worthwhile thing I've ever done, *Annem*. You of all people should understand."

"I understand a woman who gets involved with a man like him regrets it the rest of her days. I speak from experience. Look at me."

"Yes, look at you!" She gestured at her mother with the back of her hand, and Flora saw herself through her daughter's eyes: a fearful woman with graying hair, no money, no husband, no prospects, living alone on an island with a houseful of bastard children.

Yasemin sucked in a long breath, trying to control her voice. "*Annem,* you're being ridiculous."

"May God strike him blind!" Flora sank backwards down onto the bed, cursing them both. Massaging her temples, she stared stricken at her daughter until Yasemin turned and left the bedroom. Flora's eyes grew unfocused. She saw something new there.

"I saw the family destiny," Flora explained to me. "I saw God working his patterns, but I also saw in my daughter's face the sins I had committed. I understood justice is not swift, but handed out across a lifetime. You never stop paying; and your family pays as well. Something had risen in me. To thrust this on us! Behind my back yet, with my own daughter? He knew I'd never put up with it, not for one second."

3

Songs From the Old Country

Alone in her bedroom, a sudden calm and clear-sightedness overtook her. She turned off her love music. The house was eerily quiet. No noise was coming from the other room, though the younger children must have heard them arguing. Flora washed her face in cold water, folded her towel and dressed, all the while humming a folk song in her head. Recently she'd been trying to teach herself songs from the old country — *Morning Light*, and *Sweet Mother* — but without any luck: she didn't speak the language, and could remember only the tunes, never the words. What did any of that matter now? Before the framed illumination of the Virgin on the nightstand she made her grandmother's sign of the cross. Outside she strolled down the damp streets the half-kilometer back to the Hotel Saydam Planet. Feride assured her she hadn't seen Yasemin since Yusuf came in three hours ago. Flora checked the Reks Internet Café and two of Yasemin's friends' homes without any luck. On the way to the Halim Pasha House she saw a pair of policemen awaiting their order outside the Different Kebaps Restaurant stall, and growing desperate she stopped and asked if they'd seen her daughter.

"A problem, Flora?" Officer Ceber asked.

"Ah, just some back talk. Send her home if you see her. And if you spot Yusuf, tell him I have a word for him."

"Yusuf had tickets to the match," the new officer said. "I saw him this morning. He showed me them himself. Lucky bastard." Their order was up, and through the window the two men took their overly-stuffed, tinfoil-wrapped *durum kebaps*.

"He didn't go," Flora assured them.

They glanced at one another. Officer Ceber said, "We'll bring her home if we see her."

"In handcuffs, if you have to."

They promised Flora they'd use whatever means necessary, and saluted her with their lamb *kebaps*.

Beyond the close streets of the village the cool black air was refreshing, the streetlights tinged with mist. At the gates of the Halim Pasha House she greeted the night watchmen with a friendly wave. She punched in the code, ran her ID card, and entered the garden. At that moment Mustafa Faik was hustling bow-legged down the front steps. From a transistor radio pressed to his ear the tinny sounds of the football announcer rose above the chanting of a crowd. *If I die before being champion, Let my shroud be black and white.*

Mustafa was about to deliver a scoring update (still zero-zero in the twentieth minute) to the guards at the front gate, but seeing Flora he lowered the radio to his waist. He turned the volume down, squinted at her, and asked what she was doing at the mansion at that hour. Was she okay? He looked at her belly. Was it time? Laughing, she told him she was simply preparing Yusuf a celebratory breakfast for the next morning, should

Beşiktaş win the Cup. "How sweet of you." Mustafa Faik touched her on the shoulder. "You think of everything, Flora. You really do. He can use something like that, these days. He'll appreciate it." She smiled and patted his hand. The darkness of murder was running through her veins.

Flora waited for Yusuf at the mansion, and occupied herself organizing and reorganizing the spices. Just after eleven she heard a commotion in the foyer and assumed he'd returned. She set down her jars with a bang and went to confront him, but in the front hall she'd found it wasn't Yusuf. Rather, Mustafa Faik had just let Officer Ceber into the mansion, and the policeman had brought along the Mayor of the Islands. The door was still open. Moths were swirling in.

"Someone's missing a daughter, I hear," the Mayor said to her.

He claimed he had something urgent to ask Yusuf himself. He hadn't taken Mustafa at his word that the boss wasn't home. He sent Officer Ceber to check the gardens, the pier, even out to the boat, where it was no secret that Yusuf had been known to spend nights. "Just in case," he said, with a smile that went no higher than his mustache. The policeman disappeared into the darkness and Flora, uncomfortable, led the Mayor into the kitchen and made him a Nescafe. Officer Ceber was gone for five minutes, then ten, when a sudden thud startled them from behind: the policeman pounding with his elbow against the French doors of the kitchen. Flora unlocked the door and Officer Ceber led in, by the arm, the boat mechanic, Hakan Öztürk.

"Look who I found on board."

The old mechanic was trying to maintain an innocent grin, but his broken-toothed smile seemed uncertain, even fearful. He'd begun defending himself before anyone had accused him of anything. "I was only working late. Yusuf asked me to."

"Watching the game in the boat's galley," Officer Ceber said. "On the flat screen television. With a single light on. Feet up on the table."

At the time Flora interpreted the boat mechanic's fear as simply this: a clear understanding his job might now be in jeopardy. "I had no dinner," Hakan was saying. "Yusuf's kept me working all day. A slave driver." Something was wrong with the boat's tachometer, and the old man tried to explain the electrical problem. Apparently Yusuf had trouble this week making certain the first engine was still running after the second fired up. It was difficult to gauge what the second was doing once the first was started. Flora couldn't follow.

"That's a finely calibrated machine," the Mayor said. "You weren't messing with anything computerized?"

"Mechanical. I showed him." Hakan held up both hands and said to Officer Ceber, "You heard it yourself."

The Mayor turned to Ceber. The officer lifted his chin and clicked his tongue.

"Go double-check," the Mayor said. "Show him again what's wrong, Hakan."

So the policeman left for the boat a second time, and while they were waiting Flora caught the Mayor up on the evening's events: the helicopter buzzing the mansion, her daughter's plans for the following morning. Concerned, the Mayor listened with an air of utter exhaustion, rubbing circles into both eyes with his thumb and forefinger. "I worry. Your boss has been a fool. Someone has to look out for him. He can't be too careful now."

"That's exactly what I told my daughter. You understand? I don't want her out with him." Through the open window she heard the engines of the speedboat firing up.

The Mayor's handheld had rung out, but before he answered he ordered her to go home. "You need your rest Flora, in your condition. We'll take care of this."

Back home she found Yasemin still had not returned. Flora noted this fact objectively, calmly. My daughter, she told herself, is no longer mine. In the kid's room the three boys were sprawled on two beds pushed together, and Sarp, her youngest, was moaning in his sleep. He'd had a fever the day before. She felt his head, and folded the sheet back up to his neck. It was only at this age, she thought, that a mother's love meant anything. She couldn't relax, and to distract herself she turned on the television in the living room and watched the second half of the championship match. Her headache was vicious and the cramps, when they came, came stronger. Her entire body felt bloated and bruised; everything hurt. She could hardly focus on the television. She fell asleep that way in her clothes, feet propped on the couch, resting her hands on her enormous stomach, before there was any score in the game.

"I dreamed the idiot football fans were throwing chairs at one another," she remembered. "They had lit a section of the stadium on fire. Ambulances and fire engines had to be rushed onto the field, and the referee had to delay the second half until peace could be restored. So strange! Only the next day, when I finally saw the papers, did I realize it hadn't been a dream at all."

She awoke disoriented, at five-thirty, the inconsolable light of dawn leaking gray through the shades. It struck her only then:

April 23rd, the Feast of St. George. Neither she nor her daughter had missed the pilgrimage in fifteen years.

4

That Soaring Pass

For Yusuf it could only have complicated things that the events of that evening coincided with his team's first bid in eleven years to win the Super League Cup. He had a seat waiting for him in Dr. Murat Baykan's luxury suite. There would have been parties and drinking; there would have been dancing and women. Instead, it seems, he went hiking the island alone, making a series of private phone calls.

Two *fayton* drivers had assured me they'd passed Yusuf Elmas on their separate errands late that night, and both had insisted he was by himself. One of the carriages was delivering Turkuaz water by lantern light. The driver had spotted Yusuf sitting on the steps near the Lunapark donkey corral, a ghostly figure holding his wrists between his knees. Later the other carriage, driving home a family who had arrived on the last evening ferry, nearly ran Yusuf over. He was wandering into the middle of Kadıyoran Street, coughing into his pocket phone, oblivious to the sound of the horse's hooves and bells bearing down on him. "You'll catch your death, Yusuf Bey," the driver had yelled, pulling the reigns to slow the horses. "Need a ride?"

The driver claimed Yusuf had sullenly refused, one hand over his heart. If these sightings were true, my brother must have circled the island on foot that night, a five kilometer hike through the piercing darkness. It would have been his only privacy. Many times that winter I'd retraced those final steps. Descending back into the village from the high Yılmaz Türk Road, eyes accustomed to nothing but the silhouettes of the pines and the empty mansions, Yusuf would have been struck by the light and warmth of the poor village. In windows, glimpses of children on worn couches. Balconies flashing the muted colors of television screens. Old men in the card house crowding on wooden benches. Laughter, bets, and good natured threats seeping through doorways — all punctuating the drone of the football match, which came from everywhere at once. Such fellowship in this poor winter village, and my brother could claim no part of it.

After midnight it had started to drizzle. Multiple sources confirmed that Yusuf ducked in for the final quarter of the championship match at Üzman's, the local Işkembe Salon owned by Mustafa Faik's brother, who to this day still serves late night revelers tripe soup laced with garlic and vinegar: a hangover preventive. Some village men remembered Yusuf wandering in wet, his cheeks sunken, his fair eyebrows downturned. Others had not recalled seeing him enter, but had thought he'd been sitting there, wheezing in the corner by the heater, the entire evening. All attributed his somber demeanor to his nervousness over the result of the tied, then delayed, match. On TV the fires in the stands had started, and ambulances were racing onto the football pitch. Üzman himself had recalled to me Yusuf ordering two bowls of soup during the delay of game. "He said he hadn't eaten since breakfast. It looked like he hadn't eaten in weeks. His face was gaunt and bruised. There was this emptiness in his eyes." Out of politeness some loyal customers smoking hand-rolled cigarettes joined Yusuf at his table. "Usually the salon is loud and festive," Üzman Faik reminded me. "You come here any week-end, you come here during any football match, you'll see — but when Yusuf walked in that night, the place fell quiet. It was like we knew. So strange. How can I explain? A few of my friends sat down with him. They drank three rounds of tea without a word. We sensed a doomed man. Yusuf slurped his soup. I make the best soup, and I had loaded his bowl with the largest stomach pieces. It was the least I could do."

On the flickering black and white television mounted high on the rear wall the game had resumed. It had quickly taken a bad turn for Yusuf's team. Beşiktaş suffered a string of yellow cards. In the 80th minute they lost a fullback and had to play under re-lentless pressure a man down. From our apartment in the capital I was watching those moments, in the throes of football agony, with my daughters. I had woken them with my screaming at the television, and Naomi agreed to let them stay up in order that they witness football history. I will never forget the twins' high-pitched cheers when Fenerbahçe scored its triumphant goal, or the family cheers and hugs that followed. It was a diving header off a midfielder pass, struck out of the air just beyond the out-stretched fingers of Turgay, the goalie, high into the left corner, in the final three minutes of stoppage time. The epitome of grace and beauty. Football raised to performance art, choreographed like the ballet. The slow-motion replays showed that God

Himself must have curled that soaring pass in through two defenders from an impossible angle. My girls were chanting "Goal! Goal!" and bouncing on the couch — an act strictly prohibited by Naomi under standard regulations. I'd never felt closer to them or loved them more: my twin daughters leaping in their pajamas, their golden braids flying, my handsome wife clapping along, my team at the heights of football glory tearing across the green expanse of the television. We had difficulty getting the girls to sleep after so much excitement. I finally joined Naomi in bed, and I was so elated it did not occur to me to wonder what my lost brother was feeling at the moment the ball hit the back of the net. When I shut out the lights, beneath the sheets Naomi tugged at my curly chest, and we had made laughing, hushed, celebratory love. We fell asleep happy, honeymooners again; until we were awakened by the telephone at 3 AM.

"He had stayed late, drinking tea with our other Beşiktaş fans," Üzman Faik had told me. "They were trying to comfort themselves by reminding each other of the good season, of the strong effort their team had shown. Beşiktaş was a young team yet. They were inexperienced. They had great seasons ahead of them. It was an impossibly lucky, last-minute goal. Probably offsides — everyone knew that. A few of my oldest friends were in tears; they thought they might die before witnessing another championship. Your brother consoled them, raising his voice and pounding the table. 'Everyone here will live to see one more. I guarantee it! There's next year! We're only rebuilding. Listen friends! There's next year!' The crowd started to break up. People were stumbling out, stunned. Yusuf stood and left me a generous tip. I've saved those coins in my wallet all this time. I can show them to you. And he bought a final round of soup for the three or so Fenerbahçe fans, still raising a bit of a party in the opposite corner of the salon. Then he waved goodbye." It was the last they ever saw him. Üzman Faik was certain Yusuf had left alone, no later than 2 AM.

I liked to picture my brother buying the opposing fans a round of congratulatory soup. It reflected well on me. I had seen it in Üzman Faik's eyes: the continued gratitude across these years, the way he admired me too, if only for the paltry truth that I once shared blood with such a man.

The timing of his telephone call still disturbed me. He had to have known precisely what was coming, what he had brought upon himself. It could not have been an accident. After fourteen years of silence he would not have exposed himself to my ridicule otherwise — not after his team had just fallen so dramatically to my own. Perhaps my thinking was swayed by tabloid reports that too generously fed the conspiracy theories, the suicide speculation, the vendettas and political motives. No one, after all, was ever charged with a crime. Officially, it was a boating accident. I might have long ago left it at that and moved on.

I couldn't. How could anyone ignore the obvious connections? The liberal papers recalled the Susurluk scandal, when ten years ago a top ranking Police Commander, a Kurdish Parliamentarian, and a notorious political assassin, traveling together in a Mercedes, were discovered killed in a car "accident." Comparisons were made to the murder of Hrant Dink, the brave Armenian journalist who took three bullets in the head at point blank range, and whose assassin then posed for celebratory photographs with the gendarmes who'd arrested him. Yusuf's death fell squarely into the pattern. We were being lied to, and we lived and breathed these lies, as resigned to them as we were to the lung-blackening smog of our cities. Every cancerous breath was killing us — but this was who we were; this was where we lived. What else were we supposed to breathe? What choice did we have?

5

Last Minute Provisions

He had not arrived at the Halim Pasha House until the dead hours of that fated morning. "He came walking down the street," Mustafa Faik had told me. "Yusuf Elmas, one of the wealthiest men in Europe, stumbling in the fog down the cobblestone road at four in the morning. I thought he was some drunkard. We were on heightened security, so when this figure approached the gate like that, I nearly dialed the police. But then I recognized him. He was coughing, and he was soaked."

He looked like a man in dire need of sleep, though this he would deny himself. "On his orders, I woke him an hour later myself for the pilgrimage," Mustafa Faik recalled. "Just after five-thirty, Yusuf Bey was crying out in his sleep. It was an old problem with him. He was prone to those nightmares. He would let out an empty scream, just above a whisper. That morning he was mumbling some foreign nonsense. *"Halvador, malvador."* It seemed to me something was caught in his throat. When I shook him he sprang up in bed. All the usual coughing and wheezing. His face was terribly pale you know, like those actors with bad makeup in one of our old silent movies. He complained of nausea. It was worse than usual. I asked if I should telephone his private physician. The way he looked I was afraid — what with everything going on, the deposition for his trial coming up — well, I was afraid he'd been poisoned. He told me no, clutched his stomach, and sent me to the bathroom for his antibiotics."

According to Mustafa his boss, splayed atop his undisturbed feather bed, was still wearing the damp clothes from the night before, his red silk Hermès tie wrapped halfway around his neck like a noose. But my irrepressible brother had risen and bathed and changed into a tan Ravelli shirt and pressed brown khakis with an embroidered belt; so that all the villagers who saw him after he left the mansion at 6:20 until he boarded his speedboat four hours and thirteen minutes later would remember him looking put together in his casually hip clothes, though also burnt out, as if a famed lifetime of late night debaucheries had finally overtaken him. It was a dewy April morning, with a strong salt breeze from the west, but the island's weather is prone to quick changes that time of year, and the sky to the north looked threatening. Some in the village remembered that later in the morning, as he sped off in his boat, the waves had begun to rise and the sea had grown choppy. Others contended that by then it was a perfectly calm spring day, idyllic even, and the condition of the sea had not been a factor. Personally I could confirm none of this. At the hour of Yusuf's death I was halfway across the country, celebrating my birthday breakfast with my two daughters and Naomi.

Before Yusuf left the house that morning Mustafa Faik had urged him to eat something so he would have energy for the climb, but he had refused. He told Mustafa he had no time. He wanted to be at St. George's, at the top of the island's eastern mountain, for sunrise and the dawn mass. Much of the remaining Greek and Armenian population of our city would be there too. They converged on the island like this every April 23rd for the Feast of St. George — the saint believed to have the power to make young people fall in love. Mustafa Faik had long considered this religious impulse strange. "I just figured he was putting on appearances," Faik told me. Always an obedient servant, that morning the security guard didn't argue, but fetched his boss's trainers from the foyer closet and urged him at the very least to wear those for the climb. Yusuf would have none of it.

"Mustafa, old man! Why do you worry? I'll climb barefoot, like always. Should today be any different?"

After swallowing his enzymes and antibiotics — but having skipped his critical morning breathing exercises — Yusuf left the house through the back door to gauge the condition of the sea, hurried through the statue garden to the cast iron gate, entered his code, and creaked it open. Shivering, he shuffled out again onto the wet, early morning street. At the last moment he turned and ordered the old security guard to stop fussing, to go home, to get some sleep himself, and waved goodbye. "Yusuf Bey always accused me of working too hard for a man my age," Mustafa Faik claimed, tears in the wrinkled corners of his eyes. "He used to call me a mule. It was the last thing he said to me. He deserved better than what he got. To treat an aging man, a nobody, so generously all those years!" He shook his head, and sank lower into his wooden chair. "He was one of the great men of this country. It was no way for him to go. But who are we to say? Such is the will of God." With fingers blistered from his long winter of scything Mustafa Faik had lifted his tea glass, blown into the steam, and quoted the old saying: "There is no death without its appointed hour."

"Yusuf Elmas, up at this hour?" the grocer, İlhan Saracoğlu, remembered shouting that final morning upon my brother's arrival. On the way to the pilgrimage Yusuf had stopped into the *bakkal* to check the final football statistics in the city papers, a sacred habit of his, even on the busiest of days. He had always cared most deeply about Time of Possession — to Yusuf the true measure of a team's performance, win or lose. But he was up too early for a Saturday; the papers had not yet arrived.

So Yusuf had not drunk his ritual orange juice that morning. Instead he suppressed a cough, patted the shopkeeper on the arm, and told him he would stop by on his return from the pilgrimage when the papers had come in. He left the store smiling — in determined good spirits, according to İlhan.

Not two minutes later Flora Demirkan had trudged in, leaning back and thrusting out her hips to bear the weight of her swollen middle. Her eyes were wild with fear, and she neither greeted the grocer, nor wished him *kolay gelsin.* "Has Yusuf Elmas been in yet?" she demanded. İlhan, confused, had to explain that she had just missed him, that Yusuf was on his way up to the monastery. The *bakkal* was quickly growing crowded. The six o'clock ferry had disgorged the day's first pilgrims, and they were streaming into the shop for last minute provisions of sweets, bottled water, Band-Aids, and votive candles. İlhan was pulled away to help customers locate items on the shelves. Both of his doe-eyed daughters were darting around the two aisles as well. When he next looked up he noticed Flora Demirkan at the front window beside the sacks of rice, fingering her scarf and staring outside as the sky lightened over a thick gray sea. She looked wracked by indecision. "Flora, my dear," the storekeeper asked, "can I find you something?" Her eyes fell, she glanced down at the rice, but before she could say anything the first notes of the muezzin sounded across the square. Gasping, she hitched her skirt, and flung herself through the door.

"I was distracted. I didn't know at the time why she was looking for her boss," İlhan Saracoğlu recalled with a shrug, "and I still don't know what made her hesitate when she wanted to find him so badly. If she'd just hurried down the street a moment earlier, she might have stopped Yusuf. Whatever troubles were between them might have been settled with tea and a few biscuits over breakfast."

Tea and a few biscuits! Time, I'd seen, was already simplifying events in the minds of the villagers. It was their instinct; they knew only their straightforward lives: their seasons commencing in a ritualized cycle: the island empty in the winter, the wealthy residents returning in the spring, the tourists in the summer, and then the population dwindling into fall, when the poor reclaimed an abandoned village for themselves. Their days, too, were ritualized: the calls to prayer, the visits to the mosque, the morning's catch on the pier, the afternoon fruit market on Reçep Koç Street, long nights shuffling *okey* tiles across café tables, the blurry football games on Üzman's ancient television. Ritual smoothed out the ruffles of life. Little here had changed since my brother's tragedy. The messy drama he had provoked, the descent of the press, the thrust of microphones in faces, the national television specials and trashy paperback accounts, had only momentarily disrupted a peaceful off-season in the villagers' lives. Five years on, Yusuf's last movements were already receding in the island's collective memory: events joined, names obscured, relationships simplified, so that very soon most villagers would weigh the significance of the day and dismiss it with a wave of the hand: a tragic scandal of those bastard rich, no more, no less.

6

Each Alone Again

I AWOKE TO THE sound of the bathroom water pipes slamming shut. Flora returned to the downstairs bedroom wearing my white bathrobe. Her face was unmade and scrubbed clean. She looked at me curiously, as if surprised to still find me here, in what had once been my brother's office. I was trying to grin but my lips felt cracked and heavy. "What?" she asked.

"Nothing, nothing," I said.

"I almost slipped in the bathroom." She returned my smile, but like mine hers lacked conviction. "The new tiles, when they get wet…so slippery."

"Slippery," I said.

She hesitated, but joined me again in bed; and lying next to each other, shoulder to shoulder, we could hear the distant murmurings across the universe. Horses' hooves from a passing *fayton*. Calls for water delivery. Her breaths between the tapping of the shade grew longer. My heart beat around the rhythms of her breathing, and in this steady music I searched for a peace that had eluded me since coming to the island. Instead: long minutes of silence, followed by the far-off drone of an outboard motor.

"You're convinced it was the boat mechanic. Öztürk?"

"I know it." She lay still for a moment. "Hakan was the button they pushed. I don't think he meant to take my daughter. I can't imagine it. He liked her as much as everyone liked her."

"But how are you so sure?"

"He was gone the next day. Disappeared. After eleven years of work with your brother. He lived in a hut by the marina, but no one ever saw him on the island again."

"They did something with him?"

"I think they sent him away. I've heard Northern Cyprus. Famagusta. Nılay knows where he is. She's heard from him, I'm sure of it. They had something between them."

Something with Nılay. Famagusta. *I have no friends in Cyprus.*

"Why have you never spoken, Flora? Reported this?" The moment the words left my mouth I realized my foolishness.

She looked at me unsteadily. "Who to? The Island Police? Report who? Hakan? The Mayor? The M.I.T.? Where does it stop before it circles back down to me? I have a house full of children."

I slid my arm beneath her head, and drew her tight beside me. The warmth of her body next to mine was warmer, it seemed, than Naomi's had ever been — an unnatural heat. I stared at the bulge of her hip, the way it curved steeply down the cotton slope of her legs, and further still, past the edge of the blanket, to a lone exposed ankle. My own head was pounding, my back ached, and it seemed I had pulled something in my neck sleeping. This pillow-top mattress was far too soft. You sank into it and you were lost. Flora wrapped herself more tightly in the cotton robe and turned towards me, her palms pressed together as if in prayer. I asked if she was cold and offered to shut the cracked window. "No, no," she murmured, "I like it cool."

A few moments later, I could feel her chest quivering. She stifled a sob.

"What can I do?" I whispered into her hair. "What can I do?"

I removed my arm, and propping myself beside her on my elbow kissed her dark eyes, one then the other. In the light from the window I could make out the rounded flesh along her shoulders between two raised moles. Her olive skin approaching her neck was darker than Naomi's. This spot, where neck became shoulders, had always been my favorite part of my wife's body.

Flora had closed her eyes tightly against my kisses and hadn't opened them. Now she shook her head silently. Then a sudden intake of breath. "You never forgive yourself," she murmured, so quietly it took me a moment to register.

In the growing light of the room I stared into her neck until she turned and hid her face from me. I didn't try to pull her around. The facts had converged, and against them we were equally powerless. Nothing we did or said would change anything. Our night together had been a mistake. We lay in bed in the dense cold air, alert and quiet, each alone again. A line of light angled in beneath the window shade. In it the dust motes simmered with the tension of her silence.

And then Flora was weeping as she explained.

7

Pilgrims

"I HAD ACTED THAT morning in a panic. But in a way I was relieved that I had made it through the night. The previous evening, up at the mansion, I could have shoved a knife into Yusuf's chest if he had walked through the kitchen door. By morning I was calmer. I no longer wanted to kill the man. I simply wanted to state my piece."

She'd hesitated by the rice in the *bakkal* because she didn't know if she should disturb the solemnity of the morning's pilgrimage by pursuing a condemned man up the mountain. But what she had to say could not wait. She hobbled out into the town square by the clock tower, and wound her way through the village's poorly lit streets and curving alleys. She was wearing the same kind of white, open-toed, second-rate shoes I'd seen her wearing five years later, and with her weight she could not have moved quickly. But she reassured herself: if she did not catch Yusuf at the monastery she would at least find him on his way down. The main road around the island was growing crowded. It was difficult to pass through the mobs of families all strolling in the same direction beneath the shadowed branches of the Judas trees. Flora took the shortcut known only to longtime residents: the mule-trail behind the Nïzam Mosque. By the time she arrived at the mountain's base a crowd had already gathered beside the Lunapark donkey corral. People were quietly kneeling on the damp pavement to remove their shoes. The fog was breaking.

She circled the pilgrims, looking for Yusuf. He was normally easy to spot: not many men have such blonde hair, or that idiotic scraggly goatee he thought made him look like a movie star. But Flora didn't know if she had passed him on her shortcut, if he was ahead or behind her. So she resigned herself to the climb, and followed the first groups up the slope.

It was an impossible walk. Normally it took twenty minutes to reach the monastery using the steep, uneven cobblestone path Byzantine monks had first lain a thousand years before. But that morning, with penitent mobs climbing shoeless and her baby kicking in protest and her back ready to give out, Flora could hardly keep a steady pace. Every step rattled her inside. Every meter made her ill. Throngs of silent pilgrims kept stopping ahead of her to knot shredded cloth and decorative lengths of yarn — symbols of prayers to Saint George — to the bushes and pines. Nobody spoke; if they did the prayers wouldn't come true. Again and again Flora was forced to wait, to catch her breath. Strangers offered their arms.

"Here I was, in a crowd of well-wishers, with hatred in my heart," she recalled. "I was softening the whole way up that mountain. The pilgrimage always had that effect on me. All those prayers for love. I thought I shouldn't have come."

She kept turning back to see if she could spot Yusuf. A

young woman in tortoise sunglasses, gesturing, offered her an extra white sash. With a half-hearted prayer for each of her six doomed children Flora tied it around a wild olive tree. If she looked over the cliff to her left she could see the southern coast of the island below: the strip of white beach, an oil tanker anchored not far offshore. After forty minutes, just over the steepest part of the trail, the white-washed monastery walls appeared at last. Widening, the trail flattened out; the crowd separated and no longer bumped shoulders. Flora emerged at the peak just as a blinding sun broke through the mist in front of her.

Somber pilgrims were milling in groups, waiting for entrance to the monastery to light their candles before the dawn mass. With her hands shading her eyes Flora paced the wet lawn between the cypresses, past the log cabin that served as a café, to the outhouses at the foot of the rock precipice. Normally she would have sucked in her breath at the view: the entire archipelago, all nine islands, stretched below her, an iridescent bracelet on the purple velvet of the Marmara. But she was looking now only for faces, and turning, blinking, found his at last: Yusuf Elmas, climbing the stairs from the lower western courtyard, chatting with the monastery's head priest.

Flora observed the incongruous pair: the holy man in the full glory of vestments and pectoral cross, arm in arm with her boss, tormentor and lover. Yusuf turned slowly, and started when he saw her standing there, chest heaving, hands resting on her stomach, watching them like a hawk from the cliffs. He would not have known she was looking for him with such bitter determination. He offered her a grave smile and silent nod. "May it come easy," the priest said, shaking Yusuf's hand, giving him a hearty slap on the shoulder, and turning back to the monastery. Now Flora strode forward, seized Yusuf's elbow, and aimed him to a secluded spot beyond the outhouses.

"What kind of game is this?" she was saying between her teeth. "Not for all the money in this world, Yusuf Bey, would I let you pull this stunt."

Yusuf's heavy eyes widened, but he remained calm. "A pleasant morning, Flora? You're well enough to make the climb I see."

"I've forbidden it."

His face registered a momentary confusion. "Forbidden what? Tell me what you've forbidden."

"Don't play with us. So this is your great revenge? This is the best you can muster?"

"What revenge, *hanımefendim*?" He spread his arms wide. "What revenge?"

"Why all the secrecy? For ten years I work for you faithfully. And now, behind my back, this! My daughter?"

"Yasemin manages discretion. Unlike some people I know."

"What's that supposed to mean?"

"It means be proud you've raised such a girl. A daughter I can trust."

"And you couldn't trust me enough with this to ask my permission?"

"Permission?" He looked down at her enormous stomach and frowned. "I've asked her on to help. A little Marine Science project. Mapping fault-lines, seismic risk. Some real-life experience."

"Tell her now she can't come with you. Make any excuse you like."

He threw up his chin. "Say what you have to say to her

yourself. Today of all days is not the time to settle old scores. Relax! How much you each mean to me. You know that. See, Flora, this has always been our problem. You've never taken me at my word."

"And what word is that? The word of a liar. The word of a cheat. Someone who will do anything for a fuck. You'll treat her just like you've treated me. I've spent enough time in your mansion, Yusuf. I won't let you ruin her too."

He leaned his head back and laughed a tired laugh. But registering Flora's unyielding gaze, his face softened and his eyes turned sober. The black bell at the steeple of the monastery had begun to toll: the dawn mass beginning. Yusuf took her hand in his double grasp and bent towards her. "She's helping out a bit on the boat. Do you know how exciting this is for a young woman? To play a role here? I would never, Flora Hanım, do anything to hurt her — to hurt either one of you. The girl's grown up in my house. You of all people know what I think of her." His voice had lowered into something tender — a tone she remembered from a distant life. Entwined in his, her fingers weakened. "This, I thought, would be good for her. Some serious work. Something consequential. Yasemin needs this. It could lead to something for her, some direction. Where is she?" he asked. "Did she come up with you? She told me she was coming."

Flora pulled her hand from his grasp. "I've forbidden it."

"How can you forbid it?" he laughed. "She's her own woman now, Flora. She's no child."

"She's my daughter. You listen to me, Yusuf Bey. I want you to leave her alone. If you've doomed yourself, you don't need to doom the girl as well. She doesn't need to be mixed up in your games. The only direction you can offer her is trouble. You leave her alone."

"Then she hasn't come?" He looked to his left, then spun back towards the swarming crowd, which seemed to heighten his impatience, and glanced once at the silent throngs entering the monastery. With that he fell into a fit of coughing. Flora crossed her arms, waiting with patient anger for him to catch his breath. These attacks could last for a minute or for an entire morning. She wouldn't help him. Into the back of his fist between coughs Yusuf said, "A boat ride. She's made friends with the divers. Lighten up, Flora. You can count your days left in this world as easily as I can. Don't consume yourself with things you can't control. Not in the state you're in. We've had good news this morning. You'll see! I promise you good news. You can't let everything weigh on you so much, remember?"

"What good news? Disturbing an underwater grave? How is that good news to me?"

"She's told you?"

"You think she doesn't talk. Half the island knows what you're after, Yusuf. Everyone knows where you're going this morning."

His face for the first time registered concern. "Who has she told?"

"Me." She patted her chest. "That's enough."

He took this in. Cursing, Yusuf turned and hurried off, striding through the groups of pilgrims past the monastery and back towards the mountain path. At first Flora followed, calling out to him through the hushed crowds, but she couldn't maneuver the mass of bodies surging up the hillside, and after a few steps she gave up the chase as a lost cause. A weight seemed to have been lifted from her chest. The sun, yellow now, was brilliant behind her, warming her neck. The bell was still tolling. Smoke from the votive candles had begun to trail through the monastery door. She raised her eyes to heaven.

"I put my hopes in God," she explained to me five years later. "I was already at the monastery. It made more sense to pray for my daughter than to chase your brother down the hill like some madwoman. I've wondered ever since, if I had gone, what more I could have done."

Flora attended mass, and afterwards lit her own candles. She tried to relax with three village friends on the makeshift café chairs. She took a glass of the monastery's famous white wine, which she could never turn down. Her friends shared with her some generously-sliced honeydew — a plate of which Flora balanced on the convenient shelf of her belly. Negotiating her steep descent was more difficult than climbing up had been. The ferries from the city were still spilling pilgrims onto the island. In the streets village kids were congregating with pink pom-poms and ruffled skirts for the National Children's Day celebration. Amid this clamor, at 10:45, Flora arrived back at the clock tower just as the late morning call to prayer ended. She was passing through the riotous main square, scraping sweat from her eyebrows with the edge of her sleeve, when she heard the rumbling.

Everyone I spoke to five years later still remembered the moment, for the square looks out over the ferry terminal, and all the island's balconies face the morning sea, and half the village was milling up on the mountain top, with an unobstructed view to distant horizons. At first it sounded like intermittent fireworks, then the applause of an engine, then an airplane lifting off, and finally the deafening roar of God's thunder. Across the island for thirty seconds no seagulls could be heard calling, no horse's hooves clomping, no pilgrims' feet padding — only Yusuf Elmas's black V-bottom American powerboat, fourteen meters long, wheeling around the coast, then hurtling in pursuit across the waves, one-hundred and twenty kilometers per hour, heading north, toward the city.

From the foot of the clock tower Flora strained her eyes, but she could not see who, or how many, were on board.

\

8

A Philanthropic Legacy

A CAPTAIN OF A Ukrainian tanker had witnessed the sonic speedboat crash from his chart room, and radioed the Coast Guard. They received calls like this on a regular basis, for the point at which the Marmara narrows into the straits is one of the most dangerous stretches of water in the world, Russian oil barges threaten every day to crash into our shorelines, and any number of near-misses occur each week. The foreign captain would later admit on prime-time television that he was drinking a Cherry Cappy and vodka when he had called in the accident, but claimed it was his first of the day and that he was perfectly sober. According to Interior Ministry records, coast guard officials sent two surface patrols scouting the reported coordinates. The first rescue ship arrived not thirty minutes later, but found little trace of the *Bosphorus Princess* and no sign of any survivors. Helicopters were flown in. I had followed the dramatic news coverage of the search over the next two days, as a crew of fifteen rescue divers tirelessly scoured the nearby seas.

The state wasted no time declaring Yusuf Elmas officially

dead. Less than a week later I was watching my brother's funeral coverage on Kral TV. I had no intention of attending. A host of celebrities, publishers, athletes, artists, and longtime financiers paid their respects to an empty casket. The entire crowd was wearing dark glasses, and the television announcer appeared more intent on naming faces than covering the actual proceedings. It was a secular funeral with all the trappings; yet it seemed to me one extended photo opportunity. Dr. Murat Baykan gave a baffled eulogy. A few members of Yusuf's domestic staff were there, yet faced with the awkwardness of sitting so close to so many people of distinction, plus the strangeness of a funeral without so much as the mention of God, most of them fled right after the service. Uncle Haim had flown down from Sweden with the express purpose of escorting my father. But in his grief Father lost his nerve, and at the last moment he, too, refused to go. It was entirely understandable. No man should bury his child.

A gravesite was erected in the small village cemetery up the hill from Kuzguncuk, on the city's Asian side. Five years on I would track it down for the very first time. With my bare hands I pulled up the nettles and vines the best I could. I left a rock on the already tilting gravestone. I could recall only scattered phrases of the Mourner's Kaddish, which I'd last recited at Mother's funeral, and so I scoured my memory for something else to say at the grave of my brother. What kept coming to mind was our old Ladino saying: "At the time of death the eyes are not filled with money, but with the dust of the earth."

In the final revision to his will my brother had left his helicopter to the German Hospital in Cihangir, where it's now parked among rusted satellite dishes on the wind-swept seventh-story roof. The *Bosphorus Princess* — never located — he'd bequeathed to Dr. Murat Baykan. A quarter of the remaining trust, established as the Elmas Foundation, went to the Friends of the Islands in support of reconstruction and conservation efforts. The bulk of this fund, matched by a grant from City Hall, had since been used to reinforce the fleet of high-speed catamarans now plying the waters between the islands five times a day — an unquestionable boon to commuters. Nearly a sixth of Yusuf's fortune established a private technical college on land he had purchased up by the Belgrade Forest, on the shores of the Black Sea. Four years after his death Elmas University opened its doors to a class of 250 scholarship students, from every corner of the nation. A special provision held that one-third of the school's undergraduates had to be *azınlık* — claiming Armenian, Greek, or Jewish minority lineage. In their first semester students were given laptop computers. They lived in state-of-the-art dormitory rooms with single beds and recessed lighting and wireless Internet service. Elmas University's Department of Geology now sailed Yusuf's mega-yacht for scientific excursions, and in the summer hosted Semesters at Sea on the Mediterranean. A large chunk of Yusuf's remaining fortune went to the International Physiotherapy Group for Cystic Fibrosis, which recently announced a major breakthrough. Scientists have genetically engineered DNA in piglets to match the human mutation that causes the disease. The KF piglets have been heralded as a promising hope for a cure.

And the list went on. All told, it was a substantial philanthropic legacy.

9

Miracles

Five years to the day of his death, my last morning on the island, I too would make the pilgrimage to St. George. In the half-light of dawn the Greek and Armenian pilgrims had gathered at the base of the slope, near the donkey corral, and exchanged quiet greetings. The women wore dark headscarves, the men musty long jackets and corduroy caps. Friends, coughing, slapped each other on their backs. A shrill wind from the southeast whistled through the tree tops, blowing white blossoms across the pavement like fragrant snow. I bent amid the crowd to remove my dress shoes. Pieces of ripped cloth were handed around with smiles and murmured good will. I took one from Anagnosti Raba, the old Greek butcher who remembered seeing my brother on his final ascent.

"I was younger then," Anagnosti told me. "It was an easier climb. Soon I will no longer be able to make it to the top."

"Not in this lifetime, friend," I assured him. "Not in this lifetime."

Our silent hike up the hillside began. People were pulling the wet branches of the bushes, searching for empty strands to tie their sashes in prayer for love. A colorful tangle of yarn stretched on both sides up the length of the trail. I walked slowly, stepping carefully on the cobblestone, cool and rough now under my feet, the damp pebbles jutting between my toes, the grit and friction of each step penance for the mistakes of a lifetime. Through the breaking fog clouds were fading from gray to a bluish white. Blackbirds alighted to observe the holy procession from the tops of the pines. Muffled voices. Good natured complaints from under the breath. Hunched figures straightening to rest. Twenty minutes, then thirty, of unhurried steps up the grass-scented slope.

Perhaps the climb had cleared his mind; perhaps he had focused his will to imagine the success of the morning to come, and like a penitent monk had shut out the noise of life. What need did Yusuf have for these sashes? What need for prayer? A man who had so extraordinarily achieved greatness might not have imagined events spiraling beyond his control. Even in those last hours he'd still believed each of us wields power enough to redirect the currents of our lives.

I had not been to the top of *Yücetepe* in thirty years, since Yusuf and I were kids together on this island, but at the peak I found little changed. Inside the monastery I greeted the head priest and introduced myself. He took my arm and walked me through the crowds into the church, showing me the polished icons, the marble depictions of St. George on his horse slaying the dragon, the holy iasma waters where pilgrims dab their aching muscles. As teens Yusuf and I had explored this small chapel many times in our socks, but we hadn't known what any of these Orthodox treasures meant. "I used to remind your brother how this is a spiritual place, how I pray for anyone who comes here, no matter what their religion," the priest now told me. "Miracles. There is a real power on our mountain. It's good for any illness. Yusuf believed in it too. He needed that belief." The priest showed me the iron door at the entrance to the church, built by an Iranian invalid for whom the pilgrimage had brought back the power to walk. "We don't speak here about nationality, or even worry over the differences of faith so much," the priest assured me in a throaty whisper. "Greeks, Armenians, Muslims, Jews, they all come. I pray for them all."

The bells were tolling, and I jostled my way outside, beyond the outhouses, to the rocky cliffs overhanging the sea. And there, across the field, I spotted Flora Demirkan with two of her boys — Sarp and Saim. They were milling with friends under the rustic pergolas, awaiting the dawn mass. I waved, but I wasn't sure she'd seen me, and even if she had, I didn't expect her to come over. We'd found we had nothing more to say to one another. Platitudes meant nothing. I too had known a pain and a guilt that never went away. She had consoled me with her body that night, our only night together, but what consolation could I give her? Nothing for the loss of her daughter; nothing for the man of her life. The void remained. She had not been back to the mansion since. Flora was through unburdening herself.

I turned to admire the stretch of water below. Anyone watching from these cliffs on that bright morning five years ago would have had this clear view of the final drama. Yusuf had steered straight out, directly off shore. The double engines hummed lower and lower, then quavered slightly as he circled south, beyond the ferry pier. Suddenly both engines kicked in, exploding with a thunder that must have shook the island, and all islands beyond, as Yusuf opened it up. I've tried to place myself in his head in those last moments. Was it possible that a man who had achieved so much could have felt his world crashing shut around him — his beloved team unable to win a championship, his political speeches drawing condemnation and lawsuits, his scarred lungs failing, his family estranged, his civic projects doomed, his promising search for the *Salvador* compromised? No, I liked to imagine it the other way: that Yusuf's jetting across the sea that fine morning marked only a flaunting of his freedom. He would not be tied to the petty distractions and minor disappointments of this world or any other. He had led a frantically charmed life, without limitations. Nothing prevented him from racing with celestial speed out across the waters, standing on his feet before the wheel, his hand on the throttle. In those minutes at that speed he was free of the burdens of love, free of verdicts, free of disease, free for the authorities to behold, should they be watching from above.

As he trimmed in, the Lightning powerboat surged out across the white-speckled waves. Yasemin would have joined him at the wheel to help navigate, as her mother had once done. Yusuf might have chastised her for skipping the pilgrimage, for saying too much. Perhaps they had argued. Perhaps he had grown distracted. Perhaps their vision ahead was limited. Perhaps he had simply accelerated too quickly, the double engines rigged to blow at a certain speed. Again and again he had landed, pounding the surface, planing faster and louder and higher with each dangerous leap across the crests. The rooster-tail gushed out behind them; the front half of the boat rose on its aft from the water — a glorious sight — until at top speed the V-bottom exploded, flipping them in the crash, rolling over itself in a sliding fountain of spray.

I heard the crunch of footsteps in the weeds and felt someone standing beside me. Without looking up I knew who it was.
"*Günaydın*," I murmured.

"*Günaydın*."

She was standing so close to me I could feel the warmth of her
shoulder. "A fine morning."

"Beautiful," she said.

The broken hull would have sunk to uncertain depths, settled
softly upon the sea floor. I patted my pocket, where I had the
photocopy of another wreck folded in my wallet. For so long
I'd tried to forget my brother, but here I'd found a way to live
with the remembering. From these heights on the cliffs I could
imagine them coming to a peaceful rest down there, below these
turquoise waters, beside the rust-scabbed hulk of our grandmother's cattle steamer, bound once upon a time for Palestine.

10

Wet Smoke Residues

The phone call came from the Mayor's Office late morning as I was descending the mountain with the other pilgrims.

"Mr. Benezra, we have you listed as the owner of the Halim Pasha House, number 25 Yilmaztürk Caddesi."

"That's right. There's a problem?"

"As quickly as possible," the voice said. "You'll need to return."

Down the mule-trail behind the Nizam Mosque I could see the broken line of smoke in the distance, snaking in a thin trail, curving to its left in the wind. At that distance it could have been a barbecue for the National Children's Day celebrations, someone roasting fish, the spewing of a baker's chimney.

At the Halim Pasha House: two of the island's intensely red fire trucks parked out front. A long limp red hose snaked through the openings in the cast iron fence, stretching limply up to the steps, through the now flooded garden. A sickening smell of burnt wood. The front windows broken. The entire front edifice scarred with wetness. A section of shingles blasted off.

At the sight of me Officer Ceber rose from the porch and

made his way slowly to meet me in the muck of the statue garden.

"They brought a fire boat around late morning, too. Got it from two directions."

"Where'd it start?"

"It's looking like the kitchen. Were you having trouble with the oven?"

"It's brand new."

"They suspect the gas hookup was faulty."

"Nobody was using the oven, Ceber. I've been up the mountain all morning."

"It's just a first guess. This is what happens when you modernize. We've seen it before. Cutting corners. Doing the work yourself. Breaking code. Save a little money, but these wooden homes go up like powder kegs. It's a good thing you weren't here. Your neighbors on both sides heard an explosion." He looked at me with fawning concern. "You could have been killed."

I pushed past him up the porch stairs and stepped warily over some shattered glass.

"They're still working in there. You're not allowed in just yet."

"I didn't ask your permission, Ceber."

He followed a step behind as I entered the mansion. They'd spared nothing. The front foyer black with smoke damage. The smoldering kitchen charred, the pedestal table overturned, its wooden chairs ashes. Down the foyer the old office I'd converted looked like a tsunami had passed through it. The antique rotary phone stood alone on the desk, like some unearthed charred black fossil.

I could hear firemen stomping upstairs. In the hallway the floorboards were soggy and stained dark with ashes. Beneath our feet water squished in the carpets and antique kilims. It wasn't lost on me. The house had been drowned.

Back in the smoldering kitchen I slowly circled in place, coming to grips with my astonishment.

"Whoever had access could have left on the gas," Ceber said. "And then, anything could have set it off." I saw where he was pointing. Near the oven the small appliances — a toaster, a blender, both dripping, had melted.

"No one had access."

"But who's been working here?"

"I've let everyone go. I've been working in the city myself. I'm only here on weekends."

"You'll have to leave…"

He was still talking, but I had no patience for him at this point. "Give me a few minutes alone here, Ceber."

"I'm ordering you to leave. It's not safe yet. We're bringing someone over for the investigation."

And I relented. We didn't win such battles. Outside in the mud of the torn up statue garden I sat down on the bench, contemplating the mansion's timeless empire-baroque façade. In the early afternoon sunshine the smoldering house seemed lost beneath a private fog. Two families passing on the road stopped and gathered on the other side of the wrought iron gate. Children poked their noses through the bars. Two firefighters — yellow helmets, blue unbuttoned fire jackets striped with reflectors, *Adalar Iftaiye* printed in yellow on their backs — crashed out of the house, scuffing clean their boots on the porch. The older of them, in full beard and glasses, ordered the other to work on the hose, then came down the porch and sat next to me. Two more emerged from around the back gardens and with a tumult of shouting and curses began breaking down a ladder that led above the kitchen to the main bedroom.

Beside me the bearded man introduced himself as the fire chief. He was proud that his crew had arrived on the scene and had the fire out in six minutes. "But the fire in the kitchen was very intense. In small fires like this one, the smoke damage can be worse than the fire damage."

I nodded. He eyed me for a moment. "I'm told you've taken a recent insurance policy out on the mansion?"

"I have." I'd need my own lawyer now.

"Good, good. If it was truly an accident, my guess is it could have been prevented with some basic precautions."

"Yes. Precautions."

"I've been told you've been remodeling. New appliances. New wiring. Overloaded kitchen circuitry…"

"I haven't touched the electricity."

"It could have been a thousand things. You get involved, you know, on a project this size, things go wrong. The Mayor's Office would like a full investigation."

"Of course they would. It's only proper."

Officer Ceber, the Mayor's Office, this fire chief — they already knew the results of the investigation. An accident, fully attributable to me.

He was going on now about the differences between wet smoke residues and dry smoke residues, how everything the smoke reached would have to be cleaned or tossed: walls, ceilings, hardwood floors, curtains, rugs, clothing, kitchen appliances, furniture, fixtures, photographs, bed and table linens, books, knickknacks. "Carpets," he said, "are the real problem. They're made from so many different materials, there's no telling. Silk, wool, acrylic, they each react in their own way to the smoke. And to the cleaning agent."

I was nodding at him through all of this. Finally he stood.

"Things," he said. "It's only things. At the end of the day, if a fire and smoke only damage things, then you've escaped. No one was hurt." He reached for my hand. "May it pass quickly."

He who is separated from his lover cries for
seven years, but he who is separated from his
home cries till he dies.

— Turkish Proverb

Autumn 2012

Two years later I sit in the sharp Mediterranean sun across a café table from my daughters. They are twirling their forks into their pad thai noodles, competing to see who can get the largest pile into her mouth in one disgusting swoop. The restaurant has outdoor seating year round. We are three blocks from the sea, and the breeze through the street of white Tel Aviv apartment complexes has threatened, on multiple occasions, to blow our napkins off the table. I've secured them under the condiment plates. I glance behind us at two other tables of patrons enjoying their meals, then lock eyes momentarily with a dark-skinned, mustached customer in military fatigues standing at the doorway, chatting with our Thai waitress. The city is peaceful today; but in my mind I play the coming explosion of this would-be suicide bomber, the upending of the earth, the slow motion slaughter of my girls, my feeble attempts to cover them with my body, the incapacity of a father's muscle and bone to protect them. Is this heightened anxiety something you get used to? When does the sense of siege become normal?

If we're going to deal with them bombing our synagogues, we may as well do it in Israel. They were Naomi's words, and now, four months here, they've become my mantra as well.

Sara, oblivious, has wound an overly ambitious string of pad thai on her fork and is forcing it into her mouth. Estela says, "Dad, *you* be the judge."

"No," I say. "This is ridiculous. Enjoy your food. You don't have to play with it. Sara, stop that."

I can't enjoy the food myself. My spring rolls cling half-eaten to their dish, and I have spooned a pile of rice onto my plate but have yet to serve myself the vegetables in oyster sauce. I watch the twins attacking their lunch, giggling, teasing one another. Sara swipes Estela's mound of noodles off her fork. And then both are eating shrimp off the other's plate, shoveling the food down in an unspoken race and giggling so hard they might choke.

"Hey," I warn them, "that's enough." But I'm laughing now, and Estela, the bolder of the two, helps herself to a forkful of rice off my plate as well. I steal a noodle from hers with my fingers and suck it into my mouth with a spicy slurp. "Baba," Estela yells, "That was *mine!*" She slaps my shoulder.

I had picked them up late morning from Naomi's apartment, as I have every Saturday since I arrived in September. Lunch and a walk on the beach. There's talk emerging of our moving in together again, but first we'll have to find an apartment large enough. Neither Naomi nor I are ready to make the plunge; but it remains a hope drifting loosely on the horizon.

I had come to this country to grant Naomi a legal Israeli divorce, in a *get* ceremony, with witnesses and three rabbis. After two years of fiercely avoiding the issue she suddenly wanted to remarry. An orthodox boyfriend she had been seeing — a freelance writer, of all things. In this country religious edicts were more complex than they were back home; and I was told that only the husband, of his own free will, could grant a woman a divorce. I had to bring our marriage contract from our apartment in Ankara, where it had hung, framed, for twenty years. I would have to utter the final words: "Behold, this is your *get*. Accept it, for with it you will be divorced from me from this moment and be permitted to all men." Then Naomi would have to wait ninety-two days to remarry. When we arrived at the court the dingy offices had smelled — as so many buildings in Israel did — like the synagogue of my youth: body odor, disinfectant, camphor balls, and candle matches. Naomi had dressed in funereal black. I sat with my elbows crossed in my lap. The three rabbis watched us through the drawn out proceedings, two with their chins resting on their hands, utterly bored. I was willing to do this for her. I wanted to free her to live the life she needed, the life I had taken from her. But as the rabbis questioned us Naomi broke down. I held out as long as I was able before my own eyes filled. The rabbis blinked, lifted their heads, sat up in their chairs. They suggested we talk, and that we come back when we were ready. We left the offices, returned to my hotel room, and made love like teenagers, for the first time in three years.

I wanted to stay. She seemed to want me to stay. I was happy to be close. A new life. My brother had always believed it was possible. And maybe it was.

Millimeter by millimeter, Naomi and I are reacquainting ourselves. Two weeks last month I had spent with her and the twins in the basement of their apartment building — Estela and Sara in sleeping bags, Naomi and I on army cots beneath wool blankets. Other families slept around us. Hezbollah rockets were firing an hour north, raining down on the country from southern Lebanon. But in the basement a resolutely festive atmosphere prevailed. We played canasta, we watched Wheel of Fortune, we hardly slept — and we spoke late into the nights, trying to calm the concerns of the girls. We were together, a family again, brought closer in crisis. If only the semblance of love, for now the semblance was enough.

The tiny nation, this island in a sea of Islam, was under siege. Then suddenly it wasn't: massive aerial attacks, the full weight of the IDF's might, blowing the winds of war back north into Lebanon, where families not unlike ours now crouched in basements, listening for distant explosions, whispering to frightened children. A younger Avram might have summoned outrage at the disproportionate slaughter unleashed by a bellicose government. But here the rockets have stopped, and only days later I can sit above ground, stunned by a sunny afternoon, eating Thai food, ready to stroll the pretty beach with my pretty daughters. Relief clouds my sympathies; self-preservation trumps politics. We'll meet Naomi at the end of our walk. She'll bring the girls over to a ballet recital of their friends. The privilege of a normal day.

I glance from my daughters back at the man in military fatigues. He appears to be waiting for a take-out order. My eyes return to my girls. It had been over a year since I had seen them, and on my arrival in Israel I was shocked by who I found. They seemed so mature, so well-spoken, with their mother's attitude and her family's confident zest for life. Estela was beginning to grow taller than her sister, while Sara's voice — I noticed when she blessed the Shabat bread — had grown deeper and more melodious. All the energy it had taken to bring them through their first nine years. All the board games played, all the books read, all the teeth brushed, all the ways I'd tried to protect them. And then complete abandonment. But even without me the girls had continued to flourish. I would not have believed that was possible.

Soon they'd be twelve years old. They were blossoming into young women. They had painted their toenails the same shade of red. No talk of boys yet, at least not with me; and the silence on that subject unnerved a father. It was only a matter of time. I've grown used to passing the long-haired, tan-skinned boys playing football on the beach or sitting with their ankles crossed, menacingly alert, oozing testosterone, on the curbs outside Naomi's apartment. On our Saturdays together I notice, when these boys wave, the girls turn their heads quickly — too quickly — then smile at each other and sometimes whisper. My golden-haired daughters already know the boys of the neighborhood. How was it children acclimated so quickly? They had school of course, and friends, the youth group at synagogue, and a host of distant relatives on Naomi's side of the family. Adults — we were much more on our own.

I watch them now as they polish off their remaining pad thai. Sara sprinkles more sugar onto hers. Estela spoons a dose of ground peanuts. They are nearly as old as we were, Yusuf and I, the year Father sold the house on the island. I feel aged beyond years. Was it really possible I had borne so much weight of that drama? Or had that weight been exaggerated in my memory? The twins do not seem capable of those depths of anxiety, though I know I can't fathom what goes on in their own adolescent hearts. Our island cottage, shaken by earthquakes, pounded by storms, lost to us in bankruptcy, for all that had never been the target of Hezbollah rockets.

The middle-aged waitress appears, and in broken English asks if everything is okay. Shyly, Sara requests another cola. With conviction, Estela orders a Thai iced tea.

"How do you know what a Thai iced tea is?" I ask.

"We've been to Thai restaurants, like, a hundred times Baba."

I didn't know they'd ever eaten Thai before. The cuisine is new to me. "On your own?"

"Aunt Miriam took us to one in Jerusalem. And we've been with Mom to the one near Azrieli Mall."

I nod, as if suddenly remembering hearing about it. I have to constantly remind myself they've been living a life without me. *Pasa punto, pasa mundo.* A moment passes, a world passes.

When the waitress — whom I guess is also the restaurant's owner and cook — delivers the drinks, Estela offers me a sip from her straw. It's sickly sweet, so sweet I can barely keep it down. Of course Estela would like it. This is the daughter who, for as long as I can remember, demanded three cubes of sugar in each glass of *chai*. Sara, for her part, preferred sour candy, salted cookies, pickled vegetables, a different region of the tongue.

They ask me about their grandfather, whom they love and haven't seen since the move. I speak to him daily. He is nearly seventy-seven years old and living full-time on the island — though not in Yusuf's mansion, as I once hoped he might.

Despite the fire, despite the grim condition of the real-estate market, I'd found a buyer for the property. It had been a simple matter of placing a call to Erdan Özakin, in Chicago, and asking if his father, Vehbi, the old newspaper mogul, might be interested in reclaiming an historic island villa he'd once sold my brother. I met with Vehbi Özakin at the Çırağan Palace, in the same restaurant Yusuf had taken him to. He was over ninety years old now; and came rolled in on a wheelchair by a beefy-shouldered assistant, who refused to sit down, but stood at attention for the duration of the meal. When our food came I offered Vehbi a deal. Half a million Euros for the Halim Pasha House — a pittance, but considering the damages, enough for what I had planned. Vehbi agreed, snapped his finger at his assistant, who produced a watermarked check, then and there, for Vehbi to sign as deposit.

Last summer, with a quarter of the amount from the sale, I'd bought back our old cottage, our first house on the island, on generous terms from its current occupant, a widowed carriage driver. Father moved in without a battle.

The remaining money from the sale would be enough to see him through his final years. With it I hired, full-time, Flora Demirkan, to cook and to watch out for him. She was the best caregiver I could think of, the only person on the island I could entrust him to. Retired at last, Father moved back into the very house whose roof he had once water-proofed, whose sidewalks we had once written our names in. Now he spent his days fishing off the rocks, gardening, and re-building the back porch. He's donated time, as well, on repair and upkeep of the island's Hesed Le Avraam Synagogue. Each evening he sits outside the house and takes his dinner on the modest brick patio. It faces inland, to the mountains, not outward, to the Marmara, but for my father it's all the same. He can imagine whatever view he needs.

A week ago I had received a postcard, along with a photograph of the house — of Father on the completed porch, taken, I assumed, by Flora or one of her children. They came around with their mother now and then. They've found something nostalgic in looking out for Yusuf Elmas's dad. For his part, Father likes the attentions, the yelling of Feride for her brothers, the tramping of the rowdy boys up and down the stairs, the youngest kid, Saim, kicking a football against the stone wall of the front porch. Father informs me that Flora seems content — at peace once again with her torn-up life. Late at night, after she cooks his dinner, she often stays and watches the television with him. He has Digitürk now, 150 channels, and by necessity Flora has assumed control of the remote. So it is that Father happily sits through overblown American movies, and French cooking shows, and the unwatchable romantic serials from Brazil. Flora makes him watch Desperate Housewives, a new program she's recently become addicted to, and he admits to liking it as well. He also watches Beşiktaş football matches with Sarp — still loyal to his team, despite years of the Battering Ram. My old man cannot make out the players scrambling across the screen very well, but Sarp gives detailed accounts of every attack and pass and shot on goal. From what I gather there has been some commotion this week, because Fenerbahçe just signed a famed defenseman from Real Madrid, who would play two years in our country. Father said Sarp could not stop talking about the injustice of it all; and on the phone neither could he.

In my mind the island is a different place now — the old families long gone. My dad says it still reminds him though of the summer we'd first moved into that house, thirty-seven years ago, and how excited his two sons had been. He wants to know when I'll come back to visit with the twins. "*Hijos de mis hijos, dos vezes mis hijos*," he likes to say. "The children of my children are doubly my children." He wishes — how he wishes — Mother had only been here still, to share this with him: a house on the Princes' Islands, the clean sea air, the freshest fish for dinner, a dip in the water, card games at the Watersports Club, tea in the *Belediye Gazinosu*, where families could sit together watching the ferries sail in from the sunset. It was only this life, and this simple life alone, that Mother had ever wanted for us.

At the café table I tell the girls their grandfather is happier than he has been in years. "We'll visit next summer, after school's out," I promise. "He sends you his biggest kisses. You should write him. We can mail him the school photos."

"Does he have e-mail yet?" Estela asks.

"No," I laugh. "He doesn't have e-mail."

"When are you going to get him e-mail?"

I watch the Thai waitress now as she clears our table, her dark skin, her small eyes and long lashes, a silk scarf she has wrapped around her neck, her hands hard and cracked from the cooking and washing, her posture rigid as she lugs our dirty plates back inside the open door. The restaurant is new, it seems. Wicker chairs, laminated menus in three languages: English, Russian, and Hebrew. She is trying to make a go of it, running the small café herself. I wonder if inside the kitchen she has a husband or daughters helping. Or is she completely alone? It's a pretty location she's chosen: three blocks from the beach. I can see the blue of the Mediterranean over the twins' heads. In Thailand, I suppose, there must be more restaurants like this than there are grains of sand. Smart, then, for a woman to open one here. Smart but difficult, so far from home.

I swallow a few bites of the vegetables, pay the bill, leave a large tip of twenty shekels. We have arranged to meet Naomi near a falafel stand on the southern end of the beach. On the walk there the twins go barefoot, and they skip along the edge of the water, dodging the glossy waves at first, then wading, white sandals dangling from their fingers. I follow them across the sand and eventually catch up.

After awhile Sara puts her arm around my waist and hooks one finger in the belt loop of my pants. "How are you Baba?" It's an adult question, with an adult's tone, an adult's concern.

I look down at her as we walk. I remember the playground built just outside our complex when we first moved into our second apartment. It gleamed in all its plastic novelty for a few months, but after a year the sandbox had become a litter for local cats, the swings had dehinged themselves, and the seesaws were missing seats. But how the twins had loved that playground! Estela was the adventurous one. She ran faster than I could, and she jumped off ledges and climbed up monkey bars and used the seesaws as balance beams with little fear. Sara was the cautious one. She liked to climb up and down the steps of the jungle gym, but for the longest time she would not brave the slides, not even the smallest ones. I didn't want to make an issue of it. I told her she was perfectly reasonable not to want to go down slides, that slides were frightening and probably the source of most playground accidents. Eventually her excessive caution came to bother me, and when she was up at the top I'd urge her down. "Try the slide! Baba will catch you!" or "Why don't we go down together?" or "You can't go down the slide Sara, I know you can't!" Nothing worked. Only after months of watching her sister go down the slide and (despite my warnings) turn around, climb back up, and (despite further warnings) fly down head first like Superman, did Sara herself sit on the baby slide. Without any encouragement she pushed off. I rushed to her. At the bottom, her feet dangling from the edge above the sand, she looked up at me with eyes full of wonder. I lifted her, yelling, "You did it!" I tossed her into the air, caught her, and placed her soundly on her feet. For the rest of the morning she would not be distracted. She must have gone down that same damn slide a hundred times, and I must have tossed her into the air and caught her a hundred times. It was a baby slide — all of two meters high, but she shrieked gliding down it, and her joy filled my heart.

Now, on the beach, this same girl glances up and asks, "Baba, are you lonely in Israel?"

"Lonely? No. Not at all. I look forward to seeing you. I like being close. I'm busy looking for work"

"We missed you when you weren't here. Did you miss us?"

We've never spoken of my absence. Sara was the quieter of the twins. Eight minutes older, a world shyer. Now she's the more mature of the two.

"Yes," I answer.

"Will you stay?"

"Yes."

"With us, I mean. Will you come and stay with us?"

"Soon." I peer straight ahead.

I can feel her looking up at me. I see in my daughters' faces my own mother's prophetic eyes, that iron will, that ability to find the center of a person and tell what they are made of. I squeeze her to me mid-stride, hold her there for two steps, then let her go. She jogs ahead to catch up to Estela, who is bent over the surf and pointing to a dead jellyfish. I join them and we poke the cellophane corpse with twigs.

Up the beach ten minutes later we spot Naomi on a bench on the paved path that runs parallel to the road. She is wearing a white sweater with a light scarf tied loosely over her hair. Sketchbook on her lap, clenching a short thin brush, she is painting the surf. She doesn't notice us approaching. Her concentration when she is painting is as intense as any I've ever seen. Another gallery in Haifa is hosting an exhibition of her work in a month's time. Old stuff, things she's told me she can no longer look at. Recently she's moved from still lifes to trying to capture motion on the page, a skill she'd never believed she possessed. "I'm getting old," she said. "If I don't learn now, I'll never learn." The surf, on this sunny winter day, seems as fine a subject as any in the universe. I glance out to see if there is something special in the waters she might be trying to capture, but the Mediterranean is empty, no islands or boats blocking this view to the horizon, nothing there, an open expanse. The White Sea. It was this very shore the passengers aboard my grandmother's boat had been trying to reach. A short journey, around the corner of a continent, only a few hundred kilometers, but impossible all the same. For us it took three generations to arrive.

Naomi stands to greet us, kisses each of the twins on the cheeks, and to my surprise kisses me on the cheeks as well. "Hello Avram," she says, "Did you have a nice lunch together?"

Kisses on the cheeks. The first time since my arrival that she has done this in front of the twins. I stare at her handsome face. We used to joke with each other that the girls had been conceived on Naomi's drafting table. In those days, the desolate early years of our marriage, we each had kept our own office. At night I would put a cassette tape in the stereo in our bedroom — jazz or *arabesk*, something without words to distract us — and we would spend the early evening apart in our separate rooms. I was still working on practice sketches: our dream vacation villa in Bodrum that we would one day build, a loft for the ten children we would one day have. (We'd been trying for six years, with no success. Naomi's mother accused us of doing it wrong.) Naomi worked in her own office, putting paint to paper with her light touch, scenes of the Anatolian countryside and horses and fields and the gorges that dappled our homeland, but always with an element of the unexpected: a splotch of red, bloodlike, over a picnic blanket, a hint of fear in the expression of a woman picking apricots. The paintings stole your breath and unnerved you as well. After an hour or two I would pull myself from my blueprints to go change the cassette. On one occasion I stopped by Naomi's office to see how she was making out. She'd just finished a boating scene on Lake Van and was examining it as it dried. I stood over her shoulder, admiring it with her, teasing the back of her hair. She turned to me, grabbed me around my neck, leaned herself up on the table and pressed against me. She unbuttoned my shirt, then her blouse. I tried to push her paintings to the side, but she stopped me and I was lost with her. In our urgency she slipped and placed one hand on the painting she'd just completed; and laughing, she pressed the colors to my face. She smeared blue and black and yellow across my neck and across my chest as I kissed her. I turned her around and painted her back as I made love to her; then she faced me, serious and wide-eyed, and hoisted herself up the length of the drafting table and drew me into her once again. Such a mess we made. Nine months later the twins were born.

Now we help pack Naomi's sketchbook, pencils, and charcoal. The girls ask if I will walk them to the ballet recital with their mom. Four blocks from the water we come upon a run-down art house movie theater. Recently, to pass so many nights alone, I've taken to going to the theaters, but I have not yet made it to this one. It's in dire shape, with bricks crumbling off the siding and holes in the glass marquee and a rusted turnstile beside the ticket window. I pause in front of this window to note the schedule of an upcoming film retrospective. Sara stops with me; Naomi and Estela have walked ahead. I'm struck for a moment by a title among the list of films: *The Struma, Canada.*

"What is it?" Sara is asking.

Dr. Ayda Subaşı had mailed me a pirated copy, and I had watched it twice on my computer. The film runs seventy-nine minutes. It begins with a series of interviews with Israeli politicians, historians, poets, and émigrés, all of whom relate the story of growing tensions in 1941 Romania. Slowly it details the failed dives for the wreckage of the *Struma*. At first it's a dry film, made up of well-trodden Holocaust material, a straightforward work about familiar people and lives lost in familiar ways. It breaks no new ground. But unexpectedly, in its second half, the film leaps to the personal histories of three of the families whose relatives had fled Romania aboard that boat. The movie picks up energy. Across generations the storm-tossed families have wound up in Los Angeles, Sydney, and Toronto. I've always approached movies (and books and plays) like I have architecture: you inhabit them, you walk that space and experience it with hope from the inside. Much as my favorite buildings have each time I've returned to them — the miraculous sweep, say, of the Aya Sophia,

or the spare functionality of the Bauhaus I've come to admire
in Tel Aviv — the second half of *The Struma* moved me both
times I sat through it. The narrated family histories accumulate
personal weight. It is here the film has a broadness of scope. You
come to know the contemporary interviewees and the depths of
their families across three generations. Unlike most films I see
nowadays, it does not run overly long. Nor, despite the tragic
story at its heart, is it entirely bleak. It offers a vision of a vibrant
life for these families of lost refugees, a way to move forward.
There's one memorable scene of children playing cricket in their
Sydney club teams. In another, two families — having once fled
the violence of the same Romanian village — find themselves
reunited at the memorial service for the bombed ship on a Black
Sea fishing vessel. A young teenage vocalist has just recorded
her first album, which fuses Sephardic music with contemporary
rock and folk. Her songs play in the background for much of the
film, and her amusing dance performances in a punk coffee shop
in West Hollywood serve as transitions between the three family
stories. By film's end the interviewees have become true screen
characters. I found myself rooting for them. I wanted to know
how their lives played out. I wanted to fast-forward beyond the
film to see how these people might further spite the cruelties of
history. The movie's rhetoric is subdued; nobody mentions contemporary politics. Much of its charm lies in this restraint. It is
by no means even-handed or well-paced; and the three or four
critics who took any notice dismissed it, claiming it did not say
enough about the mass slaughter at its heart. But watching these
people on the screen, these children and grandchildren of survivors, this punk girl dancing, closing her eyes and wriggling her

hips to the pleasure of her own bizarre song lyrics, it's impossible to deny their existence, or claim their stories are other than what they are.

At the window I'm trying to see if they've listed the date it will play. Maybe I'll take the twins. The poster advertises two independent films I've already seen, with show times at 7:30 and 9:45. Another poster in an adjoining window reads COMING SOON, in bright yellow capital letters, the two O's unevenly spaced. And beneath it, behind smudged glass, *The Struma's* poster. An image of a sinking ship, wracked by waves, above the tagline: *Only A Survivor Can Tell.*

I look for his name buried in the fine print. At first I cannot find it. I can't find his name, and it seems for a second these last seven years never happened. Life is an illusion. The man who'd once accused his nation's leaders of muffling history has done just that with his own. Retracing the credits word by word, I spot it at last, buried deep in the list of Associate Producers: *Yusuf Benezra.* I cannot take my eyes off the twelve simple letters, and the colors and text surrounding it fade.

My daughter is pulling me by the shirtsleeve. "Dad," she says. "Come on already!"

I run my finger over the glass-framed poster, across his surname, as one might touch a gravestone.

"Let's go," Sara says, dragging me by the other hand. "Mom's waiting. Walk, Dad! Use your feet."

Acknowledgments

This novel could not have been written without the generous support of the National Endowment for the Arts, the Black Mountain Institute, the Iowa Writer's Workshop, and Bucknell University. I've benefitted greatly from the wise feedback and counsel of Alan Drew, Dorian Karchmar, and Helen Atsma. My colleagues at Bucknell's Department of English and The Stadler Center for Poetry have never wavered in their support of my writing. My students in Istanbul, New Delhi, and Pennsylvania have been a constant source of insight and inspiration. I am especially indebted to Paula Closson Buck for her advice, example, and grit. My deepest thanks to Marc Estrin and Donna Bister of Fomite Press, both for their literary activism, and for so enthusiastically offering this novel a home.

For their love and confidence: Dan, Sharyn, and Livia Rosenberg, Lori, DJ, and Andrew Ruschman, Steve Hamm, Todd and Barbara Marsh, Linda and Jerry Marsh, Ron and Teri Rosenberg, and Marilyn and Howie Crain.

For all of this, and all else beyond: Gabriella, Alexey, and Michelle.

Fomite

A fomite is a medium capable of transmitting infectious organisms from one individual to another.

"The activity of art is based on the capacity of people to be infected by the feelings of others." Tolstoy, *What Is Art?*

Writing a review on Amazon, Good Reads, Shelfari, Library Thing or other social media sites for readers will help the progress of independent publishing. To submit a review, go to the book page on any of the sites and follow the links for reviews. Books from independent presses rely on reader to reader communications.

For more information or to order any of our books, visit
http://www.fomitepress.com/FOMITE/Our_Books.html

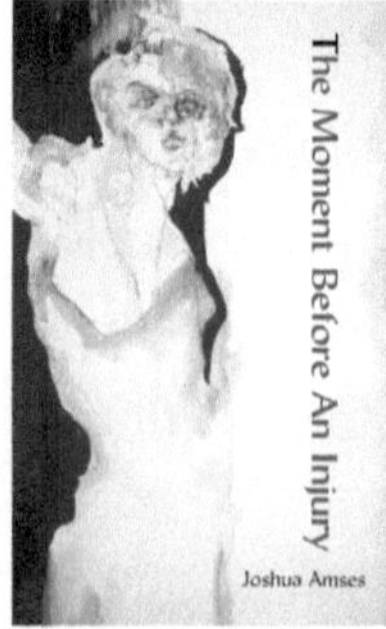

*The Moment
Before an Injury*
Joshua Amses

*Nothing Beside
Remains*
Jaysinh Birjépatil

*The Way None
of This Happened*
Mike Breiner

Victor Rand
David Brizer

*Summer on the
Cold War Planet*
Paula Closson Buck

*Cycling in Plato's
Cave*
David Cavanagh

Fomite

Picking Up the Bodies
James F. Connolly

Unfinished Stories of Girls
Catherine Zobal Dent

Drawing on Life
Mason Drukman

Foreign Tales of Exemplum and Woe
J. C. Ellefson

Free Fall/Caída libre
Tina Escaja

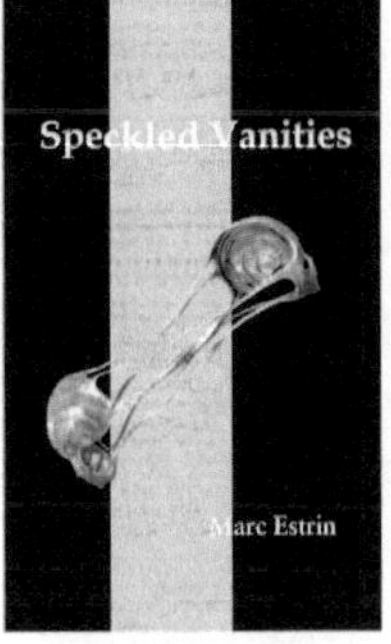

Speckled Vanities
Marc Estrin

Sinfonia Bulgarica
Zdravka Evtimova

Derail This Train Wreck
Daniel Forbes

Off to the Next Wherever
John Michael Flynn

Fomite

Semitones
Derek Furr

Where There Are Two or More
Elizabeth Genovise

The Hundred Yard Dash Man
Barry Goldensohn

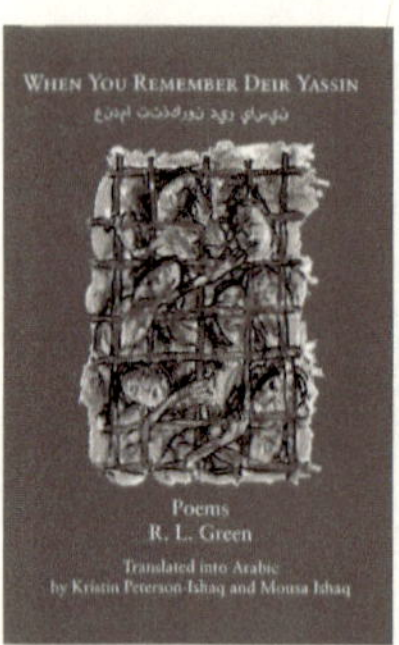

When You Remember Deir Yassin
R. L. Green

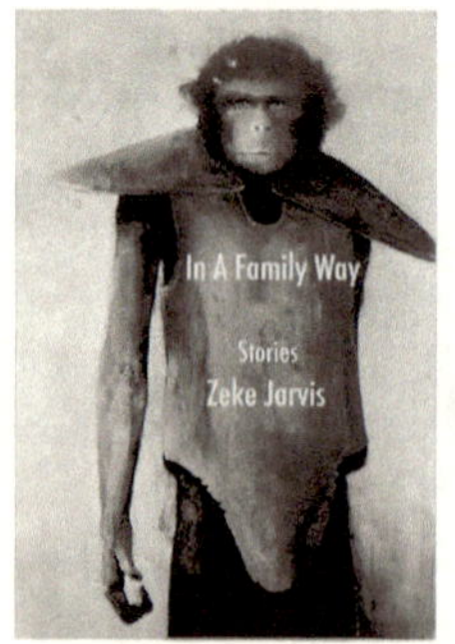

In A Family Way
Zeke Jarvis

A Free, Unsullied Land
Maggie Kast

Feminist on Fire
Coleen Kearon

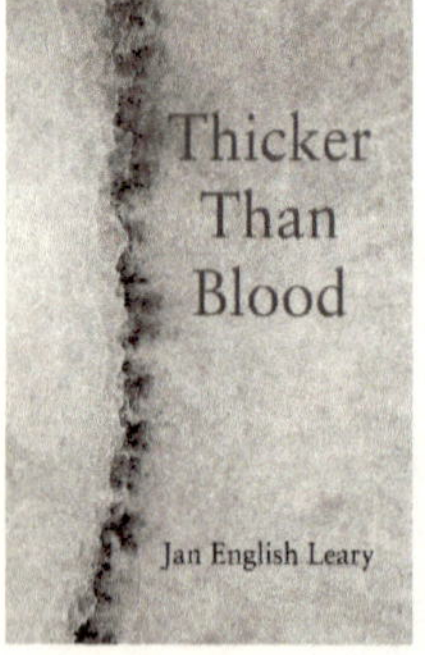

Thicker Than Blood
Jan English Leary

A Guide to the Western Slope
Roger Lebovitz

Fomite

Confessions of a Carnivore
Diane Lefer

Unborn Children of America
Michele Markarian

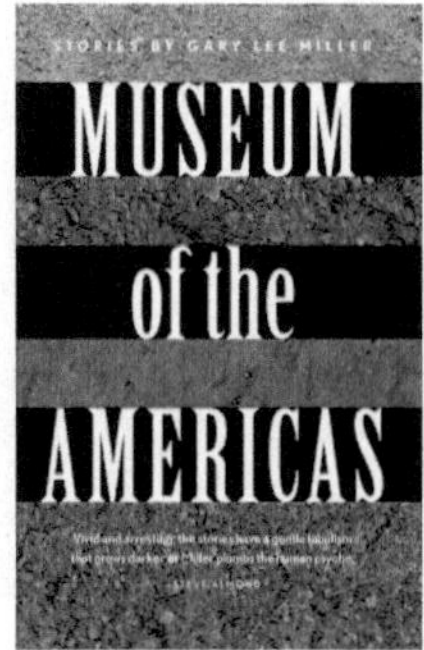

Museum of the Americas
Gary Lee Miller

My Father's Keeper
Andrew Potok

The Hole That Runs Through Utopia
Joseph D. Reich

Companion Plants
Kathryn Roberts

Rafi's World
Fred Russell

My Murder and Other Local News
David Schein

Planet Kasper Volume Two
Peter Schumann

Fomite

Bread & Sentences
Peter Schumann

Industrial Oz
Scott T. Starbuck

Principles of Navigation
Lynn Sloan

Among Angelic Orders
Susan Thoma

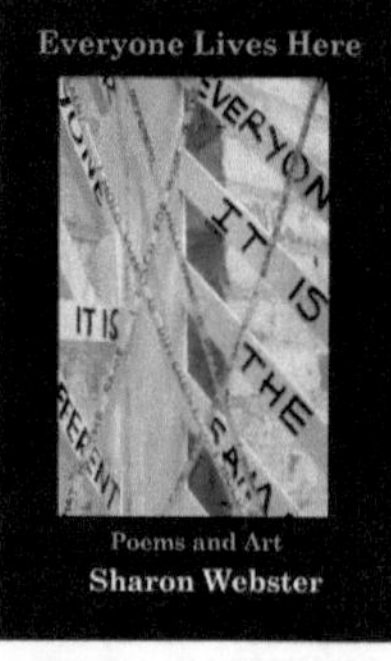

Everyone Lives Here
Sharon Webster

The Très Riches Heures-
Tony Whedon

The Falkland Quartet
Tony Whedon

*The Return of
Jason Green*
Suzi Wizowaty

*The Inconveniece
of the Wings*
Silas Dent Zobal

More Titles from Fomite...

Joshua Amses — *Raven or Crow*

Joshua Amses — *The Moment Before an Injury*

Jaysinh Birjepatil — *The Good Muslim of Jackson Heights*

Antonello Borra — *Alfabestiario*

Antonello Borra — *AlphaBetaBestiario*

Jay Boyer — *Flight*

Dan Chodorkoff — *Loisada*

Michael Cocchiarale — *Still Time*

Greg Delanty — *Loosestrife*

Zdravka Evtimova — *Carts and Other Stories*

Anna Faktorovich — *Improvisational Arguments*

Derek Furr — *Suite for Three Voices*

Stephen Goldberg — *Screwed*

Barry Goldensohn — *The Listener Aspires to the Condition of Music*

Greg Guma — *Dons of Time*

Andrei Guruianu — *Body of Work*

Ron Jacobs — *The Co-Conspirator's Tale*

Ron Jacobs — *Short Order Frame Up*

Ron Jacobs — *All the Sinners Saints*

Kate MaGill — *Roadworthy Creature, Roadworthy Craft*

Ilan Mochari — *Zinsky the Obscure*

Jennifer Moses — *Visiting Hours*

Sherry Olson — *Four-Way Stop*

Fomite

Janice Miller Potter — *Meanwell*

Jack Pulaski — *Love's Labours*

Charles Rafferty — *Saturday Night at Magellan's*

Joseph D. Reich — *The Derivation of Cowboys & Indians*

Joseph D. Reich — *The Housing Market*

Fred Russell — *Rafi's World*

Peter Schumann — *Planet Kasper, Volume 1*

L. E. Smith — *The Consequence of Gesture*

L. E. Smith — *Travers' Inferno*

L. E. Smith — *Views Cost Extra*

Susan Thomas — *The Empty Notebook Interrogates Itself*

Tom Walker — *Signed Confessions*

Susan V. Weiss — *My God, What Have We Done?*

Peter Mathiessen Wheelwright — *As It Is On Earth*

www.ingramcontent.com/pod-product-compliance
Lightning Source LLC
Chambersburg PA
CBHW050947210726
48287CB00004B/1176